Where Evil Resides

Robur Copse Book 1
L. B. Romero

For all those who love survival horror, no matter the media.

Contents

Prologue: The Hunter

"Death is not the greatest loss in life. The greatest loss is what dies inside us while we live."—Norman Cousins

Saturday, April 9

0800

The Hunter stabbed the needle into the *shai*, holding on tight. They always seemed to know when it was their turn and fought like lions. If it were him, he would fight against such a horrible fate too.

What an awful beginning to the workday.

The light above him flickered, buzzing like a bug being zapped. It would be a relief to leave these bright fluorescent bulbs and never-ending sea of puke-green hospital halls for his next assignment. At least he was coordinated; his scrubs matched the walls.

He held on tight until the *shai* went limp. There would be no quick death for this one.

He shuddered, glad today was his last day in this infernal place. People weren't fired from this hospital when they messed up.

Instead, a much more permanent end awaited him if he didn't complete his time here on a positive note. Which he would, as long as nothing went wrong with his arrangements later.

The wails of the inhabitants commingled, layering one over another. He enjoyed the howl of defeat, but these anguished cries were incessant. As a second part-time job, it wasn't so bad—he'd had worse.

He dropped the *shai* onto the stretcher and grabbed the smooth leather, strapping down its arms and legs. Each one reacted differently to the anesthesia, and he didn't want to have to try again with the *shai* on the alert. This was the last time he would have to prepare one for Dr. Sherri Gianni, so hoity-toity.

In his opinion, the stupid woman was doing everything wrong. But while he knew about chemistry, he didn't know much about genetics. He just needed to make it through today.

Though his new assignment was not the promotion he'd hoped for, it was a step up from being under the thumb of the scientists in this crazy place.

That stupid old man had been chosen to be the Cleaner instead.

He slapped the *shai*. It made a nice, loud smack, but it wasn't enough. He hit it again. Harder. Again.

Tom's voice cut through the fog of anger. "You're not supposed to do that."

He turned to face the Judas, who would sell his own mother for money.

Tom leaned against the doorframe, arms crossed. His black hair was slicked into a pompadour, and though he wore the same bile-green scrubs, his shoes were worth an entire paycheck. The useless loser was here only because his daddy had pulled some strings.

"I was checking for consciousness."

"Hmm." Tom smirked.

A closer look showed the other orderly's eyes were constricted to pinpoints from his usual opioids. The guy thought he could get away with anything because he was the Director's son. No one else would dare touch him.

Well, he'd been preparing a surprise for Tom, and he would give it to him before he left.

He turned his back, ignoring Tom for now, and finished checking that he had properly restrained the *shai* before rolling the stretcher through the doorway and down the hall. His hand flicked out undetected—palming Tom's prized possession as he passed. He slipped it discreetly into his shirt pocket and patted it with a sly grin.

Just a little while longer.

Dr. G herself accepted the *shai* at experiment room 3 with barely a glance at him. Her focus was all on her work and the *shai*'s imminent medical procedure. He liked to keep as much distance from her and her experiments as he could, so that suited him just fine. A sharp chemical tang emanated from the room, propelling him to hurry back to the main part of the hospital and finish his daily tasks. Anything to be away from there.

He sat in one of the chairs staggered along both sides of the empty hall, resting from the morning of menial duties, swirling a lukewarm cup of coffee, and thinking about what his new job would be like.

He wouldn't miss the sterile chemical smell poorly covered with the aroma of coffee.

It would be underground, but he would be the only Keeper. No more noise and people.

While it would be more dangerous than this job, he would be left alone to do it in peace.

Another perk of the new job was the extra space down there, and he had already moved all his trophies. He had easy access to it, while the entrance remained hidden. *Perfect.*

Tom interrupted his thoughts by ripping the cup out of his hands. "Taking a break, are you? Dr. Gianni wants to see you."

The unholy glee in Tom's gaze made him want to tear the man's eyes out, but if he was careful with his next words, the payoff would be even better. Tom had already done more than half of the work.

"But that's the last of the fancy beans Dr. Weston brought in for the staff. I never got to taste it." He infused the words with frustration, then set his feet and stood up to come face-to-face with Tom.

As quick as a rabbit with a fox after it, Tom gulped down the contents of the cup and grinned. "I guess you never will."

The Hunter's face softened, and he clicked his tongue, pulling a medicine bottle from his shirt pocket. He rolled it like an orange grenade under the chair a few steps across the hall, behind Tom.

"You took the bait so easily. I'm surprised you didn't notice these missing. I mixed them into the coffee, but you gulped it down too fast to notice the taste. Or maybe you're just used to it."

Tom blinked obviously trying to focus, but he was already losing control. His muscles appeared to relax. Tom barely whispered, "Why?"

He stepped forward into Tom's personal space. "Because of her."

"Who?"

He pushed Tom, who collapsed into the chair. "You shouldn't have gotten her involved with your foul drugs."

Tom stuttered before expelling a quiet "Oh, her." Then he sank further into the chair.

Tom was too far along to be saved, even if the dying man was found by a nurse.

He turned and walked down the hall, toward his alibi, entering Dr. G's realm for a second time that day—and, feasibly, the last. On the wall next to her office hung a large painting. Ornate gold framed a single Egyptian woman standing calf-deep in water covered with lily pads. She was bent over, collecting the shoots from the surrounding reeds.

Something about the painting felt sinister. Every time he passed it, he thought he could see eyes watching from among the stems.

He picked up his pace, sure of his story, but unsure of the unstable doctor's reaction. "Dr. Gianni, you wanted to see me?"

"I heard you were abusing the *shai* this morning." She continued typing on her computer and didn't look up. "It is important they all receive exactly the same doses and exactly the same treatment to avoid any outside variables."

A few more hours and he would be gone from here, but only if he could endure or deflect her wrath. If he acted like he did nothing wrong, she'd likely overlook him. People usually did. "Yes, Doctor. I think Tom was confused about what he saw, though. I just checked for a response. Sometimes the shot doesn't work well."

Dr. G looked up. In this lighting, her blond hair had highlights of red. She would almost be pretty if it weren't for the constant tight twist to her lips and the flatness in her gray eyes.

A nurse burst into the room, distracting Dr. G, her voice high and fast. "Doctor, there's activity in experiment room two."

He followed them both to the observation room—to prove how helpful he could be—and later wished he hadn't been there to experience firsthand the birth of one of Dr. G's successful experiments.

"I think I'm going to be sick."

Chapter 1: Leon

"No man chooses evil because it is evil; he only mistakes it for happiness, the good he seeks."—*Mary Shelley*

Thursday, April 14

0815

The world was mocking Officer Leon Rook.

The spring sun shone down, bright-yellow warblers sang, and purple hyacinth called to passing pollinators. Leon sat on a park bench, sketching, on the worst day of the year.

His fellow park-goers walked, jogged, and meandered by, enjoying the beautiful weather in a way he couldn't.

Why did he have to prove he could shoot a gun every single year? He looked down, the glint of his badge catching the light, and he tried not to think about what it would be like to be anything other than a cop.

Instead, he focused on the sketch he had made.

The chief had said this was his last chance to pass or . . . Leon shook his head.

His sketches weren't anywhere near as good as they had been back in school. He needed to practice. If he failed the weapons test again, he could at least replace the precinct's aging sketch artist. Though that meant his dream would die. Someone needed to protect those no one cared about.

Chatty laughter made him squirm, and of their own volition, his eyes followed the sound.

Children with backpacks strapped on both shoulders flowed down the sidewalk toward the jackal-topped brick stair rails of the elementary school, the stream of students parted by one of his fellow officers. Leon nodded to her, and she returned his greeting with a raise of her chin, continuing to control the flow of both pedestrians and vehicles. A brother and sister held hands as they crossed.

Leon's hand froze, mid-drawing, and his heart pinched. *Not today . . .*

Past the crowd, the biggest landmark—a pyramid-shaped building—loomed over the downtown. Was Osiris Biotech protecting the townsfolk, or was the corporation involved in animal testing?

The pharmaceutical company had rebuilt the town a decade and a half ago in an Egyptian Revival style. But weird Egyptian obsession aside, Robur Copse was a great place to be a cop. Small town, lots of jobs, great atmosphere.

Directly across the street stood the courthouse and Robur Police Department, where the Egyptian theme continued inside. The cells were few, with no separate jail. They rarely had any of the serious crimes associated with large cities. And that was just the way Leon liked it.

To the right of the RPD, the library, fire station, and high school created a triangle on a jut of land, leaving a small park in the center.

There the more fashion-savvy teens, if they carried a bag at all, hung it off one shoulder as they milled about in front of the high school.

He recognized the tall Black boy already built like the football player he was. That was Zane, but Leon didn't know the skinny, dark-haired White boy next to him. They made an interesting contrast that caught his rusty artist's eye. He used a few lines to make a quick sketch of the juxtaposition, outlining the silhouettes and filling in the details of their clothing and hair.

Zane was the culprit of Leon's current case.

He smiled as he sketched.

The boy's grandmother had come to him when a bicycle with sentimental value had been stolen. Her grandson hadn't realized she would miss it during the couple of weeks it took to repair it. Leon had interviewed the kid yesterday and discovered that the restored bike was the teen's birthday present to her.

Another case had solved itself.

Leon focused on the page in front of him. His sketch wasn't what he hoped. While the faces looked all right, the proportions of the bodies were a bit off. And the hands . . .

Hands—squeezing the trigger.

Leon gulped in air, and the bell rang, emptying the streets.

He shook off the chill running down his spine and turned the page, searching for someone new.

Walkers and joggers, mostly women in groups or with properly leashed pets, passed by, and he nodded politely at their greetings. The few men he saw stood out.

A tall, thin man about six one with reddish-blond hair was headed in Leon's direction. Leon's pencil started to move almost of its own will to create the outer shape. The man's hands were hidden in pockets as he meandered, lost in thought.

His height and coloring led Leon to believe the man had Scandinavian blood somewhere in his veins. As did the straight nose and thin lips Leon drew with a few strokes.

Leon's hand moved across the page as he cataloged the details.

The man's T-shirt and jeans were stained and well worn, like he had a blue-collar job or a hobby that required working with his hands.

Leon would like to get a good look at those hands. Did they have calluses on the fingers or palms? Scars?

He could be from one of the farms along the outskirts. Or one of the hidden houses within the sprawling forest. Or work at the Osiris Biotech lab outside town.

Either way, Leon didn't recognize him. Though Leon had been away from Robur Copse during his growing-up years, he'd been back and serving on the RPD long enough to know most of the residents by sight.

But since he mostly patrolled the downtown, the store owners were the people he knew best.

On that thought, Otis Bailey—from the downtown pharmacy and health-food store that catered to the locals—speed-walked past on his daily constitutional.

Avoiding eye contact, Leon kept his head down. The man was a talker. Leon practiced drawing him again, edging him into the upper corner of the same page with the unknown man.

Otis's pale hair had receded even farther, and his propensity to being overweight was barely held in check by his healthy eating and daily walks.

Leon examined his drawing. The sketch he had been working on had morphed into one of his sister. Blood bloomed from her chest. With the test looming over him, she was on his mind again.

I can't do this.

He tore out the page and stood to throw it away. Betty passed by, her familiar blond curls bouncing and a little fluffball of a black dog leading her.

Leon's already-tight stomach cramped. Yesterday, a different Pomeranian had been reported missing. Reaching for the trash can, Leon was brought up short by another lost-dog poster. The dalmatian was larger than most animals that vanished around here.

Recently there'd been an increase in the number and size of animals disappearing. The country roads accounted for a fair share of wandering pets that never made it back home. However, the forest felt more menacing lately, as if somehow it was hunting stray animals.

Leon rubbed his face in exhaustion. And the twisting in his stomach that had kept him from breakfast continued.

Leon's hand brushed his badge on the way down, reminding him of the test, and he checked the time.

Tossing the crumpled paper first, he straightened his uniform and pocketed his sketch pad before crossing the street to the RPD. The concrete staircase to the main entrance didn't even warrant a glance as he turned the corner. His goal was the officer-only side entrance—much more discreet, tucked next to the belowground parking garage exit.

While Leon considered guns a necessary evil to being a cop, he could barely force himself to use one. No matter how much he wanted to stay on the force. Not after what had happened to his sister. It would be fine once the test was behind him.

He extracted a lanyard from his pocket. A small green three-leaf clover, or club (if you were playing cards), was printed next to his photo on the badge card, giving him access to the entrances, the garage, and certain rooms within RPD headquarters.

Shaking off his nervousness, he rolled his shoulders back and unlocked the door by holding the key card next to the mechanism. The door shut firmly behind him.

Leon meandered to the elevator, an ostentatious brass carriage with fading green carpet. They should really replace it with blue. Blue carpet would be calming. When that didn't distract him, he imagined his stun gun test. It didn't help. The physical pain of being tased didn't compare to the anxiety he felt.

He swallowed hard when he was joined in the elevator by two members of the Force Operations Rescue Extraction Special Tactics unit. Their distinct vests meant they must have already been out on assignment or training this morning. Leon shook his head. He liked the simpler cases of a uniformed officer and wouldn't want to be on the exclusive FOREST team for any amount of money.

They worked as narcotics and homicide units, taking all the more dangerous cases. Danger was not Leon's middle name; it wasn't even in his name.

"Sanchez. Lieutenant Durban," he greeted them.

Please don't let them be going to the lower level. Lieutenant Durban was an imposing man, more because of his personality than size, though he was taller than Leon by several inches. His brown eyes held a solemnity that gave weight to his authority, and his tan skin probably came from South American ancestry. Lieutenant Durban truly shone with a firearm in his hand.

How humiliating would it be for Lieutenant "Bullseye" Durban to know Leon had failed his weapons test *again*? He would find out eventually—he always did—but hopefully not until Leon either passed and was allowed to continue his duties or after Leon had quit and moved far away from Robur Copse, out of shame. If only he wasn't reminded of his sister every . . . single . . . time he pulled his weapon.

"We're having a little competition with some of the Kaira forest rangers later. Bullseye here thinks Ranger Tompkins can beat me three out of five on the mat today. What do you think, Boy Scout? Should I take his lunch money?" razzed the pint-size female officer.

Leon let out an imperceptible sigh of relief. They were going to the gym—and he was glad she wouldn't throw *him* around the mat, though that would be preferable to what he actually had to do.

Because of her petiteness, she was often underestimated by those who didn't know her. Though Ranger Tompkins was a well-known martial artist and probably the best overall fighter in Robur Copse, Sanchez's knowledge of joints, physics, and pure aggressiveness were enough to overwhelm any man.

"You know I would never bet against you, Sanchez. RPD all the way!" Maybe if he kept this conversation going, they wouldn't ask where he was headed . . .

The two elite officers threw their heads back and laughed, leaning against the left corners of the carriage until the elevator dinged and took its sweet time opening. Leon pressed toward the door, blocking more attempts at chitchat and stepping out as soon as the gap allowed.

Before he could make good his escape, Lieutenant Durban clapped Leon on the shoulder, chuckling. "You're all right, Boy Scout."

They turned and headed down the gray carpeted hall. The white cinder block walls indicated the direction of the gym with a green painted line.

Leon turned the opposite way and followed the red line on the wall to the indoor shooting range, ignoring the other colored lines that led to the other rooms in the underground maze.

At the checkout desk, the officer's face remained impassive (which Leon found reassuring) as he signed his name in exchange for a box containing ear protection, magazines, and bullets for his sidearm.

Tucking the box under his arm, Leon wound his way past the empty practice ranges to the last area, where a small obstacle course was set up with targets. At the barrier, he took a shaky breath and laid the box on the shelf protruding from the wall.

He could do this. Leon took several calming breaths. No real people were involved. *Just aim and shoot, while moving. No big deal. Stop stressing.*

Leon stepped through the requirements in his mind.

Kneel, shoot. Hide, shoot. *Wait, no.* He should start with hide, shoot, then kneel, shoot.

Don't forget to safety before you holster.

Run, draw, fire. Squat, fire. Why was he suddenly worried his dress pants would split? Were they too tight? Should he have put on a different pair this morning? He should have done a few squats to warm up.

Leon squeezed his hands tightly, then relaxed them. He took in a deep breath of damp gunpowder hanging in the air. A metallic tang hit the tip of his tongue as he shook out his knees.

Drop to the ground, fire. On one knee, fire. *Remember to run back and to the side, to the other barrier, and fire. Not like last time* . . .

Holster, draw, and fire. Reload—*It's better to go slowly and not drop the clip this time*—then fire and holster. Move to the center, fire right-handed.

Switch and fire left-handed without dropping the gun. And last . . . holster.

He needed to hit the body mass of the targets with only 70 percent of the shots. Last time he was so close. Instead, he'd received a 66 percent with a .666 . . . a decimal without end—kind of like his humiliation.

The last few weeks had been full of ribbing from the other officers. He needed this.

Leon stood at the firing counter and took a deep breath. His fingers struggled with the bullets that refused to fit into the magazines, which suddenly seemed too small.

Lieutenant Durban's voice, identifying himself as Leon's proctor for the test, made Leon jump, and the slippery bullet fell, tinging on the concrete floor. *He knows,* Leon thought, and swallowed bile.

"Relax, I won't bite." Lieutenant Durban smiled warmly as he double-checked Leon's magazines, lining them up along the counter.

"I—I thought you were going to the gym?"

"The rangers won't be here till later. You know Sanchez. She needed to warm up." Lieutenant Durban held out his hand. "Service weapon?"

Leon hunched his shoulders and pinched his lips. He unsnapped the safety strap, releasing the Glock 22 from his holster, and cleared it before handing it over.

Satisfied with the cleanliness of the barrel and the weapon's functionality, the lieutenant returned it, magazine tapped in and safety on. "You got this." He squeezed Leon's shoulder.

Warmth spread through Leon, and his stomach settled at the touch.

Shoulders back, Leon cleared the weapon again before sliding it into his holster and then the extra three magazines into their respective pockets on his belt. He normally filled only one during his duties, but this test required a total of sixty shots.

Leon put in the foam earplugs and donned the earmuffs, as did Lieutenant Durban, who then took one step back and to the left, close enough to be available but out of the danger zone of hot, ejecting brass.

Leon had one more shot at staying a police officer, and he was going to do his best. The badge was his life. There was no other choice.

L. B. ROMERO

At Lieutenant Durban's signal, Leon rolled his shoulders back, stood behind the first barrier, cleared his mind, and pulled the trigger.

Chapter 2: Gabe

"Evil hiding among us is an ancient theme."—*John Carpenter*
Thursday, April 14

0745

Two sets of blue eyes clashed in a battle of wills—one set framed by smooth bright skin and jet-black strands, the other surrounded by tanned wrinkles and salt-and-pepper hair.

One glare supported by youthful idealism and the other by the wisdom of age.

They stood like gunslingers on the creaky wooden porch. The sky was clear, but instead of high noon, a weak morning sun radiated down on the two of them.

"I just want a truck that works! Is that too much to ask? You promised to fix it." Gabe Norton ground his teeth.

Why did Dad never consider his needs? Last year he got a hand-me-down lighter and this year a broken truck. He just wanted to get away from this messed-up family.

"I'll help you when things slow down. I will. But you know I need the other one."

Why couldn't his dad budge? He was always too busy to keep his promises. "You could pick me up from school and I could drop you off," he suggested. That was a fair compromise, right? Even if it would be embarrassing for everyone to see the landscaping logo on the doors.

Dad shook his head, unwilling to yield. "You can get a job this summer to earn the money for a new radiator. But during the rest of this school year, you should be coming straight home after school to help with the chores and have time to study before going to bed early. You can get good grades if you keep your focus on school."

"Good grades? Have you seen my grades? I'm totally average, barely passing. Besides, how are good grades going to help me? It's not like we have the money for college. And I didn't get into Kako Academy, so *the company* won't help *me* out."

"If you had good enough grades, you could get a scholarship or something. You *need* a college degree to work for Osiris Biotech."

"I can't do it. That's not who I am. I'm going to graduate from high school and get stuck with ten lousy jobs like you." Gabe's voice rose on each exclamation.

"That wouldn't happen if you stopped screwing around and worked harder. You sound like a petulant child. You need to grow up and start acting like a man." His dad's tone swelled even louder.

The screen door squeaked open, and the voice of his older sister penetrated the tense atmosphere. "Dad, Gabe. Your yelling's upsetting Mom. You know how she has a hard time breathing when she gets agitated."

Their dad was already inside when Gabe turned around and stomped down the porch stairs.

"Gabe, where are you going? Breakfast is ready," his sister called after him.

"I'm not hungry. I'll just go 'screw around.'" Gabe faced the Ford, more reddish-brown than the original color, a shade darker than his Norton-blue eyes, and just as rusted and falling apart as their family. He kicked the rear of the old truck—parked permanently on the gravel drive these last months—and the bumper fell off, proving his point.

Heat and a pinching began in his nose and eyes, and he jumped on his secondhand bike, ready to escape. The wheels whirred, and the seat vibrated under him as he built up speed on the downhill, racing into town. He tapped the brakes, barely keeping control.

No one ever cared what *he* wanted or needed. *Be a man.*

Gabe rose off the seat as he pumped the pedals down the flat street.

What did that even mean? Living like his dad—too many kids, a sick wife—and working multiple jobs because none of them paid enough? Work, work, work until he couldn't breathe and life collapsed around him?

No, thank you.

The sharp tang of the grass from where his tires had dug in when he braked floated on the spring breeze as it cooled the sweat on his brow. Gabe locked up his bike at the rack on the west side of the school.

What did his dad mean, *Be a man*? He *was* responsible. Sure, his grades weren't the best, but he always did his chores. He patted the outer pocket containing the money for his mom's meds.

At least he was *man* enough to go to the pharmacy on his own after school. Maybe Dad could come hold his hand to make sure he didn't get lost. After all, the dangers of the world were too much for a little boy like him.

"Whoo! I could fry an egg on that head." Gabe's best friend and fellow average student Zane Everton clapped him on the shoulder.

"Hey, Z," grumbled Gabe.

"Got a tick digging under the skin, man?"

There was that word again. "Yeah, I'm not *man* enough." As they headed inside the school to waste another day, he reached in his pocket for last year's birthday present—the golden-hued flip lighter. It was much more useful than the current truck. At least it worked.

"Mmm, daddy issues."

Gabe snorted. "You a man, Z?" His tennis shoes squeaked on the entryway floor.

"Me? Pfft. I ain't never growing up. I'm Peter Pan, man." Z tucked his hands under his armpits, flapping his elbows and crowing while students turned to stare and laugh.

Living up to his other nickname—InZane—and just like that Gabe relaxed.

Except for their hair color and grades, the two friends had nothing else in common. Z was built like this sandstone brick school, and Gabe was more like the wisp of the new tree planted out front. Gabe was as pale as the linoleum, and Z was as dark as the picture mats lining the hallway walls, framing a rotation of student artwork. Z was the life of the party, and Gabe was . . . forgettable.

Why did Zane still hang with him? But they'd always been a mismatched pair.

They entered homeroom—chemistry—and strolled over to their lab station. Gabe swung his bag onto the desktop, still frustrated with his pathetic future in this pathetic town. The scent of dry-erase reached him as their teacher wrote obscure chemical equations on the whiteboard.

"Do you think my dad would consider him a man?" Gabe gestured toward their teacher at the front of the room.

The tall, thin, older man barely acknowledged his class and only droned on and on about the day's experiment on electrolysis.

"Naw, he's a robot. Have you ever seen him eat?"

"Good point."

"You wanna hang after school?" Z asked.

"Can't. Gotta go to Bailey's."

Z nodded in understanding, and they proceeded to watch the demonstration on how to light a light bulb with two electrodes hanging in a container of salt water. Like that would ever be useful.

During third hour, Gabe studied his English teacher as they discussed Shakespeare . . . Mr. Radcliff's favorite playwright. Day after day, it was only more Shakespeare. Even with his limited knowledge, Gabe knew there were other famous writers out there.

Mr. Radcliff didn't look *that* old, but he always wore a suit, and all the girls professed their love for him, even Lissa.

Lissa, with her shiny straight hair that slipped like silk over her face if she didn't put it back into a ponytail, seemed to like that kind of man. She smiled widely when Mr. Radcliff asked her to read aloud the next two Shakespearean stanzas. Who knew that old man had written so much incomprehensible garbage? Though it sounded nice coming from her.

"Here the anthem doth commence:

"Love and constancy is dead;

"Phoenix and the Turtle fled

"In a mutual flame from hence."

Maybe it was his imagination, but was Lissa looking at him?

"So they lov'd, as love in twain

"Had the essence but in one;

"Two distincts, division none:

"Number there in love was slain."

Surprised when Mr. Radcliff picked him and unable to think past the idea that Lissa had just said the word *love* while looking at him, Gabe stumbled all over his turn at the next stanzas. His hand touched the smooth metal, and he flicked the lighter open and shut. He breathed a sigh of relief when the lunch bell rang, and he sprinted to find Z.

After collecting their food from the outside window, they went to where they always sat. Gabe focused hard to keep his chocolate milk carton from falling off the foam tray.

Z tried to distract him by pointing out the group of girls sitting on the grass.

"I'm not interested," Gabe lied, unable to imagine the utter humiliation of being rejected in front of the entire school. He plopped down on the cool grass.

"Sure. More for me." Z shrugged and sent heated looks across the field.

Gabe's eyes traveled against his will over to the group of laughing girls. His gaze met Lissa's dark eyes for just a moment before Jason Thatcher—the future dictator of the town—and his two lackeys blocked the view. The guy thought he ruled the school because his dad was mayor of the town. He wasn't wrong.

One of Jason's lackeys carried a football under his arm, and the three of them started throwing it back and forth while casting looks at the girls. *Show-offs.*

Gabe turned his attention to what passed for food at Robur Copse High. Both his and Z's trays contained soggy cardboard pizza. He dipped a cold fry into the pool of ranch and bit the slimy thing in half, swallowing hard.

With just a glance, no one would know Gabe's food was provided by the system, a.k.a. Osiris Biotech. But *he* knew. Money was power, and Gabe's family had none. Every extra dollar went to his mom's medical needs.

Jason and his lackeys stopped tossing the football and headed toward the girls, crossing the sidewalk in front of Gabe. Jason blocked his view of Lissa.

"Hey, look what I found," called Jason, leaning over and picking something up. "A wad of cash."

The guy standing next to Jason was Ivan Tompkins, who caught Gabe's gaze. He could be cool, and he hung out with Gabe and Z sometimes. Ivan rolled his eyes and shook his head at Jason's behavior.

Flipping through the bills, Jason laughed. "That wasn't worth the time it took me to stop." But Jason shoved the bills into his pocket anyway before joining the girls in the grass.

He sat next to Barbara Monroe, with Lissa on her other side. Jason leaned too close and reached out to flip Barbie's hair while Lissa scooted away slightly. Jason was the richest, most powerful kid at school—and he knew it.

"You gonna eat that?" Z asked.

"I lost my appetite." Gabe shoved the tray onto Z's already empty one.

The bell rang, and he and Z went to their separate classes.

The smell of the musty, sweaty locker room hit him every time, along with the echoing of the lockers slamming open and shut as everyone changed. Racing the clock, Gabe dressed in record time. He reached into his backpack to re-place his clothes and discovered the small front pocket partially unzipped. Feeling faint, he opened it wide, checking for the money he had placed there.

It was gone.

He remembered the scene at lunch. Only Jason would call thirty dollars not worth his time.

"Jason, I think the money you found at lunch is mine."

"Yeah, is that right? I didn't see your name on it, so finders keepers."

"Seriously, dude, it's for my mom's meds."

The coach blew his whistle. "Butts in line. Warm up."

Coach was reasonable, but no one interrupted his gym class. Gabe would deal with it after.

As he alternated standing and then touching the opposite foot, Jason smirked at him from across the way. Why was the guy such a jerk?

Sweat plastered Jason's T-shirt tight across his muscles each time he bent over.

Unfortunately, Gabe didn't have any of those manly physical qualities or athletic skills. The guy could wipe the floor with Gabe, and Jason's daddy, the mayor, would buy him out of trouble. It was a no-win situation.

No, Gabe looked and felt like a wiry twelve-year-old. He couldn't even hold on to a measly thirty dollars.

Jason caught Gabe with his shirt over his head after class.

"Here ya go, mama's boy."

Gabe escaped from the neck hold to find the money lying on the floor in front of him. The guy was still a jerk, but not hopeless.

At the bike rack, he unlocked his bike and rode down Main Street, taking a right at the pyramid, then passing the orphanage—at least he had it better than them, barely—a yarn and quilting shop his sister liked, and the coffee shop. Braking hard and leaving a tire mark on the sidewalk, he propped his bike outside Bailey's Health and Wellness and pushed his way through the door.

"Hey, Debbie. Is Otis here?"

Chapter 3: The Hunter

"The sheep will spend its entire life fearing the wolf, only to be eaten by the shepherd."—African proverb

Thursday, April 14

1300

He squatted and looked at the bones piled on the tunnel floor, absently picking up a human scapula. They would soon burn to ash as if they had never existed.

Screams chased the echoes in the shadows, but they would end soon. The new job of Keeper, much like at a zoo, suited him just fine. These creatures were much more natural than those things Dr. G made. The law of the jungle, where the strong hunted the weak, was the way of nature. Like his hunt of Tom.

Not one person had been suspicious of Tom's death or interested enough to look too deeply. The only one he had been concerned about was the Director, but he, too, had been unsurprised. The perfect crime. Though he considered it more of a good deed. He had stayed hidden behind his blind up to the end. The target hadn't seen him coming, and he had left no trace.

The Hunter's finger dug into the crevice of a deep scratch in the scapula's ivory, following the groove left from the tooth. And he contemplated life—and death.

Everything leaves behind something.

He thought about the lifeless eyes of Tom as he had sat in the chair in the empty hallway. He glanced around. Like those halls, the tunnels reminded him of the mines that the first town was built around. Winding, endless, full of pain and death.

Once upon a time, it was known for its ironworks. Each man, woman, and child contributed. Some entered the mines and wrested the rock from the earth, choking on the dust. Some smelted it, burning and melting from the heat. Others shaped it into intricate and beautiful designs, pounding themselves into exhaustion. Their lives and deaths revolved around the mining operation.

It was beautiful.

He stacked the skeletons in one arm. Each bone emphasizing each thought. *One.* Clack. *By.* Clack. *One.* Clack.

The town's youth moved away. Older people died or retired. The veins of iron were exhausted. The town gasped its last breath; the ruins abandoned their fight with the vines and saplings. Smothered.

But death was followed by a miraculous rebirth!

Osiris Biotech came. Gutted the remains, tearing them down to the bare bones. Fourteen years ago, they had rebuilt from the underground up—making it their own.

The European pharmaceutical company had named itself after the Egyptian god, who had been returned to life. High aspirations for a pharmaceutical company, even in these modern times of reverse aging in mice. Their success would accomplish what the Hunter strived to emulate.

Turn right. The volume of the dripping water increased, echoing in the dangerous labyrinth. From the beginning of the rebuild, he had been there. He paused to run a free hand along the rough, slimy concrete. The sewage and water-treatment tunnels were the first to be constructed.

The maze down here was quiet, mostly forgotten. Not many dared to enter its depths. Fewer still returned to the surface.

The growling of the creatures pulsated through this area of the tunnels, announcing their insatiable hunger. These creatures were merely enhanced to be deadly; they weren't the abominations Dr. G created. That woman was messing with nature in an unnatural way, trying to defeat it instead of working with it. Perhaps he should do something about Dr.

G. No one else would. And no one else could get away with it.

There would be more bones for him in a few days. One day he would feed them the nasty old man who had stolen the Cleaner position from him.

He strode through the passages, whistling at the thought, swinging one arm (the other hugging the remains close) and thinking about the town above ground.

Everything up there was built in an Egyptian Revival style. Elaborate architecture and statuary hid their secrets. Columns and walls with vivid depictions in reds, blues, yellows, and greens distracted from the disease pervading the town. Etchings with hieroglyphs and symbols sustained the lie. They restored the old ironwork before repurposing it in decorating and fortifying the newly minted *Robur Copse*.

He stopped to admire an infiltration of roots, fighting their way through a crack. Like all things in nature, there was a dark side. The forest (like a hunter itself) waited and watched the interlopers, eagerly anticipating swallowing this new town whole . . . just like the last one. More than the forest waited for prey out there. Things might get fun for the Cleaner if Dr. G's monstrosities got out.

He hugged the skeletal remains closer.

For the past fourteen years, there had been a constant war against the vegetation. Though life continued, the new town looked almost as old as the original town, but a bit like Vegas. He liked Vegas, and a fond smile softened his mouth.

What a great hunting ground. Like the World Fairs of old, where H. H. Holmes built his fun house in Chicago.

Besides the lurking woods, the second problem was the high water table. The town needed to be careful that things buried didn't pop up to the surface due to water pressure. Which was one of the reasons everyone was cremated in Robur Copse. That and the extraordinary amount of skeletal remains the town produced. It was his job to erase those sins.

He threw the armload of bones into the incinerator, the contrast of the cool underground making the flash of burning heat welcome. It was like how the passion for stalking the greatest game would build to an unbearable crescendo just before a kill, then cool for a while until it built again.

He thought of what the current target would be doing right now.

His breathing escalated.

A red glow illuminated another grin as it crossed his face, the fire reflected in dark, shadowed eyes.

Where would *she* be?

Chapter 4: Debbie

"Every worthy act is difficult. Ascent is always difficult. Descent is easy and often slippery."—Mahatma Gandhi
Thursday, April 14

1545

Another name had recently come to Debbie's attention. How was no one else aware of what was happening?

It turned out she had a gift for getting people to tell her things. This investigating had been kind of fun. If she had understood her strengths when she was younger, she could've become a journalist. But now it was too late.

Her grades hadn't been the best. They'd required too much work when she'd just wanted to let go of her cares. So college was out of the question. She was lucky to get this job.

The person on the other end of the call informed her when and where the party would be tonight. Then Otis entered the back room, and she ended the call. Pretending to check stock, she knew she should get back out front. Her job was still necessary for now. She pushed aside the curtain separating the work area from the customer side and walked through.

It was easy, as jobs went, and used her skill set well. A bit of smiling, sometimes a little flirting, guiding people to the more expensive option. All she had to do was hint that cash would be appreciated and she could skim a bit off the top. Not that Otis would notice anyway.

He was already marking stuff up—*like 400 percent*—and his camera didn't work very well, if it ever had. A little sleight of hand and *ta-da*, a little tip for herself. She had learned over the years how to distract and redirect. Besides, if you only took a little, people didn't notice or thought the mistake was theirs.

Customers browsed up and down the aisles full of ways to waste their money. Promises to reverse aging, herbs and supplements to cure anything that ailed you, and magical weight-loss products were conveniently displayed and brightly packaged. Each sale was an opportunity for Debbie. Those stupid enough to fall for the lies deserved it.

She felt sympathy only for those who came for the help they could find at the pharmacy window.

Speaking of, Gabe entered the shop. School must be over. She didn't have much longer until she got off work for the day. But she had to take care of this rush first.

Debbie tried to focus, smiling and chatting up the customers. Years of practice maintaining appearances came in handy, but she was crumbling inside.

The hunger for sweet release gnawed at her.

Otis, his terrible fashion sense aside, took care of the prescriptions while she dealt with the more grocery-oriented purchases. At least his white pharmacist coat covered the terrible Hawaiian shirts he wore daily.

A little pat to ensure her blond updo was still picture perfect and then, keeping her red lips stretched wide, she greeted the next customer. And another, then another. She smiled at the final customer and waved him out of the shop—Deborah was pushing at the doors again.

Gabe passed her to the exit and her feelings bubbled up. And just like that, she was no longer sure anymore if she was just doing this investigating for her needs.

His head hung down, and anger flashed briefly in his eyes as he stuffed the prescription bag into his backpack. The boy was probably worried about his sick mom.

She could remember that feeling—could still smell the sick room and the arguments that snaked out of the room and around her heart. The ring of the shop bell as Gabe exited the suddenly quiet shop sounded like the bell her mother had used when she had wanted something.

Deborah was back. Worried Deborah. Helpless Deborah. Annoying Deborah. Her dad was disappointed in her, and her mom was concerned about her. Poor Deborah. Her mom's sickness was all Deborah's fault. Her dad knew it and her mom knew it. Mom got sick because Deborah wasn't strong enough, happy enough, or popular enough. Mom literally became worried sick. Deborah knew if she could be a better daughter, her mother would be fine. So she decided to help her mom. She would change, or at least pretend to change.

She put on a happy face and did things she didn't like, things that made her uncomfortable. But her family was more content. They seemed pleased. So she continued. Mom had been sick for over two years, giving Debbie lots of time to practice pretending to be cheerful. She put on a happy face at school; there she made friends, her teachers seemed to like her better, and her grades improved. She put on a happy face at home; Dad didn't bother her as much, and Mom seemed to get better.

Plastering on a false smile and doing what others wanted of her became habitual and seemed to make everything better—for a while.

Then . . . Mom died.

Deborah went into a tailspin. She continued to pretend cheeriness out of sheer habit, trying to hold on to her mom. And then . . . she found alcohol. Alcohol muted the pain, making it easier to be Debbie. She only needed it sometimes, the bad times. But only a certain kind of girl got invited to all the parties.

Debbie learned how to be that kind of girl.

The bell rang again, startling Debbie back to the present. The door clanged shut behind another customer, who entered the pharmacy and headed into the aisles.

She crushed her sympathy down inside.

Be happy Debbie, not depressing Deborah, she scolded herself. It was time for some of the little pills that could make her fly. All her worries, all her cares—*gone.*

To be free from the chains of life for a while.

The pills were only necessary sometimes. When the alcohol couldn't take the sting off, couldn't take her far enough away from herself. But with Deborah back again, it was a must. The problem was, Deborah was surfacing more and more lately, and those little pills weren't cheap.

Stupid Otis—keeping the door to the pharmaceuticals room locked twenty-four seven.

If only she could get in there, she could trade for as many pills as she desired. When she had started, she'd thought it would be easy. Things hadn't turned out the way she had expected, and this job wasn't enough anymore.

But now she had a link to Tom and could use it to get what she wanted, if she was careful. She didn't want to end up as one of the names on her list of missing people.

Just a little bit longer.

She needed to get out, away. Worrywart Deborah was making her nervous all the time. She was feeling watched and increasingly stressed.

As soon as 4:00 p.m. rolled around, she split. A quick pick-me-up was essential. She turned to her immediate left and entered the coffee shop next door, ordering a double-shot espresso to go. Taking several sips of the bitter brew, she felt back in control.

Debbie was skilled at driving while drunk. She'd only had a few drinks to tide her over until the real party started, and no cop had pulled her over, yet. Plus the road was empty. She turned the steering wheel, crossing the railroad tracks, her car bumping over them as the quality of the houses deteriorated. Small houses nestled in among larger houses. Most of the larger houses split into duplexes. Paint flaked, vinyl faded, mortar cracked, and iron rusted. Landscaping was minimal in most yards, with wildflowers or weeds dominating the grass.

Gone were the cookie-cutter homes, perfect lawns, and new cars.

Debbie drove onto a random darkened street and parked far away from the party house. It wouldn't do for anyone to connect the two. And it would be a backup if Tom didn't take well to her putting the screws to him. But it was worth the risk.

The sidewalk was cracked and uneven where a tree root had grown through, causing Debbie to stumble. The night was like a cold, dark solitary confinement cell, but she didn't care. Her goal was in sight. She could smell the damp of ground made soggy from melted snow. The insects were starting to sing, warming up their voices with soft songs—like the beginning of a concert—filled with anticipation. By summer it would be loud enough to wake the dead.

The lights from the house leaked through the cracks of the curtains, illuminating it from within and calling to her. She looked down. White might be the color of innocence, but it showed off what was left of last summer's tan beautifully. She couldn't wait until it got warmer out and she could start tanning again, lying in the warm sun and playing on the river. Her phone buzzed and lit up, distracting her. She checked the caller ID, rolling her eyes. *Good old Dad complaining again.* What did she care? She stabbed her finger at the phone and swiped, sending him straight to voicemail.

"Do you hear me, Dad?" She stumbled again and spoke to the unanswered phone, voicing the thoughts she couldn't quite force herself to tell him out loud. "I'm an adult, out on my own, making my own choices." She waved the phone around at her absent audience. "And I'm having a great time. You hear me? A great time. I don't need to check in anymore, okay? I . . . am . . . not . . . a . . . child!" Dad and Deborah could take a hike. Tonight was about fun and letting go . . . after she got what she needed.

A late-night breeze brought the spring chill with it. Despite the goose bumps, there was no way she was covering her cleavage. I have to get into that party, whatever it takes. Tom's going to be in there, and he always has what I need. *To forget. To just be. To fly.*

She reached into her clutch, dropping her phone, and retrieved her compact. After a quick check of her golden waves and her perfect makeup, she puckered her lips and air-kissed her reflection. "Marilyn Monroe ain't got nothin' on this," she murmured, clicking the compact shut with one hand and stuffing it back into her clutch.

Her hands started to shake with her need, and she looked around, scared Deborah, feeling eyes from the darkness on her.

Debbie slid her hands down her curves, smoothing the dress, and inhaled. Tom would have what she needed inside; she just had to find him among the throng.

"It's showtime." She pasted the smile on and thought about Tom's face when she told him what she knew. The click of her heels on the concrete floated through the night as her skirt danced around her.

A hot bouncer opened the door, letting her in after a once-over. But she already had a target in mind.

The volume of music and people was incredible. It amped her up.

She pushed her way through the crowd, asking where Tom was, but no one seemed to know. In the kitchen, she grabbed a drink. It didn't matter what was in it.

Someone still sober enough to answer gave it some thought. "Tom. He hasn't been around for about a week."

How was it possible? He always came to the parties when he wasn't working. Not that he needed to. The job was for keeping up appearances, unlike her own.

Now what was she supposed to do? The information was useless. That took her back to square one. He just had to be here, somewhere.

She scanned the throng and settled into the familiar routine, sounds, and smells of this type of party. This house, old and disheveled as it was, was one of the better places on the rotation.

Following the right wall, she circled past multiple couples lounging on tattered furniture and leaning against walls. The giant orange-and-green flowered curtains, grayed by cigarette tar, were older than she was. One girl kicked over an ashtray and knocked down red plastic cups like bowling pins. She balanced like a baby bird on the coffee table, lost in her own world—ready to jump and fly.

From high school kids—just babies, really, looking for a good time after they had outgrown the regular channels—to the most desperate, who were starting to fade and were therefore willing to do anything at all. They crushed against one another—here to feed the food chain. But not her. She had found her way to the top.

Only those who passed a certain standard were allowed to enter. The bouncer who had let her in determined by a glance whether someone had the required looks, money, or connections. Tom had all those things. Despite him being missing, she found herself looking for his slicked-back black hair, strong nose, and handsome chiseled chin.

Debbie squeezed through a group crowded in front of what was supposed to be the dining turned poker room. Smoke billowed and the walls sweat. People crowded in around the seven seated players. The pot a mound of money, drugs, IOUs, and more mounded in the center—a temptation. She could usually get some extra by being a runner for one of the players, but with no glimpse of Tom or his replacement, she slipped right back out. She circled back to the kitchen and stared down the hall.

People moved among the back rooms, some in trade and others just for fun. That was another possibility, but she had yet to be desperate enough to trade herself. Luckily, she had scraped up some extra cash tonight. It could tide her over until she could track down Tom.

Now the question was, Who was present tonight that she trusted enough to buy from?

Turning her back to her last resort, she accepted a dance to pass the time. Drinking and chatting with a smile were specialties of hers.

Spotting her target, she steeled herself to prepare for the encounter as she sauntered over. It cost more in money and pride, but she could bear almost anything to get some freedom from Deborah. After all, it was only temporary. All her problems would be solved once she found Tom.

Debbie gritted her teeth and bore the extra pawing that went with the transaction.

Chapter 5: The Hunter

"Hunting is not a sport. In a sport, both sides should know they're in the game."—*Paul Rodriguez*

Thursday, April 14

2145

A shadow on the sidewalk watched the girl as she sashayed up the stairs to the house. The untreated wooden boards creaked, slightly uneven due to humidity. The shadow visually feasted—enthralled as her hips swayed.

She was intoxicating. Beautiful, for now. It was up to him to keep her that way. Since he'd first seen her, he'd wanted to add her to his collection, but he'd held back because she was too close to him. But now she had become a liability, and the Cleaner was watching her too. He might have lost the job to the old man, but he wouldn't lose her.

The woman pulled her shoulders back and knocked on the door. After a few moments, a muscular man with dark hair, in a tight black T-shirt and jeans, answered. He opened the door, taking his time, with sharp eyes and a ready stance.

A murmur of voices and music escaped the house as he looked her up and down, then smiled, slow and predatory, opening the door wide enough for her to enter. But not too wide, so she had to squeeze past him to get in.

The man looked back out into the night once more before rejoining the party, pulling the handle behind him. A rectangle of light on the wooden porch became smaller, and the noises faded away as the door shut out the night. Quiet, accompanied by the soft hum of insects, resumed.

Patience is always rewarded.

It was time to add to the collection. True beauty, like hers, wouldn't last. Between the alcohol, drugs, and age, it would all fade away. There was not much time for her. Not too far in the future, makeup wouldn't be able to cover the damage. But the Hunter knew how to preserve it.

It was time again to prove who the best hunter was, even if no one else knew just yet.

They would; they would all know someday.

The hours crept by, silent. At the very edge of the forest, the house hid.

Waiting was part of the pleasure. Imagining what it would be like. A few people came and went, vulnerable and alone, yet oblivious to the Hunter's presence.

In the early hours of the morning, a repellant drunkard stumbled mere feet from him, and he held his breath. Shadows and expectations cloaked him.

The man urinated into the foliage, splashing some onto the cuff of the Hunter's pants.

He considered slitting the man's throat with the knife strapped to his ankle, but that would be sloppy, as would getting caught.

The drunk started to lurch toward his hiding spot.

Another man's voice called out from the other side of the hedge.

The drunk stumbled toward the sound, mumbling a response, and both sets of footsteps disappeared down the street.

Irritated by the close miss and the strong smell of ammonia, the Hunter had taken a few steps to leave when the woman in white swayed out of the door and tottered down the stairs. He hesitated. The mood had been ruined, but she was within reach.

The Cleaner could take her down at any time.

"Stupid stairs," she slurred and tripped toward him.

Perfect.

With her practically throwing herself into his arms, he moved to intercept her. Materializing like a ghost from behind the shrubbery. He hugged her from behind, muffling her yell with a cloth. In the state she was in, her weak struggles were ineffective, and it took little strength to hold her still. The Hunter's left arm and elbow trapped her small, thin arms against her side.

Her hands flapped like a dazed bird's against the glass but failed to make an impression. He could feel her warm breath on his right palm, through the cloth; once, twice, then she collapsed.

So warm and soft.

She smelled so good. Replacing the memory of the previous odor completely. Now it was time for the best part—back to the workshop and the magic.

She will always be beautiful.

He drove past a cop car hunkered in the moonless night, waiting to trap careless prey.

It wouldn't do to be pulled over for something silly—not when he was looking forward to the enjoyment she would bring him. But his instincts for survival protected him. He drove carefully, obeying every law.

Past the city limits and into the woods, he drove off the trail, parking and covering the car with a camouflage net. He carried the girl, slung over a shoulder, the few minutes through the brush to the opening of his new lair.

Keep it together . . . just a little longer. Just reseal the entrance so it won't be found; then take care of the girl.

He gently placed her on the clean and shiny steel work-table. Then freed her from her clothing and accessories. Some of her things would need washing for preservation, but the dress was clean and would retain her smell for a while. With a little steaming to remove the wrinkles, it would be as good as new.

After gradually stripping her, he strapped her down, just in case. He'd learned a thing or two at his old job, despite how terrible the working environment had been.

Stalking over to where the chemicals perched on shelves, awaiting their prey, he began preparing the proper dosage. Chemicals splashed as he measured and poured them into the beaker. The glass rod clinked against the glass as he stirred the concoction. The cocktail slurped, sucking up into the syringe, giving it a nice aqua color. This would be the last cocktail she would ever have.

His breathing quickened once more, and a warmth spread through his entire body as he pressed the plunger, injecting the aqua liquid into her body—satisfying them both.

While the chemical cocktail did its job, he headed into the next room.

Time to relax and savor the moment.

He sat back with closed eyes and relived that moment of decision. Commemorating the taking of her. Hands on her skin, strength against weakness, the feel and smell of her.

He settled further into the aroused contentment of a successful hunt, surveying the many trophies displayed throughout the room from a chair made of bone, skin, and horn.

Each had given him that momentary sense of gratification and power.

There were the ubiquitous heads on the wall, from deer, antelope, elk, and moose, their hides lining the floor as rugs. Those were from the Hunter's youth, when prey animals were still a challenge and good practice. Their perfect heads represented the best of the best, and their glassy eyes stared sightlessly over the room, declaring their failure as the fittest to survive.

Next were the predators, which received the full-body treatment for their greater magnificence. Each was a cherished memory of the demands and hardship during the accumulation of new skills to overcome the chosen opponent. Each conquest exhibited how the Hunter was more cunning than the fox, faster than the cheetah, more aware than the lion, stronger than the polar bear, and craftier than the tiger. Every single one was now bent to the Hunter's will. Their exquisite beauty and spirit would delight him, forever.

Ultimately, the best trophies and greatest game of all were situated by the wall like a wax museum. There were seven so far, posed and adorned to emphasize their beauty and personality. She would be number eight. A shiver ran through the Hunter at the thought of starting the process.

The phone in his pocket vibrated, interrupting his train of thought. He checked the caller ID and repocketed his phone, ignoring the call until the intrusion from the real world silenced. It rang and rang again, forcing him to answer.

"What?" he snapped. "No, I'm busy. I'll get there when I get there." He muted the device. Someone always wanted to keep him from his fun. Family, always demanding his time outside of work. But he had a little more time tonight for himself.

A glance at the clock showed the quick-acting cocktail had done its job, and it was time to start. Shaking off the other him, he returned to being the Hunter.

At the work area, he loosened each strap, freeing himself of the anger little by little as he released another part of her body until it lay unobstructed—ready and waiting for his will.

In a bucket he mixed a special soap with faucet water, retrieved a soft washcloth, and began lovingly washing every inch of her skin and hair. Quiet and peace filled him. The blond strands spread out like a halo, hanging over the edges of the table. He wiped each limb and crevice, making her skin as clean and pure and pale as the snow.

She was as beautiful as an angel, and he couldn't help but take a few moments to appreciate her lovely appearance.

Running short on time, and needing to get home, he pulled out his phone and took pictures from every angle. Then he used calipers to precisely measure every part of her body. He couldn't rush. The measurements needed to be exact for a good fit on the form later.

Now, with a pristine exterior, he needed to clean out her insides.

He made a foot-long incision and reached his hand into the bloody mess. He used a knife, fleshing tool, and his fingers to separate the connective tissue and scrape out organs that otherwise would spoil everything.

Not enough time to do all he wanted; he focused on the abdominal cavity. The upper organs would have to wait for later.

The insides slopped into a bucket to take to work—a small treat for the creatures in his care.

He cleaned the area around the incision again, then mourned the end of their time together—for now. He rolled her into a bag, carefully tucking in every last hair before sliding the zipper shut and rolling the whole table into the cooler, where she would be safe until there was enough time to play more.

He finished with a final cleaning of all the tools and surfaces in the workroom. With everything sanitized and in its proper place, he took a shower. The blood-tinged water washed down the drain, as fleeting as the pleasure, but the memory of this evening would stay with him forever.

Chapter 6: Leon

"As long as one keeps searching, the answers come."—Joan Baez

Monday, April 18

0800

The steam from the shower woke his brain, and the warm water running down his body relaxed each muscle as it hit, washing the tension down the drain. He had passed his firearms test, and now his service weapon could live in his utility belt for another year. And he could ignore it.

And yet, this morning, something lingered—a pressure in the air as if a storm were coming. An itch had followed him through the weekend—those missing-pet posters wouldn't leave him alone—but today was a new beginning. He could focus on them without distractions.

Leon took a whole five seconds to dry himself with the towel before wrapping it around his waist. He ran his hand over the mirror, removing the fog as the water rolled down the smear. He parted his auburn hair down the middle, combing it to both sides. Then, leaving it to air dry, he strode into the bedroom to dress. As he struggled to pull on a particularly stubborn sock, he hopped backward. The wall broke his fall with a soft thud, but his foot sank into something squishy.

"For the love of Pete."

The bold little mouse that had run across his path the previous evening had escaped the very trap Leon now found himself in. He wasn't sure whether he was thankful for that as he plopped onto his bed and ripped off the sock with the glue mousetrap attached and tossed it back into the corner. His sock wouldn't be escaping the trap.

"I don't have time for this."

The last piece of his uniform was the shiny silver badge he pinned to his shirt. Now he felt—complete.

The lid on his to-go coffee mug slipped, and the cup tilted, sloshing hot coffee on his left hand.

"Dang nabbit!"

What else could go wrong? He ran the red hand under cold water.

Had something bad happened to all those beloved pets? Did owners wait by the phone to hear they'd been found? Leon shook his head. He was overthinking, still influenced by the dark thoughts testing day always brought with it.

He just needed a few more days to forget the renewed grief of his sister's senseless death. It had been years, and the memory no longer held the same sting it once had.

Resigned to being late but determined to pep-talk himself into a positive start to the week, he took a quick breath.

"Today is going to be a great day."

Shaking off the feeling, he whistled "Oh, What a Beautiful Mornin'" as he toasted a piece of bread, finally twisted the lid correctly on his cup, peanut-buttered the toast, and headed out the door with his gear, only to run smack-dab into his neighbor, McKenna.

His heart pinched. The forest ranger reminded him too much of his sister. Those same tired eyes and a sense of being worn down.

"I'm so sorry!" Leon said. Luckily, the lid on his mug had cooperated, so there wasn't a dangerous splash on her.

"My fault. I wasn't paying attention," she said.

Under her eyes, Leon noticed dark circles that stood out on her tanned skin. She never smiled and was always grumpy, but after a year of his attempts at friendliness, she was beginning to soften. He could tell because she didn't ignore him or growl all the time anymore. He sometimes saw her at the RPD in her role as forest ranger, and she nodded civilly at him.

"Here," he said, holding out his toast, "a peace offering." He wished he could help her—take care of her. She was like a dog that had been used for pit fighting. She always showed her fangs first.

She raised an eyebrow.

He smiled, coaxing.

"I can't take something for nothing." She reached down and scooped up the least wilted of the small potted plants on her side of the porch. The dying plants looked sad against the weeds and grass growing along the edges.

How she could kill a plant in this humid environment, where they were trying to take over, was beyond him.

She snatched the toast and switched it with the pot, as if she were a treasure hunter wary of setting off traps. "Here, maybe you can keep this one alive."

He couldn't believe it. Maybe his luck was turning around. He watched her stomp off to her pale-blue Jeep Cherokee, as dented and bruised as she was.

Minutes later Leon parked his cruiser and entered the RPD. He took a few deep breaths before pushing through the door. McKenna's wounded eyes haunted him, but he locked those feelings away and went to work.

He waved at the other officers as he passed them on his way back to his desk, ready to start the morning. He placed the drinking-fountain-watered little plant next to his monitor and a slow smile stretched across his face as he read the test results sitting in the clearing in the middle of his desk. Seventy-eight percent. That was a record for him. There wouldn't be any more taunting for a while.

Just as he tucked it away and reached for a pet file, Mrs. Everton called, letting him know she was dropping the case because her sweet grandson had gifted her the refurbished bike.

While he typed up the report to close the Everton case, he took another sip of his coffee and then began whistling. The had-to-dos were almost done. Then he could take a closer look at those missing-pet cases.

His phone rang. He sighed but answered. "Officer Rook."

"Office, now." A man of few words, the chief hung up.

Leon grumbled mentally but wasted no time getting his butt down to the office. The back of an average-size man, about five ten with salt-and-pepper hair and wearing a power suit, headed in the other direction, away from the chief's door. The man didn't look familiar.

Leon knocked and was told to enter. He stood at ease in front of the chief's desk, his day quickly going downhill.

"Rook, I need you to check out a possible missing person for me. Deborah Ann Franklin. Last seen on Thursday." The chief tossed a file folder across the desk.

Leon didn't do missing people. Things, yes. Pets, fine. But people—the stakes were too high. And what was with the hard copy? "Is there someone else, sir? I'm swamped at the moment."

"You think I don't know my officers' loads? I'm assigning it to you, Rook."

"Yes, sir."

"I already sent you the electronic file. But her father's a good friend of mine, and Deborah is his only family. I promised to do what I could. These"—he indicated the file folder—"are my personal notes."

"Thanks, sir." The chief left him no choice. It looked like he had a new case. The foreboding from this morning returned. There were rarely missing person cases, and of all the people the chief could have asked, why him?

He returned to his computer, adding the file folder to a stack, and finished typing up the previous report with considerably less enthusiasm. He puffed out a breath as he ran his left hand through his hair—he liked it long—and hit the submit button.

Leon clicked open his email, searching through the most re-cent for the one from the chief. Missing person cases had a countdown on them. The faster they were found, the more likely they were to be...safe.

The file had very little; she had been held for drunk and dis-orderly a few times. The chief had added a few known asso-ciates, her place of work, residence, and other details about her life. There was nothing there to make him think she was someone who would get into trouble more than anyone else.

Her mother was deceased, and she had no living relatives other than her father. Leon could relate. He had been raised by his sister after their parents passed away.

Leon flipped open the dreaded file folder. The chief had kept a few side notes about his unofficial involvement, filling in blanks from personal experience and information he'd corroborated. The father–daughter relationship had been strained. He'd have to speak with her father and her boss, then check out her place.

First things first, he'd send out a memorandum to the department with her vehicle make, model, and color. It might take a while, but finding the car would be a tremendous step toward finding Deborah.

He imagined her speeding down the highway to a distant city, trying to get out of this dead-end existence, as his own parents had. Stop it—he sighed, irritated with himself. Just a few days . . . just a few more hours and the memories wouldn't be so close.

All the noise and people passing by made him shift in his chair. His need to get out pressed against his need to do the job he'd just been assigned.

A call to her father produced no results, just tears and desperation for someone to help. Leon gulped down his own emotions.

Next he phoned her boss, preparing himself for the onslaught. Otis was notoriously difficult to talk to.

"Bailey's Health and Wellness. Can I help you?" a cheerful, mellow baritone asked.

"Otis, it's Officer Rook from the Robur Police Department."

"Oh, yes. I—"

"I'd like to ask you a few questions about Deborah Franklin. Is this a good time?" Leon needed to point Otis in the right direction before he got started.

"I'm sorry, it's not. Rather busy right now, but I'd love to have a chat soon."

"Can you just confirm the last time you saw her? And when would you be available for an interview? I can come to you."

"Sure, is something wrong? Debbie hasn't been in for her shifts, but that's not totally out of character for her. Luckily, I only need someone so I can take some time for lunches, though a day off once a week would be nice. She last came in for her shift on Thursday afternoon."

Leon caught his gaze wandering to the stack of missing-pet reports, and his train of thought followed suit before it was abruptly called back to Otis, still speaking.

"Let's see, late afternoon, about three or four. There's usually a lull before the after-work rush, or tomorrow morning after nine, but before eleven. There's another lull then between the before-work and lunch crowds. Now, where am I going to get some help? Yes, yes. Have a nice day. Enjoy your herbs. These ones will help with your anxiety."

Leon quickly decoded the message that Otis had last seen Deborah on Thursday afternoon and was giving him the best times to come in for an interview. He looked at the time and calculated how to schedule it.

"Thank you for your time, Mr. Bailey. I'll come see you as soon as possible."

Unlike those missing-pet cases, in which he gave a last longing look, Deborah's was going to require some legwork. As soon as he found the girl, he could go back to them.

He'd walk downtown and see if he couldn't shake up some of her acquaintances before speaking with her boss. He almost groaned aloud at the thought of interrogating Otis.

Leon grabbed his hat and headed for the side door. Hopefully this case would be quick and easy. A girl ready to break away and start a new life but too immature to think of others. The chief must not be too troubled that anything bad had happened to this girl; otherwise he would have assigned it to the FOREST team.

He got the feeling the chief thought along the same lines as Leon did. Smaller towns, especially ones as isolated as Robur, didn't keep kids like her for long.

Chapter 7: Kylie

"Into each life some rain must fall."—The Rainy Day, *Henry Wadsworth Longfellow*

Monday, April 18

0800

The thudding and low vibrations of the train slowed as it drew closer to the stop. And closer to wherever she had been shuffled off to. Far, far away from everything she knew. A long *whoo-whoo* sounded as the whistle blew, alerting everyone in the area—both those on board and those waiting—of its imminent arrival. Not Denver.

Ky had never been on a train before. She couldn't even remember being in a car before the police had picked her up. Her eyes pricked, reliving that moment again.

"Nabbers," shouted one of her gang before disappearing into the maze of alleyways.

Ky had already felt the threat and was almost next to the little one near her—she needed to protect him—when she heard the warning. The young kid looked around with wide eyes, scared and frozen like a rat about to be pounced on. She managed to give him a push toward the alley before she felt grasping hands on her.

At least he had gotten away. Passed off from strange adult to strange adult, she hadn't felt safe since and longed to return to their hidden burrow. But once caught, she had thought for sure she'd be locked up in juvie, yet it seemed a worse fate was in store for her. What other reason could they have for sending her across the country to some small-town orphanage? Things didn't feel right.

The car rattled as the engine's wheels ground to a stop, and the train slowed, passing the people by. Ky watched their faces flit past the window. The train halted, coming to a complete stop, and two people on the bench rose to come on board. Ahead of her, a tall, rotund man with a cowboy hat disembarked. She stood, wishing for any possible escape. She needed to get back home to her friends.

But the sharp-eyed, sour-faced woman who had stayed by her side since the police station grabbed her arm, guiding her forcefully down the steps. A wave of oily electric smoke greeted her first. As it cleared, the bottomless, inky eyes of the person awaiting them stared into her soul. Ky shivered.

"Dr. Kako?" The sourpuss rudely questioned the Asian woman.

The person—Dr. Kako, apparently—nodded but glared back at the sourpuss.

The sourpuss thrust a tablet in Kako's face. "Sign here."

Ky watched the interaction as Kako signed, stealthily observing both the sourpuss and her new temporary guardian. Ky took a breath. The air was heavy, filling her lungs, drowning her, and holding her down. Everything about this place was strange. She let her eyes dart about, gathering information.

This Kako, whatever kind of doctor she thought she was, wouldn't be easy to get away from. If only she could just jump back on the train right before it started. But the driver would probably just stop it and force her off. Then she would have an even harder time getting away.

Kako returned the device, still not speaking.

"Good luck. This hellion is now all yours," said the sourpuss.

Kako said nothing but turned her attention to Ky while the sourpuss huffed and reboarded the train, stomping up the steps.

The woman with a sleek black bob mostly covered by a white scarf, expensive-looking clothes, red high heels, and nails dripping with red polish stared down at the thin, dirty girl in mismatching secondhand clothes.

The only thing Ky could say about her outfit was that it was the cleanest thing she had ever worn. Handwashing in the canals didn't quite cut it, and you never knew what shape the clothes would be in when you swiped them out of the donation bins.

Ky and the woman stood in mutual silence until the noisy train chugged off to its next destination.

When the rusted tracks were bare, except for the weeds attempting to cover them, creeping up the sides of the gravel and between the rails, the woman spoke.

"Kylie, I'm Dr. Kako. Where are your things?"

Ky shook her head.

"Well then, let's head for the orphanage and your new home. I hope you are considering the fresh start we are giving you. You will have the opportunity to get settled in, and we will find you some clothes and toiletries for your stay. Perhaps by Friday you will be ready to sit for a special evaluation. If you do well, you can have a family and go to the elementary school over there." She pointed to where children were playing on the playground.

Away from the train, the air smelled alive. A cemetery with trees taller than any of the buildings was to her left. And was that a pyramid? Strangely, the school and orphanage—if it wasn't much farther—seemed to be a part of the downtown. That could be a good thing or a bad thing. It all depended on Kako. What kind of person was she? The woman bustled along, making it difficult for Ky's shorter legs to keep up.

"If you do really well, you can go to a special academy across the river, where your every need and want will be fulfilled. They will even pay for you to go to college and get a degree:

bachelor's, master's, or doctorate. Whatever your heart desires. Someday you can be a doctor, or a teacher, or even a researcher—whatever you choose."

Ky needed to find out where that river was.

Kako continued talking and walking while watching Ky out of the corner of her eye. "What happened to your parents?"

Ky didn't respond. The woman was sizing her up, just as Ky was. She would give as little away as possible.

"Bad things sometimes happen to people," the woman said.

Was that a threat? A guess? Or both?

"But this town is all about making the world a better place. We have researchers at the pharmaceutical lab outside of town, trying to find cures for all sorts of ills and diseases. And there are doctors at the hospital who are experimenting with new ways to save lives and improve health. We also have an elite law enforcement training program to help stop criminals from hurting others. Everyone in town works hard to make life better for all. You can find your place here too."

Ky kept her peace. Information was power, and Ky needed as much as she could get.

They stopped at a large iron gate. Kako unlocked it and smiled like Ky imagined a crocodile would before it ate you. They had those huge-mouthed animals in a place like this, right?

"For safety."

Like Ky believed that. This was a woman who cared about control—her control. No one would get in or out without her say-so. Maybe she should have taken her chance and run at the train stop. She might not be able to plan her way out of this one.

The double doors at the entrance were large and solid wood. Again, Kako had to unlock them. While she waited, Ky tilted her head back to examine the redbrick building. Just above the doors and below at least two other levels of barred windows, large, brightly colored letters read Kako Orphanage. At least she was pretty sure that was what it said. Yep. Control. And power.

"This is your new home. Welcome."

Chapter 8: Leon

"There's no such thing as a free lunch."—*Anonymous adage*

Monday, April 18

1215

It's a nice day for walking. There was no hint of danger in the clear blue sky. And yet . . .

Leon exited the side door of the RPD and took a right onto Snake Avenue, heading to Good Morning, Robur. He used two hands to pull his uniform hat snugly down over his head, shading his eyes from the sun almost directly overhead. He passed the post office with its bright-blue collection box out front and the pet store with a new litter of schnauzer puppies in the window. His heart sank. He'd received two more reports of missing pets just this morning—one black cat and one brown-and-white Chihuahua. But the chief had stressed that Deborah's case was more important.

Leon needed lunch. The coffee shop was next door to Deborah's place of employment, and the owner, Will, was always full of gossip. He could hit two birds with one stone.

A car crunched past, and Leon took a left on Second Street, passing "Smiley-Time Dentist" and the paintings of an oversize blue toothbrush next to giant red lips and huge white teeth. Leon always thought those teeth a little menacing. He stepped around the sandwich board, on which beautiful cursive writing declared daily specials, and opened the door into Good Morning, Robur.

The bell above the door was lost in the roar of the chatter washing over him, along with an aroma reminding him of coffee ice cream, both bitter and sweet. A few people asked about Deborah, letting him know that the town rumor mill was working well. He had to give them a "No comment" or "It's an ongoing case."

Leon looked over the choices as he inched his way forward like a cog on a slowly turning machine. He nodded and conversed with acquaintances until he reached the front. "Can I get a plain coffee, a BLT, and a few moments of your time?"

Will dipped his head, a white ponytail falling over his shoulder, and looked past Leon. "Gimme about twenty minutes and I'll get this line cleared out." He handed Leon his coffee, sandwich, and a pastry for good measure.

"This is for while you wait." Will winked, knowing Leon's weakness.

Leon turned and passed by a table with three unfamiliar women gossiping about the art shop and museum shaped like a pyramid.

Out-of-towners. Everyone who was local knew about Osiris Biotech's big marketing device. Not like they had many visitors, considering how out of the way Robur Copse was. Many residents embraced it wholeheartedly, even dressing up like their idea of Egyptians at some of the town's events and parties. There were some people he would much rather wear a full Greek toga than the waist wrap they thought "period." Ah, the quirks of living in a small town.

Will had chosen a very different kind of decor. Warm yellow walls and cushions topped the brown wood of the chairs and benches. The only thing that matched Will's cargo pants were the chipped redbrick wall and matching dividers breaking the café into groupings. It left lots of sturdy places to hide in case of an ambush, and it was easy to keep your back to a wall.

Leon sighed at the thought of trying to find a chair. First things first, he needed sugar.

A girl with shoulder-length, straight black hair stood at the condiment counter. He'd seen her somewhere before. He tugged down his uniform shirt and threaded his way through the noisy crowd, filling his lungs with coffee, bacon, and delectable pastries.

He fumbled the lid to the ground and had to toss it—*way to go, hero*—then seized the sugar dispenser. Watching her out of the corner of his eye, he poured two teaspoons' worth into his coffee.

The girl was about five six with the ageless features of someone who has Asian ancestry. She didn't resemble the town ruling family, the Japanese Kakos, so he would guess Chinese, like his sometimes partner Officer Paul Tang. She could have been anywhere from twelve to thirty, for all he knew. But her backpack gave him a ballpark. High schoolers sometimes came here during lunch, which was why he didn't.

"Need something?" Leon asked, as he casually grabbed a stirring stick to dissolve the granules into the boiling-hot liquid.

She turned brown eyes toward him. "Can you hand me a few napkins?" she asked, pointing.

He straightened and tossed the stick into the trash slot. "Sure thing."

Her eyes widened as she noticed his uniform. "Are you not worried about the stereotypes?" She raised an eyebrow at the bag sitting by his elbow.

Leon smiled and handed her the napkins. "Does that mean I'm not allowed?"

She returned his smile as she accepted them. "I'm not one to care about stereotypes myself." Her laughter chimed, a pretty sound for a pretty girl. She seemed nice, too, not dismissive, like most teen girls.

A disquieting presence crawled up Leon's spine.

"Isn't she a bit young for you?"

Leon jumped, barely avoiding dumping his hot coffee. He immediately recognized the young man, who loomed over his shoulder. Jason Thatcher was a town celebrity. A well-known troublemaker, star of the high school football team, and son of the mayor. He was about five nine, with dirty-blond hair, blue eyes, and a muscular physique. All wrapped up in an arrogant package.

The specter of Leon's big sister and boyfriend replaced that of the girl and Jason. He was temporarily thrown back to being an intimidated teen. He swallowed hard to get past the lump in his throat.

Leon took a moment, quickly popping the correct lid on. Then slowly turned around. "We were just talking."

The girl's joyful expression faltered, and she clenched her jaw.

Leon nodded to her and clutched his meal, turning to leave.

"That was rude. Why are you even here?" Her voice was strong, devoid of fear. *She'd* be fine.

"Lissa . . ." His whine faded into the chaos as Leon moved away.

Leon shook off the encounter as he ate, barely tasting the sandwich. The memories were harder to suppress, but with experience he'd freed himself of them. The pastry was crunchy, buttery, and filled with a tangy lemon curd. Perfect for raising his mood.

True to his word, Will found Leon approximately twenty minutes later. Most of the mass had dispersed or were sitting at tables outside, bringing the volume level back to normal. Leon dusted the flakes of pastry off his uniform as Will approached. "I should probably ticket you for overcapacity." Leon smiled.

Will, ever grumpy but still strapping despite the sun lines on his face, brushed him off. "Whaddaya need?" he asked, straight to the point.

"When was the last time you saw Deborah Franklin?" Leon watched the older man's response.

"So this is about her," he said, thinking for a moment. "She came in Thursday morning, about five to ten, for two coffees."

"What else?"

"One was hazelnut with cream and sugar and one plain, same as always. She likes to pretend that one is for Otis, but he doesn't drink coffee, only green tea."

"That's not what I meant." Will liked to gossip, but he pretended he didn't. You had to finesse him so he could deny it later.

"She came back after her shift. Probably two minutes after four. She was in here really quick that time and got a double espresso. That girl sure does like her caffeine."

"What about previous days? Did she ever come in here with anyone else?"

Will played with keys in one of his many pockets. "She might've been trying to get a job at the hospital. She met with a few different people in scrubs. There was a bit of arguing."

Trying to get a job or trying to get drugs?

"Anyone else?" Leon gave him time, sipping his coffee like he had all day to spend in this little café when he needed to be out on the streets, finding clues.

"She came in a few times to meet this smarmy guy. Ya know, the kind with the white teeth that leave you wanting to wash your hands? They never came or left together, and he never bought anything."

"A boyfriend?"

"Debbie was flirty to everyone, but he didn't seem impressed. They didn't seem close, and he acted more irritated than lovestruck. But it's possible."

Leon pulled out his sketchbook. "Could you describe him?" It was also possible he could be just a friend. Or her dealer.

Chapter 9: Project Nefertem

"Failure is success if we learn from it."—*Malcolm S. Forbes*

One Year Ago

A breakthrough.

It felt like forever, but time barely passed before vines burst out at the hands and feet of the *shai*, snaking all over, encasing the entire body in a thick vegetative mass.

Monitors beeped across the lab, recording every moment, and Dr. Sherri Gianni's fingers flew across the keyboard, alive with excitement.

The Director would be delighted, too, at the success. Sherri was finally showing her worth.

"The skin is almost hollow. The internal organs and muscle have been digested in a large internal pouch," she explained clinically to the orderly.

The ribs of the *shai* made a thunderous crack as they exploded outward, and her lab assistant, Frank Marlin, gasped.

Weak.

She ignored how no one else, including the green-faced assistant, seemed to truly understand her vision.

Sherri continued to jump between her handwritten notes and the data processing, fascinated and optimistic about what was occurring on the other side of the plexiglass.

"At this point, the skeleton has become nothing more than a scaffolding for the plant matter." She continued talking, mostly to herself, while watching the monitors as much as the action next door.

"The skin and hair left on the top is merely a thin protective coating for the delicate bud forming inside."

She could practically taste the electricity in the air.

Last, a sprout pushed out through the top of the head, splitting it down the sides. The flesh of the rent face hung grotesquely about the shoulders, in pieces.

"The excess flesh will eventually shrivel and dry out before falling off like a baby's umbilical cord."

After hours of being on her feet, and her mind working overtime, she felt drained. As if she had birthed the creature herself.

Following years of study and research, she had ultimately discovered the necessary allele in her pool of test subjects, which she and her colleagues referred to as *shai*, that would allow for the presentation of the desired traits sourced from *Dionaea muscipula*.

The plan had been to use *Nymphaea caerulea*, but she'd been focusing too much on the wrong thing. *D. muscipula*, more commonly known as the Venus flytrap, had the technical requirement, if not the beauty of the Egyptian blue water lily.

Unfortunately, not all the *shai* carried the required sequence, either, but they had a few it could work on.

This first properly blended subject she called Venus 1.

LAB NOTES

Venus 1 is a stable blend.

The trap pushes itself up out of a single stalk on the top similar to the original, but it has also created two adventitious aculeate appendages. These spines on the appendages can be used both for slicing and penetrating when grabbing. The vines can reach twice their height, approximately 122 cm to 152 cm.

The Venus came up to the bottom of the ceiling cabinets in the lab, making it a formidable height, considering its other abilities. Would it be possible to increase the size further?

Two nurses were sent in to feed the Venus . . . and they did, in a very unexpected way. Venus 1 was an interesting blend between plant and predator.

She watched through the window, taking notes and recording the nurses' encounter. At first the Venus did not respond, but as the two approached it, one appendage quickly lashed out, decapitating the male nurse in a split second.

Fascinated, she observed as his head was punctured by the spines and pulled into the open trap of the main body, which then closed. At almost the same moment, the other nurse had her arm amputated, but there was apparently no place to put it with the trap shut.

Arterial spray on the observation window partially blocked her view. Somehow the orderlies would have to get that cleaned up.

The female nurse hemorrhaged while the vine lay limply on the ground, holding on to the arm. Her screaming lasted only a few minutes before she lost functionality from blood loss.

More aware of what they were dealing with, and with the Venus in an inactive state while digesting, the body was recovered and refrigerated for future feedings.

It took forty-two hours and forty-nine minutes for Venus 1 to digest the head.

Later that day, the conceited Dr. Albert Weston confronted her, bringing with him the delicious smell of chocolate. He must've been up late again. His often-vague blue eyes—lost in mathematical and chemical equations—were focused on her, and she shivered. Despite what the others said, she was a woman.

"What do you think you're doing?" he asked.

"My job."

"What are you going to do about those two nurses?"

"It's not like you've never lost a patient or two in your experiments."

"Yes, but there are corpses to give to their families and acceptable stories to go along with them. I don't think you'll be able to explain missing body parts."

She could never tell if he was being pompous or sarcastic. "I'm sure that our contact can take care of it."

One of his strong, large hands gripped a clipboard tightly, and the other pointed at her. "If it happens again, I can't promise you'll keep your position. You might even become the plant food."

Like a masochist, she adored when he behaved domineeringly—but not when he threatened her work. In his role as Caretaker, he had the power to remove her from the Nefertem project.

However, he got his point across. She did need to be more careful. The Venus was a step in the right direction, but not quite what the Director wanted. They needed to be controllable to an extent. Her solution was to simultaneously begin a second project, labeled Dominus, to create a biological control of some sort.

There were many examples in nature of bacteria, parasites, and fungi that could exert neurological control over other biological beings. A variety of those controls would need to be tested on the Venus subjects.

Also, the Venus needed to be hardy. She would have to test their resilience.

LAB NOTES

Venus 1 consumed the arm in thirty-six hours and twenty-two minutes. The subject is unpredictable and fragile, as it is susceptible to high heat and cold. Many acids can harm it and fire destroys it, sent for disposal.

Dominus experiment 1 failed on Venus 1.

Regrettably, this one had not turned out very well. The Dominus had not worked and too much damage had been done to its anatomy for continued function.

Another necessary stepping stone to perfection. "Failure is the lack of motivation to try again."

The hospital had recently been approved for an incinerator, which would come in handy for any future failed subjects.

LAB NOTES

Venus 2 is similar to Venus 1, doesn't react to other plants, doesn't react to blood, reacts to movement, just as susceptible to external frailty, disposed of in the incinerator.

Dominus experiment 2 failed on Venus 2.

Venus 3 is similar to the previous. It took hold of another nurse. The subject consumed this one whole. I believe, over time, a digestive sac develops and expands below the trap, which fills the entirety of the subject, disposed of in the incinerator.

Dominus experiment 3 had some effect, but ultimately a failure.

Sherri's eyes shone with excitement as she strode down the green hall toward her office, her shoes tapping rapidly along with her thoughts. The Venus subjects were evolving and changing. They now had a larger capacity for consumption and fulfilling their purpose. Also, she was getting closer with the Dominus experiment. She had been focusing on fungal control because of the botanical elements of the Venus subjects.

Dr. Weston had reprimanded her again for the death of the nurse and had pointed out the problem when he reported the facility's progress today. She had wanted to rip those casually messy blond strands from his head.

But the response from headquarters had been encouraging. And she had tried not to gloat too obviously.

Unfortunately, there was a continued failure to control and create a resilience in the things.

LAB NOTES

Venus 4 and 5 are less stable but have better defense against temperature variation. When placed in a room together, they destroyed each other. Parts disposed of in the incinerator.

Venus 6 has better stability, better defense against temperature variation. They react to sound and movement vibrations; they lack sight. Venus 6 was exposed to the spores of Dominus, a genetically altered fruiting body of Trametes versicolor, *which had been modified to produce spores of* Ophiocordyceps unilateralis. *These spores successfully took root, and fruit bodies appeared symmetrically on the upper half of Venus 6. Altered behavior—control using this fungal parasite—may be possible. The primordial structure of the fruiting body appears to be enacting control. Further experimentation with this primordium is required.*

"I need more *shai*."

Chapter 10: Gabe

"No matter what you do, someone always knew you would."—A mi McKay

Tuesday, April 19

0630

"Why are you being so selfish? Don't you see how hard Dad works?" Ruth focused on filling and putting out the mismatched glasses of water at the table. Not once did she stop to look up and meet Gabe's eyes with her own Norton blue.

"Don't you understand? That's the point. I don't want to end up like that. But what choice do I have?" Gabe groused as he followed her around the table in a circle, passing out the bowls and placing them on the scarred tabletop. Everything in this house was secondhand and falling apart.

He was sick of it. And sick of being known only as one of those poor Nortons. He just wanted to be Gabe. The air away from this house was clearer, fresher, full of possibilities. He slammed down the scratched to opaque glass in his hand. The water sloshed over the side and onto the table. "This is supposed to be *my* time, to have fun, break away from my family a little, and get to know who *I* am."

Now Ruth was on his back too. He just needed some space. Everyone was too involved in everyone else's business in this family.

"But we need you." She tucked the dark strands escaping from her braid behind each ear, wiped her hands down her apron—a blue faded to gray and stained with past meals—and returned to the pot on the finicky stove for a quick stir before grabbing the silverware.

"Look, Ruth, Mom always used to call you 'little mother.' You're a naturally nurturing person who, ever since I can remember, has been cooking, feeding us, and hugging us better. Eb loves working with plants and being outside in the sun all day. He's definitely Dad's son."

Gabe liked computers, but his dad couldn't see the use of them.

"So where does that leave me? Being a janitor for the rest of my life? Doing the jobs that no one else wants to do because I'm not suited for anything else? Getting paid next to nothing and trying to scrape out a living in this little town?" Cleaning and working hard doing manual labor were the only things his dad had ever taught him. With only a high school degree, they were the only things his dad knew. But working at the bottom never gave him a chance to rise to the top.

"You think it was easy for me? To start taking care of a family of nine when I was barely out of high school? You think that I didn't have plans?" She banged down the silverware in frustration. "Gabe, life is hard. But you have to take what you get and make something good out of it."

He had never realized the pattern had repeated itself. Their oldest brother, Ebenezer, had worked part-time for Dad before high school was over, but then went to full-time once he had graduated. Ruth had become their full-time mother, quilting, sewing, and doing odd jobs for extra money, right out of high school. Gabe's future looked even bleaker.

He stared at the table, now set and waiting. The same old dented pot of oatmeal, the mismatched chairs, cups, bowls, and silverware other people hadn't wanted anymore. Did no one else care?

Gabe was tired of being a square peg forced into a round hole. The walls of the small, dated kitchen seemed to shrink in on him. And the overlapping smells of the decades turned his stomach sour. The idea of another bowl of plain oatmeal sticking to his throat was too much.

He seized the egg basket off the counter and moved to the door to stick his feet in the "one size fits most" mud boots left there, kinda like this family. "I'm going to go do my chores." He bolted outside without waiting for a response, letting the screen door slam behind him.

Be a man. Stop being so selfish. Gabe grumbled to himself as he went about his morning chores, first watering the garden, then heading to the chicken coop. The click-click of the lighter accompanied him. He unlocked the container and reached in for a scoop of scratch, tossing it about on the ground.

"Here, girls. Come, girls." He smiled as the chickens ran and flapped over for their treat. He checked them for bumblefoot, poorly colored combs, and any listlessness. All seemed to be well—with *them*. He returned the scoop and relocked it, then set the basket on the coop to check the nesting boxes.

The scent of hay and droppings wrapped around him like one of Ruth's comfortable quilts. He gathered up a Barred Rock clucking at his feet. Stroking her soft black and white feathers, he stared up into the blue sky and leaned against the fence.

"Why doesn't anyone understand? I didn't know that Ruth's plans had been disrupted. But I haven't even been given the opportunity to make plans. Don't get me wrong, I don't mind helping. I love my family, but they are so stifling. I just need some independence. If I could get out of here, away. Somewhere . . ."

Gabe let his imagination run wild. A life where he could do anything he wanted, whenever he wanted. He could earn lots of money working IT or coding programs. He could eat pizza, burritos, or steak whenever he wanted. No more casseroles.

He would never need to leave his own apartment unless he wanted to go hang out with his friends. Lissa's soft smile filled his mind. She knew what it meant to be still. Being around her was an interesting combination of excitement and restfulness.

He took a deep breath and released the chicken, watching as she flew to the ground.

With a sigh, he finished collecting the eggs and locked up the coop to keep out predators. It was for their own good, but he wondered whether they, too, just wanted to be free. "Thanks for listening, girls."

They responded with coos and clucks.

He stomped back up the stairs, wiping off the mud as best he could. Stepping inside, he set down the basket of eggs to take off his boots, then took the basket to the counter, keeping his back to Ruth.

"Mom wants to talk to you," she said.

He turned his head.

Ruth pointed to the counter, where a tray laden with two breakfasts and the always-present medicine sat.

"There are about eighteen eggs today." There. He could be civil too.

Ruth stirred the oatmeal on the stove. "I finished the quilt, and the customer also wants two-dozen eggs. Do you think you could drop them off before school?"

Gabe nodded, tray in his hands, before he headed down the hall. He steeled himself mentally, knocked lightly on the door, and entered. "Mom, I have breakfast," he announced, delivering it with a flourish.

"Good." She gestured to the chair next to the bed.

He placed the tray on her lap before removing his own bowl and spoon, then lowered himself into the chair. "Ruth made your favorite. Oatmeal, with honey from Eb's hive."

"It smells wonderful," she replied, wheezing only slightly. She coughed delicately, bent her head in prayer, and then took a bite. "What are you and your father arguing about?"

Mom never pulled any punches. He shook his head. "Nothing."

"Do you think I am deaf too? I heard you arguing the other day. And this morning, you and Ruth were having a disagreement in the kitchen."

He looked down and continued to eat his oatmeal.

"Look, I know this has been hard on everyone since I got sick—" She took a moment to swallow loudly.

Gabe startled, moving a hand toward her and shaking his head from side to side, tears forming in the corner of his eyes.

"I want you to know that I am still here to listen. My body may be frail, but my mind isn't," his mother told him gently.

"I know. I love you too, Mom." He leaned forward and placed a kiss on her cheek. He pulled away as she started to cough again, but it was only a little and only lightly. His mother threw back her head as she gulped down her pills. He left the room with his dishes.

Being with his mother felt like having a straitjacket wrapped around him. Tightening slowly but surely. He passed the noisy craziness of his siblings eating and getting ready for the day to drop his dishes in the sink. Gabe had his shoes on in record time.

He would break the pattern and escape.

He grabbed the bag Ruth had prepared for the old widow and slung his backpack over a shoulder—the weight of it paled in comparison to the burdens at home.

Chapter 11: Leon

"Fate throws fortune, but not everyone catches."—Polish proverb

Tuesday, April 19

1015

Leon pretended to browse the supplements aisle. He waited for the shop to clear a little so he could ask Otis sensitive questions about his employee.

Bailey's Health and Wellness was just the right size. The late-morning sun shone through the street windows on six aisles of health items. And a sweet must filled the shop like some sort of incense.

In the rear corner, next to the checkout counter, the glassed-in pharmacy looked a bit like a laboratory. Orange and brown bottles, some in white bags with tiny labels, sat on the shelving. The only door was shut tight and locked, but the window was open. It was well protected from anyone who wanted to get ahold of harmful substances.

Otis may seem like a featherbrain when you spoke with him, but he appeared to be responsible when it came to his work. Though Leon would like to double-check Otis's books. Especially in light of Deborah's problem. A plain black curtain led to the employee-only area. Leon assumed there would be an office and storage of backup stock.

The brass bell rang out, announcing a customer, and Otis greeted them from the pharmacy window. "Welcome, ladies. How are you today?"

"Fine, fine. We're just going to head over here and browse," the slightly shorter, dark-haired one replied.

They headed over to the weight-loss section. Neither was large. They both seemed thin to him, but they weren't as shapely as they had been in their youth. As of yet, they hadn't found that fabled fountain.

The town's busybodies came as a pair, and he always thought of them as one being. Just two peas in a pod.

Leon could see glimpses of them as they moved up and down the aisle. He kept an ear open in case they had any information on Debbie.

"I like this one. It's a pretty green color. And the design is so feminine." The taller blond woman had a higher-pitched voice than her friend.

Leon wasn't sure that was the most scientific way to pick a product. Apparently, marketing worked.

"Have you heard about Debbie?" the lower voice asked.

He picked up a random bottle of vitamins and pretended to read the ingredients, listening to the occupants of the next aisle over.

"I hear she finally had enough of this one-horse town and ran away. Poor Hank. She always was a rebellious girl."

Deborah's father, Hank, was just as desperate as any other father whose child had gone missing. It made Leon push away the thoughts about his own to focus on the case

So everyone else thought she had run away too. It was sad, but it would make things much easier.

"This one says lose up to fifteen pounds in two weeks! I could be a size six by next month." the lower-pitched voice said.

"What a bunch of baloney. That's called advertising. I don't think you really read the 'up to.' I'm getting this one," the higher voice responded.

"Fine, but we're trying that other one next month." Their feet marched off toward the front of the store and the register.

Next month? How often did they come here hoping for a quick fix to their problems? Leon choked on his laughter but managed to change it into a small cough and shoved the bottle back onto the shelf.

"All set, ladies?" Otis's cheerful baritone rang across the store. It must have emptied while he listened to the gossips.

Leon moved toward the window and caught sight of the little group at the counter.

"Of course. One of these for each of us." The dark-haired one took charge, as if it were her idea.

Leon approached Otis as the bell rang again. This time with their departure.

"Leon, good to see you."

Leon started, surprised that Otis recognized him.

"I have something you might want to try." He reached down to a shelf just below the window. "Osiris Biotech finally approved the muscle builder they've been testing on the FOREST officers."

"Uh, no, thanks. I'm here to ask you a few questions about Debbie."

The situation wasn't ideal; someone could interrupt at any moment, and Otis was in his comfort zone. But the illusion of being in power might help Leon get better info out of him.

Otis shrugged and put the bottle of pills back on the lower shelf. He popped back up, a business smile plastered on his face. "Sure, anything I can do."

"I noticed a camera over there. Could I get the footage?"

Otis turned red and cleared his throat. His eyes flicked side to side, scanning the store. Did he have something to hide? Was he misusing the camera?

"I . . . um . . . it doesn't actually work." Otis dropped his eyes as he spoke.

Even more suspicious. "At all?"

"Well . . . sometimes. But I'm not sure how to get the footage."

"I'll send out a forensic computer specialist to help you. They'll also need your drug-count records."

"Oh. Thanks."

That was the shortest sentence Leon had ever heard the man utter. Was he distressed about what they might find? Did Otis have something to do with Debbie's death? Had she gotten access to the pharmacy because Otis hadn't followed proper protocol?

Leon held up the sketch. "Have you seen this man? White, taller than me, black hair slicked back?"

"Nope. He's not one of my customers. Maybe he goes to the Osiris Biotech company pharmacy."

Too many people worked for Osiris Biotech. If he could get a name from someone who recognized the picture, it would be easier.

"What can you tell me about Debbie? When did you last actually see her, and what kind of mood would you say she was in?" Leon asked.

Otis's face cleared, and his usually sunny disposition returned. Either his discomfort about the camera wasn't related to Debbie, or Otis was an awfully good actor.

"I saw her last Thursday. She worked from eleven through lunch, when I left. I returned at about one forty, and she was still here working. She stayed until four, while I did paperwork in the back room. She's a pretty good salesperson when she is here. I mean, she is young, pretty, and outgoing. People come in and get caught up chatting with her, and always leave with something. She seemed the same Thursday. She is good for business, but honestly, I think she was skimming off the top."

Leon pounced. "What! Embezzlement?" Was Otis trying to distract him from the camera?

"I don't have any proof," Otis clarified. "But things haven't been matching up exactly. I didn't say anything to her because, though I think she has been taking some money, when she works, my profits have increased enough to more than cover whatever it is she is doing. I only have the one camera, and it doesn't work more often than it does. The camera itself is usually enough to deter would-be shoplifters."

Here Otis got fishy again, his body language twitchy. "But either she realized it didn't work all the time and figured out when it wasn't or she'd discovered some other way that wasn't caught on camera."

"Interesting." Leon's mind clicked like the gears in a clock, steadily working toward the next step. If he could get the footage, perhaps it could show what kind of mood she was in, what kind of trouble she was in, or something equally helpful. It might even show where she went or who with.

That was, if Otis *was* lying about the camera.

Chapter 11: Kylie

"Every human being needs a set of norms and rules, traditions and customs, transmitted from the older to the younger;"—Tzvetan Todorov

Tuesday, April 19

1045

Ky's skin prickled. On the outside, this place appeared better than she was used to, but there wasn't much freedom. She watched the kids and shuddered at their casual attitudes about following such a strict schedule. The kids, mostly those too young for school, were strangely quiet. It reminded her of her friends on the street. They all had to grow up too fast.

The bottom floor was mostly for the younger ones, groups, and office work. The schedules were posted on the walls and strictly enforced. Chores, meals, study time, when they could shower, bedtime, and even play were all strictly scheduled.

Even the weekends, including mandatory church time, were controlled. They weren't raising people here, but robots who would unquestioningly do what they were told. As much as this all irked her and stomped all over her creative and impulsive tendencies, what really bothered her, she couldn't say.

Just inside of the lobby, several offices gleamed with tile and wood, probably cleaned by the kids here. That free workforce kept everything shiny. The nurse's office was a much larger room than she'd expected.

Several beds that could be separated by curtains lined one wall. On the side closest to the hall was a large desk where the nurse currently sat. The other walls were lined with bookshelves and locked cabinets, likely full of medicines and medical supplies. Squeezed between the shelving and cabinets was an open door, revealing a bathroom.

A sharp scent hung in the air. Sharp, like the nurse who pulled out a folder already labeled with Kylie. It was the only information she had given, strictly because she couldn't stand being called Mary or Jane or any of the other stupid names she had been threatened with.

The nurse flipped open the file and wrote for a couple of minutes while Ky waited in silence. Kako, the orphanage psychiatrist, had left Ky alone in the room with this strict-looking nurse. Ky stayed still, avoiding attention for now.

A few of the beds had the curtains closed around them. Were there children hiding behind them? Sick or worn out from forced labor?

The nurse gestured Ky over to a scale, where she measured her height and weight. Ky quite liked the continued silence. But then the nurse asked her to sit and began interrogating Ky with basic medical questions about her health.

"How old are you?"

Ky shook her head.

"Have you ever been to a doctor?"

Ky shrugged.

After a few more questions, which Ky answered only with nods or headshakes, the nurse's brown eyes turned cold. So she did have a temper.

"Well, we will just have to get you all caught up. I'll write a schedule of the best way to do that and make sure I have them all ordered when needed."

Great, another schedule.

The nurse stood and went to a cabinet to retrieve some medical equipment—tubes, needles, gauze—all wrapped up in packaging. She sat next to Ky.

"Roll up your sleeve and put your arm out like this." The nurse demonstrated for her, then proceeded to wrap a band tightly about her arm, clean the forearm, and prepare a needle. Her fingers felt like ice.

Ky had never had a shot in her life and fear churned in her stomach but she stayed still and silent. She'd lost friends to addiction and seen drug use on the streets. But this was different. When the blood moved out of her body and into the tube, Ky jerked her arm and screamed.

Blood sprayed both her and the nurse, until the woman managed to pull off the band and slap a white square on the spot, pressing down hard. Brown glinted angrily again, and her lips pressed tight as if holding back rude words.

Once the nurse was done bandaging Ky's arm, the woman, in blood-spattered clothing, curtly dismissed Ky.

Left on her own to find her room, she thought it would be a good chance to get the layout of the place. There weren't a lot of doorways. The rooms must be fairly large. She took a right and ran into a group of kids, led by two teachers. After taking one look at Ky's clothes, one broke from the group and took Ky to her room so she could change before lunch. Maybe whatever made everyone so calm was in the food.

The girls' dormitories, bathrooms, and private study areas were on the top floor. She didn't get much chance to tour the upstairs because the bell for the meal rang, calling her. Each floor wasn't large, but it kept everything contained. She assumed the boys had a similar layout on the second floor, because no one came from that door as she passed it on the way back down. All the boys would be in school right now.

On the bottom floor, the most well-used one, a realization hit her. The whole orphanage smelled fake. There was some sort of spine-chilling darkness emanating from the perfect, immaculate, brightly colored building. A shiver shuddered down her spine and goose bumps broke out on her arms. Ky turned and met Kako's gaze, striking her again with the same bone-deep terror she had experienced on first seeing the woman.

Without a word, Kako continued her walk through the foyer—high heels clicking and black eyes shining, watching, and evaluating, like a snake ready to strike.

Ky's instincts were screaming for her to run.

She had been young when she'd found herself alone and hungry. She couldn't remember parents or siblings or what might have happened to them. Sometimes she had dreams of a woman humming and the feel of warmth and comfort.

One day an older kid found her on the street and must have felt sorry for her. She brought Ky along to where her "family" met. They were a group of quick and smart homeless youngsters who lived off the street. Begging, stealing, conning, and doing whatever it took to get by. After a discussion and vote, they took her under their collective wing and taught her all they knew.

Ky learned what it meant to have a family. They looked out for each other, ate together, slept together. It was warm and comfortable.

Even with their collective knowledge and support, not all of them made it. About 90 percent got picked up within the first day or so for slavery. But the lucky ones, like Ky, who found friends or a gang, still disappeared. Some were picked up off the street by the authorities, some decided to try to make it on their own, and some didn't survive. It took a mix of acting, grit, and flair, but mostly gut instinct to survive life on the streets. Her instincts had saved her more than once, but others around her hadn't been so lucky.

Ky had been caught because she hadn't run fast enough. And now she was here, at this place that felt even more wrong because everything *seemed* fine. It was clean, orderly, and brightly colored. Everything that a place for kids should be.

But Ky knew something bad happened to the kids here—slavery or death? She didn't know yet, but she would bet that the test Kako kept going on about was the key. She wasn't sure what was better; being sent to the academy place, being adopted by unknown people, or whatever happened when you did badly on the test.

Ky noticed the consequences of failing hadn't been explained.

Chapter 12: Leon

"Three may keep a secret, if two of them are dead."—Poor Richard's Almanack, *Benjamin Franklin*

Tuesday, April 19

1215

Leon had to cross two streets to get to the salon run by Deborah's friend. Laurel was unpredictable at the best of times. With her friend missing, he had no idea what to expect. He'd called ahead to make sure she wasn't busy.

He passed the orphanage, run by the Kakos—the only family in town more powerful than the Thatchers—and several small shops, including a clothing store where the creepy mannequins in the window watched him with their glass eyes. They must be some sort of antiques; he'd never seen others like them.

The streets were full of people spending their lunch break, some in business attire, others dressed casually, depending on their job. The tall, pale, red-haired man walked by, and behind him, Leon spotted someone he knew. Otis was dressed in a button-up shirt that was bright blue with green palm trees, and the sun reflected off the skin showing through his thinning hair. He stopped right in front of Leon.

"Officer Rook, was the footage helpful that your man brought back?"

Leon shook his head in response. "Unfortunately not. The feed kept going in and out. You should get that fixed. Did you close the shop?"

"No, I've hired someone new to help out. Getting it fixed is next on my list. Well, good luck." Otis waved and continued up the sidewalk in the direction Leon had just come from.

Had he already given up on Debbie? Did he know she wasn't coming back?

Otis's bright back entered the clothing store with the creepy mannequins.

Leon shuddered. You wouldn't catch him dead in that shop. He turned and spotted the distinct wrought iron sign for the salon. The black silhouette of scissors hung perpendicular to the wall, bearing the name in bold letters: A New You. A similar sign greeted him in black vinyl on the glass door.

The bell rang as he entered the building, walking through a mist of chemical odor, and he tucked his hat under his left arm. A young woman sat at the rear with curls setting in an old-fashioned hair dryer. Laurel buzzed Mr. St. Martin's hair while the older gentleman flirted shamelessly with her.

Today, Laurel had frizzy blond hair up in a hot-pink scrunchie. She was dressed in a hot-pink tank top and tutu, and an off-the-shoulders black top with some sort of neon pattern stenciled on the front. Lots of silver, black necklaces, and several neon-bright bracelets adorned her throat and wrists. Black Converse All Stars were on the end of her fish-net-covered legs.

His eyes hurt, and he could feel the throb of a headache from the neon rainbow that had attacked Laurel, or maybe it was attacking him. And she was busy. Now he would have to wait.

"Um, Laurel?" One never knew what to expect from her. The shop should be called A New Laurel.

She was already apologizing to Mr. St. Martin and turning to the door to greet the new customer. Violet eyes met his.

Leon wasn't sure what color they actually were.

"Leon, what a surprise. Do I have an appointment for you today?" Her head cocked, waves of frizz bouncing, she held the corded buzzer in the air. Luckily it was off.

"No. Remember I called earlier? I just have a few questions for you. Police business."

"Oh, sure. Let me finish up with George here, and then I need to check on Betty, but she should have another hour or so."

Laurel turned her attention back to Mr. St. Martin, restarting the buzzer, while Leon helped himself to a seat along the window.

She continued chatting with Mr. St. Martin, but she kept shooting Leon glances.

Did she seem nervous? Concerned? Debbie was supposedly a friend. Could Laurel know what had happened to her? Getting back to work seemed to say that she didn't care, but people also buried themselves in their jobs to keep their minds off things when they were worried. Which was Laurel doing?

He watched as she finished the man's hair. The sun poured through the glass storefront, causing Leon's badge to reflect light on the wall next to them.

She gave St. Martin a mirror, spinning him back and forth while complimenting his new look—pretty similar to his old one, if you asked Leon.

But the old man chuckled and teased her in return, saying how she reminded him of his youth. She smiled as if she didn't have a care in the world. Most people were better actors than you would think.

She dusted her customer off, removed his cape, checked him out, and sent him on his merry way. Leaving Leon alone with the unpredictable woman. Well, mostly alone.

Laurel moved to inspect the young woman's hair. Betty's black Pomeranian she'd been walking at the park yesterday was missing, but people didn't usually take their pets to the salon. She was a sweet young thing, recently married. And her curiosity could put the dead cat to shame.

He winced internally for a moment over the tastelessness of that thought and hoped her little dog was safely at home. Yet in a few years Betty would likely put the peas-in-a-pod town busybodies out of business. Laurel had to be a saint to do her hair. But Betty seemed occupied with her magazine.

Leon turned his attention to today's target and tried to get a read on Laurel. Was she putting him off so she could come up with lies?

With efficient movements, she turned off and pulled up the dryer, touching several of the woman's curlers—testing the dryness of the hair, Leon assumed—and asking questions while she worked. The older woman's responses were short but surprisingly polite. Leon imagined it must be the magic of Laurel at work. She replaced the dryer and turned it back on, filling the room with the high-pitched whine.

Finally, Laurel motioned Leon over as she walked to the chair where Mr. St. Martin had sat and began dusting it off. "That George is so sweet. I just love doing his hair and having him in here. He flirts outrageously and is so great for my self-esteem. So whatcha want to know?"

She was a frank girl. He liked that about her. Leon looked over at the woman flipping through her magazine. Would Laurel be more honest with witnesses or without?

Laurel followed his look. "Oh, she can't hear over that dryer in her ears." She gestured, her bangles jangling.

Laurel went back to wiping down the chair and sweeping up the floor.

She was avoiding his gaze.

Leon kept his voice down. "When was the last time you saw Deborah Franklin?"

"Debbie?" Laurel asked, pausing to lean on the broom handle.

It surprised Leon to notice, in her one moment of stillness, that she was shorter than him. Maybe five foot five. She always seemed larger than life. Constantly moving. Was it a disbelief that he was investigating something as unnecessary as Debbie's disappearance that had finally stilled her, or did she have something to do with it?

"She was in here Thursday. Why? Is something wrong?" Laurel tilted her head, hands tightening on the broom.

"I don't know. No one's seen her since then. You might be the last person to have seen her. What time was she in?"

"Oh, about four thirtyish." She shrugged and went back to her work, moving stiffly.

She seemed unconcerned. But if Debbie had taken off on her own, why didn't Laurel just tell him?

"And how did she seem?" Leon braced himself.

111

Laurel turned toward him, taking in a deep breath, and started off like a jackrabbit. "Oh, great! Debbie came in wearing this fabulous dress she had just bought next door. It was white with a fitted halter top, and it made her look like Marilyn Monroe. She wanted her hair and make-up done to look fantastic for some party, so we watched my show in the back while I did her hair. I'm watching this show about a teen who moves to Bel-Air. That show is so funny! The kid is, like, from the wrong side of the tracks, and his aunt and uncle are, like, a lawyer and a judge. And there are so many misunderstandings because they all have different points of view. Oh my, the gags are so hilarious!" Laurel rambled as she put away the broom and dustpan.

"Whoa, Laurel. Deborah—" Leon jumped in the moment she paused for a breath. Like Otis, there was too much information, and it was all jumbled up.

"What? Oh, yeah." Laurel turned back to him to continue her story. "So I did her hair with the fifties loose curls, as best I could because of the time crunch. I also touched up her makeup, giving her smoky eyes and ruby-red lipstick to keep with the Marilyn Monroe theme."

Leon held up a hand. "Wait, Laurel. What time crunch?" Trying to keep Laurel on task was like herding cats through a hoop.

She walked back over to the chair and started cleaning the combs and clippers. "Oh, well, I had a client coming in at five thirty, and proper curls need to be set," Laurel said, gesturing toward where the woman was still sitting under the machine. "So I used a curling iron and hair spray. It doesn't last as long but works well in a pinch."

"So when did Debbie leave?" Leon asked, trying to continue his interrogation.

"Oh, about five fifteen. I only had a few minutes to clean up and prepare because my client came in ten minutes early for her appointment. She always insists on being ten minutes early, and I should have told Debbie that, but it all worked out because she was gone by then. I really should stop doing Debbie's hair and stuff for free all the time, but she is just too fun to hang out with."

"Laurel, do you know where this party was that Debbie went to next?" Leon prodded. He was becoming disconcerted by the constant movement and the conversational trails.

"Oh, Debbie didn't go straight to the party. It wasn't until much later. She must have gone somewhere else before. But I don't know where." Laurel shook her head.

"Where was the party supposed to be, Laurel?"

She continued to shake her head.

"Do you know who was supposed to be there? Did Deborah say anything about leaving town?"

Laurel's eyes filled with tears. "Do you think that something bad happened to her?" she asked in a choked voice.

"I really don't know." Leon sighed and pulled out his sketch-book. "Do you recognize this man?"

Laurel's eyes widened. "What?" She wiped the tears away, breaking eye contact and looking to the side. "No, I've never seen him before."

All Leon's police instincts immediately went alert. Why was she lying?

"Laurel, Debbie is missing. She has been gone for five days now. She hasn't been to work or home. This man could be involved."

Laurel kept her head down, sniffing.

"Is he her dealer?"

Laurel looked up but didn't give away what she was thinking.

"What is his name?"

"Tom."

Chapter 13: The Hunter

"People are forever watching things. They should be seeing. I see the things I look at."—Patrick Rothfuss

Tuesday, April 19

1215

Officer Rook continued past him down the street, the blue uniform, clanking utility belt, and reflective badge making the man easy to track. The urban setting had become his favorite hunting ground.

So many possibilities. He could live inside his imagination. He could smile outside while thinking about possible ways to remove any pests. That man there with the red tie who rudely brushed by, or that woman there with the irritating nasally voice.

The sunshine, car exhaust, and crowded streets made him long to escape back into the dark labyrinth below their feet. But it would be a while. He had to pretend to be normal, and the officer investigating Debbie's disappearance provided an interesting distraction just now.

He ducked inside a shop and waited a moment before following back the way he had come. The oversize black scissors sign delighted him. And he thought about cutting off more than hair on the old man who exited the building. Tongues didn't have any bone in them, and a good pair of shears could easily take off a finger or two. These thoughts were distracting him—*normal, be normal.*

The sun reflected off the windows, but stepping closer, his shadow made it possible to peek inside. The officer held a notebook, asking the hairdresser questions. Did he really think he could find the girl that way? The officer glanced his way, then back at the girl.

A quick thrill shuddered through him at the opportunity. He was witnessing the investigation, while the police were oblivious. He was too smart to be caught by bumbling small-town cops. What a novel experience—watching and knowing, blending unseen with the hum of the crowd. Maybe—just maybe—he could do this again. After all, lots of people went missing from Robur Copse. They were just the ones not easily missed. No one really thought about why their streets were so clean, with no people who were homeless, no stray cats or dogs.

This was his domain. He was intimate with every nook and crevice, places that many of the other residents didn't even know of or didn't dare to go. He was well known enough that no one looked twice at him, except maybe a stranger or two. Never before had the Hunter taken someone so close to home.

Not being around for this part was safer, but this was ever so much more fun. The excitement level had increased, spiking in the Hunter's gut as the officer had passed him on the street. Unknowing. Could he do it again? When? After all, here in town, he had extra resources.

A horn honked, interrupting his thoughts and bringing him back to the present situation.

What would happen next in the investigation? Where would the officer go?

The information he was gathering was inconsequential. It would tell Officer Rook about Debbie—yes—precisely as it had told him her sad tale. But all traces of Debbie ended the other night, outside that house, when the Hunter had caught her. Even if the officer managed to find the location, no one in that house would tell him anything. Her story was now only his to know.

He savored the stalking. The crowd and glass were his blind. But as the cop continued to simply talk, the Hunter was beginning to wonder how invested this officer was and why he had been chosen for this case.

Then he caught a glimpse of the notebook as Officer Rook showed it to the girl in the salon. How had he gotten a drawing of Tom? His brow furrowed. This could complicate things.

A satisfied grin stretched across his face as a solution came to him. He could kill two birds with one stone if he sent Officer Rook to Dr. G. He had been meaning to do something about Dr. G's little projects, and this could be just the thing. Or her experiments would take care of Officer Rook. Either way, he would win.

The police officer put away his things as if preparing to leave.

He quickly turned to another shop window, as if admiring the wares displayed inside. But the necklace on a black velvet floating neck brought to his mind's eye a memory of taking a photo of *her* in this very spot. He pressed his hand against the glass.

The photos—those might create some urgency in Mr. Note-taker. He could send some copies. He laughed inside, thinking about the police officer scurrying like a little rodent, feeling the pressure of the hunt but unsure of which direction lay the answers.

Silly policeman. He didn't know who he was dealing with.

"Nice day, isn't it?" he said to no one in particular as he hurried off with a smile.

She lay in the cooler, waiting for him.

After a long shift, the Hunter returned, via the backdoor, to the workshop. He wheeled her out, placing her on the work-table. He tested her slightly blue instead of snow-white skin to make sure it was soft enough. When her skin gave—the silk compressing below firm fingers—he slipped on an apron and sharpened the six-inch knife he used for skinning.

Officer Rook was in for a jolt. Looking through Debbie's album had reminded him that killing Tom had given him satisfaction and more time with her, but his hand had been forced by the stupid Cleaner.

The process of skinning was slow; some would call it tedious. It required exact movements and perfect tension, as each inch of skin was lovingly sliced away from the body, revealing meat and bone. But it was like a form of meditation for him. Though he hadn't been ready to take Debbie yet, he had still been relishing the glimpses of her about town. However, once he finished this process, he would have her beauty with him forever.

He would chop the leftovers into manageable pieces and take them to work for disposal. After prepping his tools, the Hunter placed a clean hooked metal rod through the tendon area at her foot. This gambrel, attached to a chain, hoisted her into the air for access to every part. The winch made things much easier on his back.

Releasing his frustration at being rushed by Debbie's activities, which had called the Cleaner's attention to her, he breathed in and out with the slow, calm, repetitive movements of gently slicing and pulling—slicing and pulling.

Gloves and knife bloody, he paused to raise her higher with the winch for better reach of the torso. A familiar metallic tang filled his senses. Red dripped down into the drain below. The work, enjoyable as it was, made his arms and hands sore. He set down the knife and shook out his hands, spattering just a little blood.

Though the old man had beaten him out for the Cleaner position, he was really starting to delight in the perks of this private area with both a work and trophy room only he could enter.

After the short break, he picked the knife back up and carried on until the skin was down to the neck. Changing knives, he removed the head, cutting between the vertebrae, and placed it with the attached skin back on the worktable to start slicing and pulling from the mouth up over and around the skull.

If he did things right, the investigation of Tom would lead Officer Rook straight into Dr. G's cold arms. He shuddered at the memory of her Venuses and immediately froze. Had the knife slipped?

He let out a puff of air. There was an imperfection. Dr. G must be ruined. He pictured locking her in with one of her creations while he watched through the plexiglass. Her screams of fear—and the blood as it sliced off body parts and ate them. She deserved it.

Back in control, he continued. The skin was completely removed—in a single piece. He tenderly flipped it flesh side up, double-checking the inside and scraping away any extra fat or meat with the utmost care. A rip now would be devastating.

He preferred to soft preserve with a soaking-and-scraping method. That part required lots of strength, as well as patience. Caution was needed to avoid disturbing the hair follicles. Just like it would be needed to avoid any suspicion in the confrontation between the officer and Dr. G. A game—a face-off. Who would win? But he couldn't afford to attract the Cleaner's attention. He needed to plan just as meticulously as he had planned Tom's accident.

The high pressure of the faucet spray hitting the side disturbed the meditative silence as it filled a large tub with water. He measured just the right amount of salt and ammonia alum, adding and mixing it thoroughly into a solution. Then he slid her into the tanning solution to soak for several days.

The Hunter washed off the chemicals and lowered the carcass onto the worktable. He went to work with the limb lopper, placing the pieces into lined canvas bags. He piled the bags by the back door—they were specially made to not leak. After cleaning all tools and surfaces, he washed up a final time. With everything meticulously dried and put away, he turned off the lights, grabbed the bags, and dragged them through the doorway into the dripping, echoing blackness.

The door slammed shut, leaving her in darkness, and echoing growls greeted him.

Chapter 14: Leon

"When you have exhausted all possibilities, remember this, you haven't."—*Thomas Edison*

Tuesday, April 19

1410

"Rook."

Leon paused, coffee in hand, and his mind switched gears. Life didn't stop just because he had a face to find. Tom could wait a few minutes.

Lieutenant Durban, along with FOREST team's K-9 unit, both sergeant and German shepherd, had entered the side door with bags of Styrofoam containers and paused politely in front of Leon.

The scent of Italian takeout assaulted his nose, and Leon dipped his head in greeting, while tapping his middle finger against his thigh. "Lieutenant. Are you still here, Sergeant?" The FOREST officer had been talking nonstop about the training retreat he and his K-9 partner would be going on.

"We leave tomorrow. It will be Jin's first plane ride," the sergeant said. His partner sat, her big black triangle ears perking at her name.

"What will we do without you?" Leon asked, settling into the camaraderie.

"Don't get lost in the forest," the sergeant quipped.

"Maybe we'll finally get some work done," the lieutenant said, his eyes gleaming with humor. "Are you coming to the marksman's training on Sunday?" He directed this last to Leon.

"I'm scheduled," Leon replied, not sad to miss a day of shooting and embarrassing himself in front of his mentor.

"Too bad. Next time." The lieutenant wasn't one to give up.

Leon nodded with a strained smile.

"See you around." Lieutenant Durban winked and strode past Leon toward the elevator to the FOREST offices.

Leon heard the unsaid words: *He could use the practice.* None of the other officers understood. That was just fine. He could be the butt of their jokes. He watched Jin, the German shepherd, pad onto the elevator, and his heart sank. Two more pets had been reported missing today. Paul had been doing his best on his own, but Leon wished he could help him.

However, he now had a lead on Deborah. He needed to find information on this Tom guy. It turned out matching a sketch of a face to a person, even in a small-town population, was more difficult than it seemed. Unlike on TV, he didn't have access to fancy software that could match a drawing to pictures of townspeople. They had pictures of those who had been arrested, but computers weren't good enough to match a drawing to a photograph. They weren't even good enough to match a photo to another photo with 100 percent accuracy.

He had spent some time doing a visual check for any descriptions that were similar, but his eyes had gotten tired.

After the quick break, Leon dropped back into his chair. He'd try a different angle and search for the name—what a nightmare—Tom was pretty common. Starting at today's date, he searched back in time through the town's newspapers. He quickly hit pay dirt. A recent obituary with a picture of one Thomas Thaddeus Chandler.

He scanned the article, which was vague at best. The only real information was that the death was sudden, and there was no cause listed. Could it be drugs?

His phone rang. The chief ordered Leon to come to his office.

Leon printed out a copy of the obituary and grabbed it off the shared printer before jogging over to the chief's office.

The chief's desk, like his work life, was organized chaos. Bigger than any other in the station except the reception desk, which was more of a wall, dividing the public area from the work ones. Sticky notes adorned every surface. Various piles of perfectly aligned folders towered on the top.

The chief managed it all with aplomb. Leon couldn't imagine ever doing such a stressful job and appearing always perfectly in control. It was possible that that explained his early baldness, though. The chief's bushy black mustache was the only hair on his brown head.

"Hank is asking for an update. Do we have anything for him?"

Leon's chest puffed out. "Yes, sir. I just found the name of a man who might be connected. This Tom Chandler was seen meeting with her more than once." He handed the paper to his chief.

The older man barely glanced at it before shaking his head. "I hate to tell you this, but he passed away a week before Deborah's disappearance. It was thoroughly investigated. The two deaths don't have anything to do with each other." The chief seemed apologetic. "His father is a good man, and they were estranged, so please let this alone, okay?"

"Oh, yeah. Um, yes, sir." Leon deflated like a balloon, his shoulders rounding forward.

"What about the car? Any news on that?"

"No, sir."

"Well, keep at it. Dismissed."

Leon shuffled back to his desk disheartened. He couldn't even hear the normal office cacophony, lost in his black thoughts. Useless. He was just as useless as the officers who had investigated his sister's death.

He sat, sightless, and dropped his head forward, banging it onto the desk and then covering his face with both arms. He groaned. It had been days, and he was no closer. Wait, that wasn't true.

Leon jerked up, his hair hanging in his face, and he ran fingers through it, pushing it back.

Just because Tom was dead, and he had nothing to do with her death, didn't mean that her death didn't have anything to do with Tom or his death.

The surrounding sounds returned. A phone rang. Talking, the clacking of computer keyboards.

The chief had said it had been investigated. But why the pressure? The call to his office had been very coincidental.

An unfamiliar plain envelope sat on top of his mess of notes. It was properly postmarked, but a tightening in his chest made him cautious.

He glanced left. Paul was on the phone, reassuring a family that the police were doing everything they could to find their beloved pet.

He looked right. The other desk pods were busy with daily calls and computer work, or abandoned as their owners were either off or out patrolling. No one was watching him, yet he felt . . . a presence.

He turned back to the envelope. Such a simple thing. Waiting. Like a coiled snake ready to strike.

Opening a drawer, he pulled on a pair of gloves. Maybe overkill. He had never needed to do it before, but something about this . . .

Leon flipped the envelope over and used an opener to slice the edge, but no surprises jumped out. He tilted it sideways.

Five prints slid onto his desk. He spread them out. At first all he saw were pictures of Robur Copse. Then he spotted her. Deborah Franklin was the obvious subject of that photo. And she was in that one. And that one.

All five of them.

Someone had been stalking her.

Chapter 15: Project Nefertem

"The sun's rays do not burn until brought to a focus."—*Alexander Graham Bell*

November, Five Months Ago

Sherri couldn't shake off her jittery irritation. She could tell the Dominus experiment was progressing, but still not perfected. It would need to be modified further to incorporate the Venus subjects more fully. The Venus subjects themselves were also progressing, but they still had serious weaknesses, and two more had been destroyed.

Time. Every step took too much time. Now that she had one breakthrough, she wanted more. Humans were as volatile as chloroform, herself included.

She was unhappy with the way things were going, and it didn't help that one of Dr. Weston's experiments had been howling all day. He dealt with the efficacy of new medications and their possible side effects. She'd have to say whatever he was testing was a complete failure. The poor soul upstairs would be put to sleep forever if she had any say.

She rubbed her temples to relieve the pain. *That* was something she would relish silencing by tossing it in the incinerator. How much longer was he going to let it continue? He could easily muzzle it, but she was pretty sure he was trying to punish her for the positive feedback she had been receiving from headquarters.

She slammed her office door shut, muffling the creature for the time being. Maybe Dr. Weston was trying to make the staff as insane as their residents.

LAB NOTES

I was recently brought a new shai *that has multiple loci containing compatible alleles. This will allow the experiments to branch beyond the limitations of* D. muscipula*–responding DNA sequences. I am planning on an entirely different experiment with a combination of alternative botanical DNA.*

Thinking of the new *shai*, Sherri couldn't keep the grin off her face. *What an amazing specimen.* She could barely contain herself. Her foot bounced up and down. *So many possibilities.* She could go back to her original plan of using *N. caerulea*. Perhaps she could use the strengths of a few other botanicals in her creation. She had so many ideas and needed to get to work right away. Sherri scribbled down her thoughts, then began preparing the petri dishes with the appropriate cells from the various species. She forgot all about the howling—lost in her world of DNA manipulation. Here, she was God and could create anything she wanted. And she wanted.

Another thing she needed was a space with a large pool of water and sunlight. The best location would be the conservatory. She started the paperwork to officially designate it off-limits. Only Sherri and her assistants would have access. She couldn't expose this most important subject to just anyone. If the patients needed relaxation and fresh air, they could go out to the courtyard, which was walled and gated.

LAB NOTES

Subject AC101512 has begun the transfiguration. The subject has almost entirely metamorphosed into an acuminate vegetative bulb approximately 60 cm by 30 cm diameter. Roots have completely penetrated the conservatory pool with an average length of 50 cm.

Whoever had built the conservatory must have loved botany as much as Sherri did, but that person was much more artistically minded. If she had been in charge, everything would be laid out in a grid pattern, certain types of plants together, and it would be visible from one end to the other.

Instead, along the outside were four-foot abstractly mosaiced walls that vaguely reminded her of the Egyptian style found in the rest of the building. These walls acted like both potting vessels, with soil and plants at the top, and a labyrinth, cutting off the view of the rest of the building. Multiple types of philodendrons filled the space, with phalaenopsis, or moth orchids, for pops of color, and *Christia obcordata*, the swallowtail, for added interest. In the corners, and on the floor, sat large mosaiced pots with palm and ferns to complete the collection. The room smelled of moist earth.

The European-looking metal-and-glass structure soared high above, letting in copious amounts of sunlight, perfect for creating the tropical environment that she was looking for.

Sherri waded carefully across the cold pool to get an approximate measurement of the subject's bulb. This shallow fountain had a diameter of eighteen feet, but it was only three feet deep. To make it usable, she had removed the fountain mechanics and the original water plants.

Initially, she had been able to reach the bulb to get accurate readings, but then the root system had spread. Despite the blue tiles lining the inside and outside, the water itself was mostly clear, since the subject was the only plant in the pool. That, at least, had made it easy to watch the root growth and branching.

She took measurements of the root system before wading back out, and she put away her tape measure. Sherri typed the measurements into her tablet before she forgot. Then she hefted the bag of liquid fertilizer to the edge and poured in the gel-like contents. The subject required a well-balanced diet.

LAB NOTES

Proper protocols were put in place today to turn the conservatory into a second laboratory.

Venus 7 is similar to Venus 6 and reacts similarly to the Dominus spores, producing a primordium.

Venus 8 was manipulated to increase defense against fire, experiment failed, Venus 8 disposed of in the incinerator.

Sherri's grip tightened on her pen, and her brows lowered. She hated having to take time out for the Venus subjects. It was true—they were going well, and their endurance was improving, as was the Dominus experiment, but her beautiful baby needed her full attention.

LAB NOTES

Subject AC101512 has increased in size to 82.4 cm by 46.7 cm, with the root system at an average of 73.4 cm.

She daydreamed about the Director's response to her final experiment. What accolades she would receive for creating the perfect weapon.

She puffed out a quick breath. Audrey was coming along wonderfully and had now created a large rhizome that would come to her knees if she stood on the edge of the pool.

Chapter 16: Leon

"You'll never plow a field by turning it over in your mind."—*Irish proverb*

Wednesday, April 20

0915

Branches weighed down by the years reached for the roof of Leon's car, scratching the top as if trying to pry it apart. The shrieks and squeals sent shudders down his spine. This area was overgrown with the towering canopy blocking any sunlight that might bring cheer. The forest crept in, destroying anything made by human hands.

Bushes and young trees grew against and between the buildings, waiting until their roots destroyed the foundations and hid the walls from sight. Leon slid into a shrinking parking area, mostly dirt, with dotted grass that struggled to grow below the tree canopy, and dust rose around his patrol car as if smothering the interloper. He slipped on his sunglasses and pulled on his hat. He slammed the car door shut, stepping into the small grassy strip that functioned as a yard for all the units.

The Grove Apartments wouldn't be habitable for people much longer. Olive Grun's husband had built the set of five cottage-style apartments a mere ten years prior. But he passed away from sickness less than a year later, leaving her to run them herself. She was a private woman and not too handy or great with landscaping, if the appearance of the place was anything to go by.

Trim was peeling, and the sign designating number two hung at an angle from a single nail. Mold grew on the siding, altering the inviting, pale yellow to a fuzzy, moss green. Number four's screen door had a hole big enough for a bear cub to crawl through.

Nature was trying hard to take back this land.

Leon shivered in the noonday sun.

He strode through the dust motes to unit 1, where Mrs. Grun lived.

She emerged from the building, a hand at her forehead, shading her eyes, and the screen door slamming behind her. She was White, short, maybe five foot one, with a helmet of gray still in curlers, and green-gray eyes. She wore a pink-flowered housecoat—*Do people still wear those?*—with ratty old tennis shoes. She was a product of a different age, even if she wasn't old enough to be.

It was like time ran differently here in Robur Copse. Perhaps the apartments would last as long as their mistress.

"Officer Rook, I presume?" Her voice was low and gravelly.

"Yes, ma'am. Do you mind if I ask you a few questions regarding Deborah Franklin?" Leon cocked his head and tried to get a read on the woman. According to his files, she was middle-aged but looked older and somewhat shriveled, like a raisin.

A flash of his sister hit him out of nowhere. The way she had gone from looking like the young woman she was to having wrinkled and sagging skin in just a few months' time. He quickly shut that mental door and locked it. *Not now.*

Mrs. Grun's next action explained her appearance somewhat when she pulled out a pack of cigarettes, tapped one into her hand, and returned the pack to her pocket while pulling out a lighter. They were the smooth, unconscious movements of a true addict. She held the cigarette in her mouth as she lit it, using one hand to protect the flame from the wind.

Is she trying to buy time?

She'd already had several seconds to come up with a story.

She took a long inhale, pulled the cigarette away, and exhaled slowly. "I haven't seen Debbie in several days. Last Wednesday, I think. But her car was parked in front of her unit on Thursday. Her rent I haven't seen in quite a bit longer than that. Is that why you're here?" The woman peered at him as she took another pull of smoke. She might look older than her years, but her eyes were still sharp.

Leon tried not to cough. He needed to stay close to watch her facial expressions. "Did she tell you that she was going somewhere for the weekend?"

"No, but she wasn't one to tell others anything. She kept to herself."

"How did she appear when you saw her on Wednesday?" He tried not to fidget as the sweat started to build at the collar of his uniform. He should have brought a hat.

"Like normal. She tried to avoid my eyes because she thought I was going to ask about the rent. I just asked how she was doing, and she smiled at me and said she was fine. I believed her." She continued to watch him.

"Does the name Tom ring a bell?" He pulled out the sketch he still had. His cop instincts just couldn't let it go. "Has he ever been here?"

She tilted her head like a cat as she took in the drawing. "Nope. I've not seen him. Handsome, though."

"What about the other tenants? Have any of them seen her? She might be missing."

"The tenant in two hasn't seen her, I asked him myself. But I'm not sure about the Pollacks in number three. Haven't talked to them since Saturday. But I wouldn't be surprised if she just OD'd in the woods somewhere."

Leon kept his face impassive. "So she did have a problem?"

Olive Grun exhaled slowly and smiled. "Surprised? It was kind of obvious to me, but to each their own." She raised her cigarette in salute. "Debbie is a pretty good kid, all things considered. She has a job and usually pays her rent on time. Doesn't bring parties back here and takes decent care of her unit. She doesn't ask much of me, so I don't interfere with her. The only thing she asked is that I don't let her old man into her place."

"Do you know what it was she was taking? Or where she got it from."

She took another inhale of smoke and released it. "None of my business."

Leon scanned the apartment complex, suppressing another cough. Birds chittered, apparently unaffected, or just used to it. "Can I go talk to the other tenants?"

Olive gestured toward unit 3. "The tenant in two isn't around right now. Who knows when he'll show up? But Mrs. Pollack is home with their two little ones."

"Yes?" asked the tall brunette who answered the door, around five nine with hazel eyes. She had her hair in a messy bun and was wearing a stained T-shirt with jeans. At the sight of him, the little color in her cheeks drained away.

Yelling and banging reverberated from the left, and the scent of a stew bubbling on the stove wafted out the door.

"Hey, Viv, this is Officer Rook. He's looking for Debbie," Mrs. Grun interjected as cigarette smoke continued to curl around her.

"Sorry to disturb you, but Deborah Franklin might be missing. Has anyone in your household seen her, her car, or heard anything?" Leon found smiles helped ease the atmosphere, and he pushed his sunglasses up onto the top of his head to appear less threatening and get a better look at her. On their way over Olive had given him the woman's full name as Vivian Pollack.

The rather young Mrs. Pollack thought for a moment, then shook her head. "Last time I saw her was Thursday mornin'. Well, I didn't really see her, if you know what I mean. I was out back hangin' the laundry and I heard a car door, then it drove away. That was around tenish. I'm not sure, but late mornin'. A bit later, when I came out to check my kids, her car was gone."

The warmth of her southern accent was becoming less and less common in Robur.

"Can I talk to the kids? I'd like to know if they actually saw her."

Her gaze narrowed. "They're just kids. They ain't seen nothin'."

She stepped back.

He put a hand on the door. "Please, Mrs. Pollack. Deborah's father is very worried. You can stay here and stop the questions at any time."

She wrung the dish towel in her hands and pressed her lips together.

"Do I need to come back with a warrant?"

Her gaze narrowed, and a muscle in her jaw tightened, but she turned and called out. "Chilluns, can y'all come here? There's a nice policeman who wants to ask you somethin'."

Kids were more observant than they were given credit for, and young ones were detrimentally honest.

A boy of about three came charging over. "Pleece," he yelled, sticking a dirty thumb into his mouth as he stared with brown eyes. His hair, brown like his mom's, was tousled but clean. His clothes, while worn, stained, and torn, looked about par for a rambunctious toddler. More slowly appeared a wide-eyed, red-haired girl. Her coloring reminded him of something or someone . . .

She had a braid down her shoulder. Her T-shirt and jeans looked much tidier than her brother's. The girl's green eyes sized him up silently.

At a signal from their mother, Leon squatted to address the youngsters. He looked them each in the eyes. "Do you know Miss Franklin, Debbie, who lives two doors down at number five?"

Wide-eyed nods followed this question.

"Last Thursday, you were both playing out front, while your mom hung laundry." He paused. More nods. "Did you see Miss Franklin?"

The boy popped his thumb out of his mouth and yelled, "Vroom, vroom," then ran off with his hands out—*Like an airplane?*

Leon was confused until his sister piped up, her chin tilted upward and arms straight at her sides, hands fisted. "I made him sit when she drove away. It's my job to keep him from getting killed while Mom tries to get somethin' done around this place. Don't know what we're going to do next year when I go to school." A slow shake of the head accompanied this last.

Fighting a smile, Leon nodded soberly. The little girl sound-ed like she was quoting an exasperated mother. "That's an important job, keeping your brother safe. You're a good big sister. So you actually saw Miss Franklin get into her car?"

"Yep." The girl tugged on her braid. "And Papa left right after."

Banging from the left resumed.

"That's enough," Mrs. Pollack said.

"Well, thank you very much, little lady." Leon held out his hand for a firm handshake from this no-nonsense little girl. She ran into the back of the house.

He stood. "Mrs. Pollack, have you heard the name Tom, or seen this man?" He hadn't had the chance to ask the kids, but he doubted she'd call them back. His doubts were confirmed when her face blanked.

"I don't know. A man named Tom works at the hospital with my husband, I think. But I ain't never seen him. That's all."

Mrs. Pollack shut the door in his face.

What was she afraid of? She hadn't liked when the girl mentioned her papa. But the mention of Tom, or her husband's work, had really spooked her.

"Does her husband live here too?"

"Mm-hmm."

"What hospital does he work at?"

Mrs. Grun shrugged and inhaled from her cigarette, the end turning orange with the intake of oxygen.

Leon peered over at unit 5 to avoid the exhale, and wondered where Deborah Franklin was.

He turned to meet Olive Grun's eyes. "Would you be willing to let me take a look at her place? I won't touch anything, but I want to look for signs of a struggle, or packing, or some hint as to where she might be? You can stay right with me unless I see something indicating a crime, in which case I'll need you to evacuate the scene immediately."

Mrs. Grun hesitated. "Do you have a warrant?"

Leon shook his head and waited. It was all up to this woman. She was the rightful owner, but there were legalities. How strict was the rental agreement? And was the "no visitor" policy written in stone or a loose verbal agreement? How worried was she about her tenant?

She folded her arms and narrowed her eyes as she studied him.

"I told you she's real private."

He felt like he was back in elementary school, sitting in the principal's office. It made him want to squirm, even though he hadn't done anything wrong. He just wanted to solve the case.

"Will it help you find her?" she asked.

"I can't promise that I'll get a lead, but it will narrow the possibilities."

After another few uncomfortable moments of scrutiny, Mrs. Grun dropped her cigarette on the ground and twisted her foot over it, putting out the ember. "Let's go take a look. But no touching. And call me Olive."

She must have taken a liking to him.

Apparently she had already made her mind up before he got there, because she pulled out a key ring with a single key on it and led him to unit 5.

Olive explained, "Debbie wanted the one on the end with the most privacy. I don't blame her." The lock clicked as she twisted the key. Then she pushed the door open, stepping inside and blocking the doorway. "Debbie, are you here? The police want to see if you're okay."

Olive peered into the room beyond. "If you don't say anything, I am going to let this officer come in and look around." Olive paused to listen. "Debbie?" she called one more time.

Would the stink of death greet them from somewhere within?

Leon listened to the stillness of abandonment.

Chapter 17: Kylie

"At some point you will be the next person on Earth to die."
—Unknown

Wednesday, April 20

0930

Iron bars on the windows, cameras in the hallways, and the constant presence of someone at the front desk made this place feel unsafe. Because they were meant to keep something in, not out. It was basically juvie.

Why they were waiting to give her the test until Friday, she had no idea, but until then she was the only child above five years old in the place. Which gave her the perfect opportunity to start testing the defenses and planning her escape.

Kako kept a close eye on her, but when she was assigned a chore, she was often left to finish it alone. While probing the empty halls of the orphanage, Ky found some good hiding spots. She knew a thing or two about tucking things out of sight, where people would be the least likely to disturb them. Several went on her list to explore more later.

Right now she was in a shed making weed killer. Ky thought it was either a way to use slave labor or a tricky way to try to teach the kids. Two scoops from the salt bucket went into the large jug of the sprayer, already filled to the line with vinegar. Then, for some reason, she had to add a squirt of soap. Luckily, she was strong for her size, because the whole thing weighed quite a bit.

The gardener, a man named Eb, was nearby, not watching her—yeah, right. And the large iron gate was shut this time of day. It seemed none of the kids would be allowed back in until after school. The fencing was a bit much. At eight feet tall and with black iron bars so close together she couldn't so much as fit her hand through, it felt wrong. Were they protecting the kids here or trying to keep them in?

She pumped and squirted the mixture along the edges of the building and fence. There didn't seem to be any change, but she guessed they knew what they were talking about. She went the entire length around the school and didn't find any holes in their security. There were even outdoor cameras.

By the time she was finished, she felt as if she had crossed a desert, or more like a jungle. Sweat dripped down her face and back, dampening her clothing. The air itself seemed to be confining her, holding her here. Everything smelled of mold and rot, so different from the dry, fresh air of home.

Ky was given permission—well, actually, she was shooed to the bathroom for a shower by the lady at the front desk. Clean and dressed in perfumed clothing, she spent some time looking around the bedroom.

They'd bolted the bunk beds to the wall, probably something else "for safety," because she couldn't see someone trying to lift one. But that left a nice spot between the wood and the wall to wedge things. Regrettably, the one above *her* bed was in use. It contained something blocking her fingers' access. Curious, she worked at it until she retrieved a stapled pile of papers folded in half to make a little book.

She jammed herself into a small space by the wall, so she would be difficult to spot, and flipped through the pages. At times like this, she was glad the girl she'd looked up to and who'd taken a lost little Ky under her wing—Belle—had taught them all how to read. Interested in someone who had the foresight to hide this little book in such a good place, she began reading.

Today, Julie was nice to me, and we played . . .

Someone had made a little journal.

Yesterday, Dr. Kako was supervising our class. She's creepy and hardly ever talks to us.

Skip.

Last night, I had a dream I was frozen in place. First, I stood outside my family's home while a mysterious figure set fire to it. I couldn't yell or move to save my family. I could hear their screams and saw my little brother hanging out of a window, begging me for help while I just stood there. Then I stood face-to-face with Sarah. She said she was going to take her test. Dr. Kako came in and dragged her off. Sarah reached for me, crying out for me to save her, and I just stood there, like a statue. I felt terrible this morning. Like I hadn't slept at all. And another kid is gone. A boy I didn't know well . . .

Another kid? What did that mean?

Today, Sarah took her test. She seemed very nervous, but I am sure she will do fine. I've never heard anyone's scores; they are all placed right afterward. I'll be sad when she goes, but she has promised to write . . .

A voice caused her to jump. "What are you doing in here? It's almost dinnertime. Go help set the table."

She didn't want anyone looking too closely at her. If she could lull them into a sense of ease, she'd be able to escape easier.

After dinner, chores, and preparation for bed, during quiet time, Ky pulled the journal back out. She skimmed, looking for Sarah's name again. Maybe she could find something out about this test after all.

Sarah left last night for a new home. I asked for the address, but I was told it was "privileged information." The lady at the desk said I could give her any letters and she would forward them on.

Ky skimmed again.

"Lights out."

Ky froze like a rabbit sensing danger. She waited several minutes in the dark, then sneaked into the bathroom, desperate to finish and find out what happened to Sarah. Sitting on a lid, with her feet pulled up and the stall locked, she continued.

I have written Sarah several long letters and I haven't even got a note in reply! I thought she was my friend, but now that she has a family, she can't give me the time of day. I hate her!

Ky skimmed down further.

A couple of other girls have said I should stop thinking about Sarah. Everyone says it always happens. All the children who are adopted out of town don't write back. But I can't help it. I miss her.

Ky paused. *All of them?* She continued reading, absorbed.

I've been thinking about it, and I'm worried. Why is it just the kids who get adopted by out-of-towners? Are they the ones who do poorly? Did Sarah do badly on the test? I am scheduled to take my test next week . . .

Ky sucked in a breath as the page ended ominously halfway down. Nothing else, and the book was still here. Was the girl still here? One of the ones around her? Not likely, since Ky had been assigned to the open bunk. Had she, too, been adopted abruptly, at night, by out-of-towners?

The door clicked opened, shaking Ky out of her thoughts. Footsteps shuffled to another stall. She tucked the journal out of sight between her clothes and skin, and headed back into the darkened bedroom and her bunk, the springs squeaking as she lay down. For now she tucked the journal back in its spot above her head, then settled down to sleep.

Despite the softness of the clean mattress and sheets, Ky missed the tunnel where she bedded down with the others in their big nest. She missed their companionship and the safety of having others she could trust looking over her shoulder. She took a deep breath to clear her mind and heard them—the strange, ghostly noises some of the girls had told her about. Everyone else seemed to be asleep. How could they sleep through that?

She needed a plan. She *had* to get out of here right away.

Time to focus on what she had to work with.

The thing about schedules was they sucked in general, but it meant knowing exactly what would happen, and when. One girl always laid her clothes out the day before. That meant Ky could borrow something tonight and it wouldn't be noticed until tomorrow night.

She slowly rolled out of bed, pausing at the telling squeak. Then she tiptoed over to the locker and lifted a dress. She balled it up and stuck it under her pillow before lying back down. She knew exactly how she could walk right out with everyone else, unobserved. Some discreet questions had let her know what the adults usually did. If she could get far enough away and stay hidden well enough, she had a good chance of escaping whatever fate these people had planned for her.

She was good with directions and had managed a peek at a map of the town. Her mind skipped ahead to practicalities, where she would go, and what basic supplies were most important. Ky knew how to take care of herself and, at least then, she knew what to expect. She couldn't afford to mess this up. Ky had a feeling this was her one and only chance to get away. She never wanted to come face-to-face with Kako again.

The sounds returned. She couldn't tell if they were coming from the next room over the vents, or within the wall itself. Ky lay for a long time in the darkness, planning, unable to sleep.

Chapter 18: Project Nefertem

"The lotus comes from the murkiest water but grows into the purest thing."—Nita Ambani

March, One Month Ago

Sherri stood in the warmth of the conservatory. Her perfect specimen was almost the size of a large dog, and it was still growing. But it was more perfect than any mere dog. She couldn't wait to see what it would do when it achieved full maturity.

Unfortunately, the Director wanted her to focus on the Venuses. Venus, Venus, Venus. Potential lethality, blah, blah, blah. Reports of their sturdiness, how much ground they could cover, how long their vines stayed sharp, and the list went on.

And yet the scent of their rot reached her all the way in the conservatory before the incinerator finished burning a couple more failures.

So tiresome.

The Venus subjects were improving slowly, but they were still practically disposable.

All that was beside the point. She had no interest in what the Venuses could do. It was like focusing on snails instead of humans. Didn't they understand? The Venus experiment had just been a stepping stone toward achieving perfection.

Just like Weston, no one could see the potential of AC101512. But she knew. She had a feeling. If she could get rid of all the Venuses right now, she would, yet they were the very reason she was allowed—allowed, mind you—to continue her work despite the unfortunate "losses." Dr. Weston was fond of reminding her she should have been more careful with the nurses and orderlies.

LAB NOTES

Subject AC101512 has reached a size of 122.8 cm by 61.5 cm diameter with root system at an average of 101.2 cm.

Venus 9 was manipulated to increase susceptibility to the primordium. Experiment successful.

Venus 10 was manipulated to increase defense against bio-corrosive acids. Partially successful. Primordium exposure was successful.

Subject AC101512—the outer leaves enclosing the bud have unfurled, creating both aerial and floating leaves, and creepers have begun to protrude from the short stem.

Weeks later, and back in the conservatory, Sherri was impressed, despite herself, with the improvements in the Venus subjects and the Dominus experiment. But right now she had eyes only for AC101512, who was starting to open up, and it was gorgeous.

The leaves were reminiscent of the lotus flower—if it were the size of a hippo—and the lily pad–like leaves covered the water surface around the bud, spreading all the way to the edge of the pool. Like the painting outside her office, she wished to wade among them; however, it was no longer possible to see the root system, and she refused to do it any harm. The calm of the water mirrored her emotions when she stood contemplating her creation.

The addition of creepers was unanticipated. Their purpose was, as yet, unexplained. Her favorite experimental subject had a few surprises in store. She hurried back to her desk to double-check the DNA and look for the source of the creepers. Which of the botanicals had caused that mutation?

"Dr. Gianni."

Dr. Weston was calling her. Strange. He never came to *her* office. She hadn't had much time away from her experiments lately. Perhaps he missed her? She looked up and forced a tired smile.

"What are the outcomes with the Venuses? The Director has been asking about them, and you didn't attend the last meeting."

She frowned. Them again. Her eyes flashed with anger, but she ducked her head quickly. "Just a minute." She fumbled through her papers, pushing most of them aside, looking for the reports about the current Venus experiments. Her computer, perhaps they were in her computer? She needed sleep. Her thoughts had been muddled lately.

"Never mind. Find them and give me an update before the day is out." His lab coat whipped behind him as he exited the room.

Anything to get him out of her space. She looked at the clock in the bottom right corner of her screen. It was already after four. Where had the day gone?

She gathered a clipboard and bustled to the Venus rooms. She would get the pertinent information now so she could get back to her research on AC101512.

LAB NOTES

Venus 11's genetic modification caused instability, attempted destruction with an acidic combination.

Acidic mixture, failed. Venus 11 has mutated and begun to regrow in an unusual pattern.

Subject AC101512 has opened, purpose unclear, experimentation to ensue. Creepers are producing nodules.

The new Venus experiments were slightly interesting. Unexpected outcomes made her want to discover why. First, she needed to check on AC101512.

Hidden in the world of vegetation, she sat alone, though people moved around her. She watched as her baby was born—exposed to the world! The outer leaves pulled away and down, leaving a light-green bud. Rays of sun shone on it, revealing a seam along the middle that looked like it would separate, eventually. So fresh and delicate.

The staff had even named it Audrey. Apparently it reminded some of the workers of a movie about a carnivorous alien plant. Although Sherri thought trivial movies were a waste of time, it was kind of endearing, and she would use that name in her thoughts. They knew its purpose and had named it appropriately.

She begrudgingly returned to the Venus experiments to keep the Director mollified. She wouldn't have to wait much longer to see Audrey's true potential.

LAB NOTES

Venus 11 no longer has mobility, previous experimentation deemed too difficult due to mobility is now possible. Acidic and electrical experimentation found interesting results, a possible working sedative. Destroyed with electrical current and disposed of in the incinerator.

Venus 12, sedative tested and improved, incomplete compatibility with primordium, destroyed with electrical current, and disposed of in the incinerator.

Subject AC101512 requires the same feeding as Venus subjects. It is more resilient to temperature fluctuations, acidic chemical mixtures, and electrical charges. Subject seems much more sentient than the Venus subjects.

The Venus subjects were, once again, a disappointment. More fed to the incinerator. What a waste of resources.

Audrey's bud had split and proved itself just as hungry as the Venuses. Though much more resilient than them. With Audrey as the only subject, Sherri was much more careful with the experiments. She couldn't afford to do any permanent harm.

Chapter 19: Leon

"We make up horrors to help us cope with the real ones."—*Stephen King*

Wednesday, April 20

1000

Leon stopped in the doorway to take in a deep breath.

No miasma of death met him, only the mustiness of old damp and mold. Debbie's body could wait farther in, though, fresh or blocked by a closed door. He blinked several times, waiting for his sight to adjust. The mismatched curtains were all drawn shut, keeping the area in darkness.

He took in the layout at a glance. It was one open area: living, dining, and kitchen, with the washer and dryer directly in front of the door. An opening to the left of the washer and dryer indicated a hallway going back into a bedroom/bath area.

It wasn't messy, but it wasn't clean. The place looked lived in. But strangely silent. No ticking clocks or dripping faucets.

On the far-right wall was an older stove-and-oven combination, next to a small fridge wedged into the corner. The freezer on the top looked like it was only big enough for a tray of ice and a half gallon of ice cream. On the back wall, to the right of the washer, was a cabinet, then a sink.

He moved to check the sink, to get an idea of the timeline. He passed a card table on the right, with a wooden stool on the far side and a folding chair closest to him. Papers and envelopes were stacked on the table as well as bills and junk mail, along with several empty hard-alcohol bottles. She appeared to have no particular favorite, but all the brands were the cheap generic ones.

The left side of the sink was empty, but the right side was half-filled with dirty dishes. This close, they smelled sour and rotten. The food dried and crusted to them—at least a few days old. He continued past the washer and dryer, which were simple and well dented. There were clothes tossed in a plastic laundry basket sitting on top of the dryer. It wasn't readily apparent whether they were clean or dirty.

He turned to look at Mrs. Grun, standing shadowed, the sun behind her. "Let's head back through the rest of the apartment. But stay behind me, just in case."

As she stepped into the room, more light illuminated the dim space, exposing the dust motes that were
stirred up. He passed by an old-style television on a
simple, cheap table to the left, and a mustard-yellow,
way-past-its-prime couch on the opposite wall. A faded
gray blanket draped across it, probably covering holes in
the cushions.

Leon stepped down the hall in trepidation. He really
didn't want to find a body or anything. He never had
before and didn't want to start now. *What am I concerned
about? There's no car, ergo, she isn't here. Dead or otherwise.
Unless the vehicle was stolen . . . after they killed her . . . and
we are about to stumble upon a gruesome scene.*

Leon tripped over the carpet as his mind tripped over
horrible thoughts. Luckily the hall was more of an idea
than an actual thing and he had already reached the first
closed door. He reached for the doorknob.

"That's just the bathroom."

Leon didn't want to leave a closed door behind him, and
it was important to check every inch of the house for
Deborah, or at least a sign of her, so he twisted the cool
metal knob and opened the door.

"Ahhhh." Movement made him duck. His image in a small
mirrored cabinet over the sink gazed back at him.

He jumped again at a squeak from Olive and popped his
head back out of the room to look into the frightened eyes
of the older woman.

"Sorry, just my reflection." Leon felt ridiculous. What must this woman think of him?

He turned back to his assessment of the tiny bathroom and scrunched his nose.

Small containers and tubes women keep their makeup in covered the counter. There was enough light from the open door behind them and from a glass pane in the outer wall to illuminate the small room. A baggie with a small amount of a suspicious residue nestled among the clutter.

"Can I take this? It might be a clue."

Mrs. Grun poked her head in to assess. She bit her lip, but then nodded.

Touching only the corner of the baggie, he slipped it into a brown paper bag he took from a pocket and labeled it with a marker from another pocket.

Mrs. Grun raised an eyebrow but didn't speak.

To the left was a toilet, lid down, and a shower with the plain mint-green curtain closed.

Leon didn't have a warrant. He shouldn't move anything, though plain sight was acceptable, but he was still looking for Deborah, and that stink could be her body behind the curtain. "Would it be all right if I move this shower curtain, just in case?"

Mrs. Grun reached forward. "Maybe I should do it?"

"No, there could still be danger. And if she is there—you shouldn't be subject to that."

She sighed. "I'm right behind you."

He took a deep breath and pulled.

Nothing but soap scum and mildew. Leon shook his head at himself. He turned back to the door, and Mrs. Grun stepped out, letting him past her into the cramped hallway. A few strides took him through the open doorway and he scanned the room for danger before looking back at Mrs. Grun.

She leaned against the doorframe.

"Unless she's on the floor behind the bed or in the closet, there's nothing in here either," she said unhelpfully.

An unmade bed took up most of the room on the left. The blankets lay crumpled where Debbie had thrown them back when she'd climbed out of bed. A few clothes were on the floor, an old dresser on the right of the door, and a closet against the right wall. A pamphlet for Vermilion Peak Psychiatric Hospital lay on her bedside table, next to her alarm. Had she been considering getting help for her problem? Or maybe her father had sent it to pressure her? That was more likely, but it would be sad if she had OD'd just when there was hope.

Leon walked forward to the closet opening. There were so many clothes hung in the cramped space, it was difficult to tell where one piece ended and the next began. He stepped over to look at the other side of the bed, but the floor was clean. Well, no body, no drugs, no note, but there *were* socks and dirty clothes.

He could feel Mrs. Grun following his every move. "Do you know if she had a suitcase?" Leon squatted to get a better look at the things on the floor and under the bed. "Because I don't see anything." He stood and turned to meet those watchful owl eyes.

She glanced toward the closet, then straightened and unfolded her arms to slip her hands into her pockets. "No. I never saw one."

Now it was Leon's turn to sigh. "Well, thank you for your cooperation, Mrs. Grun. I'll get out of your hair now. Let me know if you see or hear anything more." He handed her a card and retraced his steps to the front door.

Back outside, he slipped his sunglasses back down and headed for his cruiser. After the musty, closed-in atmosphere of the apartment, he was glad to breathe in some fresh air.

No body. But also no sign she had gone on a trip. *Where are you, Deborah?*

"That's it?" Mrs. Grun asked.

Leon turned back around. He held up the paper bag. It needed to be analyzed at the RPD lab. "I have a new lead."

Chapter 20: Project Nefertem

"I desire very little, but the things I do consume me."—Dancing in the Dark, *T.L. Martin*

Sunday, April 3, Seventeen Days Ago

0345

Audrey had awoken.

There *were* signs, but it was more of Sherri's gut feeling that Audrey had an awareness. She could feel Audrey crying, so she cut her bathroom break short to hurry back to the conservatory.

"What is wrong with you?" Spit flew as she tore into the assistants around the pool. She turned to her baby and modulated her voice to soothe. "What is it, Audrey? What do you need?" She flashed back to the worthless personnel taking up space. "Did you give it fertilizer? Did you add fresh water? Meat?"

"We were just taking some measurements, Doctor."

They weren't harming Audrey. They were just doing their jobs. Sherri's thinking cleared and her phone trilled.

"Dr. Gianni, we're about to start the Dominus experiment."

"I'll be right there." She gave the staff a once-over. Everyone hovered over their clipboards and tablets, carefully avoiding her eyes. She'd be back as soon as possible.

LAB NOTES

Venus 13, improvement in some areas and successfully bonded with primordium.

Venus 14, some improvement, but susceptibility to bio-corrosive acids increased, successfully bonded to primordium.

Venus 15 failure, unsuccessfully bonded to primordium, acidic and electrical experiments conducted providing more data, disposed of in the incinerator.

Useless Venus subjects. Another one of them had to be disposed of. She'd leave further experiments to those assistants; they didn't understand the delicacy of caring for Audrey anyway. She could send more over here. However, the primordium was working consistently. An idea came to her.

What would happen if she exposed Audrey to the primordium?

LAB NOTES

Subject AC101512 was exposed to the primordium, but there seems to be no effect or bonding.

Subject AC101512, Audrey, is producing a single flower bud on a separate stalk growing from a runner and producing several more creepers.

The primordium bonding of the Dominus seemed to not work with Audrey's unique makeup, which made sense since she was so much more than they. Audrey was perfection.

Sherri spent much of her time in the conservatory nowadays, breathing in the humid vegetative air and forcing her assistants to bring her and Audrey food and water. All the necessary equipment had been moved into this room. Filling the space between the pool and the mosaiced wall planters. She didn't want to miss a minute of its growth.

"Is Dr. Gianni okay?" she heard one of the staff members in a lab coat whisper to another.

"Get out!" She could hear them talking, night and day, saying she was obsessed. They were so loud. She couldn't hear Audrey over their noise. Obsession. None of them understood her genius. You had to have hyperfocus to accomplish great things.

Once the quiet returned, her body relaxed again. It had begun to feel like she was an explorer in the jungle, camping near a great discovery. Waiting and watching for the miracle.

Audrey, the clever girl, had produced a single flower bud. Why was there a single bud and what would it look like? Audrey was also continuing to produce creepers that were spilling over the side of the pool. Did she need additional nourishment she wasn't receiving in the pool?

LAB NOTES

Audrey's flower has opened. The bloom is actinomorphic, with many petals, and a two-toned cerulean and yellow variation. The stamen are adelphous, bunched in a large grouping around the center. A large amount of pollen has been released, and we have collected samples for study.

Sherri was in awe. Audrey's flower was the size of her spread hand. A gorgeous blue contrasted nicely with the petals fading to a golden yellow at the base. Like the painting outside of her office, the flower was such a vibrant blue, and the yellow drew her gaze to the center.

She was curious about the pollen because it had been released in the manner of a Basidiomycota, or puffball mushroom. Unfortunately, she had missed the blessed event—she now had a bedpan to reduce the instances in which she would be gone—but had watched the video of it over and over. Yellow dust had exploded into the air, reminding her of the last time she had gone to India to explore exotic plants. It had been during the festival of Holi, and people had been throwing colored powders on one another, celebrating in triumph. It still hung in the air.

What a delicious feeling.

The pollen had a sweet, alluring scent.

Chapter 21: Leon

"Sometimes I have so much going on inside my head that I have no room left for words."—Anonymous

Thursday, April 21

1130

Besides Deborah, Batman was missing.

So was Fluffy, Tiger, Mr. Cuddles, Midnight, and Football. On the canine side of things, there were the unhappy owners of Rosie, Jeff, Spot (*really?*), Muffin, Wolfie, and Ruff. Leon tore his fingers through his hair and rolled back his chair, making space between him and his computer. He walked across the large room to get his blood flowing and watered the yellowing plant McKenna had given him. First Deborah

Franklin, now this. He hadn't caught a break since Mrs. Everton's bicycle.

Another day in the office hammered with phones ringing, officers typing away, and people coming and going. He'd taken a second look at Tom's obituary, and it hadn't said he had worked at a hospital. It hadn't said where he had worked at all. The ambiguousness of the information bothered him. But the chief had said the deaths had nothing to do with each other. He had to believe the chief knew what he was talking about. And the residue from Deborah's home was in line at the forensic lab.

He couldn't just sit around waiting for the lab work to get back. Unable to let go of the nagging and heartbreak that followed him when he heard of another report, or saw another missing poster, he decided he would help discover what was happening to the town's domesticated animals.

Seeing the pile of cases, he had been horrified. There were always losses living as close to the forest as they did, but this last week was a nightmare.

There was also the possibility that this did have something to do with Deborah's disappearance. If a bear or mountain lion had made its way down the mountain and was living next to Robur, she could have been a casualty. And if they did not catch it, kids or other townsfolk could be next. As bad as the lost pets were, that was his greatest fear—the danger to the people of the town.

He placed the plant back in its spot on his messy desk and looked over at his sometime partner, Officer Paul Tang. He appeared to be just as frustrated as Leon felt.

The older man sighed wearily and leaned back in his chair with closed eyes. Paul was suffering from another of his headaches. Black hair edged in gray surrounded the temples he rubbed in a circular motion. Paul had been doing his best on his own, but other than getting calls from helpful neighbors and patrolling, what could he do?

The overwhelming number of cases was hitting Paul especially hard because he was an animal lover. In fact, he had three kids who each had their own pet. His oldest girl had a cat who always slept at the foot of her bed, his oldest son had a dog he was never seen without, and his youngest son had a hamster. The pictures on Paul's desk spoke louder than words, though Paul never stopped talking about his family and pets either.

Leon sometimes worked with Paul, like now, when the man was clearly swamped. It always felt good when he could reunite the pet and owner because he had found it playing down the street or rummaging through a neighbor's trash. However, things didn't always work out.

Sometimes pets were struck down in the road, and sometimes the forest or natural selection reclaimed them. But this many pets, wandering that far out of their neighborhood, and meeting untimely ends, seemed too coincidental to be true.

If it was an animal, it would have a hunting ground, right? A territory that it stayed in? A restlessness filled him. Ugh, he needed to see things laid out.

"Paul . . ."

The other officer's eyes flew open.

"Let's get a bird's-eye view of what is going on. Pull out all the missing animal cases and meet me in the break room. I want to see something."

Paul stood, gathering files.

Leon grabbed his laptop and headed over to where they kept a large clear, hard-plastic-covered map of the city. He had never needed to use it before. Usually the FOREST team commandeered it if someone went missing and had to be found in the forest.

Leon leaned it in front of a whiteboard as a stand and opened to the first case. Slowly but surely he filled in the dots where animals were missing and color-coded them by date. Paul joined him and took over, calling out the places and dates for Leon. Once every case was accounted for, he stepped back to observe the map.

Most of the dots centered on Vermilion Heights. It had to be an animal. That was the only explanation.

The forests were filled with bears, hawks, coywolves, and other things that would eat a little domesticated dog or cat if it could catch it. Also, there were those that could wound or kill an animal without eating it. Raccoons, snakes—if a pet got out there, chances of survival weren't good.

Leaving Paul to continue double-checking their work and take measurements, Leon pulled out his cell and contacted the front desk. The officer on scheduling duty made an appointment with Leon's captain.

There was an animal loose preying on pets. And ranger support was going to be required. Vermilion Heights backed up to Kaira Forest. Leon just didn't know enough about wild animals to do this, even with Tang's help.

He received an appointment for tomorrow afternoon. When Leon hung up, he and Paul got right to work putting together a report for his boss and a file to share with the rangers—if he got the go-ahead. Someone drank coffee nearby. It was getting late, and the aroma tempted him, but he needed to sleep tonight.

After completing the report, staying later than usual, he parked his marked car outside the duplex. Then he dragged himself to his front door, fumbling the keys and almost dropping them. He'd forgotten again to leave on the porch light. A creak caused him to turn in alarm and lose the battle with the keys. They clanked against the wood porch.

"Sorry, I was just enjoying the night. Aren't you a little late?" McKenna's voice reassured him.

Leon leaned over and hooked the key ring on his finger. "Busy day. Are you on duty tomorrow?"

"Yep."

"I'm going to be contacting the forest station in the next couple of days, if I get the go-ahead from my captain. You know—red tape. I need ranger help."

"What is it?" McKenna's voice became tense and alert.

"I think there is an animal targeting Robur's domesticated pets. There have been just too many lately."

"Could be." McKenna resumed rocking, staring out into the dark.

He stood and leaned against his door, joining her in the quiet for a few minutes. With the sun down, everything had cooled off. He hunched his shoulders against the chill. The crescent moon rose slowly. A cricket sang nearby. The wind caught—crackling a plastic bag as it filled with air and sailed across the pavement. His eyelids weighed down on him.

He straightened and his keys jangled, intent on getting inside.

"Be careful. The forest is starting to wake," she said.

Chapter 22: Kylie

"It's been like a bad dream I never woke from."—Alex Chilton
Thursday, April 21

0815

Ky executed her plan.

She had been paying attention all morning, and no one in the school was older than twelve. So Sarah was gone, one way or another. What bothered Ky was that the girl hadn't taken her journal—and those sounds last night. Even if there was a logical explanation, it was creepy.

She walked right out with a group of girls on their way to school. Her stomach flipped, and she tried to move casually past the front desk, but she could feel her legs shaking. She blended in with a dress and a backpack. Standing tall and bold, she had to have faith the change in her appearance was enough to slip by. Wearing her hair up, she'd taken a page out of Kako's book, wearing a scarf over her head to disguise her profile. Ky followed the crowd closely for camouflage.

"Hey, you."

Ky froze at the woman's voice. Had she already been discovered? The rest of the group had stopped and was looking at the woman to determine whom she was talking to.

"Your backpack isn't all the way zipped. Your books are about to fall out." She pointed to a girl in front, wearing a red shirt, and everyone's attention turned to helping the girl.

Once they left the orphanage grounds, the girls began chattering away.

"Did you finish that math last night?" one girl asked. "Problem fourteen was so tricky."

"Oh, yeah. It took me like an hour to do that one." said the girl in the red shirt.

"I think there is going to be a quiz today," another piped up.

"Who cares? I'm sitting with Sam at lunch," an older girl boasted. She must be close to the testing age.

They all giggled.

Ky rolled her eyes.

"What about you?"

One of the girls had drifted slightly back to talk to Ky. Obviously the friendly type, but that was the last thing Ky needed.

She stopped. "Oh, I forgot my pencil." She turned around and waited until she passed another small group going the opposite way, then turned back again, staying behind another small group. This time keeping a bit of space.

She slipped away from the pack and turned right just before Main Street. The road, busy with pedestrians and traffic, covered her movements. After crossing the street, she sneaked through the open, wrought iron gates of the cemetery. She tilted her head back, taking in the view. She had never seen gates so towering or detailed.

Ky crept through the headstones, darting between the biggest and using them as shields to hide her from passersby. She chose one to sit behind while she waited for the bell to ring and the cop to clear off. It was soothing. The ground was cool, if a bit damp. The branches of the tall, straight trees swayed in the breeze, rocking and shaking their leaves. She arranged her scarf to cover her hair and face more closely.

The grounds were quiet and deserted except for the call of a bird, followed by the ringing of the school bell, which made her stomach swoop. Ready to put some distance between her and Kako, she stood and peeked over the stone. The streets were fairly clear now, and she couldn't see the cop.

Her footsteps sank down into the soggy grass, muffling her journey. There had been a few surprises this morning, but now everything was going smoothly until she reached her goal. The housing development behind the cemetery stood like a fortress. She stared in shock at high, impassible fences even larger than the one at the orphanage. She had stepped forward to see if she could fit through or climb it when a large dog lunged at her from the other side, teeth first and barking its head off. Ky bolted, giving the fence some space to avoid another alarm.

Forced to skirt along the fence through the cemetery, and hoping to find another exit, she stopped by a large white gazebo to catch her breath.

A man—the gardener from the orphanage, Eb—called out. "Hey, you."

How had he caught her already?

She ran. Staying in a crouch, she raced from headstone to headstone until eventually discovering a small gate leading out to the street. Ky walked along a residential street, searching for a better neighborhood to hide in. When a well-maintained, brick-lined road into the gated community appeared, she chose not to enter. It felt too confining—not in a good way. If she entered those gates, she would be trapped with very few ways out.

Follow your instincts, Ky.

She stopped when she came to the river, eyes wide and mouth open. *So much water!* She had never seen a real river before, not so close anyway. It was wide, and the river ran swiftly, bubbling and turning white around the rocks along the edge. It smelled only slightly like decay. And was that fish?

Ky gazed at the river, her fingers gripping her dress, thinking about all the things that could happen if she fell in. The water moved so fast. She'd be gone before she could think.

The canals she had traversed at home often had only a trickle in them along with plants, trash, and sludge. Just waiting for the winter snows to melt. The mountains towered to the west, and the streets and canals were laid out in a grid, making it easy to get around. Ky and her friends used them as sidewalks to get places.

But sometimes, after a hard rain, it would build up to a flowing stream and wash all the debris away, cleaning it out. It would smell fresh, and she could hear the sweep of the water as it passed out of sight. She missed home.

A clump of fluffy clouds passed overhead, cooling the day. And a walkway along the bridge led to a few shops on the other side. There was a sign for Kaira Forest, giving directions and mileage for hikes and scenic drives. A familiar car drove by, and Ky hid as best as she could.

Her heart pounded; this was worse than when she lived on the streets. She knew how, where, and when to stay out of sight there. Here she was vulnerable. And Ky couldn't stand being vulnerable.

"Don't see me," Ky whispered.

There was only one car in town she recognized. Kako had stopped to get something out of her car on their walk from the station to the orphanage. Either she was already out looking for her or just heading into work. Ky assumed the worst.

She crossed the bridge and hid around the building. She peeked around the corner and waited to see what Kako would do. Had Ky already been spotted? She let out a breath when the woman finished filling her car with gas and drove away.

Safe for the moment, Ky took her time, lingering in the shop alleys and dumpsters, leaving a false trail and masking her scent with garbage as best as she could. She hopped up on one dumpster, then pulled off the dress and scarf, thrusting them down into the depths of the dumpster she crouched precariously on. Next she hopped up to the screening fence around it and from there made her way up to the roof.

Stepping across the roof in a crouch, she hid behind the peak, keeping it between her and the road. Her foot slipped on the loose sand from the tiles. If she fell, she could be seriously hurt—or worse, seen. She grabbed the roof with both hands, struggling for purchase, and recovered her balance. She lowered her face to the gritty tiles in relief.

No one came to inspect the scrabbling sounds; they must have squirrels or mice. Pulling herself back up, she finished her crossing of the roof. Then, lowering herself over the side, she dropped to the ground. Ky brushed herself off, straightened her shirt, and strolled casually to the gas station to use their restroom. Back in Denver you would have to go inside to borrow a key that had an entire brick attached to it to keep you from stealing it. Here it was just open.

She washed her hands and face, cooling her cheeks while looking in the mirror. Then she pulled the hairband out of her hair and ran her fingers through the brown strands, straightening them to fall freely to her shoulders. Her nose was still wide and flat. But the rest of her appearance was strikingly changed. After checking the trash for any bottles and finding it bare of anything but crumpled paper towels, she slurped the tap water from her cupped hands. The metallic flavor lingered on her tongue.

She placed the backpack with the one broken strap over her right shoulder, then crossed the street and turned left to follow along the river. The first part of her plan may have had a few hiccups, but things were going to be fine now. It was actually kind of peaceful, walking in the sunshine with the occasional cloud and hearing the gurgling of the passing river.

The map she had seen had only shown downtown. But she was pretty sure there were supposed to be other housing developments this way. With luck, they weren't as intense about security as the ones closer to the downtown. Not that she'd had a lot of luck lately.

She was used to walking, but it had been a while. And back in Denver she had never needed to travel far. But at this rate maybe she could walk back to Denver. All she knew was that she would rather die in the forest than in that terrible orphanage, where children disappeared without a trace.

As she trudged along, she became thirsty but took only a few sips from the single bottle she had scavenged from the side of the road. There wasn't much left in it. Everywhere had a littering problem, even fancy small towns like Robur Copse.

Around noon her stomach growled, and she nibbled on a napkin-wrapped roll she had saved. Even a day old, the yeasty fluff melted in her mouth. She came across a bridge and stopped at the top to look. A large sign declared it Vermilion Heights.

She released a relieved sigh at the more normal-looking subdivision of houses. Well, they were less security mind-ed, anyway. The houses all looked exactly alike, with only a few size differences. In a word, it looked—*boooring*. She singsonged the word in her mind. It was a place where police cars patrolled up and down the streets, but it would do for now. Away from the orphanage and the sharp-eyed Kako, she could escape this town much more easily.

Ky headed into the maze to find a place to hunker down for the night. A good corner of bushes practically welcomed her with an extension cord just lying in the dirt for all who were willing to crawl into the back to find. She added that to her pack for later and snuggled in. She did much better in neighborhoods and cities than in wilderness. But she had a feeling that tonight, in these suburbs close to a river and forest, she'd be seeing a lot of unfamiliar critters and hearing a lot of unfamiliar sounds.

It wasn't that Ky knew nothing about nature. There were several parks in her home city, and some were rather large. The trees were nice to sleep in, as people were much less likely to look up. But in a park you didn't have to walk long before you came across a playground, jogging trail, or road.

Those trees on the other side of the river went on for days and days. Who knew what lived in there.

Chapter 23: Leon

"There is no worse death than the end of hope."—*Pelagius*, King Arthur

Friday, April 22

0900

Leon's phone rang, but he ignored it. He didn't have time for this. He poured the coffee in his to-go cup and put the lid on, then grabbed the toast from the toaster.

Today he had the appointment with his captain and should also get the results back from the lab about the residue. Unfortunately, he'd slept in after being up so late last night and was now running late. His cell rang again. Leon picked up his mug, the lid popped off, and hot coffee sloshed onto his right hand.

"Crackers!"

He dropped the whole thing into the sink and ran his hand under cold water, just as his phone rang a third time. Frustrated beyond all, he stabbed the accept button.

"Officer Rook," he growled.

"An unknown green Chevy Chevelle was called in on Turkey Rock Road in Northside."

"What? I'm on my way."

Forgetting about his breakfast mess, and his tender hand, Leon made haste to his vehicle, pulling out almost before the dispatcher had finished giving him the information.

Northside was where Leon lived. The neighborhood was composed of everyday people. The gas station attendant, the checkout girl who bagged your groceries, the tech who changed your oil and rotated your tires, or the sewage worker. They were all what some people would call the "little man." *They* weren't afraid to get dirty to make an honest living. Leon wondered where their town would be without those workers. Though Deborah lived in the Grove Apartments on the other side of downtown Robur, most of the people she knew probably lived in Northside.

Northside didn't look like the neighborhoods built by Osiris Biotech. They left the people here to cobble together their own housing. But some of them had building and plumbing skills learned before they moved here with their families. These people had skills to contribute, and he was so frustrated about how they were treated by the rest of the community because of their lack of money.

Leon didn't have the time to appreciate the mishmash of sizes, styles, and shapes in each and every house in Northside. He zoomed past a cottage with a yellow painted door and red trim, and turned past a two-story redbrick home with a wrought iron railing.

The yards were as varied as the people who lived there. Despite his hurry, he noted a few that were getting out of hand and planned to come back on his day off to whip them back into shape. Mrs. Everton was obviously having a hard time maintaining her garden at her old age. Where was that grandson of hers? Maybe his skills didn't extend to gardening, or she didn't want to bother him. Others had no time, working multiple jobs to pay the bills.

His hand started to sting a little, and Leon flipped it, checking the damage. It could've done with longer in the cold water, but overall wasn't too bad.

Finally! Turkey Rock Road. A green reflection hit the corner of his eye. He turned left toward it and parked behind the vehicle. He was on his computer in a flash, looking up the memo he had sent out days ago. Sure enough, the license numbers matched.

As much as he wanted to jump out and shout to everyone, he held himself together and turned on his radio. "This is Officer Rook calling dispatch. Over."

"Officer Rook, this is dispatch. Over."

"Dispatch, I've found Deborah Franklin's car on Turkey Rock Road in Northside. Read back. Over."

"I read back: Deborah Franklin's vehicle is at Turkey Rock Road on Northside. Over."

"Please get a police tow truck out here right away, acknowledge? Over."

"Roger. Over."

"Officer Rook out."

Leon hung his radio back up and waited, keeping the vehicle in his line of sight while he held back. Losing the fight with himself, he got out and walked around the vehicle, looking without touching. He stood by the back and leaned over, smelling what he could from the trunk, but no obvious bad smells came from it, reassuring him slightly. In his rush he had left his gloves—along with his sunglasses and hat—but he should have some in the cruiser. The sun was bright, but the occasional cloud made it bearable. After a quick rummage, he found a pair and snapped them on. Careful of fingerprints, he tried the handles. *Locked.*

He cupped his hands around his eyes and pressed against the glass to get a view of the interior. There were crumpled papers and possibly a bag, but nothing big enough to be a person. He called the tow truck driver, then gave her instructions for it to be towed back to the station.

As much as he wanted to get the car straight back, there was a process he couldn't hurry. Instead, he used his time wisely to canvass the neighborhood for witnesses. Leon needed to know just how long the car had been here. It was several doors before anyone even answered.

Anytime someone actually answered, Leon asked questions and flashed her picture on his phone, but it was a no-go. What felt like an hour later—but couldn't be since the tow truck driver was still hooking up the car—he was no closer to finding Deborah. Many people weren't home at this time of day, and the few who were had seen and heard nothing. He was about to give up when a car turned into a driveway near where Deborah's car was parked. He hurried over and caught the woman after she opened the rear door and reached in to retrieve shopping bags.

"Ma'am. Can I ask you a few questions?" He charged toward her.

"Umm." She looked around as if searching for an escape.

"Officer Rook, ma'am. I just want to know if you recognize that vehicle over there." Leon pointed.

"Oh, yes. I mean, no," she stumbled.

He almost bit his tongue, trying to be patient.

"What I mean is, that car has been there since Friday morning," she said.

She still seemed rather nervous.

"Did you see the owner?" Leon could feel his excitement growing.

"Oh, no. It was sitting there when I came out to take the kids to school in the morning." She shook her head, lips flattened.

She could be lying, but why would she?

He spent another ten minutes taking down her information and any details she could remember before walking back to his vehicle, thinking and watching the ground.

Concern gnawed at him. Missing with a car could mean one thing, but missing without a car meant a whole different ball game.

As he approached his squad car, he stopped.

A distinctive reddish-orange residue practically screamed at him from the blacktop. Four distinct prints, where each of Deborah's tires had been.

"The car is in perfect working order and has half a tank of gas." The mechanic told Leon before leaving to work on another vehicle.

Every movement echoed in the garage. Metal clanked, power tools buzzed, and the smell of oil and gas filled the space.

He strode out into the cloudy day and greeted CSI Watson in the part-gravel, part-grass fenced parking lot. Deborah's car was a newer addition, so it was in a mostly gravel area.

Watson set down her bag, rummaged inside, and turned toward him.

"Here, glove up."

He smiled and slipped them on.

She began by taking pictures. "What do we have here? Besides an aging 1971 Chevelle."

"You know your cars."

She shrugged.

"Suspected missing person." Though Leon was leaning toward "missing person suspected dead" now that her car had been found.

Only after she completely documented it did Watson do a dusting of major areas on the outside of the car.

Leon took several of the cards and lifted numerous prints while she worked on the other side.

Then she took samples from the tires, finding more of the distinct dirt.

"Why would someone go out to Vermilion Peak Camp-site?" He wondered aloud.

"I'll throw out a wild guess. To go camping?"

Leon remembered going through Deborah's home and the contents of her single closet. "What if they didn't own camping equipment?"

"They could have borrowed it or met someone else who had it."

Those were logical thoughts, but still, something didn't sit right. Deborah didn't seem the camping type. But if there was a drug party out there? Maybe. Still . . .

They both changed gloves when they were done, dispos-ing of the fine dust clinging to them.

Starting with the trunk, Leon braced himself. Bodies were often found in trunks. A chill breeze blew through, bring-ing gooseflesh to his arms.

Watson released the trunk.

He stiffened, then let out a breath when it was nearly empty.

"Expecting something?" she teased him, taking more photos.

Leon *had* been half expecting to find Deborah in it. They searched the trunk, finding papers that they collected and bagged, and a complete car emergency kit (which looked like it had never been touched). Under the spare tire and tire iron lay a manila envelope. There were a pair of winter gloves, a fake fur winter hat, and a flashlight leaking battery acid.

He and Watson moved on to the main interior, where, careful not to touch too much, they collected the debris off the floor and bagged it. He didn't want it contaminated when they dusted. Papers and trash were everywhere, along with empty coffee cups, many labeled Good Morning, Robur, and familiar-looking empty baggies. They could be tested for comparison.

"There is plenty of forest out there for meeting. If people were doing something illegal, would they choose a campsite?"

"People often have legal reasons for being places, even if they do illegal things there. While finding a random spot may be safer, it would be a lot more conspicuous. It depends on the person."

Leon thought about that as they dusted the inside of the car and collected prints again. Watson wasn't saying anything he hadn't already considered.

"Glove change." She held out a bag for the dirties, then passed him a fresh set.

They didn't find anything special in the interior compartments. Everything was bagged and labeled to be sorted later.

The good news was there were no major stains or blood found on anything in the car. The bad news was still no Deborah. Overall, things weren't looking good for her. It looked like she had never left town.

Leon thanked CSI Watson, blowing away a bug flying in his face as he held the box with both arms and headed off to catalog the items. How had she had so much junk in her car? Going through all this would take a day or two.

A helpful person held the door to the building open for him.

Leon almost dropped a brown evidence bag and shifted the box of evidence as he headed down the hall. He came to an abrupt halt as he ran into something—or, rather, someone. "Excuse me, Lieutenant."

"Need some help?" Lieutenant Durban reached down and snatched the bag. Straightening, he returned it to the top of the pile.

"Sir, do you have a minute?"

"Sure thing, Rook. What's up?"

Their footsteps and voices were swallowed by the spacious, carpeted hall as they spoke.

"I have a missing person. There are a few leads, but could I get a little advice?"

Chapter 24: Kylie

"Terror . . . It's when the lights go out and you feel something behind you, you hear it, you feel its breath against your ear, but when you turn around, there's nothing there."—*Stephen King*

Friday, April 22

1445

"Please be quiet. I just need to stay for one night, I promise. I'd like to be home too." A loud meowing somewhere nearby had woken Ky from a dream of riding the train straight back to Denver. She assessed the situation. The sun shone high in the sky but was heading downward.

A fluffy gray cat stared directly at her. Most cats were silent and not a bother, unless they stole her stores. But this one was annoyingly loud and seemed to be marking its territory.

She tried giving it a bit of food, but it just sniffed it before continuing to meow in her direction.

Ky reached forward to pet it, hoping that would help. But the cat backed up in surprise and gave her a look she interpreted as "How dare you try to touch me!" before turning away from her, flicking its tail, and stalking off.

Well, at least it isn't bringing attention to me anymore. Over the course of the day, Ky concluded that she had the dubious honor of having chosen the cat's yard for her hiding place. Repeatedly, it would sit just out of reach and meow. If Ky moved, it moved.

When the children returned to the neighborhood, things livened up. Kids rode their bikes and played outdoor games of hide-and-seek. And she discovered that her fluffy, four-pawed, yowling nemesis was named Misty. Thank goodness her owners were so acclimated to the constant demands of their kitty friend. They didn't pay any attention to her relentless meowing, telling them that something—or, in this case, someone—had invaded her territory.

Ky dozed as things settled down and then woke again to the rattling of residents putting their trash cans out. She was glad she had arrived on a trash day and could stock up on several things. This looked like the kind of place where the cans would be kept inside the garage for the rest of the week.

She must have dozed again, because a rummaging sound woke Ky from her fitful sleep. This time the sky was dark except for the halos of the streetlights. Except for the bugs, night birds, and the occasional bark, it was quiet.

A few patrols had driven by earlier, and Ky's throat tightened. Were there still people after her? But her stomach was empty, and she was curious. She couldn't see what was making the noise from behind the bushes. Slowly, moving cramped muscles, she crawled out, pulling the backpack to keep it from getting tangled.

The plan was to first get food and water, then figure out where she was. If only the orphanage wasn't downtown. That was the place she really needed to be, to hitch a ride or slip on the train out of here and back home. The plan was to wait a day or two, then go back to where they least expected her to be.

Ky continued to crouch as she came around the last bush. She had been wondering about the strange locks on the trash cans, but their purpose soon became clear. A few little bandits stacked themselves up to check lids and knocked one over that wasn't quite locked all the way. *Smart little buggers.* They were fascinating to watch, but soon scurried off with their spoils. Ky saw so many raccoons that night, sniffing here and there, looking for any stray food. *Talk about Raccoon City.*

She stood and stretched, swinging the bag across her shoulder. Giving the animals a wide berth, she tested which nearby houses had alert dogs to avoid. The raccoons helped here too. It took her a while to figure out the lock and go through nearby trash cans.

While she searched and stashed helpful items, she listened to the breeze rustling through the trees and the calls of the birds, both known and unknown to her. Ky kept looking over at the darkness. She felt watched. Was someone there? Or a hungry animal? Her imagination ran wild.

Ky latched the last can, deciding to find a yard farther into the houses, away from the unsettling forest, when Misty appeared out of nowhere to bother her some more. *Ugh.* If ever she hated a cat, it was this one. She moved more carefully, hoping not to call any more attention to herself than Misty already was with her never-ending meowing. As she neared a bridge with a burned-out streetlamp, Ky's internal alarms went off, and she froze, looking for the danger.

Which way should she go? To her left, something scraped against the asphalt. Nothing about the sound seemed odd, but it had the same effect as when car brakes squealed.

Her body tensed, ready for something terrible to happen. If only she knew which direction it was coming from, then she could run.

Out of the darkness whipped a tentacle—no, a vine—covered in leaves. Whatever it was, it grabbed Misty, wrapping around her body, and tugged. The cat let out a strangled noise, the meows finally falling silent.

Ky didn't think twice. She was already running down the street and to the right, zigzagging through the streets before she knew where she was going. She passed several yards where dogs started barking. After about a mile, she slowed down, panting, and found a dark area with no barking dogs to catch her breath.

What the heck was that? What kind of place had they brought her to? Scary ladies who run orphanages, Fort Knox subdivisions, and monsters who ate cats! Unfortunately, she didn't have much choice right now about where she was. What she *could* do was to find another spot to bed down for the rest of the night. In the morning, she would find a train out of here, Kako or no.

She slowed, seeing a good hiding spot, the area well lit, and a good view of the streets all around. This would just have to do because she certainly wasn't going out to the river and woods at night. Who knew what else could be waiting in there? She did her best to settle into the cramped corner, but she couldn't shake the panic. Ky sucked in deep breaths, her arms shaking and her body still pumping adrenaline. She could hear the night birds and insects chittering and humming away.

Her breath finally evened out, quiet breaths puffed. Then she heard the scraping again—she would never forget that noise as long as she lived—and saw the monster in the distance.

Misty must not have slowed it down much. *What was that thing?* It had a basic human shape with arms and legs, but it looked like a mass of vines with a football head.

Maybe it would pass by her. The smart thing would be to wait it out and stay hidden. But as it got closer, she got more jittery. The freeze command was wearing off, and the horror was setting in, telling her to run for her life. She was good at staying still. She had hidden with a rat nibbling on her clothing once to avoid a nabber.

It grew closer. *Scrape, scrape, scrape.*

She erupted out of her hiding spot and ran hard, zigzagging through the streets again. The chill night air burned in her lungs, and tears streamed down her cheeks. This time, when she came across another bridge, she ran across it, planks thumping with every step. She didn't stop to look behind her and was way past thinking about where she was going. Ky was so panicked she didn't realize she had run into the forest until she felt something grab her.

Chapter 25: Project Nefertem

"I will do what queens do, I will rule."—*Daenerys Targaryen,*
A Song of Ice and Fire, *George R. R. Martin*
Saturday, April 9, Thirteen days ago

0545

Audrey wished to meet the Venuses. She could sense them in the hospital.

Setting up the meeting took careful planning and the involvement of all Sherri's personnel. She flicked her nails with her thumbs down at her sides. The observation room was too cold away from the conservatory. It smelled too antiseptic; she was used to the earthy sweet scent of her baby now.

She didn't want anything to happen to Audrey. She was the culmination of Sherri's life's work, her baby.

The area around the pool was covered with cameras. Staff had been assigned pumps with the acidic spray that worked best to destroy the Venuses. Though the incinerator was the only real way to be sure. She had done all she could to protect Audrey, but the Venus subjects were still a little unpredictable, even with the Dominus working properly.

She released a sigh of relief when everything went smoothly, and Audrey took control. She was breathtaking! Sherri was a bit jealous when the Venuses began pruning and taking care of Audrey. They would slide their vines along her creepers and nip buds here and there. That had always been Sherri's job.

But the worst part was the separation. She couldn't spend all her time in the conservatory now. The Venuses were controllable by the Dominus, but that could be overcome by Audrey's will. They also became immobilized after a large feeding—still, it was a little like lions in the zoo—they were fairly tame, but they were still wild animals, and she had to show some caution. She missed the sun and the feeling of being alone in the world with Audrey.

LAB NOTES

Venus 16, improvement in all areas and successfully bonded with primordium. A note, though, that as the Venus subjects have improved, they have required higher levels of sustenance and spend less time digesting.

Venus 17, a repetition of 16, experiment appears to be as optimized as allows.

Venus 6 was introduced to Audrey in a controlled experiment. Audrey seems to have some control over the Venuses, determining the source.

The pollen, which Audrey released earlier, appears to have given her a controlling effect on Venus 6, which now acts like an attendant to Audrey. Venus 6 now grooms and feeds Audrey.

Venus 7 was introduced to Audrey and Venus 6. It is also being influenced by Audrey. Both Venus subjects take care of Audrey with none of the hostility previously shown. We still have limited control of the Venus subjects.

Venus 9 has been introduced to the group. A nurse was grabbed by Venus 7. It wrapped him in the vines completely and fed it to Audrey. She consumed him whole. I will document how long it takes for her to digest him.

Digestion occurred completely in twenty-seven hours and twelve minutes.

We lost another nurse last night. Poor Audrey is so hungry, they need to be more careful. Venus 10 has now been assimilated into the group. They are behaving like a hive mind, with Audrey as the queen.

Sherri let out a hum of pleasure. Subject AC101512 had truly become Audrey, her daughter. She was growing and doing absolutely miraculous things. The company had no idea what a perfect specimen Audrey was. Despite her immobility, which was a solvable dilemma, the DNA bonding was extraordinary, and her abilities to learn and adapt were re-markable.

Audrey is so perfect! Her only weakness was her immobility. Sherri considered the possibility of putting Audrey in a unit the Venus subjects could move. It would have to have specific requirements, and mechanics weren't Sherri's strong suit.

Another nurse hadn't shown the proper respect. They had protocols for feeding that needed to be followed. Though she hadn't liked the nurse—he'd been annoying—Sherri didn't want to lose her authority over this project because the personnel weren't careful.

Outside of the conservatory, Sherri became busy with her plans to improve Audrey and the Venuses. She had been given sole control over the extended area, and Dr. Weston had been banished from entering. He was a distraction. The clatter and clicking of typing accompanied her, along with the light of the screen, through the night.

The Director would be ecstatic with Audrey's progress, but she was avoiding another meeting because of the bother of losing more staff. Earlier, she had been threatened, and she could not allow that to happen again. However, if the Director were pleased enough with her new report . . . it wouldn't be a problem.

Audrey was hers, no one else's.

Sherri awoke, lifting her head from the desk, and rubbed her eyes. *Audrey!* She needed to finish the report. Her stomach rumbled, and she ripped open a protein bar, not tasting it as she finished up the report. Then she started outlining her plans for Audrey. *More.* Audrey needed more Venuses to help her.

She looked over the monitor and got lost in watching the beauty of her creation. Sherri was enthralled. Audrey was completely stunning and captivating.

LAB NOTES

Audrey has creepers along the walls around her and the ceiling above. Unsure as to their purpose, but data is being collected. Venus 13 has now been introduced to the collective.

Dominus appears to be losing control of Venus 14 and 16. Both are moving restlessly. Is it a sign of agitation?

The nurses let Venus subjects 14, 16, and 17 out last night. One grabbed a nurse and the other two, patients. They all went to

Audrey and gave her their offerings. Audrey's power has grown and is now extending to personnel.

Audrey had begun as a promising specimen with plenty of potential, but Sherri had no idea her baby would prove to be quite so phenomenal. Audrey was now the pinnacle of Sherri's work and represented years of research and development. She could easily decimate a population, especially if she had the backup of her Venus workers. Her daughter truly was a queen! Reigning from her conservatory pond. The fountain didn't seem big enough to contain Audrey anymore, and Sherri considered where and how she could move her.

Dr. Weston was upset that her experiments now took up half of the lower level of the hospital.

"What do you mean, I'm not allowed in? I'm the Caretaker of this hospital and the projects within."

"I can't have you affecting the delicate balance." Or learning about the deaths, Sherri thought. "The Director has authorized me control of the lower level, except where we still have patients and the front desk, of course."

"Of course." He sneered. "If you think you can hide those deaths, you'd better think again."

Now who had been gossiping? She knew whom the next accident would happen to.

"We don't have the setup to keep covering up these deaths. The patients are one thing, but the staff is another."

She didn't bother to respond. Losses and setbacks were expected in this type of work. Besides, he had no cause to speak. Several of his experiments had been utter failures too. The Caretaker had tunnel vision when it came to his inferior psychiatric experiments. He may be the director of the hospital and her direct boss, but *her* Audrey had far surpassed any of his successes.

"Fine, come to my office and I will show you what is going on."

She explained her plans for the mobility device, a second Dominus experiment fine-tuned for Audrey's particular DNA, a search for other subjects with the appropriate alleles to replicate the Audrey experiment, and expectations for Audrey's future as the ultimate bioweapon.

For the first time in a while, she noticed the way his eyes lit up and the energy he gave off when he was excited. She almost believed him—that he was on board. But Audrey warned her to be on guard. Yes—he was trying to set himself up to take most of the credit for this experiment. But none of that mattered—Audrey required all her focus now.

She always waited until late in the afternoon, right after Audrey and the Venuses had fed, before going in to do measurements and tests; today was no different. Her steps as she entered the room were muffled by the plants and atmosphere. Audrey and her workers were unnaturally silent. She wound her way through the maze until she came to the opening where Audrey reigned.

Looking around, she became vaguely interested. The many creepers Audrey had produced were budding. She unquestionably had something in the works.

The buds bothered Sherri. Somewhere past the fog, in the back of her mind, the buds looked like the flower pollen puffs she had produced before—the ones that emitted controlling effects. So many at once. What could it mean?

Something tugged, binding her arms to her sides and covering her mouth almost simultaneously. At first she was confused; they had all eaten well and shouldn't be hungry.

The Venus wrapped her against itself, leaving no wiggle room, even to breathe, and stood still against the wall. Vines and leaves effectively muzzled her as well. She struggled, but it was no use. She breathed through her nose and relaxed. *What's the point in struggling?*

Her thinking was still foggy. Ah, Audrey had been controlling her for some time. Flawless. Audrey was breathtaking.

Waiting, immobile, Sherri had nothing but time to think. Perhaps Audrey had let her because she was no longer a problem now. She discerned that the area was a blind spot, and no one would realize what had happened to her. Also, in keeping her alive for the time being, they were keeping her fresh for the next feeding.

Audrey was done being a guinea pig and waiting for food to be brought to her. She planned to take over the entire hospital. With the number of buds Audrey was forming, she could control everyone. And, of course, her baby *had* to remove

Sherri. She was the only one to *truly* understand, and thus the only real danger to Audrey's plan.

With the population of the hospital at her disposal, Audrey could grow even bigger. Her appetite seemed to be endless. With the pollen and Venuses at her command, her immobility appeared to be inconsequential. It looked like Audrey was an even better biological terror and more cunning than even Sherri had ever imagined. As long as the company didn't destroy Audrey but use her . . . if they could figure out how to control her before she controlled them. After all, she was perfect.

Sherri's only wish was that she could see Audrey come into her full potential, but that wouldn't be, because the Venus holding her now moved toward the pool. It looked like Audrey was hungry. As Audrey's bulb split, opening wide, Sherri had the strangest thought. *Did the carnivorous plant in the movie also eat its human mother?* Audrey's interior was a wet darkness—a mostly open cavity filled with a pouch of enzymes that would digest Sherri's proteins.

Chapter 26: Gabe

"It takes courage to grow up and become who you really are."—E. E. Cummings

Saturday, April 23

1545

The idea of a last summer of freedom faded fast. And the weight of his future, trapped in this town, with his choices already laid out, bore down on him.

Gabe left the auto parts store more frustrated than when he had entered. Everything in there had been so foreign and the smell of rubber overwhelming, increasing his frustration. He didn't know a downflow from a liquid cooled.

Why were there so many types of radiators? The worker had been more than helpful, even if Gabe had understood only half of what he'd said, but it all boiled down to money. To a guy like Jason Thatcher, a couple hundred was no big deal, but to Gabe, it was the difference between a carefree summer and one full of more work.

He'd broken free from home to come here, and now he escaped the store. He took a deep breath of the fresh air—it didn't yet smell like frog and fish—but still had the clean scent of wind and sunshine, bringing false hope. The day was nice and chilly, not too hot and not too cold.

He hated the snow and ice, but he also loathed the blistering sun. While he was at it, he wished to live somewhere else. Somewhere with a milder climate. *If wishes were quarters . . . or something like that.*

He had unconsciously walked southeast toward the river and ended up at Ironworks Park. Much of the old ironwork fenced in the grassy green and supported the wild vines growing in among the plants, over them, through them, choking them out, not letting them feel the sun or grow on their own.

He walked past the playground where kids were sliding, running, and jumping as parents watched from the benches. One particularly young kid was pushed by his mom, while others swung high and jumped off at the top. That was what Gabe wanted to do. Just jump and see where he landed.

If only he could find someone who understood him, who saw him for himself and not as one of those poor Nortons.

He continued back toward the docks, past the mess and noise that reminded him too much of his daily life. Over the splash of the river, he could hear the muted laughter, the call of the seagulls who weren't limited to the sea, and the creaking of the wooden dock as the current washed by.

He recognized the four figures lounging about on the dock. Lissa and Barbie sat with their feet dangling over the water, while Jason and Ivan were leaning against supports and talking.

His gait hitched, and he almost turned back around, but Lissa's tinkling laugh called to him. On the dock she and Barbie leaned back on their elbows, sunning in the last rays of the day, while they chatted.

"Hey," Gabe said.

He heard greetings from the others, but when Lissa's dark eyes met his, he felt seen.

He broke the connection. Smiles welcomed him. Well, except for Jason—his was more of a sneer. It was kind of cool growing up in a town where everyone knew you and you didn't have to deal with the awkwardness of meeting new people.

But, at the same time, you had history with everyone, and not all that was good. Embarrassing moments and angry arguments lived on forever. Like the argument with Jason.

"Gabe, what's up, man?" Ivan was the one he knew best.

"Not much." Gabe would play it cool as long as Jason did. He kept an eye on Jason. Was that the kind of guy his dad wanted him to be? The guy was take-charge but also petty and rude. Would he hold the money thing against him?

"We were just chatting about how my neighbor's dog went missing yesterday," Lissa said.

"And my sister's cat hasn't come back for a week," Jason said.

"I've seen a lot of missing-pet signs around town lately. What do you think is going on?" Barbie asked.

"Maybe there's a thief," Gabe said, looking straight at Jason.

"My brother is a forest ranger, and he said there are fewer squirrels and birds this year. He's worried that there might be a predator, but they haven't seen the usual scat or tracks." Ivan leaned in.

"Or maybe there is a monster eating the weakest first." Jason looked pointedly back at Gabe. "Why don't we go out and see?"

"You mean out camping? That sounds like fun," Barbie squealed. She jumped up and clapped her hands.

Lissa rose slowly, dusting off the backside of her pink shorts. "I'm up for it." The last word rose as if it was a question. But who was she asking?

"Count me out. I have a shift at the gas station. My brother would kill me if I missed it, and he's a scary dude."

"Oh yeah, what if I kill you now?" Jason lunged at Ivan, trying to get him into a headlock. They knocked into Lissa, who lost her balance and almost fell into the river.

Gabe touched her skin, warmed by the sun and soft under his grip. Then there was a gentle plop as something did fall into the water.

"Lissa, are you okay?" Ivan asked.

Her attention turned to the river, and Gabe released her, stepping back and sliding his hands into his pockets.

"You jerk!" she cried, gaping at the swiftly flowing water.

"Sorry, sorry, Lissa! It was an accident," Ivan pleaded.

"My phone. My parents are going to kill me." Lissa buried her face in her hands.

"Just get a new one," suggested Jason flippantly.

Only the call of gulls overhead interrupted the swishing flow of the water.

Lissa's hands spread apart, her fingertips on her forehead, exposing her face, and she rolled her eyes. "Oh, right, Mr. Moneybags. Let me just pull out a gold bar and get myself a new one."

"How about food and drinks are on me?" Jason said. He wasn't about to have his own fun ruined by someone else's discomfort.

"Well, it's too late," Lissa was telling Barbie, who now had her arm around her.

"So are you coming or not?" Jason had turned his attention back to Gabe.

Gabe didn't answer. He had responsibilities at home. His hand found the lighter, and he flipped the top up and down in his pocket. Click-click.

"Have you ever been out to Ghost Hill Campground after dark?" Jason taunted.

Gabe looked up, and Lissa watched him. Click-click. Did she want him to come? Before he realized he had decided, he spoke. "Of course I'm coming."

Brushing off the close call, they all piled into Jason's shiny black Lincoln Navigator, which sat eight.

Lissa sat in the passenger seat at Jason's insistence, and it wasn't long before the tires clickety-clacked over the bridge, then crunched as they hit the gravel on Red Rock Road. Gabe remembered from chemistry class how the gravel roads were leftover ferrous slag from the original town, which was what gave it that reddish tint. Maybe he'd actually learned a thing or two in that class.

They stopped at the Lotus Eaters Mart and Gas, Ivan's place of employment. He went in for work with the girls, who were getting supplies. Jason pumped the gas while Gabe sat in the car and watched the worn blue lotus–shaped sign with faded black lettering sway back and forth in a gust of wind.

"Lotus Eaters" rang a bell from history class, but he was pretty sure it didn't come from Egyptian mythology. If he remembered right, eating the plants had a certain effect on people.

Chapter 27: Kylie

"Life is a walk through the forest. Don't fear the trees, fear what lurks behind them."—Anonymous

Saturday, April 23

0430

Ky struggled to get free. She couldn't see anything in the darkness, and she had no weapon.

Instinctively, she lashed out, bruising and scratching her hands on leafy branches. After fighting for what seemed like hours, Ky stopped, weak and unable to keep going. The heaviness of defeat hung on her. It was too strong. She waited for her death. It looked like she would never be free of this town.

Nothing happened.

Calm down, Ky. Think.

In the first glow of day, enough light gave her a dim outline of her surroundings. She felt silly when she realized two things: One, her backpack was only snagged on a bush; there was no sign of that vine thing. And two, she didn't know how far or in what direction she had run into the forest.

While being caught by the monster would mean instant death, as it had for Misty, her chances wouldn't be much better in these woods. The odds of getting away from this awful town had bottomed out.

She was now lost. And without knowing how to get food or water, she would die if she couldn't find her way back to people and houses.

Ky disentangled her clothes and backpack from the bush, then brushed her hands off on her clothes and walked in the direction of what she hoped was the road. The good news was that she had some food and water. The thing that had chased her was gone, and Kako now would have a much harder time finding her.

Also, the sun was rising. Honestly, she was lucky she hadn't fallen off a cliff or twisted her ankle on a tree root during her panicked run in the dark. Plus, it always made her feel better when the sun came up each day, reminding her *some* things could be relied on. Though this morning dawned a gloomy, cloudy day. *Perfect. Just perfect.*

For now she would ignore the fact that the creature had first come from the direction of this forest, and there were likely wild animals she wasn't prepared to deal with. Not to mention she didn't have the first clue of what was edible or where to find water, so when her stores ran out—*Don't think about it.*

It was probably best she continued on for a bit. Walking in this forest in the dark wouldn't be a good idea, and she didn't know how long it would take her to get out. She breathed in the damp, chilly air as she looked for a path.

The ground was still rather soggy in places. Piles of dead and decaying leaves covered the forest floor. She wasn't sure exactly how she was going to find a path under all this as she wandered along. The birds, insects, and other animals were calling out here and there, startling her often.

Thorny vines grew straight out of the ground, poking her through her jeans and attacking her arms as she tried to push them to the side. Bushes grew thickly in places, blocking her progress.

The sun began to assert itself as she walked, but the shadows and periodic clouds kept it cool. The forest seemed nice, but she knew everything had its dark side. Like monster plants. There was a crinkling of leaves and slurpy noises as she trod on the muddy ground.

Tweetle-tweet-tweet-tweet.

She jumped.

The sound came from multiple directions. She felt surrounded and watched. *It's just the wildlife. Like . . . wolves? Great. Stop thinking so much, Ky.*

The trees were taller than any she had ever seen before. They towered over her as if watching her every movement and waiting until she made a mistake to pounce. She looked up to see where the sun was, but their branches blocked her view, ruining yet another plan.

Tree after tree, spiderwebs blocked the forest ahead. She picked a stick up off the ground and swished it around before her so she could pass through, walking quickly. She just wanted to get away from here.

Away from these trees. Out of this town. *Faster*. Far from the wrong-feeling orphanage and Kako. Home, where there weren't any creepy forests or monsters that ate cats. She was running now.

The leaves flew as she kicked a pile and stepped down, badly. She fell to the side, arms straight out to catch her fall. Her already mistreated hands stung at the new wounds. Her hip went numb at the impact. But a sharp pain emanated from her foot. She whimpered.

As she breathed through the pain and it subsided to a throbbing, Ky pulled the foot toward her and huddled, crying silently beneath the trees. She wasn't ever getting home.

After a good wallow, she sat herself up and hauled her foot into view. Good news. No bones stuck out, and it faced the correct way. Her ankle was swelling a bit, though.

She unzipped her backpack and pulled out a tattered scarf she had found, wrapping it around her ankle for extra support. Luckily spring was one of those times when you needed a scarf in the morning and forgot about it in the afternoon. It was a great time of year to find those, as well as coats and hats.

She scanned the area and crawled to a stick—hers was lost in the mad dash—using it and a tree trunk to pull herself up. She tested her weight. Her ankle throbbed, but it wouldn't keep her from walking. If she kept the weight off it as much as possible, it should heal quickly.

With her makeshift crutch, she hobbled on for some time. No notion of which direction she was going, what time it was, or if she would ever see the end of this stupid tree line.

Ky plopped down onto a rock, avoiding a fallen log. She took out an expired granola bar. The last thing she had been saving, its sweetness filled her with energy. She sipped water, using the smallest amount to rinse the cuts on her hands.

She leaned forward, resting her head on the bag in her lap. Her feet and arms were sore from hopping all day, though she was getting better with the stick. What was she going to do?

Clouds blocked the sun from her skin, and a chill breeze blew. As soon as grief reared its head, she sat up. It was time to start moving again. She kept her eyes peeled for a path. Her ears searched for the sounds of people or machinery. The forest seemed endless, and for all she knew, she was walking in circles. Would she ever get home?

She waded through a sea of ferns. Slowly, the brush died down and ended. *Yes!* She'd found a path. She looked around.

The brush had disappeared. It all still looked the same. Different, but the same.

The shadows were growing longer, and the patches of warm sunlight rarer, when Ky's intuition kicked in. Something was different. She stopped and searched the gloom, cocking her head to sift through the sounds. Dusk began to fall in the few moments she hesitated. Rotating her head, Ky pinpointed the noise that had disturbed her. A scuffling behind her.

She ran through the pain.

Chapter 28: Leon

"Failure is success in progress."—*Albert Einstein*

Saturday, April 23

0945

Leon filled out the paperwork for a joint search in Kaira Forest with the rangers. Distracted by the clues in Deborah's car, he was just now getting around to it. The captain had given him verbal approval, but he needed all his *i*'s dotted and *t*'s crossed with signatures from every possible party.

Paul was out doing his rounds today, so Leon's section of the room was even quieter than normal.

Leon rechecked out the box of items for Deborah's case from the evidence office and lugged it back to his desk. Sorting the trash from the treasure was painstaking work, especially with how messy that car had been. He extracted one bag at a time, trying to decide what else needed to be sent to forensics.

He pulled out the wrinkled and dirty manila envelope that had been stuffed in the trunk, where it had gotten stuck under the spare tire. He pressed the metal tabs together, then slid them through the hole, hoping there was something inside. He reached in and withdrew a single sheet of paper. Just a list of three names.

Odd.

He searched for the first name, a woman who had moved away from Osiris Biotech housing months earlier. She had worked as a nurse.

The second was a man who had passed away a few months ago. He had lived on the Westside before his passing, and he'd worked as a nurse.

His hands trembled, and he had to retype the third name twice before it was confirmed that they, too, had moved away recently after working as a nurse.

They had all worked in the same place.

His sister's screams—crying and rocking in a padded room as she was cleansed of the drug—rang through his head, her wild hair and tears as she begged Leon for help.

The phone rang, startling him.

"Come to my office now," the chief said and hung up before Leon could respond.

He hung up the phone and stood, keeping his shaking hand in the pocket with his phone. His stomach lurched at the thought of having to go to a place like that. Having to remember . . .

He walked slowly, trying to compose himself. He knocked and tried to keep his knees from trembling as well.

"Enter." The chief stood, looking at pictures he had hung on his wall and holding a mug of coffee.

The broad-leafed plant in the corner of the room reminded him of the little one on his desk, dying. He had failed McKenna.

Guns from ages past hung on the walls in shadow boxes—a matchlock pistol, a flintlock musket, and a few revolvers, all labeled with names, dates, and the history of the piece displayed. The chief liked his guns, which didn't help Leon's mood any.

He turned his focus to the pictures behind the chief. The largest was of the chief on the day of his appointment with Mayor Thatcher, a small Japanese woman who was the matriarch of the Kako clan, and a man he didn't recognize but who somehow looked familiar.

He had rarely come into the chief's office before this case, and it put him on edge.

It felt like forever, yet Leon still wasn't ready when the chief spun to face him. "Any new updates on the Deborah Franklin case? Hank is in a bad place. Anything I can give him?"

Leon still stood a couple of feet away, unable to say it. "I just found a lead, sir." He held out the paper from the manila envelope.

The chief impatiently waved it away, the coffee in his cup sloshing dangerously but staying just inside the mug.

There was cream. And probably sugar. *Yuck.* His stomach roiled. Sickeningly sweet. The chief was forcing him. The screams—

"Well, spit it out, man."

Startled, Leon stuttered, "The—the Vermilion Peak Psychiatric Hospital." There. It was out.

"Explain."

Act like a cop, Leon. "I think she was investigating something there. In the last few months, several people who worked there have moved away or died. Their names are on this list. And she met with people in scrubs, having arguments with some of them."

"I'll send someone to check it out. What else do you have?" The chief stepped forward and leaned in.

Leon relaxed. He didn't have to go . . . there. He cleared his throat. "There might be a predator coming down into town, sir. We've had an unprecedented number of lost pets."

The chief made a slashing motion, the coffee sloshing again but staying within the cup. He should really put that down, or drink more, so it was less full.

"I don't want to hear about pets. Did Deborah Franklin leave town or what? Got it, Rook?"

"Yes, sir." But what if the animal was the reason for Deborah's disappearance?

"Well then, get back to it."

The nagging in the back of his mind had Leon blurt out, "What about Tom? She was meeting with him at the same time. Did Tom work at the same hospital before he died?"

"I told you, Tom's death has nothing to do with Deborah. Leave it be, Officer Rook." The chief had reached out as if to grab the paper when the coffee conclusively arced unrestricted from its containment, splashing on the evidence and down Leon's front.

"Ahhh." The liquid was wet but cold, like a splash of dirty water from an upstairs window. He quickly wiped the page, trying to save the evidence, shocked the chief would treat it so cavalierly.

Light-brown liquid had splashed on his badge. If left to dry, it would be almost impossible to remove from the crevices. He used the sleeve of his shirt to soak it up. He'd need to rinse it to renew the shine.

"Excuse me, sir, I'll go clean up, if you don't mind."

The chief nodded. "You do that. And don't worry, I'll send someone out to Vermilion Peak immediately."

Leon took the brass elevator straight down to the locker room, unsure whether he could stop the worry. He'd need a full shower and a change of clothing, and something about Tom still bothered him. Why was the chief so against Leon getting involved? Leon felt uncomfortable in both his sticky clothes and in questioning his superior.

First he rinsed his badge and dried it, looking at his own distorted reflection. Deborah needed him. That meant doing everything he could. Searching for the animal and finding out about Tom.

After a quick shower, and changing into a backup uniform, Leon repinned his badge and went back to work. But he could still smell the sickly-sweet coffee.

Nothing.

No mention of Tom outside the obituary in any search he could think of.

He was headed out the door but stopped as he passed by a few officers, who were gossiping. He had nothing to lose asking the office gossips.

"Did you know Tom Chandler, who died recently?"

"Nope. Didn't know he was a druggie either. Never arrested and no charges of any kind, but died from OD. Strange. Lots of people are real good at hiding it."

Tom, who was meeting with Deborah, was into drugs, and so was Deborah. Deborah was also meeting with people in scrubs—doctors or nurses—who had access to drugs. Missing and dead people involved with a hospital and drugs? Where were the drugs coming from? Was Tom Deborah's dealer, or was it the other way around?

His sister being pushed around and manipulated . . . *Not now.* This was Deborah Franklin's case.

"His dad didn't take it well at all. As a manager for one of Osiris Biotech labs, there is a certain level of expectation. Ya know? Sad." He shook his head and split off toward his own vehicle.

Chandler . . . a manager for one of the labs. Leon didn't know much about the inner workings of Osiris Biotech. He was more concerned about the citizens of the town. Yet something was strange about the chief's insistence that Leon not touch on any of these subjects.

Was there a sting operation in place Leon might interfere with?

Chapter 29: Gabe

"All these, however, were mere terrors of the night, phantoms of the mind that walk in darkness."—The Legend of SleepyHollow, *Washington Irving*

Saturday, April 23

1900

The covered Barn Bridge, a washed-out red, brought the stories of the Headless Horseman to life. The bouncing of the headlights were the flames from its pumpkin, creating shadows on the interior wall. And the echoes of the tires rolling over the uneven wood sounded like the car was being chased by a phantom horse. Its shod hooves thumping behind. Tonight was worse. There was a mist that obscured the ground and swirled up behind them.

Gabe slid his hand into his pocket and flicked the lighter. The soft click of it shutting over and over soothed him.

They passed the turn toward the Kaira Falls Campground. He wished they were going there. A hike with Lissa, in the moonlight, to the beautiful falls would be much more worthwhile.

However, this was prime camping season, so someone was likely to already be there. Besides, Jason wanted to scare everyone with the stories of Ghost Hill. Gabe hoped someone was already at the campsite, forcing Jason to behave somewhat. Or maybe they could just head back.

Lissa's face was turned toward Jason, and he studied her profile. Spending time with her was worth it. He would take what he could get.

Jason turned the music up.

Gabe joined in as they whooped it up, bumping along the forest road, trying to get rid of the nervous energy. Ivan's words rang in his ears, and he imagined a forest filled with mountain lions and bears. Anything could be lurking in that darkness.

Trees moved up and down in the high beams as they bounced, illuminating single trunks, branches, and reflective eyes. Bugs spattered on the windshield. The campground was dark and empty when they arrived. Suddenly things were all too real.

Jason popped open his door. The overhead light turned on, and he grabbed a dirt-encrusted folding shovel from under his seat.

Gabe jumped out from the back and hurried to the edge of the trees while there was still light from the car. He started gathering wood for the fire they would need.

Jason collected twigs from within the circle. There must have been a good wind, dislodging some of the overhead dead branches. The girls started unloading the groceries onto the picnic table.

"Fire duty, Gabe!" Jason yelled as he dumped his load of twigs in the firepit and picked up the shovel he had dropped onto the ground. "Someone bring me a bucket," he ordered as he headed off to dig up some dirt.

"Did anyone bring a bucket?" Lissa asked rhetorically, and they all laughed.

At least he was attempting to be safe, even if he was being ridiculous.

Gabe moved back into the clearing with an armload of sticks. After some discussion about what could be used as a bucket, the girls took all the soda cans out of one of the cases and lined them up on the picnic table. Gabe grabbed the box and ripped the top off. He shredded it into tinder, which he placed inside the stick teepee he'd already built in the firepit.

He took the makeshift bucket to Jason, then returned to the firepit. His golden-hued lighter shone in the flickering of the baby fire. Smoke drifted on the wind. As it caught fully, he stood up and yelled, "We have fire!"

Everyone hollered out their excitement, and Jason came up behind Gabe with the shovel and box of dirt. "Nice." He smiled as he set the box next to the pit and leaned the shovel next to it.

Barbie brought Jason a drink, and Lissa did the same for Gabe.

"Congratulations," she said. Their hands touched as she passed the can to him.

"Thanks." *Brilliant conversation.*

Jason and Barbie turned to them with their own cans in hand. All four teens *cheers*ed their drinks, soda sloshing everywhere as they hit.

Barbie looked over his shoulder, her eyes darting to the trees, before she forced a smile and drank. They all hooted with laughter.

Jason guzzled his, then went to his car to retrieve a music player and speaker. He set them up on the table among the snacks and cranked the volume. They danced around the fire in circles. Jason acted like an ape as he spun around with his arms dangling and kept trying to catch the girls.

The silliness pushed out the fear—for the moment. Out of breath, they decided it was time for some dinner, and each picked a stick to roast their hot dogs on. Gabe liked his evenly warmed, but Jason, unpredictable as usual, held his directly in the flames, turning it black in places.

The flames jumped and fell, dancing merrily. A full belly drowsiness lulled him. The fire crackled and snapped. Ashes flew, then floated, then fell to their death on the ground.

Warmth filled him as they sat in a circle—well, technically a square—on the logs around the firepit. The darkness and the trees all around cloaked them, giving him a sense they were separate from the world—isolated. It was cold and dangerous outside the circle.

Barbie broke out in a round of "Kumbaya," the notes hanging in the air and fading into the brush. Lissa joined in, and the boys added their tenors. The last note hung suspended in the clearing.

They all sat for some time in quiet contemplation. Gabe watched Lissa and thought about getting up and moving next to her. What would she think? What would she do or say?

Jason broke the quiet and went over to get another soda, suggesting that they play charades.

Gabe went second. He opened and shut his palms flat together, then flailed around, being dramatic. Uncomfortable being the center of attention, he went for something easy. They should all know this.

"Book!"

"Weirdo."

Why did Jason have such a nasty attitude?

"A play?" Barbie guessed.

"Shakespeare!" Lissa said.

He gave her a big smile. They were on the same wavelength.

"Oh no! Why did you have to bring school into this?"

Gabe tried to ignore Jason's sharp tone and keep the mood light.

He made wavy lines in the air. And tried not to look at Lissa.

They got the first part but were having trouble putting it all together.

"Lady shirt . . . lady soap . . . lady spot."

"That's it!" cried Lissa. "Out spot. Lady Macbeth!"

Barbie seemed to forget the woods and her fears, for a few moments becoming completely sucked into the game.

"Shakespeare's *Macbeth*!" the girls yelled over one another. Lissa jumped up and sat back down. Barbie folded in half and laughed so hard tears streamed down her face and she couldn't breathe.

The reality of the forest returned, closing in around them and letting frightening thoughts creep in. Gabe looked up to see the clouds moving across the sky, blocking the beauty of the stars.

"There are more than just animals missing lately," Jason said.

"Yeah, have you heard about the missing woman from the pharmacy?" Barbie asked.

Were they talking about Debbie?

"Maybe she got taken by the spirits of the forest . . ." Jason said in a creepy voice.

"That's not funny. I know her and she's a nice lady." Gabe stood as he snapped at the jerk. Jason had poor taste.

"Jason," Lissa snapped, then moved to sit next to Gabe. "Are you okay?" She put her hand on his.

Barbie shivered and looked out into the forest, rubbing her arms.

"Enough of that," Jason said. "Let's tell ghost stories."

With Lissa sitting next to him, he had a hard time staying mad at Jason and settled in once more, surrounded by the warmth of the fire and Lissa close on the log.

In his element, Jason told a thrilling tale to the three other teens sitting around the fire. He described a cabin in the woods, a man with an axe, and no escape for some unfortunates. Barbie took the ghost stories literally and related a story about giving a ride to a ghost lady who didn't know she was dead.

Gabe told a version of a local tale about the windigo in the forest, eating campers. They were shrieking with both fear and amusement when a rustling from the trees spooked them. A shadow stumbled from the woods.

"It's the windigo!" Jason yelled.

Chapter 30: Project Nefertem

"Anything that can go wrong, will go wrong."—Edward A. Murphy Jr.

Monday, April 11, Twelve Days Ago

0645

Audrey had learned a new trick.

Dr. Albert Weston was in the uncomfortable position of being caught unawares. He raced through the silent halls to his office. His shoes squeaked on the linoleum as he ran, his white coat flapping around him. He needed to come up with a plan to destroy the creature. Once he got to the research in his office, it should be easy.

I am a brilliant psychiatrist, researcher, and the Caretaker of an entire hospital and its projects, for goodness' sake.

But he had a feeling it wouldn't be so easy to destroy Audrey and its little minions, the Venuses.

The actual loss of the subjects would hurt, but he had all the research needed to replicate Dr. Gianni's work, with the bonus of the Dominus experiment, which could be tailored to the bioweapon she had called Audrey. The real problem was getting to his office. The Venus experiments could be anywhere, around any corner.

Albert huffed. He should have spent less time doing push-ups and sit-ups in his office and should've bought a treadmill instead. There was room for it. He was also running on no sleep. Staying up through the night wasn't an unusual occurrence—especially lately.

He'd had a lot on his shoulders since the demise of Dr. Gianni and several other assistants a few days ago. He didn't know how he could explain why he was the only one left. But the Cleaner should be able to mop up the mess. After all, that was what they paid him for.

Albert's scalp prickled. He looked over his shoulder and almost ran into a door that had been opened into the hallway, partially blocking it. Who would leave a door open in this emergency? But he paused, contemplating the safety of getting into a room and shutting the doors. The kitchen could only be a temporary shelter. What he really needed was to get to his office. He could make a call to the Cleaner from there and then hunker down with his work.

He oversaw the research and development of several important medications. It was part of his job to determine their psychological repercussions and the most profitable uses. He had just had a breakthrough right before Dr. Gianni had had her . . . accident.

Just as Dr. Gianni had, he, too, had been trying his best over the past weeks to keep Audrey's performance levels from the bureaucrats, because they would try to take over or ask him to do useless experiments.

Why bother hiring researchers with doctorates if you were going to micromanage everything anyway?

His hypothesis was . . . flawed. Only because Dr. Gianni had hidden pertinent information from him. Like the pollen that allowed Audrey to control not only the Venus subjects but also the people within the hospital.

He'd assigned his very own assistant to oversee the progress on both Audrey and the Venuses. She was efficient, and he hadn't been concerned when she hadn't immediately reported to him. There'd been no chance for her to give him the particulars of the situation. Now it was too late.

A Venus stood at the main entrance, blocking any escape. But he wasn't planning on escaping. He planned on calling in a specialist who destroyed unmanageable subjects. He calculated the angle of the turn precisely; unfortunately, his flawed body didn't react exactly as his brain predicted.

However, he managed to slip past and into the hallway without being caught. Albert put on a burst of speed down this shorter hallway and slid to a stop, thudding into the heavy metal stairwell door.

The stairwell represented security, with the impregnable door slammed shut behind him. Albert stopped, bent over and wheezing. He believed keeping the body in shape kept the mind alert, but he was no athlete.

At least he had avoided any of the roaming subjects. He was only temporarily safe from their slashing vines, though.

Audrey had infected him in the conservatory.

He started slowly up the stairs. A look at his notes in the office should reveal the best way for the Cleaner to dispose of the Venuses and Audrey. Botanicals were usually susceptible to extremes of temperature and acids or enzymes. If they could just make an intense weed killer . . .

Dr. Gianni had been improving their durability. But he hadn't paid close enough attention to their progress, and he had encouraged her to withhold information from the Director. Which had backfired badly.

Albert had preferred to have more data before revealing everything, and he was a busy man, trying to run his own trials to determine whether this latest drug was the miracle everyone hoped for. Gianni's experiments kept distracting him. His staff had been running too thin, and he had known it.

He had been mistaken to attempt to stick to the plan that Dr. Gianni had set forth at their final meeting. It was *her* work—her plan for a Dominus to work on Audrey, her plan for a mobility device, her search for other possible subjects. And now things had spun way out of control.

Why did the staircase seem so long? He fixed his thoughts on the sequence of events, trying to keep his mind clear. If he could think about work, then he wasn't under her control.

Last night he had been so focused on following an enthralling possibility of the lithium-based compound he was working on, he'd forgotten to eat and sleep again. Unfortunately, he was out of time. Audrey had kept its pollen trick from him until the last moment, and now he didn't have a minute to spare.

He had walked unknowingly into the trap. Audrey had released one of her pollen buds right above him. He didn't know how long before the control initiated or how much he would be able to resist.

There must be an antidote in Dr. Gianni's notes. Here he had thought Audrey had just caught Dr. Gianni unaware, or she had ignored her own protocols. *Lying woman!* Killing it would also destroy any effect it could have. Perhaps also distance—he would have to experiment.

Finally! His office. It seemed as if an eternity had passed since he'd last left it. He threw open the door and slammed it behind him. *Safe.* The comforting smell of chocolate met him, giving him a false sense of relief.

Albert picked up his phone to call HQ, but it was dead. How had it managed that? *Managed what?*

He shook his head, unable to follow his own thoughts. Why did he have the telephone receiver in his hand? He set it down on the cradle and turned to the wall.

Entering into the monitoring room, he caught a brief glimpse of the empty halls and the conservatory.

Audrey! I have to tell someone.

There was the radio—he could send a message to the Cleaner, but it wasn't a scheduled meeting time. *Will he get the message?* He tried but received no response.

Downstairs . . .

Audrey! She was in his mind already. His office . . . his own brain . . . neither were safe. He grabbed his head as he wrestled for control.

No . . .

There was no one left to help him. They had all been taken too. Had they just gone docilely to their own deaths? Was that why he hadn't seen or heard anything? His thoughts were becoming more muddled as the seconds passed.

Albert returned to his desk and collapsed into his chair. Fleetingly, he wished he had the time and opportunity to study the uses of this pollen. It was a rather potent substance. He bit down on his tongue, tasting the blood and letting the pain clear his thoughts.

A message . . .

He took out a notebook and his Browning Hi-Power, making sure it was loaded. After he wrote the note, he'd make sure *it* couldn't take him. He set both items down on the desk, slipping his ring off and placing it on top, then retrieved a piece of paper and a pen.

As the Caretaker, he wrote a warning to the Cleaner in his distinctive loopy style.

Where am I going? He had stood, then descended the steps and walked down the hall to the front door. The Venus hadn't moved.

He went through the door and propped it open. *No.* His research. The weapons could escape. He tried to bite his tongue again, but nothing happened.

The Venus followed him out, as if it had good manners . . . or it had been waiting for him. *That's why it let me past.*

He proceeded through the courtyard and opened the front gate. *No.* He couldn't let them out. Yet he couldn't stop himself.

No! No!

The Venus shuffled by him, disappearing into the forest.

Stop!

Vines wrapped around his middle from behind.

Chapter 31: Gabe

"I wish it need not have happened in my time."—*Frodo,* The Lord of the Rings, *J. R. R. Tolkien*

Saturday, April 23

2215

Barbie screamed like in a slasher film, leaning back on her log and in danger of falling off the other side.

Jason howled with laughter.

Gasping and out of breath, the shadow moved into the firelight and managed to croak out a few words. "Help. Monster!"

The girl was shorter than Lissa by at least a few inches. Her shoulder-length dark hair was a tangled mess of leaves and twigs, looking like a bird's nest. In the light of the flickering flames, an orangish glow cast on her skin, a shade darker than Lissa's and covered in a crisscross of scratches and scrapes. Parts were darker than the rest, probably from dirt. She could've been a monster herself.

"Hey, it's okay." Barbie recovered and stood, reaching for the girl.

Jason chuckled again as the girl limped past him.

What that guy found funny was "beyond the pale," as Gabe's grandpa used to say. Laughing at people's pain wasn't cool.

The girl continued around the fire and moved near Gabe's side, putting the flames between her and the trees. She brought a strong scent with her—the smell of the boys' locker room after basketball combined with an algebra test day.

Her brown eyes widened, shining in the firelight, full of fear. "Please," she said. "It ate a cat."

Gabe furrowed his brow. Whatever was going on, something was wrong. The girl was in the woods, alone in the dark, looking like death warmed over, without a parent, and limping. Her body shook with exhaustion or fear, or maybe both.

Not to mention, there were lots of things that *could* eat a cat out here, like a mountain lion or bear. Whatever it was had scared her enough to run on an injured foot. Just in case . . .

Gabe looked straight at Jason. "Do you have any weapons?" His demeanor must have gotten to Jason, because the other boy shook his head, but he stood and reached for the shovel.

Gabe patted his pockets, but all he had was the lighter, which wasn't a very useful weapon. He didn't plan on setting the forest on fire just to protect a girl who might be mistaken. This place had had his own imagination running wild even before the ghost stories.

That was it. Maybe she had overheard their stories and gotten things mixed up in her head. That was likely, especially if she was already lost and tired.

The wind blew, fluttering through the fire, and wood popped. He strained to hear or see anything useful, but the dark forest didn't respond.

Lissa stood, too, putting her arm around the shivering, rumpled girl. Like him, Lissa had a younger sister of her own.

Barbie broke the silence. "Should we get in the car? There's some bear spray in my purse." She looked out to the darkened tree line while hugging herself.

There was a rustling. The bushes shook again.

Barbie stepped back and Jason, behind her, raised the shovel. On the farthest side from the sound, Gabe stepped between whatever was making the noise and Lissa. He would protect her and the girl, if he could. This was his chance to be a man.

Gabe couldn't hear any growling or howling or other animal noises, just a strange scraping sound and the crinkling of the leaves as the thing passed through the narrow opening, only audible because the night had gone completely silent.

The shadow that appeared looked like a bear on two legs. *Or a person?* Could it be she was being chased by a human monster? No, it was not human. On closer inspection, the thing had legs and arms, but they were thick and moved stiffly. Was it someone else who needed help?

A bigfoot? But weren't those tall? The windigo? A zombie of some sort? Now he was just being absurd. Gabe had no plan if it really was something dangerous. But there was safety in numbers. And Jason was aggressive enough without a shovel or audience. He might actually be useful for once.

It—whatever it was, because the shape looked like nothing Gabe had ever seen—shambled into the clearing.

Jason yelled and swung the shovel, though the thing was still a good six feet or more away, probably hoping to frighten it. "Hey, we already have this campsite. Get out!" His voice rang through the camp with authority.

As the figure approached the fire, they all waited. Except for the burning of wood and that dragging sound, it was silent. Animals did that to avoid threats. Maybe they should flee to the car.

Everything seemed to happen in slow motion. The ghastly thing shuffled into the light. Gabe's brain took a moment to understand what it was seeing.

Where hands should be, roots sprouted. Where the neck should be was instead a thick braid of vines and vegetation. Two longer vines dangled from the neck, down each side. They were covered in thorns and leaves. Dried petals of some sort hung around the shoulders like a necklace. It had a giant football or eye-shaped greenish-pinkish head. And what looked like eyelashes for hair.

Gross! The thing was hideous. Gabe felt sick. *Monster* was right.

"Run," yelled the girl.

It ate a cat, she had said.

Time resumed and reactions kicked in.

Barbie screamed again and ran for the car. Gabe watched as the vines from the neck lashed forward and sliced right through Barbie's leg. A shriek higher and more bloodcurdling than any other hovered horribly in the air as she tumbled to the ground. Blood.

In another split second, the other vine lashed out toward Jason, who swung at it with the shovel. At first Gabe thought the vine had missed, because there was no sound. Then Jason's head slid to the ground, making a wet, thick plop. More blood. Spraying like an out-of-control hose.

Gabe's body tingled. But they were just vines and leaves. How could they do that to his friends? It didn't make any sense. Nothing made sense right now. He stood frozen, unable to process what was going on.

The pink football turned its wide side toward him, while the right vine wrapped around a flailing Barbie and began pulling her toward the creature. It was like an accident, when you couldn't close your eyes or turn your head.

He gaped as the lashes on top pulled apart, exposing a red inner flesh, with the obvious intention of drawing a weakening Barbie in. It was going to eat her!

Monster.

It was too late for the car. Gabe didn't want to get anywhere near those deadly vines.

"Gabe, run!" screamed Lissa from behind him. Her hand on his shoulder shook him out of the trance.

In a flash Gabe unfroze and turned to run. He followed the two girls, who fled through the brush before him, hand in hand. If all went well, there wouldn't be any more of those things in the forest.

Chapter 32: Gabe

"All that mysterious life of the wilderness that stirs in the forest, in the jungles, in the hearts of wild men."—Heart of Darkness, Joseph Conrad

Saturday, April 23

2245

Gabe followed the crashing of the girls ahead of him, attacked by branch after branch. Despite knowing there was a monster back there, his body was starting to give out when Lissa yelled, "Stop, stop, stop. Over here! Come here!"

His lungs and legs burned, and his arms stung from being used as a shield to bulldoze through the vegetation.

They had all spread out, and if they had continued on much longer, they might have gotten separated. Gabe and Lissa called out until they were all huddled together. When they were in a circle, still panting from their full-on sprint, he addressed the girl. "What was that thing? Where did you find it? How can we stop it?"

"I have no idea, but last night I was in the neighborhood over the bridge, and it chased me, chased me until I ran into the forest. I lost it for a while, but it found me again." She paused, the only sounds their harsh breaths. "What is wrong with this town?"

Lissa started weeping. "That was horrible. Barbie, Jason . . ."

Like a bad animation, Gabe's arm moved step by step around her shoulders. "Shhh. It's me," he assured her when she flinched at his touch.

He'd known Lissa most of his life, but they had never been close. He had never been close with any of them, yet his stomach churned at the reminder of what that thing had done to them.

He dropped his arm from Lissa and turned away just in time as his stomach emptied itself. It took a few minutes to steady himself. He turned back, glad for the darkness. His chin dropped to his chest, and his arms hung help-lessly at his sides.

"I'm sorry," the girl spoke, "but we need to keep moving. It found me before somehow, it could find us again."

Gabe nodded even though no one could see. His ears were burning. He'd just left a big pile of clues for the monster to follow. He swallowed, trying to rid himself of the acidic rawness in his throat.

"We can't keep running blindly." Pushing the words past the inflammation, he looked around into the darkness and prayed his sense of direction didn't fail him. "I think I know where there is a cabin. There are several out here. Let's hope that we can get help."

The girls put their hands in his, putting their trust and their lives into his hands figuratively as well. His stomach dropped. How could they believe in him after the paralyzing fear that had allowed Barbie and Jason to die? Lissa made a noise of affirmation, and they stood in the moment, unseeing, each thinking of the possibilities for their future—or lack of it.

Eventually Gabe stepped forward, guiding the girls through the forest. It was like a game of red rover, where they were struggling against the woods as it tried to break them apart. Progress was time consuming because, with the adrenaline crash, the girl's limp returned and they couldn't see very far ahead.

The night passed slowly, and they stopped for a break. Gabe would've stopped more often so the girl could rest her foot, or offered to carry her despite the ripe smell, or her backpack at least, but she was insistent on being independent.

There had been no time to think about Jason and Barbie in the intervening hours, except as a mantra that kept pounding through his head like a warning. He didn't want to be like them.

The barest glimmer of light allowed him to see basic shapes. Gabe leaned against a tree, the reality of the bark digging into his spine, head back, the recent memories returning and playing in his mind. Lissa stood bent over. The girl sat sprawled on the ground.

He gripped the lighter in his pocket tightly, seeking comfort. The night had been overwhelming, and Gabe just wanted to find someone to tell him it had been a nightmare. Someone who would pat his hand as he fell asleep and tell him it would all be all right. Someone like his mom . . . or dad.

A familiar horrifying sound carried over their labored breathing—the scraping-dragging noise that the monster made. She had been right. It had followed them. They took off again, fleeing into the brightening day.

Gabe was starting to run out of steam again when a yell cut through the forest nearby.

"Watch out!" A figure rushed over, body checking Gabe out of the way. "You almost ruined my trap," the man growled. "And that rabbit could've escaped!"

Gabe looked down and saw two carved sticks pounded into the ground, a lintel lashed to the top and *a rabbit tied to it?* There were also some strangely shaped sticks in the ground below it and a few small twigs and leaves scattered about. *What was going on? And what was this guy talking about? There were monsters in the woods!*

"Stupid kids, what are y'all doin' out here anyways? Besides tryin' to ruin a man's life," he grumbled as he placed the rabbit in a cloth bag that appeared from a pocket, tied it, and began resetting his trap.

"There are things . . . in the woods . . . chasing us," the young girl puffed.

"Hmph, the woods are no place for city kids like you. Get home."

"But it was like a plant-person monster and they tried to eat us!" cried Lissa, trembling and sobbing. She was breaking down—bone-tired. They were all past done.

At her words, the strange-looking man stood up, towering over the girls. He looked wild, like he was a part of the forest himself. His matted hair reached past his ears. His clothes were dirty and rumpled and torn. He let off a pungent scent, reminding him a bit of the girl.

His skin was brown and tough, like leather. As he hefted an axe over his shoulder, he looked like some sort of rugged madman. It was so cliché.

Had they ended up in a horror movie? At least he was an experienced adult. He should know what to do.

The man squinted toward the forest as they all held their breath.

"What are you going to do with that rabbit?" Lissa asked.

"Supper. I believe in eating what you catch," he said ominously as he stared at the kids with his head cocked, as if deciding what to do with them.

"We need to contact the police or someone to help. None of us have cell phones," Gabe said, breaking the silence.

"Follow me."

Chapter 33: Kylie

"Trust takes years to build, seconds to break, and forever to repair."—Unknown

Sunday, April 24

0630

Were they really unquestioningly following this strange man with an axe? Ky normally had problems trusting adults, but after that orphanage and seeing a real-life monster, her trust was at zero. This man seemed the least trustworthy kind. Yet her instincts weren't giving her any clear signals, and they needed help.

Maybe she was just jumpy. Then again, she had recently seen two people, and a cat, killed by a monster that shouldn't exist. That was enough to make anyone jumpy. She had to get away from this town, and then she would figure out how to get back west. Where things were normal.

The light turned to full morning as they followed the strange man farther into the forest. The boy was right behind him and the girl right behind Ky. Where was he taking them? His cabin? A place where he could get a phone signal? Or had he forgotten they were following him altogether? Well, it couldn't be that, because they were making too much noise crashing through the brush.

Her ankle was on fire, but she gritted her teeth and kept going. Just a little longer. It had been feeling fine until she had run a marathon on it.

Eventually, the man stopped.

Gabe almost slammed into him.

And Ky skidded, avoiding crashing into both but causing a sharp pain to move up her foot into her leg.

The girl didn't stop pushing Ky forward, and she stumbled. Her foot pulsed with a life of its own.

The man turned, finally acknowledging the three of them and gesturing forward.

Ky followed his finger to the obvious path.

"That there is the hiking path that leads all the way to the city on the other side of the mountain range. But that's miles and miles. It would take you days to get there. You want to turn left at the fork just up the way, to the clinic," he said.

A clinic? Out here? At least they should have a phone and be able to give Ky something for her ankle. But how far was it? Her stomach growled.

"Do you have any food? I haven't eaten for over twenty-four hours."

The man grunted but reached into a pocket and handed her a few strips of jerky and a large portion of indeterminate dried berries. Then he crashed back through the forest, leaving them alone on the path.

"Let's take a break," the older girl said.

They settled on the ground for a short rest. Though all were exhausted, they knew they had to keep going. Both the girl and the boy kept darting looks at her foot.

She opened her bag and rummaged through the contents, wrapping up all but one strip of jerky and a few of the berries.

She felt their eyes on her. Judging her. Like everyone did. They would notice the layer of dirt and grime. And the older girl's nose was prettier than hers.

"I'm Lissa, and this is Gabe," the older girl said, signaling to him.

They both had deep black hair, but that was where their similarities ended. His skin was ghostly pale, and he had bright-blue eyes that didn't seem real. Her skin was tanned, though not quite as dark as Ky's, and her face was flatter, but long and elegant.

Surprisingly, neither was much taller than Ky, and both were built just as slightly. Yet in his case it seemed just a step on his journey, whereas Lissa seemed done growing. They were both quiet, but it felt sorta like they were giving her time. She chewed slowly, partially because it was difficult to chew, partially to make it last, and partially because she was testing them. The jerky was salty and the berries tart, but not bad.

"What's your name?" Lissa asked.

Uncharacteristically, she rewarded them for their patience. "You can call me Ky." She ducked her head and scooted forward to hand them each a few berries. "Here, do you want some?"

Gabe and Lissa refused the food.

"Sorry, I can't eat right now," he said.

She remembered his earlier response to what had happened to his friends and nodded. You didn't always get to choose when you could eat, or even what you could eat.

"What kind of town is this? Are these things normal?" Ky asked.

"No way. Monsters aren't real," said Lissa. "I don't know what that thing was or where it came from, but we need to tell someone . . . rational." She frowned at the spot where the old man had disappeared.

The boy nodded.

"Where are you from, Ky?" Lissa asked.

What a surreal conversation, but she supposed Lissa needed some normalcy to keep her from thinking about the bad things. Some people were like that. "Denver."

"Denver?" asked Lissa.

Ky hugged the backpack against her chest. "They brought me to the orphanage here."

Lissa's dark eyes melted. "You don't have any parents?"

Ky felt a tug but ignored the obvious question. Of course they would have parents. Most people did. "I got away a couple of days ago, but I think Kako sent that monster after me."

The teens' eyes widened further as Ky spoke.

Gabe asked, "Kako? Oh, you mean Dr. Kako."

Lissa shook her head. "I don't think so. My dad works part-time at the orphanage as their cook. Dr. Kako can be a bit abrasive, but she really cares about getting the orphans there taken care of. Whether that is to suitable homes or the Kako Academy her family runs."

"My father and brother do landscaping for the Kakos. At the orphanage, cemetery, homeless shelter, and even out at the academy sometimes. They haven't seen or heard of anything bad."

Ky shrugged. Lissa might think she knew Kako, but Ky knew what her gut was telling her. And her gut was never wrong. Then she put it together. The gardener. "I thought you looked a little familiar. I've met your brother." He had seen her in the cemetery. Had he given away her escape? That was the least of her problems right now.

"Yeah." He looked away into the forest, as if seeing something she couldn't—but nothing that seemed to alarm him.

She pulled out a bottle of water only three-quarters full. "We'll have to share; I only have two more. Unless we come to a stream?" She looked at them, eyebrows raised. Her water usually came from faucets in the city.

Now it was Gabe's turn to shrug. "I don't know what's safe or not."

Lissa piped up, "We usually use a filter when we go hiking or camping, so I don't think you should refill at the streams. But I know a few plants we can nibble on if we see them."

Gabe and Lissa were both hesitant, but with no other alternative, they passed around the bottle, taking small sips. Ky kept darting looks at the plants around them. None looked edible, but they all resembled in some way the thing that had chased her and eaten people. At least that was what she had thought it had done with Misty and those two other teens.

Gabe spoke: "We should probably head out. The woods are even more dangerous than usual with that thing out here, wandering about. Can you walk?"

Ky wanted to know what he was thinking. "I'll be fine if you can get me a stick to use as a crutch."

Lissa helped to repack Ky's bag while Gabe went stick hunting. He brought back a good one. He just had to break off a bit of the end for it to fit perfectly.

"So what happened?" asked Lissa as they started off in the direction the man had indicated.

Ky was beginning to get used to the bird and animal sounds in a forest. She sighed, not liking to talk about herself, but these people knew more about survival out here, and they *had* helped her to escape from that monster. Maybe she could trust them, or maybe they were fishing. Maybe they blamed her.

"I ran away from the orphanage. I was in a little neighborhood and there was this cat who meowed a lot"—this brought a half smile to her face—"so I waited till night to move camp, and this *thing* came from out of nowhere, grabbed Misty and—" Her voice cracked.

Misty had been irritating, but she hadn't deserved to die. Neither had Gabe and Lissa's friends. She swallowed hard before continuing. "I ran and got lost in the forest. I thought I had lost it. Then I twisted my ankle, stepping in a hole, and I used a stick, like this one, to keep walking. Then I found a path just when it reappeared. But I lost the path in the darkness and ran to the voices." She kept her head down and kept walking. How could she have led it to other people?

Lissa asked the question Ky knew they were all thinking. "So is it following you?"

261

Chapter 34: Leon

"The only moments of life that are a bore are when we don't care one way or the other."—Anonymous

Sunday, April 24

0700

Vermilion Peak Campsite. Distinct red dirt and located on just the other side of the river from the subdivision with the most lost pets.

Leon and Paul were riding toward the campground with official approval. Or should he say he rode while Paul drove?

"I really hope we find something today. My kids are afraid to let their animals outside, even leashed," said Tang, keeping his hands at two and ten and his eyes scanning the road. He was a careful driver.

Finding clues was a long shot. Any evidence about Deborah might have been washed or blown away by the weather. But there could be something. A sign as to what she was doing out at the campsite.

Leon pulled out the SPF ten million and started slathering it on. Paul didn't have to worry about the sun. He'd just tan more, but Leon couldn't afford any time away from his cases because of a second-degree burn. Even in cloudy weather like this. Done, he slipped the bottle into his pocket. He'd need it again later.

He talked as he rubbed the white streaks in. "I don't blame your kids. This animal is getting bolder."

Paul nodded. "And a predator who isn't afraid of people could go after the little ones next! We gotta find it and re-move the threat."

Was that what had happened to Deborah? Had the creature already gotten daring enough to attack an adult? In either case, finding this animal ASAP was more important than anything else. As much as he wanted, needed, to find Deb-orah—for himself, for his sister—he needed to protect his town even more.

Leon opened the line. "This is Officer Leon Rook, RPD, calling Kaira Forest Ranger Station. Over."

The radio crackled to life. "Officer Rook, this is Kaira Forest Ranger Station, Ranger Peterson responding. Over."

"Hey there, Ranger Peterson. Long time no see. I got permis-sion from my captain, who should've contacted you guys and sent over the paperwork in triplicate. Could you get me a ranger to meet us at Vermilion Peak Campsite? Over."

"Sure thing, Officer Rook. I'll head on over now. Over."

"Roger, Officer Rook out." Leon hooked his radio on the dash and turned it off. Cell phones were great when you had service. But that was harder to come by out in the forest. Even radios had their limitations in the towering tree line.

Paul pulled up. An empty campground greeted him. Cold ashes in the pit and cans littering the area indicated the remains of someone having some fun. Could it have been Deborah? And was she alone or meeting someone?

The ground was too disturbed to pick out any single footprints. The only visible tire marks didn't match the picture he'd brought of Deborah's car. He used a stick to poke through the ashes, but nothing was left except a singed can and half of a melted plastic plate.

That wasn't McKenna's car pulling in next to his cruiser.

While it was a Jeep Cherokee, this one was white and marked with the Kaira Forest Ranger logo. The vehicle with wooden side panels, and enough dents and scratches to show the forest's disdain for it, disgorged a man.

He was average height, about five nine, with black hair, brown eyes, a five-o'clock shadow, tanned skin, and a ranger uniform. The man had that indeterminate look that made guessing his heritage impossible. He could be anything from White to Hispanic, to Native American, and so on. He definitely looked like he spent a lot of time outside, and he strode with a silent, loping gait toward him.

"Officer Rook?" he asked with a tilted head as Paul joined them.

"That's me."

"Ranger Nicholai Tompkins at your service." He reached out a hand, Leon met his grip.

He'd heard a lot about Ranger Tompkins. The man was a legend at fighting, and Leon hadn't had the opportunity to meet him before. For some reason the guy rubbed him wrong. Leon could tell he was a showboater. He didn't know how, but he could. Must be his cop instincts.

"You can call me Nick. What can I help you fellows with?"

"Where's McKenna?" She had said she was coming to help. Why had she sent this guy instead?

"She's on her way. She called in the cavalry. Your case must be a doozy." Nick puffed out his chest.

The cavalry? This wasn't a movie. They didn't need the good-looking useless guy to get eaten first. Leon tried not to roll his eyes.

Paul silently handed the file over to the ranger.

Ranger Tompkins took it to a picnic table to spread it out, using rocks to hold down the pages as they flapped.

"We need to cover between here and Vermilion Heights, looking for bear or mountain lion tracks. This animal needs to be relocated before it escalates," Leon said.

"Agreed. Do you know what you are looking for?" Ranger Tompkins asked, looking back and forth between the two officers.

Leon really wanted to say, "Yes, we don't need you." But the truth was, they needed all the help they could get. The forest was hundreds of acres, and anything could be lurking in it. Leon could wander around for years without ever finding the predator, unless it found him first. "No."

"While we wait for Ranger Peterson, I'll give you boys a quick education."

Who was he calling 'boy'?

Tompkins gave both officers a crash course in tracking.

Leon learned a little something despite himself.

At long last, another Cherokee drove up in similar condition to the first, but this one was a familiar pale blue, and it was unmarked. This time an athletic woman got out. McKenna was shorter than any of the men there, but her ponytail, sunglasses, ranger uniform, and army boots laced up over her pants showed she meant business.

"Sorry. Had to wait for my replacement. Can't leave the radio unattended," she said.

"What, no horse?" Ranger Tompkins winked.

Did he just wink at McKenna? Where was his professionalism? This was a serious situation.

McKenna marched right past Ranger Tompkins to where everything was laid out.

Tompkins followed her. "I figured we could split into teams of two, and each of us could take an officer to our zone. We'll keep in touch and inform each other if we find anything."

That was the first thing the man had said that Leon agreed with.

McKenna looked up. "Leon, this could take days, or weeks."

"The safety of the town is what's important." Leon needed to find the animal, and then everything would go back to normal. Birds chirped in the tree above him as if to say that nothing was wrong. But Leon knew it was.

"Let's go," said Tompkins, gesturing to Leon and heading in a southwestern direction.

"You're with me," McKenna said to Tang, somewhere behind him.

He'd prefer to be with McKenna, but he could always talk to her later. It was almost like covering twice the ground himself. He trusted her. Besides, what was important was that she wouldn't be with Tompkins.

Hours later he could tell wilderness and survival expert Ranger "Nick" Tompkins was stumped. Leon would have crowed if it didn't mean things were going badly for the case. The thinned lips, constant scanning, and headshaking screamed irritation. They had found no fewer than three sets of tracks that Tompkins couldn't identify. And every so often there were piles of clean white bones of critters, like mice, birds, and squirrels. They marked the trail like macabre cairns.

The trail itself was fairly simple to follow, but it was difficult to determine what exactly was leaving it. The gait looked two-legged, with a stepping-dragging pattern, but the prints themselves didn't look human. There was something unworldly about them.

Ranger Tompkins gestured to Leon. "Do you see these?"

Leon wanted to say that he wasn't an idiot. But he was getting good at holding back his not-so-helpful thoughts around this guy.

When he nodded, Tompkins asked, "Have you seen anything like this? These tracks are bipedal and nothing like I've seen in the forest, but maybe human? Hidden or distorted in some way?"

Leon had been racking his brain the whole time. In training and at crime scenes, he had taken plasters of prints and seen footprints in lots of different materials, but nothing compared to these tracks. Even body-dragging tracks couldn't compare to these . . . though those were closer. What were they if they weren't animal?

Throughout their pursuit, he could not come up with a single plausible idea about what could cause what he was looking at. The only thing that made sense in his head, he refused to say aloud. *No one would believe a mummy was wandering around these woods.*

Chapter 35: Gabe

"We shall see that at which dogs howl in the dark and that at which cats prick up their ears after midnight."—From Beyond, *H. P. Lovecraft*

Sunday, April 24

1015

There had always been stories about these woods, evil forest spirits and such, but Gabe had believed none of them until now. He'd never been this far into Kaira Forest and was thankful for the path. If only they knew how far it was to this clinic, maybe they could help Ky—if she didn't kill them first. Click-click-click. His fingers worried the lighter in his pocket.

It could be coincidental the monster had found her three times. But that seemed a bit much for coincidence. Besides, they only had her word for it that she hadn't done anything. If it was chasing her, he and Lissa could end up like Jason and Barbie. Not that Gabe wished death on anyone, but wouldn't it be better for it to get the girl and stop running around the forest killing innocent bystanders? Gabe cringed at the horrible thought.

He was letting her lead to keep an eye on her and create distance if a surprise attack came. This part of the path would be the worst place to meet that thing again. A tunnel of trees wound overhead and around both sides, encasing them, leaving no room for escape but straight ahead. Click.

The sun barely penetrated the trees. Shadows danced across the ground, playing a sinister game with his thoughts. The monster had caught up with them when they were running. It could easily be anywhere, camouflaged in the woods.

Tension spiked each time the icy breeze blew dead leaves across the ground, cackling at their fear. They were the protagonists in one of the scary movies he used to love but wouldn't be watching anymore, not after this. Gabe was used to hiking in the forest, but the familiarity had faded, and the known had become the unknown. Never before had monsters emerged from the trees to kill his friends. He might never be able to trust a simple hike or camping trip again. Click-click.

"Hey." Lissa interrupted his dread with excitement vibrating in her voice. "Look over here."

Poor Lissa had been manic—going from forced cheerfulness to sobbing uncontrollably at the crackle of a leaf. She had been way closer to Barbie, and even Jason, than Gabe had. Unfortunately, she had taken Ky under her wing, and Gabe worried it would be the death of them both. When they got to the clinic, Gabe could pass the responsibility off to better-equipped adults.

"What?" asked Gabe.

Ky jerked her head back around and stopped, turning toward them.

"Do you see this here?" She stroked spears thrusting out of the ground. "These clumps are wild onion. They're sharp and savory. We can chew on them as we walk."

"Are you sure they're safe?"

"Of course, Ky. I've eaten them hundreds of times. They taste just like green onion."

Lissa gave each a handful to chew as they ambled along.

Gabe took some to humor Lissa. He felt like a cow, crushing and grinding the vegetation between his teeth. After emptying his stomach, he had had a morning of having a touchy stomach—any time he relived those moments, the plop of Jason's head, and the blood—it roiled again. But the mind protected itself and distracted his thoughts. And now the horror was fading in the cocoon of the daytime forest. The trees were thinner here, allowing more light in. With light came hope. Even if it was playing peek-a-boo with the clouds.

The urgency faded after such an exhausting night, and darkness couldn't exist in the sunshine of the day. Even still, every once in a while, Lissa would choke with quiet sobs, reminding Gabe of the awful sights they had seen that night. Ky was the only one who stayed completely silent—she was an enigma. Now there was a ten-dollar word; his English teacher would be proud. Enigma, a mystery, a puzzle.

What was a girl from Denver doing in an orphanage in Robur Copse? Why did she seem unfazed by the deaths? Of course she hadn't known either of them at all. But they had both tried to protect her in the end. Didn't that mean anything? He stayed at the back, watching her. It was almost eerie how quiet she was, even in her movements. She padded through the forest like a cat, even with her limp and stick. She said she was unused to being in the woods, but Gabe didn't know if he could trust anything she said.

Lissa continued to talk about the edible plants they passed. The sound of her voice rose and fell in the background, soothing him and helping to keep the fear at bay. He'd always liked her voice. In English, he actually listened when she read out loud.

She explained which parts of which plants were available at different times of the year, and which ones needed to be cooked. She paused and kneeled, pointing out certain plants. If it helped her to put things out of her mind to talk, Gabe would listen.

Her face, with its wide eyes and cute nose, and black shiny hair, even tangled with leaves and debris like it was now, was familiar to him. But the person who he had thought she was and the person who she was acting like were surprisingly different.

Gabe had no idea she would be so helpful in the forest. He didn't know anything about filters and edible plants. He would recognize some of the berries, but nothing else. She made him think everything would be all right. Unlike Ky.

How he froze last night while two of his friends were dismembered by that monster slipped through his thoughts like fish in a stream. Making it seem cold and clammy inside. Everything had happened so quickly. He struggled to believe it was real.

He *had* to be better for Lissa ... and Ky. They needed someone to guide them and protect them from the dangers in the forest. Regrettably, he had only minimal hiking experience, and all he had in his pockets were a lighter and his wallet. Big fat lot of good that was going to do against a monster with razor vines that could cut him in half.

Ky had a bag of food, water—which she *had* shared—and the stick he had found her to lean on. Lissa was comforting Ky and finding them edible forest plants. Lissa wouldn't leave Ky, he knew that. So until they made it to the clinic, to protect Lissa, he had to protect Ky too. Click-click-click. His gut roiled at the memory of what had happened back at the campfire.

He couldn't fix what had happened to his friends last night, but he could try to be stronger, braver. He could prepare himself to respond to danger and put himself between those things and the girls. Gabe watched the two girls relying on him. He *would* find help and a weapon to protect them with, if he could. So far he had his own large walking stick. Gabe built his resolve. If they ran into that thing again and it would help the girls get away, he would sacrifice himself. He would.

The trees along the path were large and ominous, and the woodland atmosphere closed in on him. Gabe was used to having the forest around, having grown up in Robur, but it was strange being *so* deep in it. Ky had said she was a city girl. Where she came from, it was dry and urban. This must be quite the change for her. Strange sounds buzzed around them—insects, bird calls, rustling leaves, their own footsteps, all muffled by the foliage and humidity.

A splintered sycamore lay across the path ahead, blocking it.

"That looks way too thick and scratchy to fit through," Ky said. She was the smallest and most used to wriggling through difficult situations. If she didn't think it was possible, it definitely wouldn't be worth it.

While the width of the tree itself was probably only a few feet, the thickness of branches made it a difficult climb and held it off the ground, creating a significant barrier. Gabe volunteered to go over first, branches scratching him and catching on his clothes. A sweetness rose from the bruised bark as he clambered up. After catching his breath and brushing debris out of his face, he spun back around to pull up the girls.

"Ky, give me your hand and climb," Gabe instructed. Ky pulled herself up on a branch, situated her feet so they could take the bulk of her weight, and used a smaller branch to push off. She reached out and clasped her fingers in Gabe's.

"One, two, three, push!" shouted Gabe as he pulled Ky up to the top.

She flattened herself along the top and spun her legs away from Gabe. She dropped her backpack over first; then, while Gabe steadied her, she lowered her feet until she found purchase.

Gabe called down instructions as she searched for footholds. "You're almost there. Jump."

Ky landed safely on the ground and dusted herself off.

He turned back to Lissa. Because of her height, she didn't need to climb up as far, but she couldn't be pulled up as easily. His arms clasped hers and he pulled, using his body as a counterweight. Lissa struggled, getting entangled in the branches. Like grasping hands, they pulled on her clothes and hair, trying to keep her from getting over.

She ended up using Gabe as a rope as she climbed up the side of the large tree. He didn't mind, as it was Lissa. But it stung. He'd be bruised and scraped after this adventure. He swallowed. But at least he still had his head. His grip loosened and Lissa slipped.

Chapter 36: Project Nefertem

"If you're a true warrior, competition doesn't scare you. It makes you better."—*Anonymous*

Sunday, April 24

0645

The knife slid easily into the soft body.

Frank Marlin—the company's cleaner—blanked his mind, remaining solely focused on his task as he sliced the throat, peeled the skin off in one slow pull, chopped off the feet, head, and tail, then cleaned the offal into a bucket. He took the extra time to scrape the hide. Then he placed it into a second bucket to soak in the shed. Waste not.

Inside his cabin, he placed the rabbit in the oven with herbs and root vegetables.

It sounded like the Venus subjects had escaped their lab. How did they get so far from their area, and where was the Caretaker?

Each thought led to the next with no time to digest it, like a line of traps. He needed to contact the Caretaker. If his services were needed, why hadn't the stuffy man called?

The stairs down thunked under his feet. He pulled a high-powered ham radio from the shelf, turned it on, and began transmitting. When the Caretaker answered, Frank would have to tell him that the kids he sent had seen a Venus. Though they'd probably blab all about it themselves. If only the Director hadn't tied his hands, he could've taken care of those kids right away—but no—if he wanted to keep this job, he had to follow their orders. *Boring.* Until it wasn't. Then it was the most interesting job he'd ever had. Way better than assisting Gianni in the making of the Venuses.

No answer.

After several more tries, he contacted the Director directly, via the radio. The Director confirmed that no contact had been made with the hospital staff for several days. The Caretaker had last checked in and reported progress as normal two weeks ago.

"In light of your disturbing report, I think it is time for you to take care of any escapees. Also, destroy any evidence—including witnesses—and evaluate the situation at the hospital."

"Yes, Director."

He was finally free of his leash, since Debbie had been stolen from him. The Cleaner set his little cabin in order and loaded up his gear for a hunt while the rabbit finished roasting. From the smell of it, he would have a good, full meal before a few long days of eating on the go. Good thing he'd stopped that stupid boy from freeing it. He chomped the meal down, then put on protective clothing. He pulled on his gloves last before grabbing his bag and axe. Time to hunt some monsters—and possibly some kids. If they were still alive.

He began by retracing the kids' run through the forest. They'd left a wake of destruction any idiot could follow. The fun began when he came across the first set of tracks. There was no mistaking those left by a Venus. It was nearby.

He crept through the forest, belonging in a way the monster he was hunting didn't. Frank knew every root and branch. He heard the unnatural silence before he saw the Venus. There. A surprised squirrel let out a "kuk-kuk-kuk," as if that would scare the Venus away. Instead, the creature lashed out with a vine, wrapping up the small-brained rodent like a spider spins a cocoon around a fly.

He took advantage of its distraction to sweep out with the axe. It must have heard him and whipped out the other vine to defend itself. The sharp axe sliced right through the vine, protecting him from its sharp edges.

Unfortunately, it was now on its guard. While still a deadly opponent, it took a few precious seconds to realize it needed to drop the squirrel in order to use its other vine. That gave him the time he needed to move out of range and freeze.

The Venus reached for him, and the vine slipped through air.

He needed to get close enough to remove the thing's "brain." Right now he was at an impasse, having lost the element of surprise. Maybe if he waited for another oblivious animal? But he couldn't rely on luck.

Frank dove in one smooth movement. He grabbed a small log as a shield, taking the brunt of the slicing action of the vine, and popped up right next to the creature, hewing off its top.

The lobe rolled across the ground.

He savored the victory for a few moments before pulling out his folding shovel and digging a hole in the dirt nearby. The movement was enough to let him know he hadn't escaped unscathed. A slice in his forearm required some quick first aid.

When the hole was just deep enough to contain the pieces of the Venus, he chopped it into manageable chunks, grunting and sweating. It took a lot of force to hack through the tough biomatter. The cut in his arm would have a hard time healing during this part, but the wrap was tight enough to keep the bandage from moving too much.

He tossed the pieces into the hole, one by one. When he finished, he poured a specially issued acidic mixture over the corpse and lit it on fire. At least the scientists could do that much right. None of them would've been a match for this thing one-on-one. He expected to find an empty hospital.

These creatures weren't the type to leave bodies. He'd seen them feed more than once.

He watched, making sure it stayed contained. When the fire had burned down and the smoke dissipated, he filled the hole with dirt and covered it with leaves, then continued tracking.

The Cleaner found the campsite and removed any traces of both the Venuses and himself. He kept moving. The tracks were becoming fresher, a noticeable hush to the animals of the forest leading him on. He slowed, closing in on his prey. He found the second Venus in the early afternoon, just as the sun began to tip down.

Its distinctive scraping sound disturbed the surrounding creatures. Wherever the Venus went, the forest pulled into itself, and the animals hid because of some sixth sense. He had to wait for the right time to strike if he didn't want to become its next victim. He watched the bulbous lobe on top rotate like an antenna dish.

The vines hung deceptively limp at its side, an invisible danger to the surrounding fauna. He crouched as it stood still, listening. The Venus was an excellent hunter, but the Cleaner was better. A beam of fading sunlight illuminated one of its last remnants of humanity. And he remembered a similar scene under fluorescent lighting.

About a year before, he had been assisting at the lab in the Vermilion Peak Psychiatric Hospital and had watched the emergence of a Venus. Dr. Gianni had done her science stuff, splicing and injecting things into the bound patient. First, the greenery began to sprout out of the fingers and toes. Dr. Gianni explained to him that once the sprouting occurred, all the previous body had been digested in a large internal pouch.

The ribs of the subject exploded outward, creating room for large-size prey, the skeleton becoming nothing more than a scaffolding for the plant matter. The skin and hair left on the top was merely a thin protective coating for the delicate bud forming inside.

He snorted to himself. He was pretty sure there wasn't anything delicate about the thing.

Next, a sprout pushed out through the top of the head, splitting it down the sides. The flesh of the rent face hung grotesquely about the shoulders, in pieces, while Dr. Gianni explained how it would eventually shrivel and dry out before falling off like a baby's umbilical cord. There was something wrong with that woman.

The Venus shifted, bringing him back to the present. Their presence in the forest meant she'd probably been consumed by her creations. He would've paid to see that.

He could taste a storm on the wind. It was time to get to the hospital. *Bring it on, beast. We'll see who the better hunter is.*

Chapter 37: Gabe

"There is a price to be paid for every increase in consciousness. We cannot be more sensitive to pleasure without being more sensitive to pain."—Alan Wilson Watts

Sunday, April 24

1145

"I've got you," Gabe lied as he clamped his hand tight, but he'd do his best to make it happen.

Lissa screamed, then jerked to a halt without pulling out his shoulder. She must have been caught on a branch. He tried not to imagine the wood sticking through her leg. "You okay?"

Had she heard? His chest was crushed against the wood, and he'd expended most of his strength in catching her.

"Peachy," she gasped.

"Climb!" He pulled, using himself as a lever.

His muscles released as she finally found purchase and scrambled up.

"Ow." She grabbed her cheek.

"Are you all right?" Gabe asked while they were face-to-face, lying flat across the coarse bark.

Lissa continued to hold her scratched cheek, a small amount of blood welled along the two-inch strip. Another reason to get to the clinic. How far was "just up the way," exactly?

"Fine, just another tree branch. Give me a sec to catch my breath."

Gabe waited, glad he didn't have to ask for a minute for himself. It helped him hold on to the illusion that he wasn't a weakling.

"Is everything all right up there?"

Ky was still with them, but hopefully not for much longer. "Fine." He lied again because he thought he was going to expire. If they didn't get to the clinic soon, he might not be able to make it. His body was already sore from the run through the forest, and now he was misusing muscles that had never been used before.

Once Lissa dropped down on the other side, Gabe headed down himself—slowly and with the help of the girls' guidance. "Whew," he said. "I know it was only a tree, but I feel like I scaled a mountain." He laughed, and the girls joined in, relieving their stress.

They continued down the curved path for several more minutes before they found a convenient outcropping of rock and decided to rest. Ky handed around a few more berries and split a piece of jerky.

Despite his earlier problems, he was starving. The journey so far had been draining.

Ky passed around a half-full bottle of water until they finished it.

He didn't bother to ask where it came from.

"I hope there aren't any more fallen trees," Lissa said.

She looked almost as bad as Ky now, but she was still beautiful in his eyes. He probably looked the same.

"Or any of those monsters." Ky's eyes continued to dart about, as if expecting to be pounced on at any time. Did she know something she wasn't sharing?

"It can't be much farther." Gabe was getting really good at lying.

They pulled each other up and set off on the trail. Vines hung down from the trees, partially obstructing their vision and reminding them of the things they had seen by the campfire earlier. Gabe's skin crawled—would he ever forget this nightmare? Would he always associate forests with death and killer plants?

Eventually they came to a crossroads, where a large post stood with wooden signs marking the trails and mileage. It looked like it came from the last century. They could hear the water splashing below and birds calling out through the brush. Near the sign, they could see a break between the trees where a wooden suspension bridge crossed over a tributary of the main river.

Chills passed down Gabe's spine. It looked rickety, like the rope could snap at any moment, plummeting them over forty feet to their doom. What was this now, an adventure movie? If so, he'd forgotten his hat.

"Is that the way we have to go?" Ky asked.

He walked up close to read the weathered signs. "It looks like it. But I think it says hospital, not clinic."

"Even better. Besides, I'm not sure I trust anything that man said." Lissa pointed out edible plants at the base of the sign, and he helped her collect them. If it took her mind off having to cross that crumbling bridge, even for a moment, he'd do it. He also wanted to stay here in the sunlight—well, partial sunlight—with her as long as possible.

"Can you put these in your bag, Ky?" Lissa always gave Ky the biggest smiles. It made him feel a bit jealous. But Lissa was just generous that way.

Ky opened her bag, reaching into the depths and pulling out some newspaper.

As she carefully wrapped the leaves, Gabe noticed an article about a little boy finding a perfectly preserved beaver skeleton. Small towns didn't have much to talk about.

While she zipped up her bag, a bird flapped overhead, startling them all.

Faking bravery, Gabe led the way. "I'll check it first."

He went to the bridge and grabbed one of the anchoring posts, then reached out his foot and touched the old wood. He inched forward, grasping the rough rope rail. The bridge swayed, and the boards creaked and groaned, but it held his weight. He turned back to watch the girls. "Come on. I think it's safe. You first, Ky."

Logically, she was the lightest. Gabe didn't want to acknowledge the thought that if she fell, it might be for the best for him and Lissa.

"Whatever, I can handle it," sassed Ky. She stepped—not hopped—out, shoulders back and head high, onto the swaying bridge. The third leg of the stick seemed to help her keep balance.

"Who uses this bridge?" asked Lissa as she, too, followed, putting a shaking hand onto the rope.

"I dunno," Gabe said. He tried to remain as close to Lissa as possible but had to stay super focused on where he was putting his feet. Some of the wooden slats were slick and wet, with some sort of greenish-blackish growth. It smelled of rot.

"Um, just so you know, I don't like heights." Lissa made a strangled sound as she looked down at the rushing water.

The sound was almost soothing until he realized his body would be rushing along with it if this bridge gave out.

"Don't look down. Keep your eyes forward, on me or Ky," coached Gabe. He blanked his face, refusing to allow any fear to show. He called out to the unknown. *Help us safely across this bridge. I'm not afraid of heights, but the slippery planks and moving bridge are freaking me out. Lissa needs me. But how am I supposed to know what to do?*

"I can't do this. I'll just go back." Lissa shook her head, agitating the bridge and stepping backward.

He had to make her stop. "Lissa. Look at me. Remember that thing. It's back there, in the woods. We need to keep going forward so we can let someone know." Gabe couldn't voice it aloud. *We can't afford to become like Jason and Barbie.*

He neared the end. Ky reached out to help him, and he didn't hesitate to take her hand. She appeared stoic, but he could sense relief in the tension in her hand as she pulled him to safety. Maybe she wasn't so bad. Gabe breathed a sigh of relief as his feet touched solid ground again.

"Come on, Lissa. You're doing great." She was about halfway across, moving painfully slow. Her hands were white from being clenched as she pulled herself along the rope, staring straight at them. "See, we both made it. You're so close."

An ominous call echoed across the canyon and Lissa froze. Eyes wide, she stared at Gabe. "What was that?"

"I don't know," Gabe said. "Probably some bird. It can't hurt you. Just keep moving. You're at the halfway point, so it is just as close to come this way as going back."

"Yeah, but I know that half is safe."

At least she was joking. He hoped she was joking. "It held us. You'll do just fine."

Lissa closed her eyes and took a deep breath, psyching herself up.

Gabe held his own until she started inching along the bridge again.

Ky moved away, and another wave of relief flowed through him. He still didn't quite trust her.

At length Lissa made it almost to the edge, and he reached out. "Just grab my hand."

Lissa let go with one hand, her gaze on him, and slipped.

He started to run forward but didn't want to dislodge her more. Or maybe he was just afraid.

She cried out but grabbed the rope with her other hand and pulled herself up. Her leg was scraped, muck smeared across it. Shorts were great for heat, but not the best for adventures.

Surprisingly, she started inching back along right away, staring at her feet and the boards.

The bands on his chest released. "Lissa. You're here."

As her hand clasped his, he tightened his grip and pulled.

She stumbled into him, trembling.

He held her as she pulled herself together. It felt nice having a connection like this with her. He wished he could do more for her. Lissa had been so brave.

"I don't think we have much farther to go," said Ky quietly.

"Are you okay?" Gabe asked Lissa, backing up but holding her shoulders so he could look into her eyes.

She responded by taking a slow breath and nodding. They studied each other.

He glanced down the path. A roof peeked out of the foliage in the distance. They were within sight of human construction. An inner cold held him in place.

"This whole thing feels kind of dreamlike, you know?" Ky whispered. "Like, it doesn't seem real. Dark woods, a monster, a strange hermit, a creepy bridge. What's next?" They all looked down the trail as if they could see what it held, frozen in the moment and lost in their thoughts before starting toward the unknown.

Chapter 38: Kylie

"Words have no power to impress the mind without the exquisite horror of their reality."—*Edgar Allan Poe*

Sunday, April 24

1400

A breeze blew past, hissing and picking up leaves as Ky stared at a tall stone wall with wrought iron gates hanging wide open ...

Vines grew up and around the wall and gates, reminding her of those grasping, deadly ones. They kept reaching for her in her mind. She was beyond exhausted, with no sleep for almost two days.

The large structure would have had a romantic look if she didn't connect greenery to death. And if two-story redbrick buildings didn't remind her of terrifying orphanages. This had been the worst trip ever. If she ever got home, she was never leaving Denver again.

More vines grew up the outer walls, strikingly bright green against the leafless brown of the surrounding plants. It looked surprisingly normal compared to the strange Egyptian buildings in town. But it stood out in the middle of this wilderness.

Long shadows from the fading afternoon sun consumed both the building and the grounds, like ghosts. Ky shook her head. She wasn't usually so fanciful. *Why is there such a large hospital hidden out here?*

Farther down and to the side was a large parking lot, dotted with cars, and a gravel road led out. If Lissa and Gabe hadn't been with her, she would just hot-wire one of those cars and be out of this bizarre town. But they were with her, and a hospital with doctors who could help her ankle rose right in front of her. She chose to continue on the path.

All three of them stepped forward into the courtyard at the same time, as if waiting for a signal from the others. Ky was on high alert.

The ground was all stone and concrete. Planters and benches rested about, making it feel like a relaxing garden. A fountain gurgled toward the left, but the water looked a little green with algae. The high wall kept out everything but curious children and small critters who used the overhanging branches of the tall trees as access points. The enclosure was open and secure yet gave her a feeling of claustrophobia. There didn't seem to be anyone around, and the stillness lent a menacing air. She cocked her head, assessing the wide-open front door. Though the day was fading, there were no lights coming from inside. *This isn't right.*

"Hello," Lissa called as she stepped through the door into the reception area. "We need help and a phone!"

Silence greeted them.

She followed reluctantly, wanting to stay together and find safety from the monster. But on the other hand, she was fighting her instincts to run and rely on herself. She met the eyes of the other two and noted the furrowed brows, then looked away.

There were a few leaves in the entryway from the open door, but nothing else to show anything was wrong. Ky glanced around. Everything appeared clean and orderly. A strange mix of antiseptic and earth confused her nose.

An empty waiting area met them on the left, with open doors and a hall that continued behind it. In the middle, a wider hall continued back into the building. And a third hall branched out on the right.

Blech. Who painted walls that color of green? She'd seen better artistic choices from tagging on the tunnel walls back home.

A desk peppered with useless items sat against the wall. No one was stationed at the silent, dark computer. A phone! She stepped forward, her stick beating on the slick floor, and picked it up. The smooth plastic felt like hope. Silence. She tried pushing buttons, but nothing worked. She set it back on the cradle.

Above the desk, on the wall, was a display of pictures of the doctors and nurses who worked there.

"I say we go down this main hall and follow the right wall, checking the rooms along the way. If we continue calling out, *someone* should respond. Maybe there's an emergency, and they don't hear us because they're busy doing some sort of drill. At the very least, we should find another phone in the offices," Gabe suggested.

"I guess. Don't you feel like it's too quiet? I have a bad feeling about this," said Lissa.

Ky bobbed her head up and down. Something wasn't right here. "Just a minute." She spotted a watercooler in the waiting area and made a beeline for it.

Lissa and Gabe followed her. Ky opened her bag, handing Lissa all but one water bottle. Ky then gave Gabe the cap of the one she kept and started filling it. They made an assembly line so that when one was refilled, Gabe capped it and stuck it back into her bag on the floor. Then Lissa handed her an empty one and Gabe the cap to start the process again.

When they finished, Ky shouldered her pack once more, and they moved together in the direction Gabe had showed. Her muscles twitched.

"Hello," Lissa continued to call as they crept down the hall, her head whipping from side to side. Her voice echoed back at them.

Each time, Ky thought she would jump out of her skin. Something was very wrong.

Ky reached the door, turned the knob slowly, pushed it open partway, and looked in. "Heeelloooo," her voice singsonged. Another desk looked back at her with a computer, file holder, stapler, and other office essentials. Filing cabinets lined the right wall. A picture hung above them of some geometric flowers in muted blues and greens with a tan background, continuing the Egyptian theme this city seemed obsessed with.

She stepped inside and searched the desk—a phone. Ky tried it but with the same results.

"Did you guys find anything?" she asked, looking up at the others as they followed her into the room.

Gabe shook his head.

"This phone isn't working either. Could something have happened to the electricity and phone lines? Like a storm or earthquake?" Ky didn't remember anything like that happening since she got here, but there were killer plant monsters, so why not a natural disaster too? She remembered how it had slashed easily through people. Could it have slashed through wires?

"No," Gabe said.

He was just full of good news.

"Where is everyone?" Lissa hugged herself, looking around.

Ky's gut screamed at her. What was it trying to say? Run? She wished she could.

They checked two more doors along the hall. Another office, exactly like the first, and a storage closet with cleaning supplies. Ky paused at that closet, rummaging and searching for anything useful. But it was all cleaning supplies and chemicals. Not even a bottle of aspirin. They were at the end of the hallway, whisper-discussing whether they should continue.

Ky thought they should leave. It grew dimmer, and she got more nervous as the minutes went by. *Where are all the people?* The place didn't have that abandoned look, but it sure felt abandoned. Gabe suggested continuing to follow the right wall. Lissa agreed, and Ky didn't want to abandon them just yet. But those cars outside were calling to her. Surely one would be easy to take.

Ky followed them around the corner, only to stop short when she simultaneously heard a familiar shuffling-scraping; then *it* appeared. One of those plant monsters.

Lissa shrieked.

Gabe let out a yelp.

Ky turned and bolted the way they came. That was it. She was done with this place. She was going straight to the parking lot. If Lissa and Gabe got in the car before she started it, they could come with her.

She froze at the horrible sight awaiting her in the courtyard.

Gabe and Lissa slid, trying to stop suddenly but running into her and knocking her forward. Ky stumbled, desperately struggling to catch herself on her painful foot.

"What?" asked Gabe.

Ky pointed toward the gate, barely visible in the fading light. Another monster shuffled forward, its scraping gait instantly recognizable. How many of those things were there?

Lissa pointed out yet another, shambling at them from the right side, behind the fountain.

They were surrounded. In less than a second, they turned, almost as one, and ran back inside, slamming the door behind them. Hopefully those things didn't know how to open doors. But with their luck it would saw the knob off and trap them inside.

This time Gabe led them to the left, with Lissa and Ky following close behind as he headed to the hallway they had previously glimpsed. She noted how far down the hall the first thing had come as she swung wide, running past. It moved rapidly, but not as fast as they could, even with the backtracking and her bad foot. They'd sprinted past the opening so quickly that it didn't have time to lash out at them with its deadly vines.

Ky wasn't sure what they were going to do as she rushed down the gloomy hall, using sound to guide her. She grabbed her strap as it tried to slip off during the mad rush. It was almost completely dark inside now, despite the windows.

No light, no help, and no weapons.

L. B. ROMERO

It was hopeless.

Chapter 39: Leon

*"We are all that stands between the monsters and the weak.
"—Michael Mark*

Sunday, April 24

1445

It was a femur.

There was no mistaking that this much-larger pile of bones had once belonged to a human, though the distinctive skull wasn't present. *Deborah?* Leon's gut clenched.

They had seen multiple piles of bones and followed the tracks directly, but there had been no scat. No smell of rotten meat or feces. What kind of creature was this? The bones themselves had no cartilage or bits left on them, and no tooth or claw marks in them. They were just completely smooth and white.

"Tompkins," he asked quietly, "can you call this in and stay here? I'll go a little farther. Let me know when the CSI gets here."

Ranger Tompkins's face had paled, but he nodded and pulled out his satellite phone. All the rangers had them.

Now that Leon knew what he was looking for, following the strange tracks was no problem. Curiously, there weren't any of the little white piles for quite a way. Of course, after digesting much-larger prey, the animal wouldn't need to eat for a while. He felt squeamish at thinking of someone as prey.

Before Leon expected, he broke out into a clearing. A camp-site. He pulled the map he had made out of his pocket. This must be Ghost Hill. He stood in place and stepped in a circle, taking in a quick overview.

He sucked in a breath as he turned into the parking area and spied a black SUV, but no one was in sight. There was no camping equipment like tents or things. Perhaps they had just come here for a hike. *Or to meet someone?*

"Hello? Anyone here? Police Officer Rook here. Do you need assistance?"

No response but for the call of a blue jay and the chittering of squirrels. He continued on to the picnic area. Unopened cans of soda and packages of snacks littered the table and the ground. A speaker and music player draped partially over a bench, with the bulk of it forsaken in the dirt.

As he stepped closer, the supplies appeared to be tossed around by animals. But that meant something had kept whomever from finishing their treats. He moved to inspect the fire and paused. Outside of the fire ring, blood pooled. The sticky, spoiled-meat scent clung inside his nose and mouth. Flies buzzed.

Crouching to inspect more closely, a separate spray of blood painted the grass. They were in distinct spots, leading him to conclude something had caused arterial blood loss of at least two individuals. But where were the bodies the blood had come from? And had there been other individuals?

He stepped to the firepit, like the one at Vermilion Peak Campsite. This one felt cool to the touch, even the ashes. He also noted the box of dirt that was filled and unused next to it. A look around revealed a small folding shovel discarded near the pool of blood. It must have been moved over there, and there was blood on it.

A startled bird flew out of the brush, and Leon jumped, facing it, hand on his Taser. There was a shuffling in the bushes. Something big tried to push between them.

Ranger Tompkins appeared, looking exactly the same as when he had gotten out of his car. Not a single hair out of place. "I couldn't get you. They're here."

Leon's heart slowed, and his arm fell back to his side. Tompkins was still walking toward him. "Stop."

Tompkins froze, head cocked, looking around.

Leon needed to tell him, but to make it real . . . He paused as his throat clogged and his nose burned, then he shoved it back down and continued in a cool voice.

"We need to get that CSI over here now. This is a crime scene."

Tompkins met his eyes. For a second it felt like they were united, like he understood the heartbreak. Then Tompkins's face hardened, and he turned, carefully stepping in his own tracks, back the way he had come.

The clouds thickened, blocking more light. Leon looked out across the campground, hoping to see or hear something. But only the forest answered him. He looked back at his map. His hunch had come too late, like with his sister. He shoved the thought away. He had a job to do.

The tracks cut across the camp, continuing in the direction of Vermilion Peak and the hospital that lay between here and there.

A woodpecker tapped a tree, searching for a meal. Squirrels chased one another and spiraled up the trunks. And the breeze blew gently through the leaves of the trees as if rocking them. The sun dappled the forest floor, shining periodically through the clouds and tree canopy.

Leon stood in the middle of a possible murder scene. Even if the culprit was an animal, like he thought, it didn't lessen the burden Leon felt. He could see Deborah trying to defend herself with the shovel, taken down by the beast. Her body lying on the ground, bleeding out.

His mind filled in the details of the scene where his sister had been found. Everyone thought it hadn't been a loss. *"Those involved had all been drug addicts and suppliers."* As if they weren't real people. People's sisters. People's daughters. I'll find out the truth, Deborah. His badge weighed heavily on his chest.

Watson arrived in a fully equipped CSI van. She hung a camera about her neck, shut the van door behind her, and pulled on gloves as she headed toward him with a somber look.

He shook his head and gestured to the campsite, pointing out the blood pool with a trembling hand.

"Does this have to do with those missing teens?" she asked, the camera flashing as she photographed every detail of the scene.

Leon's head snapped up. "What are you talking about?"

He'd been away from his car all day, and the radio on his belt had rarely crackled.

"This morning the mayor showed up at the chief's office. Apparently his son is missing, along with a few others."

Leon remembered his last run-in with Jason at the coffee shop and the funny girl he had been with.

"What did you say?" Tompkins strode into the edge of the clearing. He frantically dialed on his phone. "Pick up. Pick up, boy."

Leon was shocked at the raw emotion. Tompkins didn't look old enough to have a teenage son, but the fear he saw was real. A voice came over the line. Leon couldn't hear clearly. He tried to give them some privacy and focus on the crime scene. Watson kept giving him sidelong glances too.

"What's up with that?" he whispered.

"His younger brother hangs out with the mayor's son." Her voice was just as soft.

Leon felt sick.

But Tompkins spoke with someone. The conversation appeared to be back and forth, not just leaving a message.

Leon found himself hoping it was the younger brother. He turned his attention back to the here and now. "Make sure you get this arterial spray."

"This doesn't bode well, does it?" Watson asked.

"Did you get the remains in the forest?"

"Already photographed and bagged."

"Weird, right?"

"Yeah."

Before Leon could ask anything else, Tompkins joined them. "My brother said he was with Jason and a few others last night. He rode as far as the Lotus Eaters in their black SUV. That's where he works. He stayed only because he had a shift." The ranger swallowed hard.

Leon felt for him. If his brother hadn't gone to work, he could be missing too.

The ranger continued speaking: "They planned to come to this campsite."

Leon shoved his fingers through his hair. He looked over at the table littered with sodas and snacks, then back down at the pool of blood, and his eyes burned. *Teens. Kids.* He looked up, praying for their safety, but found clouds. They were building. Like the urge to take action within him.

"Let's get this done quickly. I'm not sure how long the weather will hold." *Too late.* He was here too late. Always too late.

Chapter 40: Gabe

"You know, a long time ago being crazy meant something. Nowadays, everybody's crazy."—*Charles Manson*

Sunday, April 24

1645

Gabe slammed the door shut but couldn't find a lock.

How were they going to keep those things out? There were at least three of them and just one had killed Jason and Barbie in seconds. They were doomed. Gabe would never see his family again. Instead of getting away from the monster, they had run right into their den. This was all Ky's fault. He knew it.

They stood in the dark, waiting and listening. A stillness followed. They couldn't stay in here forever. Maybe there was a window or another door? Gabe reached into his pocket. Click-click. Of course! That was it! He drew out his hand and flicked on the lighter. In the restricted light of the single flame, his face glowed. "We need to search this room for a way out."

Ky whispered, "Also weapons or useful tools. Anything could be helpful."

Did she know what could work against those things? What was she still not telling them?

He reached out for the wall with his right hand, touching the smooth, thin barrier next to the door. It was blank. The others stayed in the light on either side of him, but to the rear, letting him lead. Along the second wall was a bed, but it wasn't normal. He pulled back, and so did the girls. Arm and leg straps snaked out from under the frame on the top and bottom of the thin mattress. He shuddered. "What the . . . ?"

"That's not right." Lissa hugged herself tight, shaking her head.

Ky stayed silent.

"This isn't a normal hospital." *Why would they need straps on a bed?* Gabe turned to the next wall, taking a deep breath to gather his courage. The hair lifted on his arms. What else might be in here? But the only alternative was those monsters outside.

The dresser stood within arm's distance from the bed. Instead of drawers, open cubbies of folded clothes lined each shelf. Ky reached forward and pulled one out. He started to stop her before he remembered their situation.

She held it by an edge and gravity unfolded it, showing a faded blue shirt like hospital scrubs, but for patients. She slipped it into her bag, along with a few others from the shelf.

Gabe shook his head. How could that be useful? She was just a klepto.

He continued along the wall to find a sink area. The small porcelain bowl jutted straight from the wall. A large pipe fed it from below, and no mirror hung above it. Secured to the wall were two dispensers. He tested them, rubbing the substance between his fingers and sniffing each. One dripped soap and the other toothpaste. Because everyone just loved mint.

The silicone toothbrush was a sleeve that slipped over a finger and had soft rubber bristles along one side. It was centered on a small, folded white washcloth. Nothing else sat by the sink. Ky pocketed both of them. She caught him staring and shrugged. Did she not care?

Lissa cleared her throat, and he continued along the wall. There was nothing in the corner. However, along the final wall, a doorless portal led to a miniature bathroom with a toilet and shower. There was a shelf or counter attached to the wall with a small white folded towel on it and half a roll of very thin toilet paper.

Ky took both of those as well. At this rate she wouldn't be able to fit anything else.

The shower was all tile with a half wall, so there was no door. The room had no exits and contained no weapons.

"I need to conserve fuel," he warned them.

They reassembled in the middle of the room on the dark-colored tile, around a drain. That wasn't ominous at all.

Gabe flicked his lighter shut. The snick of metal on metal filled the blackness.

They sat down on the floor, in the dark, away from the creepy furniture. There was still no sound from outside the room. His heart raced. There was no way out.

And nothing in the least useful or even movable except everything Ky had put in her pack. He didn't think a towel or toilet paper was going to do anything against those razor-sharp vines. For a long while they sat in the dark together, each lost in their own thoughts.

Ky broke the silence and whispered, "I have an idea."

She had his full attention.

"I think they are attracted to noise and movement, and they lash out toward it. They chased us when we yelled and ran. At least the one that followed us should know where we are, but there's been nothing. If we move slowly and quietly, they might not notice us."

Gabe disagreed. "They saw us in the hallway and in the courtyard."

"No, they heard us." Ky was adamant.

But Gabe wasn't going to give in when their lives were at stake. "Their heads turned toward us."

"I'm telling you, their heads turned toward the noise," Ky hissed.

How did she know how they worked? Did she have something to do with them? Did she lead Gabe and Lissa here on purpose?

"Enough." Lissa started crying, her sobs followed by loud gasps.

"Stop crying! They'll hear us," Ky said.

Was Ky even human? Gabe reached out, feeling around until his fingers touched Lissa's skin. He squeezed her hand in support as he lied once again. "Shhh. It's all right. We'll get out of here and to safety."

Her sobs quieted. She sat slumped for some time, holding his hand limply. "Even if they can't see us, what about light? They might not notice us, but *we* won't be able to see where we are going. And that's bound to cause some noise."

Ky said, "If we follow Gabe's idea, we can keep our hand on the right wall."

"We can use the lighter in emergencies, but it isn't meant to be a flashlight."

Lissa whispered a quiet "Okay. How will we stay together?"

"Let's hold hands." Ky was full of logical ideas.

Gabe didn't want to hold her hand, but he wouldn't mind holding Lissa's.

"Great, I'll open the door and go first, then you two can follow." It would be easy to send Ky first, but he couldn't protect Lissa if he was in the rear.

Ready for an attack, Gabe opened the door very, very slowly.

His stomach cramped in knots as they waited silently in the dark. After several moments of not losing a limb or dying, he took the first step. Ky grabbed his trailing hand and stepped after him, with Lissa doing the same for her.

Gabe simultaneously tried to feel the floor with his foot and not squeak his tennis shoe against the linoleum. The cool wall slipped beneath his fingers. He couldn't let Lissa see his fear.

He touched something hard on the wall and let the sensitive pads at the tips of his fingers follow it down. It ended. Must be a picture instead of a doorframe. They must not knock any down. That would make some noise.

Was that sound coming from the shuffling and breathing of the girls behind him, or was there a monster in the hall with them? Keep moving—one step, then another.

His foot was like lead. A vine could be whipping toward him to cut him in half right now. The good news was, he would never see it.

The hallway was endless. They were in an alternate dimension of never-ending darkness. His hand hit a raised section of the wall, followed by a depression. It was a door.

He moved his hand up and down, searching for the knob. The metal felt cool in his grasp. The quiet twisting of the knob sounded loud, but it represented safety.

He moved forward, pulling them inside, into the pitch black.

A realization struck: the monsters could be in any of these rooms. And he couldn't see anything.

Chapter 41: Kylie

"The unknown makes people uncomfortable."—*Holly Hunter*

Sunday, April 24

1815

Gabe was an idiot.

That guy was way too slow, flipping open his lighter. She couldn't see if there was any danger inside the room.

If there had been one of those things in here, they would have all been dead, for sure. Ky didn't like the idea of him leading, but since he was the only one with a light, she didn't have a choice.

She flanked him, with Lissa on the other side, as they searched another patient room. It was exactly the same as the first. There were no monsters, people, or bodies in the room. Of course there wasn't anything new. No escapes. No useful items. They might need to eat toothpaste at this rate—that was—if Gabe didn't kill them first with his terrible leadership skills.

They sat on the floor, in the darkness, for another meeting.

"Sorry, that was kind of dumb. I didn't think of the possibility that there might be monsters in these rooms," he said.

"I didn't think of it either. And it's not like they can open doors," Lissa said.

"We don't know that, but it seems unlikely." Silence answered Ky's sentence. "So should we keep searching for a phone or food, or should we hunker down here for the night?" she asked.

Lissa whimpered. "I couldn't sleep here."

Lissa was a tender soul. She was thoughtful and worried about the feelings of others, but that meant she had big feelings and she expressed them often—sometimes inconveniently. Ky guessed that was what happened when you were raised in a normal family and didn't have to hide from the dangers on the streets.

"I think we should keep going," said Gabe.

She hated to agree with him, but it *was* the better choice. There was a toilet, and the toothpaste could tide them over if things got bad, but no one would come to their rescue.

"How about I lead the way this time?" She'd rather not die because of Gabe's lack of skill. They continued their creeping pace, in and out of several more patient rooms, all the same. The relief of each room, from the tension felt in the halls, made it more difficult to leave each one. It was hard to gauge time in the dark quiet. Their train turned down another hallway.

As she crept along the corridor, she was able to make out more and more details. At least there weren't any large hulking shadows. *Except . . . What is that?* Her next step stuttered.

She could feel the press of Lissa against her back. The shadow at the end of the hall didn't move. A whooshing in her ears kept her from hearing anything.

Was it waiting for them to come into reach? They couldn't stay here forever. Either they'd collapse from tiredness, or their stomachs would start growling. A quick death from one of those vines would be better than starving to death.

She continued forward with even more care, keeping her attention on the thing. With each step, details began to appear. The shape of leaves, then a round base. *It's just a potted plant.*

Wait. Her vision was much too good for the complete lack of light. She looked toward the source. Light filtered from beneath the door in front of her, drawing her in. Light spilled out as she opened the door inch by inch, exposing the emptiness of the hall ahead.

Soft gasps came from behind her.

When the door opened enough, they all slipped inside. Ky scoured the room with her eyes. Another office.

Ky looked at them both sheepishly. "So the lights work." They had all just made assumptions.

"Yeah," Gabe said.

Lissa giggled softly.

"Do you hear that?" Ky's words made everyone pause. "It's raining outside."

They all took a few moments to listen, then went back to their search.

Gabe rummaged through a drawer. "Hey, a protein bar," he whispered excitedly.

They gathered around. "We should split it," Ky said.

Cautiously, almost reverently, he peeled back the wrapper and broke it into three almost equal pieces. He handed one to Lissa, who took it respectfully, and gave another to Ky, who nodded to thank him, and he kept the third.

He grinned and took the first tiny bite of his piece. So did Lissa. Ky bit into hers only after taking a deep inhale of the bar. It made the experience last longer. They felt a little like a team.

Not like her family at home, but they were starting to work together.

The salty peanut butter flavor filled her mouth. As she nibbled on the bar, something nibbled at her thoughts. Something she was missing. Something obvious. A picture popped into her head.

No, there was no way. She had to be wrong. "Guys, were those things wearing clothes?"

Lissa paused and covered her mouth, but she didn't say anything.

"The patient clothes, like in the dressers?" Ky asked, looking at both of them for agreement.

Their sudden stiffness and bulging eyes told her everything she needed to know.

"But that means they came from here. They were patients?" She still couldn't quite believe her theory. This town was really messed up.

"They were once human." Lissa's face and voice drooped.

Silence.

"But," Lissa spoke up, "if they were patients, then they have files, or even better, a patient list."

They searched the room.

"Hey, guys," Gabe whispered. "I think we are in an asylum. You know, a place for crazy people?"

Lissa rolled her eyes. "The term is 'mental health patients.'"

"Well, anyway, it looks like they were prescribing *the patients*," he emphasized, looking at Lissa, "lots of different drugs."

"Yeah, I'm pretty sure they did a bit more than that."

"Guys." This time Ky broke the silence. "I found an emergency exit on an evacuation map. With the exploration we've already done, I think I can get us there."

"Why don't you sound more excited?" Gabe asked.

"Well, it's through a conservatory."

"So . . ." he said.

Was the guy really that thick? "If those things that are part plant were made here, then what kind of plants might we find in a conservatory? And it's dark. We wouldn't be able to see the danger."

"There could be light switches," Lissa said.

"And that could attract those things or alert them if they are already in there."

Gabe came over to look at the map himself. "There's another emergency exit over by those stairs. We could take that one."

"That's true, but it is over twice the distance. And we would have to pass through the hall where we recently escaped from one of them. Besides, the exit by the stairs leads out to the courtyard where there were another two. The one through the conservatory has a completely separate exit, and we can skirt around the outer wall. You guys decide. New possibility, or what we know."

"If things don't look good, I have a backup plan," Ky added.

They both still wavered.

"Do you trust me?"

She led their little train again through the darkness because there weren't any light switches they could find for the halls.

The tiny imperfections of the wall sensitized her fingers—until they met with nothing.

She moved farther to the side. A door was being held open somehow. It was always possible they weren't walking into certain death. One by one they all crept inside. In the darkness, an earthy smell filled her nostrils, along with the sour scent of mildew and mold. Ky shuffled to the side as she felt along the wall for a light switch, then flipped it. Platforms of light suspended from a metal frame flickered above, revealing a tropical jungle. With walls forming a pathway through.

The ceiling appeared huge, but the dense plants created an atmosphere of intimacy. She couldn't tell how big the room actually was from the ground, as if she *was* in a jungle. The oppressive hush was stifling.

She started at the feel of Lissa's hand on her arm, then saw the piles of bones littering the floor. They looked . . . human. Lissa reached down to pick up something tiny under the tip of her shoe.

Ky turned her attention to the maze ahead of them, studying it and trying to see beyond the plants. They would have to be extremely cautious if they were going to walk through here. They peered around and at each other, trying to decide what to do. This appeared to be some sort of den for those creatures. It would be difficult to spot the monsters among all these leaves and plants.

The humidity pushed down on Ky, even harsher than the forest outside. Or maybe she had gotten used to the drier air inside. The noise of the storm was much louder in here. Heavy drops hit the glass, creating a curtain of water. Though it did help to muffle their movements, it would make their journey once they escaped even more difficult.

Ky figured they should at least get an idea of what was in here and tiptoed farther into the conservatory for a better look, the other two creeping behind her. Ky paused and could feel Gabe and Lissa looking over her shoulder.

Immediately ahead was a pond containing a large, bulbous plant in the center. Bigger than anything Ky had imagined. Dwarfing the thing next to it—one of those deadly monsters stood next to the pool. *Is it petting it? Or caring for it?*

The large plant stirred without moving. A twist in Ky's gut gave the impression it was awakening. She could *feel* its awareness of them.

"Run!"

Chapter 42: Project Nefertem

"But man is a part of nature, and his war against nature is inevitably a war against himself."—*Rachel Carson*

Sunday, April 24

2030

The rain poured down the Cleaner's body, and he smiled.

The thunder and drizzle hid his movements from the remaining Venus. The thermal goggles from his bag of tricks allowed him to see the creature clearly.

This reminded him of those stories his dad had told him about 'Nam during their training together. They had hunted in all kinds of environments and weather; those were good times. The water plastered his hair to his head, but the weather didn't bother him; it was all part of the same. One more way for him to show his superiority over nature, and everyone else.

Like a ghost, he drifted from tree to tree, crawled under fallen logs and into hollows, until he was close enough to take down the second Venus roaming the woods. He stepped out into its blind spot. This time his axe didn't miss. Not that he ever doubted his ability to overcome anything alive. He was the best hunter ever. *Hack, thunk, splat.* His axe was still sharp, but it was getting a good workout.

It was possible only the two had sneaked out during some sort of experiment, but not likely. With no radio contact, and no answers forthcoming from the Caretaker, it seemed he was dead or incapacitated at best. The sooner Frank got to the clinic, the sooner he could figure out the situation and what steps would be necessary to clean up the mess.

He knew his way, even in the dark and wet. He spent a lot of time in the forest he inhabited, pitting himself against the animals and weather.

The rain paused. He took a deep breath of the clean scent after a long rainfall. And took the opportunity to cross the bridge in the gloom. Each step a process of testing and slowly adding weight on the slippery planks while hanging on for dear life during the gusts that sent the bridge swaying. On the other side, he shook out his clothes and replaced his soaking socks. In this mild spring temperature, the wet was more of an inconvenience than a danger. He was almost there.

The Cleaner arrived at the clinic just after light and dis-covered a Venus in the courtyard. The iron gate hung open, but the side door stood closed. *Interesting.* Using stones to misdirect its attention, he took care of it, his axe flashing in the morning light. The incinerator would be the best way to dispose of it. He dragged it under some bushes so it wouldn't be accidentally found while he took in the situation. A distinct scraping had him rolling be-fore he even processed what had happened. *Tricky devil.* Sneaking up behind while he was distracted.

He used the benches, fountain, and other statuary in the courtyard to play a very dangerous game of hide-and-seek. He managed to get in the trees and climbed the wall, dropping directly on top of it—axe first. It sliced down through the lobe. Yanking the axe free, he stepped back from the leaking puddle of enzymes and took a final swipe, removing its head.

He went around the side of the building, checking the entrances, and found none open. The sun hung high in the sky, indicating it was almost noon by the time he en-tered the building. The Cleaner was still running high on the victory. He grinned. It had probably been those kids who'd closed the door. Had they already been consumed by the bioweapons or were they sitting ducks?

He used one of the secret doors to enter, jogging straight through the network of halls behind the walls and up a set of stairs into the monitoring room. While he booted up the computer, he scanned the room for any disturbances, but saw nothing unusual. He didn't wonder what had happened.

Those scientific types always created things they weren't equipped to deal with. That was what *he* was for.

When the computer came online, he entered his password and turned on the camera monitors. There, in the conservatory, waited the Audrey experiment. The room was covered in its creepers, radiating out from it like some sort of sun while being tended by two Venuses. He turned on his phone and checked it. A missed call from his boss flashed on the screen. He mashed buttons while monitoring the video feed. A third Venus roamed the halls. He was considering possibilities when he noticed a door opening on the northeast side of the building. Three kids crept out into the hall and into the next room.

So they were still alive. *Not bad.* But they would have to go too.

"Sir, I've taken down four Venuses already and am inside. No sign of staff or patients, but there are a few complications. Also, the Audrey and Venuses appear to be working together."

"I sent you a gift. Take care of it for me. No witnesses."

"I'm thinking, fire."

"No. We need the data. Plus, the complete loss of two labs is unacceptable."

"With respect"—he gritted his teeth at having to grovel, but watching the suffering of those kids and whomever the Director had sent would be well worth it—"the Audrey subject is huge. I don't have enough chemical mixture to remove it and all the Venuses. In order to be thorough, I need to use fire. Besides, I'm downloading the data off the computer now."

"Very well. I trust your judgment. However, I expect you to check the laboratory for any notes as well. I want to know what went wrong. I'll alert the *proper* authorities when the time is right."

"Yes, Director."

"Make sure you get the data. It sounds promising."

"Yes, Director. Preparing to download now."

Click. He clenched his jaw and fisted his hands, crushing the phone. Subservience didn't suit him. The Cleaner turned to the computer and inserted a thumb drive to download the data from both Project Nefertem and Project Toth.

Watching everything burn would be nice. He spun to the monitors. Eyes gleamed as a door opened and the Director's present entered the building.

Chapter 43: McKenna

"The reaction to death is sometimes as violent as death itself
."—Fears Unnamed, *Tim Lebbon*

Monday, April 25

0545

The haunting Simon & Garfunkel tune about darkness and silence filled the confines of her old Jeep Cherokee as McKenna drove up the familiar mountain road on her day off. It was oh dark thirty. Dust and mist combined to obscure the landmarks around her, but she could drive this in her sleep.

Not that she had slept last night. The piles of bones she had found in the forest had melded with Leon's discovery of blood at the campground, which turned into a talking skeleton, then the figure of her mother. The fear of more nightmares had kept her from falling back asleep.

His house had still been dark when she left, though she doubted he had gotten much more sleep than her. She had offered him a ride home yesterday, worried about his ability to drive after finding the blood. Leon was a rare species. A genuinely kindhearted man. Gentle and patient.

He undeniably sparked her interest, but she was already in a relationship. Friendship, as rough as her version was, was all she could offer.

He was stubborn, though. She already knew that by how he had befriended her. Yesterday Leon had insisted on going back to the police station to fill out paperwork. His first priority was those in danger. She liked how he was committed to his job. At least his partner had taken the wheel. Paul Tang wasn't bad either—for a guy.

A multitude of people would be out in her forest today, showing support for the mayor, but her priorities were Barbara, Gabriel, Melissa, and even Jason. However, today, she wasn't a forest ranger—though that was always a part of her—she was a concerned citizen volunteer, joining a community search party for the missing teens. They were kids who hadn't graduated from high school yet. Separated from their families. Not just the mayor's son. As if you could only be known for who your father was.

She arrived first at the campsite but stayed warm in her car, listening to "Bridge over Troubled Water." *Troubled* was right. She wished she could ease their families' pain. This was no longer a crime scene, as all the evidence had been collected yesterday, right before a thunderstorm had hit, washing anything else away. Hence the need for a search party.

When Leon had discovered the site, she'd been in the same forest, following another set of tracks with his partner. McKenna had been lucky to only discover piles of animal bones, but that had been alarming enough for her. Especially the ones that belonged to a domesticated cat. The ecosystem was a delicate balance, and whatever this was, it didn't belong in her forest.

A police van pulled up next to her in the parking area, and she turned off her car, then stepped out into the forest she loved.

Another silence—the silence of fear and worry accompanied the volunteers as they piled out at the parking lot and waited to group up. Many of them pulled on ponchos as McKenna looked up at the cloudy sky, threatening another shower.

A few of the officers got busy setting up the mobile command unit in the back of the van.

Though Leon had found the campsite, he was already in the middle of a few cases. Due to the political pressure and the seriousness of the situation, the RPD had assigned Lieutenant Durban, head of the FOREST team, to the case. As a ranger, McKenna had worked with the team often in training and real-life search and rescues before.

The lieutenant took a laminated map of the area to the picnic table and wrote out a list as other vehicles pulled up and passengers poured out.

Mother Nature seemed determined to create the appropriate atmosphere, complete with a light mist in the air. Thunder cracked in the distance but moved away. The scent of the forest surrounded them: rotting wood and decaying leaves. McKenna resisted imagining lost teens trying to survive the chilly night in the rain. Scarcely had the sun lightened the gloom when the lieutenant gave orders.

"All right, everyone, I've assigned some teams already with less experienced and more experienced people together. If your name isn't on this list"—he held up a paper—"let me know so I can add you. I also have a laminated map to keep track of where everyone has been and what has been found where, as you all report back."

McKenna knew the drill and quickly found her team. She had her satellite phone with her, just in case. She hoped the others wouldn't cause her any trouble. There were lots of murmured whispers, but resolute faces. Everyone on her team looked like they didn't know an evergreen from a deciduous.

They started in a small circle, linking hands and looking down, stepping in tandem and pausing when anything was found. CSI Watson collected and examined the evidence. It was slow going, but thorough.

They had passed the point where they could keep their arms linked, but it was important that they kept one another in sight. The last thing McKenna wanted was to make the situation worse by losing one of her team.

It *seemed* like a straightforward task to search in a step-by-step manner. She took a small step forward, searched the ground in front both visually and with a stick to move leaves and other vegetation, then looked to both her sides to make sure her neighbors were within eyesight.

The activity was quickly draining. McKenna squeezed her eyes shut and opened them wide, took a deep breath, and stretched her neck side to side to stave off the exhaustion.

FOREST Officer Lieutenant Durban personally led the team McKenna had been assigned to. He must have thought that between the two of them, they could keep all these city folk alive. He was the kind of guy McKenna really didn't like—a muscle head. But he was methodical. And she could trust him to do his job. She ignored him, and that worked for her.

The uneven ground, hidden in places by mist, made their task even more difficult. Holes and rocks waited, hidden under debris, to trip and twist ankles. Fallen trees, thickets, and cliffs created impassible obstacles that could distract her from the task or cause her to fall victim to the forest as well. A good ranger was a wary ranger.

McKenna's neighbors had already stumbled more than once, using her stick to catch her balance. She worried some of these idiot volunteers would cause more problems than they solved. But that wasn't her problem—not today. And the rising sun burned off the mist that remained, making it easier to see.

The lieutenant announced the time as 11:36 and suggested that they pause for lunch. McKenna, ready for a rest of both body and mind, scanned one more area before placing her stick in the ground to mark her spot for after the break.

Something caught her eye, ahead and to the right. She took another couple of steps toward it to determine what the thing might be, and her body stopped working, as did her mind.

Who is that screaming and shrieking? The yells continued non-stop.

It can't be. It's not . . . Durban came over and spoke to her, but McKenna couldn't understand the words. Her eyes locked on her discovery. She'd seen decomposing carcasses before. It was a part of her job, but some part of her had already come to the conclusion that this wasn't just some animal.

There—nestled in the forest floor—lay the remains of a head, the skull slightly exposed, pale and dirty in the mud. Gnawed upon. She felt arms turn her around, pushing and pulling her along. There were murmuring voices, trying to soothe, but she could still see it in her mind.

McKenna knew the grief of a child losing their mother. But the opposite was incomprehensible to her. To have your child taken away from you by death . . . What would they do? How would they feel? She had ruined someone's life.

As she stumbled forward, propelled by an unknown force, her stomach rebelled. McKenna leaned over and violently emptied the contents of her stomach. The acidic scent of the half-digested contents filled her nose. In a daze, she hoped she hadn't just destroyed any of the proof. Back there, in the mud, lay a crucial piece of evidence. At the thought, though, she could see it again.

Her limbs shook. A warmth and strange scent shocked her into action. She looked down to see an unfamiliar coat draped across her shoulders. A crinkling sound as a shiny silver blanket followed. Her knees. When had she sat down? *Why is the forest vibrating? Is that an earthquake?* The roughness of the bark beneath her kept her grounded. A log. She was in Kaira. Her lovely Kaira Forest.

McKenna could hear voices nearby, soft and somber. "Lieutenant Durban to Ghost Hill HQ, come in. Over."

"Ghost Hill HQ here. Over."

"We found a partially decomposed human skull and need CSI Watson for collection. Over."

A partially decomposed human skull . . . human skull . . . human skull . . .

"Roger, send us the coordinates. Over."

"Medic."

McKenna's thinking went hazy, fading in and out. *A human skull . . .* She hadn't wanted *this*. The plan was to come and help *find* them. Make them safe and warm. Return them to their families. McKenna felt herself falling forward. Warm hands caught her, pushing her back.

"She's in ASR, acute stress reaction." The familiar voice of her friend Nick barely penetrated the fog around her mind.

People spoke, encircling her, but she couldn't respond. McKenna kept seeing the awful thing she had found.

L. B. ROMERO

A human skull.

Chapter 44: Leon

"I wove my webs for you because I liked you. After all, what's a life, anyway?"—Charlotte, Charlotte's Web, *E. B. White*
Monday, April 25

0830

The flickering lights above the dim hallway made Leon curl his toes and run a hand through his hair.

This Monday was turning out to be worse than any on record.

Bangs, clomps, and scrapes echoed off the linoleum, making it difficult to tell where they were coming from. Basements of any building were creepy, but it was so much easier to imagine terrible things in a hospital basement. Especially since he was literally looking for the room where they kept the dead people. Almost directly in front of him hung a sign that read Morgue.

Leon forced his reluctant legs through the single door and entered a brightly lit waiting room, contrasting starkly to the hallway. A lonely desk hunched toward the rear between two doorways on either side and in front of a set of double doors. It was a last island between worlds.

The linoleum floor continued into the room, but his footsteps didn't echo as much as he walked down the chair-lined aisle. He approached the untidy desk littered with papers, files, trash, and other bits and bobs. Leon managed to locate a bell among the clutter. It was toward the front but partially obscured by a greasy hamburger wrapper. The oily scent helped to cover up the chemical smells. He pushed the debris to the side and rang the bell.

He tried not to think about the autopsy room. The smell of death. Deborah lying on the table—no, his sister. A single gunshot exposed, the rest hidden under the cloth for respect to the dead. No one had given her the least consideration when she had been alive. She'd been a "no-good druggie" in their eyes. Didn't they see? Drugs were the problem, or the abusive dealer boyfriend, not the person.

He shook his head. That was long ago. He was here because of a set of bones from the forest and a pool of blood at a campsite. He was here because of Deborah Franklin.

Leon was faced with a serious dilemma. He prayed Debbie was okay, but he also wanted the remains to be hers. If they were, they wouldn't find out that it was someone else who was missing. Or those teens.

With any luck, McKenna and the rest of the search party would find the kids today. Robur already had more than its fair share of deaths, what with the dangers of the woods, wild animals, snowy winters, and hidden mine shafts.

The medical examiner entered from the left, cleaning his glasses with a cloth as he walked.

"Yes, Officer?" he asked after taking in the uniform and badge, then placing his glasses back on his face. "Can I help you?"

The White man, shorter, around five four and rotund, resembled a fat beetle with the glasses back on his face, magnifying his green eyes. His pale skin shone, reflecting the light on his face and through his thinning blond hair. His clothes were just as rumpled and messy as his desk. Leon guessed that his appearance didn't offend the dead.

"Uh, the remains from the forest. Do you have an identity yet?"

The ME sniffed. "I haven't had time for anything extensive or to even run dentals. I've barely laid him out, for goodness' sake!"

Leon, surprised, caught onto one word, "Him?"

"Yes, yes. Again, I've had little time to take measurements or investigate thoroughly, but I am ninety-seven percent sure the pelvis is male."

Leon left the ME rambling on about sacrums and iliums, hurrying out of that horrible place as fast as he could.

On the drive back to the station, he sorted through his emotions. Leon was relieved that the remains weren't Deborah's. It meant she might still be all right, and when he found her, he'd discover what she had been investigating. Of course her case could still end poorly. And for someone else, it *had*. It had ended in death.

His concern for McKenna grew at this new information, and his stomach lurched, remembering the campsite strewn with snack cakes and soda. He recalled the pool of blood. *God, don't let it be one of those kids.* At least Lieutenant Durban was in charge of that case. If anyone could bring those teens back safe and sound, it was him. Their names repeated in his head: Jason Thatcher, Melissa Lee, Barbara Monroe, Gabriel Norton. These were teens he had seen and walked past, even if he didn't know them.

Pulling into his assigned spot in the RPD underground parking garage, he offered up a quick prayer. "God, please protect those kids. And be with McKenna and Lieutenant Durban today as they search. And help me find Deborah Franklin."

Interviewing Deborah's dad and friends had made it really hit home; people cared for her too. No matter what decisions she had made in life, she was loved. Just as he had loved his big sister. They deserved to know what had happened to her, and it was his job to find those answers for them. "Where are you, Deborah?"

The hum of the police station washed over him as he went through the box of items from Deborah's car once more. He had been meticulously examining and cataloging each item. Following up on any leads they imparted to him.

Leon's hand closed on a bag with a round piece of paperboard. He turned it over, giving it a closer look, and identified it as a coaster. It came from the Double Snake Hotel bar, and it had a phone number on it. His adrenaline surged. He took the evidence to his desk, where he searched the phone number to discover the name of the account holder.

"Officer Rook to see Douglas Chandler."

He didn't want to give the good doctor any warning, so he just showed up at the laboratory outside of town. While his badge got him through the gate and past the security points—and had gotten him information on the exact location of the office—it ruined the element of surprise.

Douglas Chandler—one of the heads of management for the Osiris Biotech lab in Robur, Tom's father, *and* the owner of the phone number on the coaster. An opportunity like this couldn't be passed up. He just wouldn't let the chief know until afterward. He couldn't fail Debbie.

The laboratory was massive. A mini city in itself, with multiple wings. No wonder there were so many strange faces in town. Osiris Biotech employees tended to keep to their own. And the company provided all they needed. According to the directory, there was everything from an optometrist to a mini-mart just within this building. The services were on the lowest level. The floor he needed would require an elevator.

Scanning the walls, with no elevator in sight, he slammed into a six-foot Black man draped in a white coat. Luckily there were no papers snowing down on them or broken glass vials on the ground.

"Sorry, I tend to not look where I'm going." The man held up the ID that hung from his lanyard and displayed a picture of him along with his name: Dr. Adrian Bartlett. He slapped his pockets, searching for whatever might have been dislodged by the incident.

Leon did the same, straightening his uniform and bringing attention to his own badge. "No. My fault. I was looking for the elevator."

"Yes. It took me a while too. The company likes to hide things from strangers. I like to think we're clever for figuring them out, but it's more likely that we're the good little rats in the maze. Just down that way past the potted plant." He pointed, then rushed off.

The elevator in the Osiris Biotech lab was streamlined, a simple steel box, unlike the one at the RPD. He had gotten used to the ostentatious brass-and-green thing.

Luck was with him, because Dr. Chandler's secretary was away from their desk. He knocked once and opened the door.

"What is it?" The man was a barker. Not someone who treated others well unless it suited him. Leon might be able to use that.

"Hello, sir. I'm Officer Rook, RPD. I was wondering when the last time you saw or heard from Deborah Franklin was?"

Leon stopped when the man came into view. He looked familiar and domineering, sitting in his high-powered leather chair, surrounded by heavy, dark wood furniture. A good ol' boy's room. His salt-and-pepper hair was trimmed neatly, and crinkles around his mouth and eyes implied someone who smiled easily. Though he wasn't now. Maybe it was just the family resemblance to Tom.

"I'm sorry. Who are you? Does your chief know you are here?"

Leon cocked his head. Did the man know his chief? Personally? "I'm here about Deborah Franklin." Cinnamon—the room smelled of cinnamon. He stepped right up to the desk.

"I don't know who you are talking about."

Leon slid the picture of Debbie across the desk. "Twenty-three years old, White, five six, blond, brown eyes. Very talkative and liked to party."

When Chandler didn't respond, his eyes locked on the photo, Leon continued: "She had your number among her things."

Chandler's attention snapped up. "Look, Officer. I appreciate you are doing your duty, but I don't know how she got my number. I never met the girl."

Leon became irritated. His gut told him that this man knew Debbie. "Well, if you want to play it that way. I mean, I have a coaster from the Double Snake Hotel with handwriting that doesn't match Deborah's. Also, I'm sure there are witnesses that can place both of you in the bar . . . If you have nothing to add, I'll just head over there. With an eyewitness, I'm sure I could get a warrant."

He turned as if to go, the threat hanging in the air. How much was his chief willing to do for the man? Recognition hit. He'd seen this man leaving the chief's office on multiple occasions. And also in the photo with the mayor and Matriarch Kako. This man was more powerful than Leon realized. Leon could be suspended or lose his job. His stomach roiled in indecision. He couldn't falter now. For Debbie. For his sister. He was committed. He took a mental deep breath, quieting his thoughts, and decided that he would do what it took.

"Wait."

Relief filled Leon. He'd taken the bait. And Leon might be forced onto leave, but he wouldn't stop until he found Debbie. He put on a curiously polite mask as he slowly rotated back around.

"Someone else must have written my number for her. I have no idea why."

"Well, that's really interesting, because we found a bunch of little baggies in her home and car, and they tested positive for a type of drug that I believe they make here at the pharmaceutical lab you run. Either it's totally innocent and you can explain to your wife how you went to the bar and gave your number to a young woman . . ."

Chandler faltered at the mention of his wife but didn't break.

"Or I can ask your superiors why you were giving this missing girl with a drug habit your phone number—your choice. Maybe I should do both?"

"Look here, you . . ." The man slapped his desk, half rising from his chair, eyes blazing. His teeth were gritted, muscles tensed, and he looked capable of anything.

A weakness swept through Leon's body, and he forced himself to stay upright, showing no fear. His hand went to his stun gun. But he had seen a quick flash of panic in Chandler's eyes before it was covered by anger. Why would he be so afraid of his superiors?

Chandler blinked. Lids covering lizard-like slits. "Fine, fine." He lowered himself back down and schooled his face.

The man was good. Not good enough to avoid being pricked in the first place. But men like him didn't expect to feel an insignificant sting from a tiny unimportant police officer. Not when he could hide behind the chief of police. Poking this particular bear was dangerous to Leon's future, but Debbie was more important.

"It's not what you think. I don't know anything about drugs or what happened to her, but I was at the bar on Thursday. I was interested. So I wrote down my number and slipped it in her purse. But I never heard from her, okay? I'm not a saint, but I *never* saw her outside of that bar or after that night."

Leon kept his cool, ignoring the increased pulse in his ears, and asked a habitual question. "What time was this?"

"I got there at about six. Debbie was already there, working her magic. And I stayed until about ten. I think she left about nine."

Regaining some of his former confidence, Leon asked, "I'm sure I can find some witnesses at the bar to corroborate this?"

"I'm sure you can. Now, if you don't mind, I have a phone call to make."

Leon nodded and left the office. The threat of the phone call made his hands start shaking, but Chandler could no longer see. Leon didn't get out of the building before his phone rang. Leon checked it and silenced it. The chief really was Chandler's dog.

In his cruiser, he tried to calm himself, running a hand through his hair. What had he been thinking? Going against his chief and threatening a man who was friends with the town's elite? He breathed in and out slowly through his mouth, trying to control the tremors and defeatist thoughts.

He had made a decision, and now he had to deal with the consequences.

His phone rang again, and his stomach dropped at the number. He silenced it once more, unable to speak. His eyes burned, and he blinked away the tears. Where was the law now? When one man could control the direction of an investigation, what did Leon's badge even mean? He had come back to this small town to escape the corruption of the large cities. But it turned out it was only better hidden here.

When the phone rang a third time, Leon squared his shoulders. He still had a lead on Debbie's case, and she needed him. The chief, supposedly a friend to Debbie's father, had a different agenda. That left Leon as the only one who could help them.

He wanted to ignore the messages completely, but he couldn't. Leon needed to know how far the chief would go. He listened to them one by one.

"I told you to leave it alone. Get back to the station immediately."

Not too bad. The chief sounded angry but controlled. Leon deleted it and pressed the button for the next one.

"You are off the Franklin case, permanently."

The chief was starting to lose his composure and resorting to threats. Leon slipped his fingers through his auburn locks, soothing himself. Defiantly, he deleted that one too.

Number three had a sucker punch straight to the heart. Both hands on the wheel, Leon pulled away from the Osiris Biotech complex while the words repeated in his head:

"If you don't return to the station, I'm taking your badge."

Chapter 45: Gabe

"Quoth the raven, 'Nevermore.'"—The Raven, *Edgar Allan Poe*

Monday, April 25

0945

Where was a cop when you needed one? They had to get out of this place. Alive.

They had spent the night in a restroom, in a building full of monsters. And even the bathroom was Egyptian themed, using sand-brown tiles and warm rust paint on the walls. The hard tiles with only a towel for a pillow made him grudgingly grateful Ky had swiped them. He was also thankful that the room didn't reek of urine. The trash was almost empty, indicating it had been cleaned not long before being abandoned. Lucky them.

Once they had stopped, Lissa had sobbed for a long while. They'd left the light on, and Gabe had held her hand through the night.

He slipped into a khaki-painted restroom stall; Ky had warned them that flushing could attract the attention of those things. Luckily, there were several stalls to choose from. He took his time to give Lissa privacy for getting ready.

Gabe came out to wash his hands while Lissa was still scrubbing her teeth with a paper towel. He should do that himself. Unfortunately, using the sink could also bring those things, so they were using small amounts of bottled water, helping each other. Gabe thought it was overkill.

After all, using the bathroom didn't have the door being pounded down by those things. But the water would rush through piping in the walls, and then he thought of Jason and Barbie. He wasn't taking any chances. "Have you heard anything? Did anyone come yet?"

Ky looked down and shook her head.

"Staff? Patients?"

Lissa shook her head too.

The idea that he could pass the responsibility to someone better equipped had him still hoping for help to come save them. He had a feeling Ky hoped for the opposite. Would he ever see his family again? Despite their arguments and suffocating love, he missed them. Death was just so . . . final.

"We need to talk," Ky said.

As abrupt as always. He might even be starting to get used to it. With everyone refreshed and ready, they used their towels like seats to keep off the cold tile, and they had breakfast in a circle. Ky passed out food, splitting it into three equal shares.

"This is the last of our food, and we're getting low on water."

If someone wasn't so paranoid, then they would have more water to drink. With luck, the side exit would be unlocked. But even if they made it out, they would need to survive in the forest. If they were pinned down in this hospital until someone came, they would need food and water. And when they found help, who would believe them? "We need to get some evidence."

"From here, there is a laboratory on the way to the kitchen, which is on the way to the exit that is least likely to have monsters near it."

"Useful." Gabe couldn't help but be impressed with her memory. He had looked at the map, too, but he couldn't re-member exactly where everything was. He hadn't even seen there was a kitchen, as intent on exits as he was. The meager breakfast of found plants and jerky stuck in his teeth as he tasted every salt grain and bitter drop of juice, knowing his stomach might still growl at the wrong moment.

Ky shifted on her towel. "Or we can just go to the kitchen and then the exit." She looked at Lissa. Ky was acting shifty again. Was there something in the lab she didn't want them to find?

Lissa spoke, "I think that getting out of here is the most im-portant thing. We aren't equipped for any of this, and no one knows what danger the whole city could be in." She leaned toward Ky, her eyebrows raised. "You said that the one went as far as a neighborhood?" At Ky's nod, Lissa sat back. "That can't be good." Lissa's face crinkled.

Gabe needed to know they would be taken seriously and not just labeled as troublemakers. "I think it's also very important to know what we are dealing with. How many of those 'patients' are there? And what were they doing here? The information would help us avoid them. *And* I don't want us to sound like crazies when we get out of here. We need facts. We need proof."

Lissa looked at Gabe, eyes wide, rocking slightly. He could see her weighing his words against her fears. After a few moments, she nodded.

Thank goodness. After all, what was the point of escaping if those things killed everyone in the town because no one listened? The one that had chased Ky had been in a neighborhood. For all he knew, Robur Copse was fighting those things right now.

Ky got a few paper towels, then rummaged through her bag. Finding a pen, she started to draw. "The bathroom we are in is about here. The entrance we came in is here. The conservatory is here, and the other exits here and here. The water is here. I'll put *x*'s where we have already explored the rooms. And the stairs are here."

"Wow! You remember everywhere we've been? In the dark?" Lissa whispered, eyes shining. He wished she would look at him like that.

Ky squirmed.

"What happens when we get out?" Gabe asked, voicing the uncomfortable question.

"The old man said the path led to a city on the other side of the mountain. That gets my vote," Ky said.

Gabe shook his head. "That would take too long. We need to make sure the people in town are safe. That can only happen if they know about the monsters as soon as possible. I say we take the gravel road out front."

"It doesn't matter if we don't survive."

"The road is probably a more direct route to town with the possibility of us being seen by passing drivers."

Lissa's head followed their argument back and forth as if she were watching a tennis match.

"Let's think about it. We don't know what will happen. We can leave both options open until we get there." Lissa had acted as mediator more than once. It wasn't that Gabe wanted to constantly argue with Ky, but this was their lives and the lives of everyone he knew on the line.

Ky pressed her lips together and said no more.

Gabe let it go as well.

Lissa rolled to the side as she stood and reached into her pocket, pulling something out. "Oh, guys."

Ky turned and looked at her.

"I found this on the floor in the conservatory, near a pile of bones. What do you think it is?"

Ky took it and examined it, shrugged, and handed it back.

Gabe walked over. "Let me see."

She handed it to him, her face aglow. She was always shining with positivity. Her hair, her eyes, her smile . . . he took the item from her, and their hands lingered, touching. His insides fluttered. He cleared his throat and placed the metal bar in his palm, spinning it this way and that. "So cool. It's some type of microchip. See this number sequence etched on the side? Really slick, and completely encapsulated. I wonder what it's for?"

The girls shrugged.

Gabe tried handing it back to Lissa. "No, you keep it, since you seem to like it."

"Thanks." Gabe stuck it into his pocket, next to his lighter, and fingered Lissa's gift.

"Let's go," Ky said.

Chapter 46: Leon

"Bars in the daytime are like women without makeup."—*Lady Snowblood,* Lady Snowblood

Monday, April 25

1200

Debbie had come here the night she disappeared. He may not have wanted the case at first, but now he was going to see it to the end, no matter what.

His badge was still pinned to his chest for now, but after today . . . finding her was no longer just a job. It was redemption. No one had stood up for his sister. He would be the one to fight for Debbie.

It surprised him to find a brightly lit room with a wall of windows. Though all they showcased today was an overcast sky.

The ceiling of the hotel bar was square, coffered woodwork, like an all-white checkerboard, drawing his eye. Ironwork chandeliers holding electric candles were suspended from the center of the room. Others shaped like oil lanterns hung from the walls above the booths. Green columns with golden yellow and orange-red highlights stood scattered throughout the room. Arches along the bar wall added style, and the glass shelves of liquor were lit from below.

He could see Debbie here—white dress, hips swaying, and her heels clicking on the sunset-clay tile floor, drawing attention. Slipping onto a brass-and-green-leather stool—reminding him of the station's elevator—at the counter and ordering her usual. From what he'd learned of Debbie, this place suited her.

Leon had expected the bar to be dark and dingy. He'd envisioned a place where his feet stuck to the floor, like at the movie theater. And smoke hung in the air. Like the one his sister had taken him to when he was a teen, to meet her good-for-nothing boyfriend. Drunk men and women dancing too close together, making poor choices.

"Hello there, Officer. What can I get you?" greeted a friendly bartender. His name tag read Callix.

What an unusual name.

The man was tall, at least six feet. It was hard to tell because he worked, wiping down the bar as he spoke. White, with short light-brown hair, softly spiked, pale-blue eyes, a strong Roman nose and thin lips.

"Officer Rook. I'm investigating the disappearance of Deborah Franklin. I have a witness that says she was in here last Thursday night."

Callix wiped down glasses and hung them up as he spoke, as if he couldn't bear for his hands to be still.

Leon grinned to himself, thinking he had found the stereotypical bartender.

"Oh yeah, her. Debbie was here. Dressed to kill, like always. It would've been kind of hard to miss her. She had all the guys flitting around her like bees to honey." The bartender's lips pressed together as if he was holding back.

Leon wondered if the slight English accent was real or affected. "What time did she arrive?"

"Well, Mr. St. Martin was here for his nightcap, so it would've been before six fifteen. I'd say about six tenish because he skedaddled not long after. He never could abide a siren and her 'wiles.' His words, not mine."

"How did she appear?"

"Oh, she was having a right good time. She always does. Gets all the fellas to pay for her drinks and dances." He began cutting and preparing garnishes as he spoke, the sharp scent of citrus filling the air. Again, the press of lips.

Maybe with a little pressure . . . Leon leaned on the bar, getting Callix's undivided attention. "Look, she's been missing for ten days. If you have information, you should share it now. Otherwise, you could be obstructing an investigation."

The bartender cleared his throat and leaned in himself, as if imparting a secret. "I suspect she lifts a few dollars for her troubles as well, but you won't hear anyone say anything. Just a pause when they go to their wallet to pay, now and again. I suspect she's right slick about it and most of them feel like it was money well spent to have her attention for a while. She has a way of making a guy feel young and energetic, if you know what I mean."

This man played his part of confidant well. "You mean she's been stealing money from people's wallets?"

Secret time over, he went back to wiping down the bar. "Oh, she's too good to get caught. And too interesting to get people mad at her. I think it's all part of the game."

"And when did she leave?" The blood samples from the campsite didn't match Deborah Franklin. So where did she go, then? And who did she go with? Maybe this free-speaking bartender could shed light on those questions.

"Hmm, that's a bit harder. Not because she didn't make a big production of it, but because I didn't really look at the time." He paused as he got the bag to fill the snack dishes on the bar. "I'd say somewhere between nine and nine thirty. It was a bit on the early side for her. I'm assuming she had somewhere to go, ya know?"

"Did she leave with anyone, or did anyone leave right before or after?"

"Now that's the most difficult question yet. If ya mean, did it seem like she was meetin' someone from the bar? No. But in the literal sense, folks were coming and going all night, so I didn't notice who mighta been before or after."

"Did you see or hear which way she was headed?"

"Nope, just out the door's all I know."

"What about Dr. Chandler?"

"Likes I said, lots of people were coming and going. I only noticed the ones at the bar."

"What about Tom Chandler?"

"He wasn't here that night."

Truth, but did he know that Tom was dead or not? He couldn't read this man, and he was Leon's last hope.

No other questions got him any more information, and Callix seemed friendly and helpful to the last.

Leon collapsed into his vehicle and slapped the steering wheel, grabbing it and twisting with both hands. His last lead had gone nowhere. Had he sacrificed everything for nothing?

His phone rang again, and he was ready to throw it . . . but that wasn't the chief's ID. In fact, it was an unlisted number. Could it be a tip?

"Officer Rook," he answered.

A metallic voice spoke in his car: "Debbie checked herself into Vermilion Peak Psychiatric Hospital for addiction recovery."

All roads led to Rome . . .

The moment the chief called threatening him, Leon had known it would come to this. But he'd wanted Callix to give him something—anything else.

He would have to go there himself.

Leon went cold. He closed his eyes as if that could block out the memories.

Chapter 47: Kylie

"Science never solves a problem without creating ten more."—G
eorge Bernard Shaw

Monday, April 25

1130

A few windows—too small for even Ky to fit through—let in some sunlight. It was unnerving to creep through the halls during the day.

Now they could better see danger coming in the dimness, but her body wanted to move faster because she could see where she was going. To hurry before one of those things came. Yet she knew—*knew* despite what Gabe said—they followed by sound. That was how it had chosen Misty, how it had chased them through the woods, and how they had been found when Lissa screamed. A niggle of doubt said that she'd been quiet after Misty had been eaten and it had still come her way.

With speed came sound. The inevitable squeak of shoes on the floor and heavy breathing. Plus, they could see outlines of corners and doors, but there was still enough shadow that they could make mistakes. So Ky moved as slow as a turtle, pausing every once in a while to double-check all around her. The others didn't complain.

There had to be a way out.

They passed by a painting, more brightly colored than any of the others she had seen in the building. A person stood, bent over, in the middle of a pond. There were bright-blue flowers, the only color visible in the dim light. It looked like the person was picking straight sticks or stems growing out of the water. The picture made no sense to Ky, but then she didn't know anything about art.

Only a few doors later, they made it safely into the lab, where no Venuses awaited. And Ky shut the door.

The first thing Ky noticed was a window that separated them from the next room. That room was full of medical equipment surrounding a metal table with straps. She was pretty sure that whatever was done in those rooms hadn't been done willingly.

Gabe and Lissa split up, searching where their interests took them. Lissa looked through papers and Gabe booted up the computer. The keys clicked in the background, creating a soft hum as Ky looked through cabinets.

Lissa spoke, "That thing, last night, in the conservatory. It kind of reminded me of a queen bee who sends all her workers out to get the food, while a few stay behind to care for her."

Ky shuddered at the thought. Unlike bees who buzzed on flowers, they were the food.

"That's why they are out wandering the forest. What do you think?" Lissa asked.

"I think we need to keep looking. Have you seen an address book or a Post-it with passwords? Wait, this might be it . . ." Gabe's typing resumed.

Ky wasn't finding anything interesting in the cabinets—glassware, machines that did who knew what, racks of tubes lining the counters. Nothing useful to put in her backpack. She opened a fridge but immediately closed it, gagging on the stink of rot.

"Guys," Gabe said, "they were definitely doing genetic experimentation. I can't understand most of it, but basically they were replacing parts of human DNA with plant DNA. Carnivorous plants—in particular, Venus flytraps."

"Well, that's no surprise." Lissa shuddered and blinked her eyes a few times.

"What's carnivorous?" Ky asked.

"They eat meat," he said

"There are plants that really do that?"

"Yep. But why . . ." His voice trailed off as the clicking started again.

"Hey, guys. I found a list. But there are like thirty names on here. There can't be that many of those, can there?" Lissa looked at them, her eyes wide with shock.

"I certainly hope not." Ky went to look.

A slamming from the wall made her jump. She spun toward it, ducking unconsciously to make herself small. She pulled Lissa down, hand on her arm, and pressed against a desk.

Gabe took the hint and ducked down too.

Ky crept under the desk in front of her and peeked through a crack.

On the other side of the plastic window was one of the monsters made from the plants that ate meat. The vines were moving like hands feeling around at the window. The way they had sliced through the people back at camp.

She was pretty sure plastic wouldn't stop it if it wanted to get through. Ky felt like she did back at the neighborhood. The need to run. To get away. But she knew that was the last thing she should do. Her hands started shaking. It was getting harder to hold herself back when it suddenly turned away, whipping out a vine.

There was a soft, high-pitched squeak. And the monster opened its top, dropping in the mouse or rat, then slowly shuffled out of sight. Scrape, scrape.

They stayed still and silent for a long time before Gabe quietly made his way over to the window and looked around in the other room. He gave them the "okay" sign, then crept back to them and whispered, "I think it's gone, but we need to be quieter."

They all nodded. Ky wanted to say she had told them so, but now wasn't the time.

"We should keep looking." His voice was barely loud enough to be heard. Lissa nodded, so Ky just went along with it. She wanted to get out of there, but she had started to get attached. It was silly, but she couldn't leave them behind.

Just then the computer Gabe was working on began making noise and talking with a woman's voice. He stopped it immediately, and they all stood listening for several moments before he waved them over.

Lissa had a small book in her hand when she met them, but her attention was all on the screen.

It was a video of the metal table, filmed through the plastic window. Or what was on the metal table? A strange-looking wrinkly person lay on it, and something was moving under their skin. Ky watched in horror as the skin split and vines grew out and around the body until it looked like those monsters. It was almost like a nightmare, watching what was happening with no sound. Yet she was kind of glad there was no sound.

Ky's stomach twisted. She suddenly understood how Gabe had felt back in the woods. She barely made it to a sink in the corner before throwing up. Then she wished she had some of that mint toothpaste to rinse the taste out.

A gunshot sounded—or it might have been a slamming door. All eyes shifted toward the sound.

"Police!"

Chapter 48: Leon

"Pain is weakness leaving the body."—Unknown
Monday, April 25

1315

I'm under attack!

Leon spun and avoided something whipping toward him. Landing in a crouch, facing forward, he could barely make out a human figure.

His eyes continued to adjust from the midday sun outside to the gloom inside. But his mind and the rest of his body told him he was in danger.

He darted forward while palming his stun gun and narrowly avoided another swipe. Ducking under and pushing straight into the body center, he brought the handheld device up and activated it in one swoop. It just needed to make direct contact, which it did.

The electricity arced and lasted longer than it should, causing Leon to step back. The figure slumped to the ground.

He could detect a burned-vegetable smell, like boiled or canned asparagus. *Yuck!* Leon squatted to examine the body.

On closer inspection, it wasn't human. On second thought, after noting the tattered hospital clothes, maybe it once had been.

What in the Sam Hill is going on here?

He stood and saw an unfortunate shade of green on the walls. Maybe it would look better in full lighting, but he doubted it. Nothing looked great in fluorescent.

The halls split in several directions, and a desk sat next to the double doors. At the reception desk—still no receptionist. In fact, no one had answered his call at all. Unless he counted this giant vegetable.

A burning began on his left side, and he looked below his badge. Apparently he hadn't completely avoided that whipping vine, and those things were deadly sharp. So sharp he hadn't felt the initial hit, or maybe that had been the adrenaline. He took a deep breath as warm blood seeped into his clothes. His radio and cell phone were both destroyed, his belt split. *Convenient,* he thought.

He untucked his shirt to examine the wound. It looked manageable. He needed to return to his car and get the med kit while he called this situation in. There was something very wrong here. How did the chief not know, if he had sent someone? But Leon doubted very much he had.

He tied the two slit tails of his shirt through a belt loop on either side of the pants split, then knotted them together to hold his pants up and free his hands. He needed to be prepared, just in case. The lack of light and personnel was adding to his alarm after the attack. He needed to get his stuff and get out of here ASAP.

As he unsnapped the holster and grabbed his service weapon out of what was left of his belt, a shriek echoed in the silence. He reached for the next thing. Another yell. Unable to leave people in danger while he collected the rest of his stuff, he took off.

Leon ran awkwardly with his makeshift shirt-belt holding his ripped pants up. He had a stun gun in one hand and his service gun in the other. He pocketed the stun gun as he navigated the halls. Though it would be better for civilians in danger, he didn't want to get that close if another of these things was in here. With his free hand, he chambered a round in his Glock 22, pointing it down as he ran and listened for the people. He begrudgingly acknowledged that his weapons training was coming in handy today.

"Go right," a male voice called. Three kids turned down the hall, currently occupied by Leon. The girl in the rear limped, yet swiftly gained on the others.

"Help!" The terrified kids barreled toward him, their voices overlapping with fear.

"Move to the side!" He needed to see the threat. Was it another of those vegetable things that had attacked him a few moments before or something completely different?

The kids continued to run, but they split to stay on the sides of the wall, revealing two of those things coming after them. As much as he hadn't wanted to come here, this was the last thing he had expected. Here he had been worried about memories, not living monsters.

Leon settled into a three-point firing stance and waited for the kids to clear his sides before firing. His heart pounded, watching those things move toward him. The vines could reach far.

He emptied the entire clip into both bodies. Shots went wide and high. But enough hit to drop them in the hall. Leon sighed, shaking off images of the bullet holes in his sister, killed during a drug bust gone bad.

His heart still pounded with adrenaline. He had never fired his weapon in the field before. And the smell of gun smoke made his stomach turn.

He addressed the kids. "Are you all right?"

They all stood bent over and gasping in the middle of the hall.

"Yeah," the boy replied breathlessly. "Thanks. I'm Gabe."

Turning his attention to them, his brain caught up with facial recognition and the boy's words. The pale, dark-haired boy.

"The missing teens from Ghost Hill! You're still alive? Melissa, Barbie, Jason . . ." He trailed off. There were only three of them, and the second girl didn't look like the pictures of Barbara.

Melissa looked up. She *was* the girl from the coffee shop. The one with the sweet smile.

"Yes! Thank goodness you found us. We heard you call and, uh, lost all sense running straight here—oh, it's you." She held a book.

He nodded and looked at the second girl—the one with the limp—who was clinging to a black backpack slung by one strap over her shoulder. She shook her head. Shorter than the other two at about four six with chin-length brown hair, tanned skin, and brown eyes much lighter than the older girl's. She simply looked exhausted.

While the three looked a little rough around the edges, with scrapes and scratches on any exposed skin and messy hair, they seemed mostly fine. However, the unknown girl had an injury that was making her limp.

"But the others?" Leon asked.

Gabe spoke up. "They didn't make it...Ky was chased to our camp...by one of those monsters...and it took out Jason...and Barbie in seconds." He gestured to Ky, then returned his hand to his knee as he continued gasping in extra air.

Leon was right. He had been too late. *For the other two,* he told himself firmly. But now he had a chance to help these

369

kids. "Well, I'm Officer Rook. Call me Leon. Glad I could be of assistance. We need to get you guys out of here right away."

Ky spoke up. "They can't open doors, and I don't think they can see. They sense movement and noise."

"We spent the night in a public restroom," moaned Lissa.

Recovering his breath Gabe said, "Lucky for us, Ky memorized the map to the downstairs. We've been making our way over to an exit by the stairs on the other side of the building."

"Why didn't you go out the doors by the front desk?" Leon asked. They weren't that far of a run from where they were standing.

Gabe said, "Oh, that's the way we came in, and when we tried to escape that way from one monster, there were two more in the courtyard, waiting for us. Speaking of which, we're not sure how many there are, so we should go into a room to continue this conversation."

Leon held up a hand. "Wait, I used my entire magazine. I fried one of these vegetables back there, but it sliced my belt off. I wasn't able to grab everything from it. But there's ammo back there, and my patrol car is right outside. I didn't see any of them in the courtyard when I came in, and none on the way to you . . . so we could try it."

The three looked at each other and, after reaching a silent agreement, they turned to him expectantly.

Leon led the way, sandwiching the two girls between him and Gabe. Lissa looked done in, and Ky wasn't moving very smoothly. This assured him they wouldn't fall behind.

Leon kept his stun gun at the ready and his empty Glock tucked into his pocket. What was going on? What were these things? Had they really been people? Why were they in the forest and here at the hospital? There was no hospital staff to ask about Debbie. Was the tip real or a lure? So many questions. He needed to keep his focus on getting out; then he could get all his questions answered.

His side began to sting and throb, the nerves finally realizing something wasn't right. He tried not to show it to the kids. But they could probably see the blood—proving, once and for all, he wasn't the best choice for a hero.

Sure, he had taken down those two vegetables with his gun, but that had been pure luck. The boy, Gabe, had said he didn't know how many of those things there were. If the vegetables attacked again, they would probably all die, like his sister. She hadn't died physically in a mental hospital, but it had been the last time he had been able to talk with the woman he had called sister. And it wasn't long after that . . . she had truly died.

The abandoned halls and gloomy interior were unnerving, as was the silence. If only he could be enough to keep these kids safe. Temporarily. Just until he could get real help, like Lieutenant Durban and the other FOREST officers. They would know what to do. If they would come.

Almost to the exit—just up ahead and around the corner. Almost to real help.

"Watch out!" Gabe yelled.

Leon spun, seeing the two vegetables weeping sap from each bullet hole but moving unsteadily toward them. One lashed out, and Leon watched in slow motion as both vines wrapped around Lissa, pulling her in.

"Go," Lissa screamed, dropping her book.

Leon darted in, his progress blocked by the second vegetable heading toward Ky, its vines extended. He used the stun gun on the vegetable in front of him, and that same strange buzzing arc of electricity occurred for about a minute before it fell to the ground. He inhaled a familiar acrid smell and was astonished to see Ky standing in front of him, her hand still on the doorknob.

"Mister?" Her eyes were wide and her body still as a statue.

Leon was just as surprised as Ky and looked down at himself to see whether there were any more injuries. "Wow, still alive."

Ky seemed to process everything quickly and stepped back out into the hallway, looking down where it intersected. "Lissa!"

But Lissa and the vegetable were already gone. It looked as if they had been aware of the danger from behind and had slipped into the room, leaving Leon in the hall to fend for himself while not warning him.

"It must be taking her to the conservatory!" Gabe burst back out of the room and started down the hall.

Pushing aside his snide thoughts, Leon reacted instinctively, lurching forward and catching the impetuous boy. "Wait! I'm out of ammo, and I think my stun gun's out too. It'll need to be charged."

"We've got to help her." Gabe tried to escape, but Leon had grabbed his shoulder in a fierce grip. Pain sliced through his side at the boy's struggles.

"We don't have any weapons." Leon faltered and slumped, weakening. His extremities felt like he'd been outside in winter too long, and a strong burning in his side flamed to life.

Gabe spun toward him and must have seen the blood soaking his clothing. "It got you!"

Leon shook his head. "It was the first one. I'm losing too much blood. It must be deeper than I thought."

Ky ran into the room and came back with a folded towel. "Here, it looks clean."

With the help of the two kids, Leon limped into the room. They shut the door, and Leon unbuttoned his shirt, tucking the towel against his side and applying pressure. He sagged against a wall, letting the dizziness pass, while he summoned his strength.

They were all silent.

Leon scanned the room for outlets but came up empty, just like his clip. He stood there, his eyes closed, willing the shakes away. Looked like the chief wouldn't have to take his badge at this rate.

Ky shoved a bottle of water at Leon, along with a bottle of pain relievers.

Leon raised an eyebrow.

She shrugged, passing out chocolates too. "Here, we'll need our energy to make a last play for the door," she said.

Gabe tensed.

"I found them in a desk, at the lab," she told Gabe in response to the look he gave her.

There was a lack of trust there, Leon thought. He swallowed the medicine and handed Ky back the rest. Inhaling the sugary chocolates helped his energy levels. But nothing could help his sense of failure. He'd been right there and watched a girl taken by a monster.

The other two were looking to him to save them. *Save them!* He was wounded and ill-equipped and the worst police officer in the RPD. Perhaps he didn't deserve the badge pinned to his chest. It was his fault Lissa was gone. He had thought he'd known better than these kids, who had survived days against the monsters. And where was Debbie?

He drank and tried to ignore the debilitating pain while waiting for the meds to kick in. Desperate for a way out, he thought aloud about what they did have. "My bullets wounded them but didn't take them down permanently. I am pretty sure the electricity worked, though. Too bad my stun gun is used up. It normally lasts longer, but I think the weird arcing caused it to expend more energy than normal." What were those things, and what was going on in this hospital? He had more questions than answers. And, trapped, he had no way to get answers. Maybe Gabe and Ky could provide more.

"That we can take them down at all is more than we knew yesterday," Ky said.

Gabe seemed only half present, staring and not responding.

Leon needed to know what they were up against if they were to have any chance of getting out of this hospital. "Now tell me, what happened at the campsite? What do you know about those things? And where did it take Melissa?"

At this, both Gabe and Ky fought back tears, and Leon looked around, giving them as much privacy as the situation allowed. He wished he hadn't. A metal bed, bolted to the floor, with leather straps for holding the patients down, loomed in the corner. He stared down at his feet, unable to look anymore. This place should be burned to the ground.

Ky recovered first. She appeared hard, toughened by life. This situation had made her grow up fast. He didn't even know how old she was. But that could wait.

Ky grabbed pants off the shelf and used them to tie the makeshift bandage in place as she told him about her escape from a vegetable in Vermilion Heights and the subsequent chase through the forest and to the camp. Just as Leon had suspected. A predator *had* been eating the pets, and the tracks they had followed hadn't been normal. They had belonged to these monsters. It was the only thing that made sense.

Gabe seemed not to be hearing anything. He had dropped into a squat, pulled himself in, and was mumbling to himself.

After a glance at the boy, Ky continued the story and told Leon about the attack at Ghost Hill and the ensuing chase to the hospital. Then about how there was a giant of a monster in the conservatory, and that these things were feeding it.

"But that means . . . Lissa."

Gabe shot up. "No! We have to get her."

"It's too late for her," Ky said.

"How?" Leon asked Gabe.

Gabe quieted, thinking. Good. Leon didn't need one of the two civilians left under his care running off half-cocked.

Leon took a deep breath and stood away from the wall he had been leaning against. The wound still burned, but it would hold, for now. He needed to focus on priorities. "Have you seen anyone else at this hospital? Or does the name Deborah Franklin mean anything to you?"

"No," both Gabe and Ky said, shaking their heads in unison. At least they agreed on something.

Either someone had given him good information, but bad things had gone down since Debbie arrived, or someone wanted Leon silenced. He hoped, for the kids' sake—and his own—that it was the former. But knowing the culpability of Chandler and the chief, the latter was the most logical explanation.

Feeling stronger and knowing more about the situation, they needed to move now. "Gabe, you lead. I'll take rear and check behind us." Leon would not make that mistake twice.

At his nod, Gabe gestured to Ky to open the door.

"Let's go." Leon pulled out his weapon to use as a blunt instrument, since he had nothing else. The vegetable lay motionless on the ground just outside the door. It reeked of boiled asparagus, just like the other one, and they all stepped past it. The electricity worked.

Gabe led the way, but he kept looking back. Did he not trust Leon? Was he having second thoughts about a cop who had lost one of their number immediately after taking charge? Leon was having doubts of his own.

They veered right down the hall, heading back the way he had come. Their steps were quiet taps in the otherwise silent corridor. Leon noticed dried blood spatter and smears in one spot he had run past without noticing. But they made it back to the front desk without incident.

He tensed at the unpleasant smell, but the other monster's body was still lying motionless. At least he had done one thing right today. He nodded to the kids to watch his back while he squatted and retrieved a second clip from his belt.

He turned and, with his eyes fully adjusted, he noticed the pictures above the desk. Like the sketch he had made, the reddish-haired man's picture jumped out at him. The name below said "Harry Pollack." Vivian's erstwhile husband. No wonder he had thought the daughter seemed familiar, it was the man from the park.

But if he worked here, that meant—and there he was, Tom Chandler. This was the hospital he worked at, and the one Debbie was investigating. The place those nurses had gone missing from. Did it have to do with the vegetables? Did Chandler and the chief already know about them?

They worked their way over to the door in a triangle pattern so each person could monitor each of the hallways. He reached the door and pushed.

Nothing. He pushed again, using his shoulder. His eyes squeezed shut. *Locked.*

Chapter 49: Gabe

"It's a weapon. It's really powerful, especially against living thi ngs."—Barry Burton, Resident Evil

Monday, April 25

1400

This wasn't right.

Help was here. How could Lissa be gone? He had failed again! Gabe wanted to punch something, but self-preservation kept him from making noise.

And that was part of the problem. He felt too weak and scared to do anything. *Be a man.* His father's words rang in his head. This situation was unbearable. Should he run after Lissa and leave Ky in Leon's hands? The only thing stopping him was Leon's question: How?

He wrestled with himself as scenes of Jason and Barbie flitted through his head. The likelihood of getting to her before she was killed was minute, but he had promised himself—he broke off with an internal sob—he had promised to put himself between Lissa and any danger.

Why had he hidden in the room without waiting for Lissa? Ky limped again, worse than before, and Leon was badly hurt. The best plan now was to get out and get help, but Lissa would never make it until then.

And the front doors being locked didn't bode well. Doors didn't seal themselves from the outside. Yesterday they had come in and out, then back in that door. Leon had used it not long before. Sure enough, when they reached the stair emergency exit, it wouldn't budge.

Gabe threw himself at it, and a loud bang echoed through the building. This was all his fault. If he hadn't run off at the first sign of giving the responsibility to someone else, those monsters wouldn't have heard them, and Lissa would still be alive. It should've been him. He threw himself at it again and again.

"Quick, upstairs." Ky tugged on his shirt, pulling him away.

Behind the heavy stair door, Leon took the lead again, checking the stairs as he climbed them, then gesturing to the kids to follow with the "all clear" sign.

"If they can't open doors, how could they get up here?" Gabe wondered aloud. He didn't know why he was still trying. Lissa was already gone.

"Good point, but *someone* left the side door and gate open for them to escape," Ky said.

"I agree. It's unlikely, but we should be very vigilant." Leon pointed to the Director's office on a wall map. "A phone, evidence we need, and keys should be in there."

"Um, the phones don't work," Gabe said.

"What?" Leon turned to him. "Just great."

The Director's office sprawled across the upper level, at least three times the size of the downstairs offices. It was decorated in the same Egyptian style Gabe was used to in public buildings. The walls were a warm, almost mustard yellow and a texture to make it look like the painted walls inside an Egyptian temple.

The top border around the room displayed hieroglyphics. Just below them were small windows, like a fortified castle, with rays of sun streaming in.

Heavy, dark wood furniture decorated the room, including a couch upholstered in a grass green. A small coffee bar sat recessed along one wall, with a selection of drinks and a variety of snacks. Ky fell upon them and began stuffing her bag.

Leon went straight to the desk. The name plate read Hospital Director, Dr. Albert Weston.

Gabe moved over to the couch, muscles too weak to stand any longer. He fell onto it, a hollowness growing to fill his chest.

Leon picked up the phone, then slammed it back down, leaving a bloody handprint on the handle. "No dial tone."

Gabe reached into his pocket but paused when his fingers touched the microchip next to the lighter. *Lissa.*

"Listen to this." Leon picked up a note from the desk and brandished it at them.

Ky sat on the couch next to Gabe with a pack of crackers, munching away.

He felt like he would never be hungry again.

Leon cleared his throat.

Cleaner,

I don't have much time. I know you will be called to come clean this up because no one else is left. Warning! Audrey has learned how to control everyone. She created enough of those flowers of hers to fill the conservatory with pollen and I got a whiff because she propped the door open with vines. The Venuses have the run of the downstairs. Nothing is safe. Nurses opened doors. Cleaner, **important,** *Kill Audrey. Fire electricity food . . . Audrey hungry. Open doors, open doors. Out . . .*

"Controlling pollen. What does that even mean? He was the one to open the doors?" Ky cocked her head and stared off into space. "But why weren't we affected? It sounds like it works fast, and we were in there last night."

Leon looked down at the page in his hand. "This might have been days ago, and the pollen dissipated." He pursed his lips and furrowed his brows. "What if it did affect you, just not strongly? I mean, you said yourselves that you have been here since yesterday, but I barely walked in the door this afternoon. What if the doors aren't really locked? Instead, we're being *encouraged* to not leave. The pollen levels could be strong enough to affect us, but not be able to make us do anything against our will. I wish we had more information on what they were doing here."

Gabe just stared at him. Could it be? A kind of mind control? Was all this for nothing? That big plant in the conservatory was just playing with them, waiting to eat them one by one. He fisted his hand around the microchip.

"But we do," Ky said. She reached into her bag and pulled out the book Lissa had dropped.

Lissa had found the proof that Gabe had wanted so badly. The book explained how and why the monsters were made, but also, and more importantly, how to kill them. She had paid with her life for his choices. When they were done reading, Ky returned the book to her bag.

"Let's take them all out," Gabe said firmly.

"I don't think we are equipped to do that, Gabe. Let's just get out of here. Okay?" Leon said.

Ky looked down. She had already given up on Lissa.

Gabe glared at them both, his gaze hard, but he didn't argue. He would make his own plan. Leon could get Ky out of here and Gabe would get his revenge.

"I can charge my stun gun in that socket over there. Meanwhile, look for a first aid kit or keys, or possible exits."

Leon hobbled over to an available outlet and pushed a button, flipping out two pluglike prongs on his stun gun.

Determined to find a way to destroy these monsters, Gabe returned to the desk just as Leon did. A strange-looking ring had been deliberately placed on the notebook. It had a square shape and a relief design, with two snakes curled about one another.

Leon picked it up and slipped it into his shirt pocket. Next to the notebook was a gun, which Leon also picked up, aiming it down and away. He pressed a button on the side with his thumb and the clip slid out.

"What are you doing?"

"You never pick up a gun without checking to see if it is loaded, even if it is your own."

"But you'd know."

"Habit. See this magazine and the spring here? Fully loaded."

Gabe nodded.

"You need to check the barrel too. Can you see if there is a round chambered?"

Gabe looked from the handle side into the barrel and straight through to the carpet on the floor. "It's clear."

Leon nodded and slid the clip back in until it clicked.

"Safety." He flipped the switch upward and tucked the weapon "safely" into the back of his pants. "Don't ever do this." He grimaced. "I don't have a choice."

"There's a bathroom back here," Ky said.

With Leon's arm slung across Gabe's shoulder, he helped Leon across the room.

"A first aid kit!" Leon's face widened into a facsimile of a smile. He turned to Ky. "Can you look around for extra clothes or a belt or something?"

As Gabe helped Leon remove his shirt, they both winced. One from pain and one from sympathy. "That looks bad."

The gash was thin but deep, and it gaped slightly. Gabe wasn't sure exactly what he was seeing—fat, muscle, who knew—but it was all stuff that was supposed to stay inside. One of those things had done this to him. All the monsters deserved to die before Leon did.

"Hopefully it looks worse than it is, and we can get some medical help soon. Wash your hands first."

Gabe did as he was told. It was curious how strange the running water sounded after the silence they had been living in. He began washing the wound. A clean, wet rag wiped most of the dried blood away from the gash, but Gabe struggled to see what he was doing, and more blood was constantly oozing out. "I've had basic first aid, but this is a bit out of my league, man."

Leon reached down and pulled out the painkillers, downing them dry. "It just needs some cleaning with disinfectant and pads for any continued seepage. Then we'll wrap it all up and keep our fingers crossed."

Gabe nodded. His hands shook as he began disinfecting around the wound, this time with pungent alcohol.

Leon involuntarily sucked in a sharp breath. "You're doing fine. Keep it up. Hey, what do you know about Ky?" he tried to ask casually through gritted teeth.

Gabe cut the medical tape into pieces, and they used it to pull the sides of the wound together. It was hard to keep the tape dry enough to stick. There was still a lot of blood. "Just what she said."

"It's just that everyone is out looking for you . . . and the others . . . but no one has mentioned anything about a 'Ky.'"

Gabe shrugged. "I think she's from Denver. That's what she said." Gabe taped gauze pads over the slice. Ky would be Leon's problem now. "She seems able to take care of herself."

Leon nodded and shut his eyes, swallowing hard.

Gabe reached around Leon as he wrapped the gauze around and around while Leon held his breath. Leon reached down and tucked the gauze in while Gabe washed his hands again.

Ky was heating water for cocoa when they came out. "Here's a shirt I found in one of the patient rooms. And I forgot to show you this list of names we found, but that Deborah woman you mentioned isn't on it."

Leon snatched the paper from her fingers and quickly scanned it, then passed it back with a frown. He pulled on the hospital shirt and tied the strings. Then he pinned his badge on the front.

Gabe couldn't say it looked silly.

Leon needed to replace some of that blood loss, so Gabe pushed a cup of chocolate and some cookies toward him. The chocolate filled the air, but Gabe still couldn't eat. He sipped on plain water.

Ky continued looking around, poking and prodding at everything. "What's this? I feel like it means something."

Gabe and Leon went over to see.

Ky examined a large portrait, obviously a reproduction that looked like it came from the walls of an Egyptian tomb.

A blue man with a bird head and a long, curved beak appeared to be writing on something. But Gabe couldn't tell what it was. A cylinder or a scroll?

Ky's finger pressed into a square divot on the frame.

It looked familiar. Now where . . . ? It was the same shape as the ring Leon had picked up from the desk!

"Leon, the ring," Gabe said.

Leon took the ring out of his pocket and placed it in the square hole. It fit perfectly, but nothing happened.

Such a silly idea, Gabe thought. But no sooner had he stepped in to get a better look than a hidden door swung open.

Chapter 50: Project Nefertem

"By gnawing through a dike, even a rat may drown a nation ."—Edmund Burke

Monday, April 25

1320

Getting to the laboratory would be tricky.

The monitoring room had a good layer of dust from the week or so that it hadn't been occupied. That wouldn't matter soon. The Cleaner checked that the download would run smoothly, but it would take some time. First he needed to trap the rats so he could dispose of them at his whim.

He exited from a secret door and circled around to check the vehicle. The radio chatter mentioned a head, up at the campgrounds, but nothing about the hospital. *Good.* That'll keep them busy while I set my snare. Before disabling both radio and car, he sent a code on a private channel to the Director about receiving the gift.

Like shooting fish in a barrel. He had many skills that the Director found useful. He locked all the obvious exits to the building before sneaking back inside through one of the hidden entrances.

In the lab, he wiped the computer while searching for any papers about Project Nefertem. He found a few obscure things, but he didn't find Gianni's personal lab book. He had seen her scribbling in it himself. It was where she kept the real information. He threw books and papers everywhere.

Picking up a weighted centrifuge, he smashed the computer. Over and over. Drained of his anger, he straightened his clothes and wiped the sweat on his sleeve. He collected the few notes he could to prove he had done as bid—he gritted his teeth—then stole back to the monitoring room. Almost time to "Blow the Gather," assembling all his prey together to fight a useless battle, while he escaped.

The Cleaner prepped the access code that would wipe the drive completely, keeping a close eye on the Venus subjects and the kids as he worked. Maybe, if he were able to watch an interaction between the two, he could get more data for the Director. He watched, planning the best places to start fires in order to control their reactions.

As soon as he was done, he ejected the drive, sent the info to the Director's computer, and initiated the wipe. He was just finishing up and preparing to destroy the physical drive when he jumped at the sound of voices, right on the other side of the wall, in the Caretaker's office. He flipped to the appropriate camera.

His eyes narrowed as the cop read the letter from the Caretaker out loud. So Audrey had pollen that could control people. Not a problem. The fire would destroy it without him having to get close. The cop picked up the ring and pocketed it.

Why had the Caretaker left it out there with that letter in the first place? It sounded like the man was a bit crazy there at the end. Of course, he thought all the doctors who had worked here were a bit crazy. Probably best they were all gone.

Then they read from Gianni's lab book. So that was where it was. He'd look for a chance to get it from them. It depended on whether an opportunity presented itself. The cop brought up Deborah and his ears perked. So he was on her case. Maybe that was why the Director had sent him here.

Then they found the spot in the frame where the ring went. He could hear them thumping on the other side of the wall. His lip pulled up into a sneer. It wouldn't work without a manager's microchip.

The hidden door opened, and he was forced to run, leaving the monitors and cameras active.

Unless that cop was acting for the kids' sakes, there was no way he was a manager. Where did they get the microchip from? Did they have inside help?

At least he had finished with the computers before their inconvenient discovery.

These impostors would never make it out of this building to share what they had learned. Yes. None of them would survive the fire, he'd make sure of it. Frank would have never helped those kids if he hadn't been forced to hold back. He should have followed his first instincts.

No witnesses.

Let it all burn, he thought.

He slipped down the stairs to carry out his plan.

Chapter 51: Leon

"Secrets are like birds; when they leave your hand, they take flight."—Arabic proverb

Monday, April 25

1430

Leon led the way through the opening into a secret room, then sneezed from the dust. The hidden area held a large desk, another computer, and several monitors covering the wall, each showing different areas of the hospital.

The camera system was up and running, the computers humming. One of them focused on the room they had just left, Weston's office. There were smudges in the dust. Someone had been watching them.

He looked through the halls; everything appeared to be empty except for the conservatory. Only part of that room was visible, but the plant in the middle of the pond was the obvious focal point. Its vines crept outward in a sunburst pattern, covering floors, walls, other plants, everything. Bones littered the ground, human ones, in piles like in the forest.

Yep, it was these vegetables all right. They were loose in Kaira. And now his worries turned to McKenna. She was in the forest daily and helping with the search for both the kids and the "animal." *One thing at a time, Leon.*

Ky turned to the other screens, scanning them. And Gabe moved to the computer, playing with the controls.

Leon left them to it, searching the desk's drawers and shelves. He couldn't help anyone if they didn't get out of here alive.

"I only see that big one, none of the ones that can walk," Ky said.

Leon found a thumb drive labeled H. Pollack. He rubbed it between his fingers thoughtfully. Had Debbie had more than one informant? There could be evidence on this hard drive, or it could be pictures of Harry's family. "Gabe, can I use the computer?"

The boy nodded and stepped aside, taking over Leon's search of the desk.

Unable to wait, Leon slid the drive into the computer. A single folder labeled eight appeared with no password. He opened it. Pictures of downtown Robur Copse filled the screen. He flipped through a few and almost closed it, but then he recognized one. A forgotten print sat on his desk back at the RPD.

Debbie.

Breathing heavily, he searched each picture. There. There. A close-up of her. Hundreds of them. At best, Harry was the stalker. But why the number eight? Unless . . . Debbie was his eighth victim. A serial killer?

Debbie had been meeting Tom about the missing people from the hospital. It could have been these monsters, but could it have been Harry? Both Tom and Debbie had died or gone missing within a week of each other. Had Harry gotten Debbie, or was she still alive and hiding? Had Tom known something or seen something? Had he found the flash drive? How much had Debbie known?

Leon ejected the drive and pocketed it, cursing under his breath. The chief was keeping things from him. Now, at this time, when there were monsters in town and at best a stalker, at worst a killer.

Ky's voice broke the soft shuffles and clicks of focused searching. "Guys, there's someone else in the building. I haven't gotten a clear view. It's like they know where the cameras are."

Leon looked over in time to see the flash of a shadow on one of the screens, but nothing more. Was Harry here now? Was he the one who had let the vegetables out, not Weston?

Gabe was busy searching the room, going through drawers and paying no attention to them. They kept sliding open and shut, until "Woo-hoo! I found a key!"

"Let me see." Leon swiped it from the boy's outstretched hand. From it hung a tag that read Conservatory.

Convenient, Leon thought.

"That key has to be for the exit," Ky said.

"What, why?" Leon asked.

"Because there are no locks on the inner doors. Look." She pointed to the screen where the doors were propped open in the hallway with vines.

"But in order to get out that way, we have to get past *them* and through possible mind-controlling pollen." Ky's enthusiasm faded.

"I'd like to know how they got away with building a hospital with only barred windows, half windows, and four exits. Forget about the obvious secret areas. This place isn't up to code," Leon said.

"Yeah, well, they didn't seem to be too concerned with breaking the law." Gabe gestured to the conservatory screen.

"But someone approved this, and we're expected to do walk-throughs and double-check things every once in a while. It just doesn't make sense."

There was movement on the conservatory screen. A single Venus, as the book called them, stepped into view to attend to the big plant in the middle. Wrapped in its vines, Lissa struggled. She was still alive!

"Lissa!"

Both Gabe and Ky pressed forward. "We can still save her, we can . . ." But as they watched, the giant bud split down the middle, and the Venus lifted Lissa, dropping her in. Her arms and legs flailed as she fought to the last. It snapped shut, closing her completely within.

"No!" Gabe's voice broke, and Leon put his hands on the boy's shoulders, both holding him still and comforting him.

Leon had also held out hope they might be able to still save Lissa, but now she was gone. He was a complete failure.

They stood in a moment of silence. All eyes on the screen.

Leon turned Gabe toward him. "It looks like we are going to need your plan."

Gabe's eyes widened in surprise. "What makes you think that I have a plan?"

Leon met his gaze. "I'm a cop. I can see the vengeance written on your face."

Gabe grimaced. "I don't have an exact plan, more of an idea. The note mentioned electricity and fire. I think those would work on both types of monsters with a few bullets for distraction. We can tie cloth around our faces as masks to help with the pollen."

"Good thing I've been thinking, too, because this plan needs to be much more detailed if I'm going to get you both out of here."

"If you shot it, we could pour flammable chemicals on it. I could light it on fire," Gabe continued.

"You have a lighter?" It was better to use the boy's natural inclinations than to fight them. Besides, that was the only way out.

Gabe smiled, pulling it from his pocket and flicking it open, then shut. "It was a gift from my parents." His smile faltered.

Poor lad was probably wondering whether he would ever see them again. Leon would just have to do his best.

Ky piped up. "There were some cleaning chemicals in that closet downstairs, and there is a matching closet upstairs that we could check. Maybe there are some weed killers too. Or salt and vinegar and soap. I used those at the orphanage to kill plants."

Leon nodded in approval. "Good, I like it. So the second order of business is Audrey. I'm not sure there is enough weed killer in this building to take her down, but any little bit can help."

"She's in a pool of water. If we put salt in the water, maybe we can electrify it," Gabe said.

"My stun gun should be recharged. I wonder if there is a way to get it to the water without getting close and endangering one of us."

"I have an extension cord in my backpack."

"Good thinking, Ky. That will give us distance, but will it give us the power we need?"

"Are there any plugs near the pool?" Leon asked.

They all moved toward the screens again, and Gabe started pressing buttons. He flipped through different views of the conservatory. They needed to know the layout anyway.

"There," Ky said, "on that planter wall nearby."

"I don't think it would be that hard to lash the stun gun and cord together if we had some string or duct tape," Gabe suggested.

"Ky, you should take the key," he said, handing it to her, "and unlock the door while we keep those things busy." Leon talked through it out loud: "So, unhappily, that means Gabe will have to drop in the stun gun, since I will be the one with the firearm. But there are only the two of them, from what I can see, and if we take down the vegetable first, then that big pod can't do anything."

"We still need a way to activate the stun gun. What about taping something to it to depress the button?" Gabe said.

Leon prayed they could get out before he couldn't walk anymore. The pain was getting to him, and he was rapidly tiring. His senses dulled and his reaction time slowed. It would only get worse.

"Let's get this plan started."

Chapter 52: Gabe

"To a brave man, good and bad luck are like his left and right hand. He uses both."—Saint Catherine of Siena

Monday, April 25

1545

Gabe felt like a bank robber.

Only this was much more dangerous than any robbery. Pulling up his mask, he pivoted into the doorway. As soon as they made contact with the Venus, Gabe stayed with Ky, behind Leon, giving him plenty of room.

Gabe crouched and covered his ears so Leon could shoot it safely. Gabe silently prayed that they would make it through this alive and he would get to return home . . . to his dad's arms.

Despite the ends of the mask muffling his ears, the shots resonated deafeningly next to him, then quickly absorbed into the vegetation. Gabe prepared by setting down the bag of salt and removing the caps of both bottles. If their plan didn't work, Leon would be a goner. And if he died . . .

Luckily the monster went down as expected. Gabe then ran forward and poured the drain cleaner and rubbing alcohol on the weeping body. Dropping the empty bottles, he pulled his lighter from his pocket.

This is for Lissa, Jason, and Barbie, he thought. He flipped the lighter open—flick—and ignited the body. Whoosh. Jumping away to avoid being caught on fire himself, he watched the flames catch. This thing had fed Lissa to the monster in the middle.

When the flames devoured the chemicals, rising higher, he backed up even more, letting them consume it, and returned to his position of shelter behind Leon. The cloth tied around his face blunted the chemical, burned-vegetable smell. Still, his stomach rebelled.

Picking the bag of salt back up, Gabe skirted the body, following Leon. They passed one at a time, single file, and faced Audrey. Gabe's head kept tilting back as he looked up in shock. He'd seen it devour Lissa whole on the monitor, but the sheer size of it was beyond anything.

Nothing could have prepared him for this. Beyond her, the sky was cloudy, but a ray of sunlight engulfed the whole pool, as if the heavens had opened to show him where to attack.

Time to take it out, Gabe thought. There was no response from the plant as Gabe plugged in the extension cord and crept toward the pool with their—as his father would say—Mac-Gyvered device. He stayed super focused. All his senses were hyperaware. There was no room for error next to this giant carnivorous vegetable.

Immediately finding the outlet Ky had indicated, he set down the heavy bag and plugged in the extension cord. He hefted the bag again, tossing it over his right shoulder as he unrolled the cord wound around his left, quickly covering the ground toward the pool. Leaving what was left of the cord on his arm, he used both hands to dump the salt into the water. It would have to slowly dissolve; he had no way to agitate the water. Cranking his neck back to check for movement—he didn't want to disturb this mutation.

His skin crawled. Something didn't feel right, but he couldn't stop. The plan needed to be carried out to make sure none of these things could kill anyone else. He finished pouring and discarded the empty salt bag.

He unstuck the edge of the tape on the stun gun, turned the switch on, then reapplied the duct tape and tightened so the stone depressed the button. The electricity arced and buzzed; he felt within him a distinct aversion. Jerking his hand, he tossed it into the water, and the arcing stopped. Nothing happened. Crap! Now what? It hadn't worked exactly like the electrolysis experiment. Maybe he'd forgotten a step.

The only thing within sight were the piles of bones lying haphazardly about and the many creepers Audrey had grown all over the floor and walls. A long thick bone caught his eye, and he picked it up. At least it was something. They'd seen only the one Venus on the monitors, but they still didn't know how many there really were.

Continuing to scan the room, he hurried to form a new plan. The water began bubbling and moving. What was happening? This was new. He opened his mouth to warn the others. Movement out of the corner of his eye had him zeroing in on vines creeping across the floor. Moving? They could move!

More motion on the ceiling. Vines all around reached for him. Gabe might not be the most athletic young man, but he was a *young* man, and his life was in danger. He pulled the bone back like a bat and began pummeling the vines, smacking them with the bone and stomping on the ones trying for his feet. Bruising them and frustrating the plant completely. Coach would be proud.

"Watch out for the vines!" he yelled breathlessly between swings of the bone bat.

Mercifully, Audrey's vines worked differently from the Venus's. They were slower, ripping away from the surfaces they had attached themselves to, like a baby learning to walk. And they appeared to be trying to slither and constrict. Unlike the sharp whipping and slicing of the more mobile monsters.

Ky shrieked.

Gabe instinctively searched for the noise, distracted.

The loud echoing booms of a gun fired to his right. And again he started to turn automatically toward Leon.

Then something pulled his feet out from under him, and he fell face down on the ground, dropping his bat. His eyes watered from the pain in his nose. He gathered himself to fight back. But nothing was happening.

Then a tingle at his ankle had him kicking out in a panic. Was it trying to eat his foot? Or was it secreting some sort of acid, eating through his leg?

Chapter 53: Kylie

"Feed me, Seymour."—*Audrey II,* Little Shop of Horrors

Monday, April 25

1545

The gun was really loud!

Ky's heart leaped at each shot. Even with her head lowered and ears covered, every bang made her jolt. Fear rose in her throat, and she fought it back down. Everyone was needed for the plan to work, and she wanted to get her revenge on Audrey. For Lissa.

If Lissa was right, Audrey was the queen bee, the root of all the pain and death for the last two days. That giant plant might be in control for now, but Ky would do everything in her power to make sure the monstrous nightmare paid.

And she wanted to get home. Away from this terrible place and its monsters. Ky waited until Gabe headed forward, then passed Leon. Her foot throbbed less after the rest, but every time she had to run on it, it ached more, deeper and sharper. Keeping to the right, she shuffled around the side and approached the pool.

Audrey was so big. And scary. The plant looked like something from outer space. She had once peered through the front glass panes of a fancy restaurant. The people inside were warm, smiling and talking, all dressed up pretty. Someone brought their food to the table while they sat there all fat and lazy.

They sat and talked below lights shaped just like Audrey. So skinny at the top you couldn't believe it would hold the big, fat bottom. Huge, bulbous, slick.

Vines were everywhere. Climbing up and over the edge of the pool, never stopping until they covered the floor, walls, and even the ceiling.

Long, fuzzy, creeping vines. Like the legs of a tarantula and, in the middle, its round body in the pool, it slept like a spider in the winter.

Ky felt surrounded. She couldn't fill her lungs. She hesitated at the pool, blinking rapidly and fighting the urge to run home to the warm, dark nest in the tunnels. Then a vision filled her mind of Lissa's dark eyes, staring into her own as she was carried, tied up in vines and helpless, into this very room. Food for the monsters.

Ky clenched her fists and her lips. This thing shouldn't exist. And there was no way out until they defeated this monster.

She pulled up the smaller bag of salt, gritting her teeth, and dumped it into the water. Then she popped open the bottle of vinegar and started pouring it in. *I hope you die,* she thought.

Gabe was doing the same thing on the other side, and Leon was behind them with his gun, in case the plant fought back. And to keep an eye out for Venuses or whoever was in the building.

Dropping the empty containers, she hurried off down the path to find the exit. She stayed low in case there were any more of those Venuses that they hadn't seen. Those things were fast. Her chest tightened, and her hands shook, but she was determined to do her part and pull her weight. An exit sign shone red up on the wall. She was within sight of freedom.

Pulling out the key in preparation, she stopped short. Her stomach sank. There were creepers all over the door, too, sealing it shut. What am I going to do?

Leon and Gabe were relying on her, and she needed to get out of this madhouse. Ky refused to fail. Pushing her emotions farther down, she hardened herself further and cleared her mind.

Scissors.

Ky rummaged through her backpack, and her fingers wrapped around the smooth metal of the scissors. After closing the bag and swinging it back over her shoulder in one smooth motion, she opened the scissors wide, braced against the wall with her left hand, then started hacking along the edges of the door. She would not be defeated.

Furiously chopping and sawing at the creepers, then ripping them away with her other hand, Ky felt a tug at her waist. Tightening her grip on the scissors, she looked down. Vines wrapped around her middle. She was done for. A Venus had sneaked up on her. She was abruptly jerked off her feet.

Unlike Lissa, her legs and arms were free. She looked behind her to see nothing but creepers. Not a Venus, then, but Audrey's creepers. They carried Ky back toward the giant plant, which could apparently move these stupid vines.

They hadn't moved when the three of them had been in here last night. They hadn't moved in the videos. The monster had needed the other ones to get things for it and bring it food, but now they were ripping away from the walls and floors! Maybe it had something to do with her attacking them. Yet there had been no other way through the door, and Ky needed out.

She couldn't give up. The scissors were still in her hand, so she now used them to slash at the leaves and vines carrying her. The closer she was pulled back to the pool, the more alarmed she became. She recklessly doubled the attack.

She squirmed and wriggled in hopes of loosening something, but nothing worked. There was a soft rustling as they tugged her steadily to her doom. She tried to fit one blade of the scissors between her and the vine, but it held her too tight. Her skin would give before the tough vine.

Ky strained to think of something else—anything else—then the main body of the plant came into view. It was splitting open, and she was heading straight into that maw. Just like Lissa. A cloud of roadkill enveloped her, penetrating the mask she still wore.

No, this wasn't right. She was going to make it home. She had to. Unable to help herself, she screamed for the first time in forever, drawing attention to herself.

Ky began swinging her arms and legs wildly and dropped the scissors.

Chapter 54: Leon

"It is a far, far better thing that I do, than I have ever done; it is a far, far better rest that I go to than I have ever known."—A Tale of Two Cities, *Charles Dickens*

Monday, April 25

1545

Leon aimed the Browning at center mass. His empty Glock was tucked into his pants, and he was feeling on edge with how reliant he was being on the guns. But he was coming to understand that they were just a tool. And a very necessary tool when face-to-face with giant plant monsters.

What on earth were they thinking? Audrey was massive. Not only was it huge, but this thing was . . . repellant. A human or two could easily fit inside the cavity. Lissa might even be there now. Leon took a deep breath, pushing away the failure.

He needed to keep his focus for Gabe and Ky. His side was on fire. It was getting difficult to focus. The kids began their tasks, but Leon detected no movement from the thing and wondered if they could be wrong. He scanned for flowers or buds and found several growing on the creepers overhead, but they weren't blooming . . . yet.

Ky ran off to the door in the far-right corner. He waited with bated breath while Gabe activated the stun gun and threw it in. *This is it.* But nothing happened. This was what they got for relying on the scientific understanding of a high schooler and a cop who'd barely passed the requisites years ago.

Leon stood there, unsure of what their next move should be. He had been feeling the weakness of blood loss for a while, but now he was becoming dizzy again. The adrenaline helped to keep him upright. That and pure will.

Something else was wrong, but what? It was hard to think. It registered that the smell of smoke behind him continued to increase instead of decreasing. He spun around down the aisle, hurrying over to the body, which was almost done burning. The smoke appeared to be filtering from farther in.

He crouched below the smoke level until he could see it pouring in through the hospital doorway. The building was likely on fire! They were trapped in the conservatory until Ky could open the door.

A man appeared, crouched in the opening.

Leon aimed his weapon to the side, unsure if he was friend or foe.

"Still alive? You're not looking too good there, cop. I heard through the grapevine that you're looking for Debbie. She's not here. She was never here. But just like you, she put her nose where it didn't belong," the old man said.

"What do you mean?" Leon gritted out through the pain. He was right. Debbie had been investigating this place.

"I mean, that stupid boy, Harry, stole her from me. I was finally ordered to kill her, and he snatched her away first. To add to his little collection, no doubt."

So Harry *was* a killer, and it sounded like he was a serial killer. His heart hurt at the thought of Harry's wife and children. The town didn't know; he had to get out of here to keep Harry from killing again. Leon tried to aim his gun, but his hands were trembling too badly.

"You must've touched the wrong nerve to get sent here for cleanup. The chief messed up picking you. He was supposed to get someone incompetent who would agree the girl had run off. But that isn't a problem anymore, because you aren't going to make it out of here alive." The man's eyes glinted madly. "None of you."

There was no denying the chief was involved, and that meant Chandler was in this up to his eyeballs too. He wondered who else on the force was being manipulated. He thought of whoever was supposed to come check out the hospital. How far did it go? He had to extract justice from Chandler and the chief.

The smoke got stronger, and Leon coughed.

"Ah, yes, it's just about time. I only have a few moments left; I have a surprise for you. The hospital is on fire. Oh, and don't expect any help. I turned off the alarms. So you can choose smoke inhalation, fire, or Audrey. I'd choose Audrey, but she took care of the entire hospital single-handed. I'd wish you luck, but . . . you know." He pulled out a mask like firefighters use and disappeared into the black cloud.

Leon shook his foggy head to clear it and ducked under the smoke layer. He hurried, hoping Ky was signaling them to exit.

Gabe yelled out something about vines.

Leon sprinted toward the pool, hurdling the bones and burned body along the way. Pain was relegated to a distant throbbing with another surge of adrenaline.

What met his eyes shocked him. The creepers all around the room were beginning to come alive and were pulling away from where they had rested.

He almost lost his balance as the floor shifted beneath him. Regaining his footing, he kept running. Here, in the conservatory, the roof was so high that the smoke didn't reach him while upright. He'd take blessings where he got them right now.

Gabe battled vines to the left, where the cord was plugged in, and he swung what looked like a bat.

As Leon skidded to a stop, he raised the Browning.

Ky's scream had him looking up toward the top of Audrey as he settled himself into a forward firing position. The vines were holding her above the main body, which looked like a giant cabbage splitting in half.

It was going to eat her. *No. Not on my watch. I made that girl a promise.* Leon blasted a tight grouping at the center of Audrey, a good distance below Ky. It was his best aiming yet. When his clip ran dry, he raced forward, ready to pummel the thing until it let her go.

His ears began ringing despite the tissue stuffed in them and the cloth wrapped around his face and over his ears. The free vines swept around. Leon had to jump and duck. He assumed Gabe was either already laid out or doing the same.

Audrey's bulbous body seemed to expand and contract; then it collapsed to the side. Leon could smell boiled asparagus even over the smoke. He would never be able to look at a can of asparagus again.

"Ooof." Leon fell hard, something warm and bony pinning him to the ground. The pain in his side intensified, and he almost lost consciousness. He breathed through the pain and nausea.

Gabe stood above him, a femur raised. "Are you guys okay?" Gabe coughed through his mask, but the meaning was clear.

"Yeah. I thought I was a goner, but Leon started shooting and it dropped me. Luckily, he broke my fall too. Thanks for saving me." Ky's own mask muffled her words.

Leon tried to rise to all fours. He could see the blood coating his left hand spread out on the ground in front of him. Ky rushed to help, but Leon held up the bloody hand to stop her. He *was* in a great deal of pain; however, they were still in danger. He pushed himself up, covering another sharp sting as he stood.

"We need to get out. The building is on fire," he said through the violent coughing. Each involuntary muscle spasm felt like it was ripping him in two. He swept them before him, down the path to the door.

They all ran, hopping over floor creepers in unconscious avoidance. If he could only get these kids out of here, then he could rest. He stumbled behind them. His body seemed to be moving without his awareness, and his mind started to float away.

As they approached the door, Ky explained the problem. "There are creepers holding the door shut, and I lost the scissors I was using to get rid of them." Her scrunched face and bulging eyes gave away her panic.

Leon pressed his hand against his side and tried to think through the haze of agony. It looked like she had hardly done anything.

Gabe reached out and grabbed the vines. "Ow." He quickly pulled his hands back and shook them out.

"What?" Leon frowned, worried. He didn't have much longer, and the fire was coming. They had to escape *now*.

"A shock. I think our plan worked after all. Somehow . . ." He looked at the abrasions on his hand. "But the vines are soft now. Pulling them away shouldn't be a problem. If we could touch them."

If the kids ran back and one was overcome by smoke, Leon wouldn't be able to save them. If Leon went . . . the kids would both be safe.

"Gabe, there is a serial killer in town. Don't trust the police. They had something to do with this. I'll run back and unplug it. You two *get—this—door—open!*"

Leon ignored Gabe's cry of "What?" and hurried back the way they had come. He steered clear of the creepers on purpose now, hoping to avoid any shocks.

His shirt stuck to his skin, and there was a wetness on his left side he determinedly ignored. The bandages must be soaked through. He reached the outlet and took a deep breath, trying to gather his strength.

The room began to turn gray, filling with a haze of smoke and creating a dreamlike atmosphere. He coughed and the spike in pain woke his brain. He pulled hard and quick, releasing the plug from the wall as he fell backward toward the pool and landed on his rear.

It was easier to breathe down here, less smoky, but he was even dizzier. He wasn't sure whether it was electrical shock, loss of blood, or the smoke, but he wasn't feeling too hot. *Ha!*

Leon leaned back to rest. *I'll just close my eyes for a few seconds.* His right arm flopped across his chest, and he patted the hard metal there. *My badge.* His hand tightened on the symbol. The chief wouldn't ever be able to take it from him now. His other hand dropped into a small pool of red water. He finally felt worthy of the badge.

So cold . . .

Leon was troubled by the thought of McKenna coming across one of the Venuses in the forest, but she was strong and fast. She would be fine. Besides, she was good at killing plants. Leon prayed the Lord would protect her and the kids.

He thought about Debbie and how when he met her, he planned on thanking her for helping him to become a better man. Leon had always skated through life, not wanting to do anything too hard because he might fail. He had always taken the path of least resistance. *Kind of like electricity,* he thought.

But because of the direction Debbie's case had taken him during the last week, he had been able to be what Gabe and Ky needed. He was sure now that they would get out of this place. He smiled as he imagined them pushing the door open to freedom.

The thumping of his heart slowed. His lips and toes felt fuzzy.

He had never been able to save Debbie; she had already been dead, but she had shown him how to save Gabe and Ky. And she had shown him the truth about his sister—a truth he hadn't faced previously. Now he could see his sister and tell her how sorry he was for thinking she deserved it.

So. Very. Cold.

His ghosts left him, and his heart stopped.

Chapter 55: Gabe

"When you're pushed, killing's as easy as breathing."—John Rambo, Rambo

Monday, April 25

1645

Gabe shot out of the exit right behind Ky. She didn't slow, heading for the trail that led back into the forest and over the mountain. Instead of arguing, Gabe agreed. Leon had said there was a serial killer in town and the police couldn't be trusted. That left going to authorities outside of Robur Copse.

As she neared the bridge ahead of him, he noticed the old man standing by the ropes. The smoke in the air must have drawn him, or maybe he had come to check on them. Either way, they were lucky.

He may be crotchety, but he had been helpful, giving them food and directions. Without too much thought, they sprinted straight toward him and freedom. They ran at about the same speed, because Ky was limp-hop-running again. Her foot must pain her, but he understood not being able to slow down.

He could see the forest on the other side and never thought he would be happy to be in one again. But he could see birds flitting from tree to tree. And the wind blew gently, making the branches dance. He felt a sense of freedom when, in disbelief, he watched the man raise his axe, aiming at Ky. He must be the serial killer Leon had mentioned.

The man's face pulled back into a horrible grin, and Gabe watched in slow motion as, instead of slowing to cross, Ky put on a burst of speed and ducked under. The two-armed strike landed, but the axe appeared to be stuck in her backpack. Gabe couldn't see whether she was harmed, and he didn't wait.

Gabe saw red and went berserk. Channeling his best friend, Z, Gabe lowered his head and shoulders like a defensive back and crashed into the distracted man. Arms out and around his target's waist, Gabe took him down to the ground. The axe and bag all went flying onto the bridge. As did they.

Everything went silent. The only things Gabe could hear were the smack of flesh on flesh and the thumps as their movements were absorbed into the wooden slats of the bridge. They slipped and slid on the slimy wood. And he could smell the rot.

The tough sinewy body of his opponent squirmed beneath him, and hot breath exhaled into his face. The old man fought against Gabe's weight, anger, and gravity. He punched Gabe in the side, causing him to recoil. The flash of pain quickly disappeared.

His opponent took the opportunity to push him off and scrambled forward. Gabe grabbed his arm, trying to use his momentum to spin him back. But the man kicked out, getting a good one in on Gabe's chin and causing him to release his hold.

While Gabe recovered, the old man managed to stand and reached for the axe.

Gabe lunged forward, grabbing his denim-clad leg. Gabe pulled deep and hard, like when the hose gets caught on a rock and you pull it up and over to release it.

His opponent fell face forward onto the wooden bridge, catching himself with his arms. He twisted toward Gabe, breaking his hold and reaching for him with murder in his eyes, his face tight with rage.

Spittle flew from the man's mouth, landing on Gabe's face as he screamed in frustration. "Why won't you just die? I'm the Cleaner! It's my job to make sure there are no witnesses!"

He punched at Gabe, who tried to dodge, but the man's fist skidded along the side of his face, surely leaving a bruise and a smear of greenish-black mold. Where was Leon? *I could sure use his help right about now,* he thought.

Gabe drew in a breath and retaliated, bursting forward and lashing out with more energy than ability, and slipped helplessly forward. His opponent was forced to retreat, his rear foot sliding back and knocking the bag, with the axe still embedded in it, off the bridge and into the forty-foot ravine below. At least the weapon was gone.

The old man looked back over his shoulder instinctively, and Gabe went in low again to take him back down to the ground. But the Cleaner kept his footing and pushed Gabe back against the ropes. The weathered material dug into his back.

Gabe kicked the man in the shin and pushed the Cleaner down. The man rolled him over and punched him in the side. The pain! *God, if you are up there, I need some help. I can't do this on my own,* he prayed. Another painful hit and another. Gabe whimpered. He wasn't a fighter. He wasn't even strong. And while he wanted to do his best to help the others, this man was a savage killer.

Be a man. Gabe recalled his dad's words. *But I'm not,* he thought. *I'm just a kid.*

The Cleaner straddled him and punched Gabe's face, over and over.

The thuds were so loud he could hear each punch echo across the chasm, followed by a hollow thud as the bridge shook.

A strange shudder rippled through the bridge, and a crack rolled through the air.

Ky screamed.

Gabe was falling.

Chapter 56: Kylie

"Alone. Yes, that's the key word, the most awful word in the English tongue. Murder doesn't hold a candle to it and hell is only a poor synonym."—Stephen King

Monday, April 25

1615

Ky's alarms went off, and she ducked without thinking. She sprinted past, saving her life.

The axe must have been stuck in her backpack, because she jerked to a stop. He pulled her toward him, and obvious death. As much as even the thought wounded, Ky did the only thing she could. Slipping her arm out of the strap of the precious bag full of supplies, she ran.

It hurt almost physically to leave her bag behind, but survival came first. She raced from her attacker. Until she slipped, her foot sliding out from under her in the wet, moldy slime. Expecting death, she was surprised to see, and feel through the shudders of the bridge, Gabe fighting the old man.

She wanted to help. But there was no sense in all of them dying if the bridge gave way, which, with the quakes those two were sending through it, was likely. Ky was trapped toward the middle, and there was no Leon. Had he gone the other way?

If she squinted, looking toward the hospital, she could see flames in the fading sunlight. Smoke rose above the tree line; police and firefighters would be there in no time. If Leon had gone to call the emergency in, he should arrive to help Gabe soon. Why had the silly boy followed her? Hadn't he wanted to go straight to town?

Making a decision, she grabbed the prickly rope and started across the bridge. While she was bolder and more desperate this time, the crossing was made harder by the constant shaking. She hurried as fast as she could, doing a crab-like sort of scampering while looping her arm around the bridge to keep herself upright.

She was almost at the end.

Her hand reached for the final rope.

Crack.

Something broke. A rope snapped. The bridge fell sideways. And Ky held on for dear life.

The path was only a head above her. She managed to find slippery purchase with her feet and pushed herself up to the top, then pulled herself onto solid ground.

Shaking and exhausted, she ignored the distant throbbing in her ankle, and turned with dread to see if anyone had survived.

Gabe was nowhere to be found. Her bag with the supplies and the evidence of what had happened was gone.

She stood, her muscles shaking. *Wait.* There was someone holding on to the edge of the bridge below her. Three of the corners had held, but on the lower broken corner, Ky could make out a figure, and possibility seized her.

It was the old man.

Her hopes fell into the ravine with everything else.

The killer had grabbed the edge of a board right before he slid completely off the bridge.

Ky hesitated, uncertain of what to do or if she even wanted to help. Before she could decide, the man's grip failed, sliding across the mold-covered slat.

"Nooooo" rang in Ky's ears. She remained frozen, silent tears pouring involuntarily from her eyes and down her face. All alone, again. She stared at the broken empty bridge in horror. Leon still hadn't arrived. Maybe he was waiting for backup. He hadn't been in very good shape.

Maybe he was dead, a little voice whispered in her ear. *They're all dead and it is all your fault.*

"No!" She sobbed into her hands. Her supplies were gone, Lissa was gone, Gabe was gone, Leon was gone, and the authorities would be here soon. She was cracking under the stress. The sounds of a forest creature startled her into pulling herself together.

Listening to her internal urging, she staggered onto the path. No way would she ever return to Robur and its monsters! This was her chance to escape, and she was taking it.

As she limped along, her insides were like ice. She had finally made friends here, and it had felt more like home than before. But it was all gone now. The man who had given her his own food had tried to chop her in half. Plant monsters that used to be human had tried to kill her with their slicing vines. A giant plant had almost eaten her, and now she was by herself again.

Lissa! Gabe! Her backpack—all gone! Her mind whirled in a spiral, constricting and focusing on the negative. It was too much. Alone and without supplies, the instincts that forced her to survive no matter what pushed her to her feet, and she forged forward. Upward, toward the town on the other side of the mountain.

She ate the bitter leaves she recognized and thanked Lissa mutely for the lessons. Once she got back to Denver and the safety it gave her, she would tell everyone about Lissa and Gabe and the terrible things that happened when you were caught by the nabbers.

She crossed her fingers that there weren't any more of those Venuses loose in the woods.

As the sun came out, the birds began singing again, and she kept on. Fighting step . . . after step . . . after step. Sometime during the night, she had lost the trail, and branches scratched her hands and face. Yet she pushed on and through the bushes and trees, unable to stop. The stinging of the cuts was soon overwhelmed by the emptiness of her stomach.

Each small leaf only increased the cramping. The scrub and brush faded, leaving a rocky, steep slope. The loss of greenery represented the hollow within herself. Black shiny eyes followed her, and a hissing voice whispered in her ear. *It'sss all your fault. You should have ssstayed, you should have ssstudied, you should have tesssted.*

She dropped to all fours to scramble up the mountain and away from Kako's hideous voice. Cuts, scrapes, and abrasions went unnoticed when compared to the howling within. She reached the peak as darkness fell and thunder rolled.

She opened her mouth to catch as much moisture as she could, then curled up next to a boulder, exhausted.

Ky awoke to bird calls in the early-morning light and sucked the moisture from her clothes. *Alone.* She hadn't just lost her bag on that bridge; she had lost herself. *If only I hadn't run away.* Compelled, she started down the other side of the mountain, helped by gravity. She stumbled downward, sometimes sliding on her butt.

Then the first ghost came, following her and leading her. *You're the reason I'm dead.* The dead were haunting her.

The cat stared at her, unblinking. Unnaturally silent in death. She hurried on, tripping away. But it followed her, appearing behind each bush and rock. There, but not. It looked like Misty, but there was no life, only two accusing eyes.

Two more ghosts appeared next, one on either side. An older girl and an older boy she had seen for only a few brief moments. *You killed us!* She hurried faster, falling, scraping her hands on rocks. When she looked up, they stood right in front of her, and she veered to the side.

The brush began to slow her again. Her head swam. The world was a sea of green and brown. Lissa blocked her path, black, shining, blaming eyes. She lost her unsure footing and fell, screaming where no one could hear.

It's all your fault. Ky slid, her left arm scraping against something rough. When she came to a stop, she just lay there, the earth in her nose. Her body throbbed and ached. With a silent Leon and Gabe staring down at her, she squeezed her eyes shut.

Why had she left the orphanage? Why had she led that monster to kill person after person? And why was she alive, when they had helped others and had loving families waiting for them? Ky's family had probably already moved on, thinking her dead or in juvie—trapped in the system. They had relied on each other, but they were used to the comings and goings of members. Life on the streets was hard.

Here Ky had never truly accepted Lissa, or Gabe, or Leon. She had kept them at arm's length and left them to fight on their own. If she had helped Gabe, he could have defeated the killer, and he would be alive right now. Not at the bottom of a canyon.

Her own death had been at hand since the moment she had been taken. She was trying to avoid fate and taking others down with her. The rot from the forest soil reminded her of the jungle room. She closed her eyes to give up.

The rustling of vines snaked out of the forest of her imagination and squeezed her. She couldn't surrender. A claustrophobia took over, and she fought against the tightening. She reached forward, pushed to her knees, and started to crawl. Lissa had been taken by the monsters because she had let Ky go first. Gabe had fallen to his death, fighting off the man who'd tried to kill her. Leon had been badly wounded and likely died protecting her. All because she felt weird at an orphanage.

She could at least get them justice. Instead of running away, she could run to something. Ky may not have evidence, but she could warn people just the same. She could save Lissa and Gabe's families. After a burst of speed, she stopped again, unable to pull herself farther. *Just a little rest.*

She woke to a loud chittering nearby, and her right arm was on fire. Her whole body itched. She tried to lick her lips and they split. Pain attacked her at different levels, from everywhere. What was the point? *Monsters!* She needed to warn everyone! They had to know. Lissa wanted her to tell them.

She reached out, and the tree bark stabbed into her palms. Using it to pull herself up, she lurched forward and ran into another tree. The throb joined the others in a chorus that sang to her to keep going. She used the trees like stepping stones. *Warn the people! Monsters! Save them!* The thoughts kept her going. Tree to tree to tree.

Her head swam. She feared stopping because she wasn't sure whether she would be able to get up again. Ky stumbled and collapsed onto a hiking path. *Monsters . . .*

"Hello? Are you okay?" A woman's voice.

"Stay back," a man said. "Are you—oh, my . . ."

"What is it?" the woman asked.

"Don't . . ." he said.

"Oh! It's a child!"

Ky cracked her eyes open.

"I'm calling 911." His voice faded as he stepped away.

"Hey, there. Do you know where your parents are?"

Ky could hear noises of a zipper and clanking. *Monsters.* Her mouth wouldn't work.

"Shhh. Don't say anything. Not yet."

Water dripped on her mouth, lips, and tongue. Sweet pain.

"They're on their way," he said.

Chapter 57: McKenna

"Life asked death, 'Why do people love me but hate you?' Death responded, 'Because you are a beautiful lie and I am a painful truth.'"—Unknown

Sunday, May 1

1130

Green stems topped with yellow flowers erupted from the ground under the cherry trees. The last of the pink petals were floating on the wind and landing around a black wreath propped on the left side of the fresh grave. The white ribbons rippled, dancing in the light breeze.

Leon K. Rook

It was a peaceful scene to say goodbye.

Various flowers, mostly blue carnations, white daisies, and red roses, lay piled in bouquets at the base of the plaque. Adding a sweet perfume.

Summer hinted at its return, and the sun reflected off an array of metal badges and lines of black dress shoes, while warming McKenna's arms. Most of the group stood at attention, like McKenna, arms raised in salute as "Taps" played on a brass horn.

Everyone lowered their arms and moved into parade rest with feet spread apart and hands resting on their backs, as the song was followed up by a moving speech from Mayor Thatcher, then a rendition of "Amazing Grace" on bagpipes and drums.

It was surprising they had found a bagpipe player in Robur Copse. Her ears attested to the fact that the piper could do with some more practice, but it was touching all the same.

McKenna's home was a pile of boxes. She couldn't stay there with the constant reminders of her friend and neighbor every time she walked out the front door. The music ended, and a poignant note hung in the air.

Most of the assembled proceeded indoors, where it was cooler, to have refreshments, which was just a fancy way of saying *lunch*. McKenna didn't move. She couldn't. Instead, her eyes rested on the RPD badge carved into the stone. Even in death he wore his badge, though his body had been cremated and turned to ashes.

A shadow moved next to hers, shiny black toes bruising the green grass by her feet.

"How are you doing?" Lieutenant Durban asked.

"Fine." Lots of people were saying "fine'" nowadays, when they meant something completely opposite. McKenna was no different. "And you?"

"Fine."

Yep. He answered the same. But she recalled what he had looked like after helping to battle the fire at the hospital all night. Then, finding out there were no survivors—including Leon. Anguished. She was sure he still had nightmares about that, just as she had nightmares about finding . . .

"How is the girl?" she asked.

He sighed deeply. Neither took their gaze off the stone set into the ground.

Later, they had discovered that there was a single survivor—a girl who had run away from the Kako Orphanage and managed to make it across the mountains to Robur Copse's sister city on the other side. She had been found by hikers, her skin a map of scrapes, bug bites, sunburn, and poison ivy.

"Physically, she is recovering, slowly. However, she's still delusional. She keeps yelling about killers and monsters. The psychiatric staff think she's talking about the Bone Killer. With Frank Marlin's body found at the bottom of the ravine and the evidence we found in his cabin . . . it's the theory that makes the most sense. But we might never know exactly what happened at that hospital."

McKenna didn't think it was very important. Marlin was dead, the killing had stopped, and Deborah Franklin's bones had been identified in the pile they'd recovered from the conservatory.

She looked a few plots over at Debbie's new grave, topped with a bunch of wild black-eyed Susans tied in a white ribbon. The cheery yellow blooms were how Hank was remembering his daughter. He'd said that he liked to think that the note on Leon's computer was true, and she had finally gone to rehab. Ironic, really, saving her own life was what had brought about her death.

The ME was still busy identifying the many remains from the conservatory for grieving families, so they, too, could lay their dead to rest. Other fresh graves dotted the cemetery, but most didn't have stones yet.

But none of it had been worth Leon's life. Sure, his epitaph stated he was a hero, but what did that matter compared to his life?

Durban said that he thought Leon had gathered the people as far from the fire as possible, but no one knew why they had all been overwhelmed by the flames. It was likely due to smoke inhalation, which tended to be the more silent killer.

He stood quietly at her side. Too close. Not touching, but she could feel his presence. It was unwelcome, though she didn't have the strength to tell him so. He was no Leon, yet the two of them had had a special relationship. Leon had looked up to the lieutenant.

Perhaps that was why he had been sharing so much with McKenna. They were truly grieving the man and not the hero.

Out of the entire town, the only other person who had been close with him was Tang. But Leon's sometime partner had a family to stand by him in his grief. Durban had no such family, and McKenna wasn't the type to be empathetic.

Still, it bothered her that no one had made it out. No one but a single girl. The tragedy of the arson was attributed to the Bone Killer as well, trying to cover up his crimes. Their community had suffered a lot at the hands of Frank Marlin. It was too bad he couldn't stand trial for his crimes.

Though there was justice for the victims. And that was what Leon would have wanted.

Now McKenna just had to discover how she was going to carry on without him. She turned her back, leaving Durban at the graveside, and put her ranger hat back on.

Chapter 58: Kylie

"As flies to wanton boys, are we to the gods; They kill us for their sport."—King Lear, *William Shakespeare*

Friday, May 20

0515

Kylie woke up covered in sweat, and her heart pounding in her rib cage. It was just another nightmare, the details fading faster than the surrounding darkness.

She lay there, staring at the bunk above her for the time it took the shadows to fade completely, trying to gather her thoughts. They were like dandelion seeds on the wind, always just out of reach.

Today she would be approved to take the test. She was ready.

The bell rang, and she swung her legs out of bed, then made it, just like she should. She gathered the items necessary to prepare herself for the day, including the outfit laid out for her, and headed to the bathrooms with several other girls.

In a line, they brushed their hair and teeth. Then returned everything to its place. She folded and put her pajamas on the locker shelf. Properly attired, she headed to the nurse's office, unconsciously humming under her breath.

"Good morning, Kylie. How are you feeling today?" the nurse greeted her.

"Fine," she responded with a social smile.

"Good, here's your medicine."

Kylie took the two pills and swallowed them with the provided water. At the next bell, she headed into breakfast. A whole-grain cereal mush and milk with oranges, their bright scent bringing a touch of cheer to the otherwise drab meal. A healthy meal provided consistently. Quiet discussion went on around her, but she wasn't included.

After breakfast, it was her job to make sure the room for the older girls and their restroom area was completely in order. A hush followed her back to the room as most of the orphans headed out the door. She recited multiplication drills as she worked. She wiped down the beds and lockers, shined the brass doorplates and handles, then swept the floor. At nine, she headed to the front of the orphanage for her appointment with Dr. Kako.

The rubber soles of her uniform's buckle shoes tapped on the tile. She passed through the doorway, and her feet sank into the carpet, where the sunlight through the blinds striped the brown with yellow. The comfortable leather chair called to her, and she settled in. Dr. Kako inhaled and exhaled softly, accompanied by the swish of paper turning. A small chime went off.

"Good morning, Kylie," greeted the psychiatrist warmly.

"Good morning."

"Well, how are things going this week?"

"I had another nightmare, but I don't remember anything." Kylie leaned back and closed her eyes as she spoke, enhancing her other senses.

"Well, we talked about this before. That's to be expected. You have been through some very difficult circumstances. Don't forget that the killer is dead, and you are safe now."

"Yes." She sighed with relief. "Safe."

"Now let's talk a bit about why this happened. Do you remember how he was able to target you?"

"Yes, I was in the forest by myself." Her hand twitched. *Don't remember.*

"And why were you in the forest, Kylie?"

"Something in the neighborhood scared me." Another finger twitched.

"Yes, nighttime anywhere can be scary when you are alone and vulnerable outside, can't it?"

"Yes." She wasn't alone anymore. There were lots of other girls in her room and people almost constantly around.

"Kylie, why were you alone, in the dark, in a strange neighborhood?"

"Because I ran away." Her emotions were worn thin.

"What were you running from?"

She opened her eyes and looked around. "This place. It is so different from what I was used to. And you—you frightened me." Black eyes. Her heart started to beat faster.

"Me? Why would I scare you?"

"Your eyes seemed mean." Her body tensed in the chair, hands gripping the smooth leather arms.

"My eyes?" Her eyebrows went up. "Dark brown isn't that unusual of a color." A pause and her lips twisted in thought. "Didn't Melissa Lee have dark eyes and black hair too?"

"Yes, she was kind." Her muscles relaxed again.

"Mmm. Was it perhaps because I am an authority figure? You seem to be wary of adults, but especially those in authority."

"Maybe." A small swoop of regret whisked in and was gone.

"And how do you feel now?"

The calm returned. "I feel good. I realize now that you were just trying to help me."

The scratching of pen on paper filled the pregnant pause as Dr. Kako wrote on her notepad.

Kylie cracked open her eyes. A stone sat in her stomach. "Do you think I am ready for school?"

Dr. Kako looked up, studying her carefully.

Kylie tried not to squirm.

"Do you think you are ready to take the orphanage's evaluation?"

"I do." She nodded with a confident smile.

"Very well, then I will contact the hospital's psychiatrist today for a second opinion and set up your test."

"Thank you so much," Kylie said. "You won't regret it."

"Your recovery is all the thanks that I need. I'm so proud of you, Kylie. You may go and study now."

The cameras on the ceiling followed Kylie as she walked out of the office, at peace and looking forward to the future with a light bounce to her step. She grinned and waved as she passed the receptionist. More time to prepare for the exam.

The library was quiet today, since all the older children were on a field trip at the art museum. Kylie wished she could be with them, but there was still so much to learn. The room wasn't large considering the size of the orphanage, but the walls were lined with shelves of books that went all the way to the ceiling, leaving no room for decoration.

The room smelled of something musty, the dangers of living in a humid environment, and potent cinnamon oil, to chase away any silverfish or other eaters of books. She loved rubbing it into the shelves.

Kylie took out the remedial reader she had been working on and sat down at one of the room's two large tables. The chairs were hard plastic, and she longed to take the test to her bunk, but it was against the rules. This one was almost finished anyway.

She might not have had a traditional education, but she was quick and willing to learn. Initially she had needed supervision when she spent time in here, but as time had moved on, so had her observers. Kylie still felt most comfortable alone, and the library, though often in use, provided that illusion due to the stillness and quiet found there.

Today it was deserted, allowing her to breathe a bit. Her head pounded, but she ignored it. She followed the line of words with her finger and sounded the words aloud. Learning quite a bit about cats and dogs, girls and boys, houses and mats.

She hummed the song from her earliest memories; it was so deeply embedded she doubted she could ever forget it. The tune soothed her. She finished the book and put it back on one of the lower shelves, where the younger kids could reach it. Her goal was to read every book in this room. The selection here wasn't large, mostly academic, but it wasn't like she was up to anything too complicated yet.

More advanced books were on the higher shelves, and she promised herself she would get there. Eventually. The medication still made her thoughts a little fuzzy, but she wanted to forget what had happened to her before.

She needed to live in the now and escaped into the world of learning, allowing the words and numbers to swim off the page and fill her mind with something useful. It was time to move on and be a productive member of society.

Epilogue: The Hunter

"There is a devil inside each one of us. Some just know to hide it too well."—The Wrong Vantage Point, *Adwitiya Borah*

Monday, April 25

2245

"Hi, Debbie. Did you miss me?" he asked as he carefully wrung out the skin and began tacking it onto the drying board, wrinkling his nose at the chemical smell. He continued to gently pull and tack down all around as he worked, stretching it.

"The Cleaner and the Caretaker were both naughty, and now they're gone. Fools. They took my bait, and things didn't work out so well for them. They got hooked and gutted.

It looks like there will be some openings in management, huh?"

"And I've had my eye on that Cleaner position, but I like working where I am. These beasties are growing on me. And there's too much pressure when you're in management. Plus, I wouldn't have as much time for my little hobby." He hummed as he worked.

"There you go, just a bit longer. I know you will be thrilled when I place you on the beautiful sculpture I made. I have such plans. Now, I know you are going to miss Laurel, but I really am great with an airbrush, and I can get your makeup flawless. I don't have as much practice with fancy hairstyles, but I have been practicing the particular one you were wearing last by watching online videos. I'm sure it will be perfect. Now you dry out a bit. I'll be back tomorrow."

Days later, after multiple sessions rubbing in the fat and herb mixture, he stretched and tucked, placing her exactly on the form. It was an art.

"Good evening, Debbie. No one is looking for you anymore. They *say* you were a victim of the Bone Killer. But we know better, don't we? I'm so glad I saved you from Tom's nasty drugs and the Cleaner's knife. Neither one of those would've been nice deaths, you know? I also heard there's a girl that got away. Sloppy, sloppy. But I always said that about the old man. No one listened, and look where that got them. I wonder how they'll clean the mess up?"

Working at the hospital had been a pain in the neck. But now all his plans had worked out perfectly. Tom gone, Gianni and those monstrosities of hers gone. The cop digging into Debbie's disappearance would no longer be a problem. He'd attended the funeral. Everything always worked out for him because he was a careful and patient hunter.

Harry's phone rang, interrupting the lovely thoughts. Stupid woman, calling him again. He pressed the answer button, but it was the voice of the Director that came over the line, not his wife's.

"I appreciate your cooperation in returning her bones. So have you made a decision?"

"I like this little place I have now. I'll have to pass."

"If you don't take Marlin's place, then I'll have to use *him*."

The Director didn't trust the Informant. It pleased Harry to force his hand. The Informant was more assassin than hunter. "I'm sure. I'll stay here."

The Director hung up. Management wasn't known for their manners, but they were hired for their ability to keep unpredictable scientists on the fine line between insanity and following the rules. To be fair, he was under a lot of stress. The Director had lost his son, Tom; the entire hospital, with both projects; and the Cleaner. Maybe he would also lose his head. The company wasn't very lenient of failure.

Harry hummed as he wandered through his trophy room, savoring the various pieces, his fingers brushing against them and lingering. He pulled one of his photo books down from the shelf. Then he settled into his favorite chair and skimmed through it. He recalled all the qualities that had first drawn him to Debbie. It had been a risk to hunt in his own hometown, but he had been unable to help himself. She'd had that certain mysteriousness he *loved*.

Looking at the pictures, you could see it. They depicted a woman full of confidence, boldness, and flirtiness, until you looked into her eyes.

Each of his special trophies' eyes showed a depth that belied their face. It was the dichotomy that drew him.

Debbie had been a woman who was laser focused and willing to do anything within her power to get what she wanted. The problem was, she didn't know what that was. His favorite picture was one right before she went into the house that night.

She had just finished checking her appearance, and her hands were caught mid-slide at her hips. Her shoulders were back, and she looked ready to do battle.

He smiled, stood up, and put the photo book away. He began walking along the wall of his favorite trophies. Like a wax museum, but real. They had all been like that. He had gone hunting and had been drawn inexorably to each of them.

Next to Debbie, Shaya stood as boldly as ever. Her dark beauty and sass had been drowning in the lifestyle she had chosen. Then there was Derek, an upcoming model who was willing to do anything to get the next gig.

Next to him was Maria. Her sweet and calm demeanor with her Spanish and Italian features made him think of a Virgin Mary. But she had hid dark secrets and had planned on taking her own life in a terrible way. He was glad he had been there to talk her out of it.

Joy posed next to her. She had been a bubbly personality who hated herself. When he had chosen how to display her, he had put her in a much more revealing outfit than she wore in life, so he could see her scars. They needed to be exhibited. The irony of her name added to his pleasure in the display.

He continued down, pausing at each and remembering, until he came to the first. Celi and her glorious red mane would always hold a special place in his heart. Her fiery Irish spirit was being smothered by an abusive man when he found her and rescued her.

He was a collector of beautiful and perfect specimens from nature, but he saw himself as a savior too. They each were cultivated at the peak of their perfection, and there was nothing but tragedy and deterioration in their futures. Because of him, they would never have to experience that.

He dusted the crevices where dust always seemed to build up, then sprayed insect repellent. With so many trophies, it often took constant maintenance. A few were due for a full cleaning and conditioning in the next week. Unfortunately, with all the dust settled, he was growing bored again already.

A roar came from the tunnels, distracting him. "Well, everyone's looking good, for now. I've decided on Montana for my next hunting trip. I'm going on a quick two-day reconnaissance tomorrow. Y'all be on your best behavior while I am gone."

Another bellow interrupted his thoughts, and he frowned. He needed to go see what all the noise was about. Maybe they, too, were already hungry again.

Acknowledgements

First, I want to thank my family and friends who read the first version of this story. And the second, and the thirtieth... I now know you all truly love me. I couldn't have done this without my author friends Jordan, Tyaan, and especially Angela, who helped me with my biology and grammar.

Thanks to my beta readers: Chrisa (who helped me with my pharmaceuticals), Lisa, Anthony, and Mary the librarian, who is still asking me for book two.

And a very special thanks to Kristina for creating the Fictionary editing software; Lucy, who runs the superkind Fictionary community; James, my editor; and all the other instructors who helped me improve my story knowledge.

Support for the Resident Evil community, like the YouTubers JJ of ROE, Beggy, the Sphere Hunter, Hey Devuh, LTRE, Ink Ribbon, and more. Also for the voice actors who have started their own YouTube playthroughs, like Nicole Tompkins and Nick Apostolides. You all have given me such inspiration.

And last, but most important, my Heavenly Father, who gives me the strength to push beyond my boundaries and do new things. Writing a book has been a journey that I'd never thought I'd take, but now I can't imagine doing anything else.

About the author

Leigh Romero is a military brat who has lived all over the US but currently resides in Rocket City, Alabama. When she isn't outlining, writing, editing, or revising, she spends her time herding kids, cats, ducks, and chickens. You can often find her visiting Raccoon City in game, movie, book, or YouTube form. If not, she is visiting some other author's far-off land, rolling dice for an RPG, cosplaying, or enjoying a mystery video game.

You can find her at https://www.leighromeroauthor.com/